Cha'risa's Gift

Written by
Ilana Maletz

DEDICATION

I am dedicating this book to my husband, Mark, and my daughters, Jamie and Natalie, who have been my best cheerleaders throughout this process. Thank you for believing in me, and in this book. You'll find echoes of the best of who you are tucked away inside these pages.

The beautiful artwork on the book cover was created by Natalie Maletz.

I'd also like to give a very special thanks to my dear friend, Caroline Lewis. I had a small group of readers commenting as the book progressed, but Caroline ran a marathon with me at the end, keeping those comments coming, providing invaluable help with editing and formatting, and taking the time to create the recipes for the C & M cookbook. She did all this as she traveled from port to port up and down the eastern seaboard of the United States. All the recipes were tested in a small galley aboard a forty foot sailing yacht named Thalia, the place she now calls home.

A special and loving thanks to all my other dedicated readers, Shelley Reed, Bill Maletz, Norman Schlager, and Judy Schlager.

1898

Cha'risa's Special Blend Hopi Tea

Harvest greenthread, as the flower buds open. Wash and dry the stems, leaves and flowers in the sun.

Once fully dried, add sprigs of dried lavender and fold the two plants into small tied bundles.

Steep in about six cups of water for five to ten minutes.

Chapter 1

Cha'risa sat just outside her pueblo home, her back pressed against the rough stones as she stared up at the night sky. She was waiting patiently for the tea to finish steeping. The familiar aroma of greenthread wafted up from her small cook fire, along with a new fragrance. She'd added a purple flower her son had given her. He'd told her the flower was called lavender, and that it was a gift to her from the woman he worked for. It was a good scent, both sharp and flowery. She breathed deep, let the smell soothe away some of her tension, and then looked back up at the vast, dark sky. It sparkled above her with the brilliance of countless stars, and its vastness was a reminder that in the grand scheme of things, her troubles were of little consequence.

She thought of Kwahu, as she often did when her heart was sore. He'd been gone four years now. She wondered for a moment, if he hadn't died so young, in such a senseless way, if he would have been able to help Ahote. Could he have shown his son a way to come to terms with the white man's world without losing himself so completely? But even as she asked herself this question, she saw it was foolish, and she wouldn't abide foolishness, especially in herself. The truth was Ahote wasn't the only Hopi struggling. All her people were floundering. Uncertainty about whether to trust the white man had split the Hopi people in two; and while they'd argued amongst themselves, their sacred lands had been redistributed and whittled away.

If only it had been the land they had lost, and nothing more, nothing quite so precious. But that too was foolish, to wonder what might have been. It was done, and now her son was torn between two worlds. He no longer knew where he belonged. In the beginning some had chosen to go voluntarily to the white man's Indian School, but that was not the choice she and Kwahu had made for Ahote. Kwahu had understood the threat immediately when the soldiers arrived in their village. He'd tried to stop the night-time raid while she'd stood by, impotent. They'd killed him right in front of her, and then they'd pulled Ahote from her arms. She still had nightmares where she could hear the sound of his screams echoing through the night as they'd carried him away. She hadn't been able to save either of them then. She was equally impotent now. Over the past four years, the white man had relentlessly worked to purge all Ahote had ever known and believed in. Now she feared they'd succeeded in killing his Hopi spirit.

As she looked skyward, she noted the seven stars of Choochokam, the harmonious ones, the stars that clung together. If only she could feel that kind of harmony, feel that closely connected to a part of a greater whole. Ever since that night of the raids she'd also become a lost soul, trying and failing day after day to find her way back from the darkness inside her. A bright shooting star slowly fell across the sky just below the constellation. Cha'risa studied its trail of light and wondered if it was an omen, a sign that she was making the right decision.

"I thought I might find you here."

Cha'risa turned at the sound of her father's voice. "I'm taking it all in one last time," she said.

Istaqa took a seat beside her. "You don't have to go," he said, not for the first time.

Cha'risa sighed. "This is best for Ahote and for me. He'll never put the pieces back together on his own. I need to at least try and offer what help I can."

Her father stretched his legs out in front of him, groaning at the stiffness in his bones. "Cha'risa, I am getting old."

"Father, don't start this again."

He continued on as if she hadn't spoken. "My time as Medicine Man will soon come to an end. What will happen if you're gone and Ahote as well? There will be no one else to teach this sacred duty to our people."

"Father, Ahote is going; there is no changing his mind. And what have I got to keep me here? The people don't trust me, and wouldn't want my help. The only way forward that makes any sense to me is to try to show my son he's not alone in this world."

Istaqa sighed. "The people need you; they just don't understand how much."

She grunted. "They fear me and call me a witch."

"You made mistakes in your anger and your grief. But who among us has not? These are troubling times for the Hopi people."

Cha'risa knew what he wanted. He wanted her to stay in Hoteville, marry her cousin, and make new babies. But what would be the point? If she ever bore a child again, the white man would take that baby too. They'd pull that child out of her arms even more easily than Ahote had been. Ahote had at least been close to manhood when they took him; he had started his initiation into the Powamu society and had learned things that now no Hopi child would be able to be taught.

Her father must have sensed the direction of her thoughts, for he sighed heavily and then asked, "When do you leave?"

"Early," she said. "The man offering us the work will meet us at Moencopi tomorrow. Ahote and I will need to leave the village before first light."

"And tell me again what this man hired you to do?"

"They're opening a lodge, and they run a cattle ranch. I'm to be their housekeeper and also help with the cooking."

Her father shook his head. "It's a waste of your gifts."

Cha'risa shrugged. She didn't know if she would ever walk the road of a medicine woman again, but this felt right to her, to set aside that mantle in order to once again be Ahote's mother.

Her father sniffed at her brewing tea, then leaned in breathing even deeper. "What have you done to the tea? It smells different."

Cha'risa nodded. "I added another type of flower to the green thread."

"I'm not familiar with that scent. Where did you find it?"

"It was a gift." Cha'risa said, stirring the pot. She breathed in the vapor and decided the steeping was done. She poured a steaming cup for her father and then one for herself. "The rancher's wife asked Ahote to give it to me," she continued. "He'd mentioned my interest in medicinal flowers and herbs to her. She grows this in her garden, and seemed to think I would find it interesting."

Her father took a cautious sip, allowing the brew to settle on his tongue. "There is a lot to this flower," he commented.

Cha'risa took a sip as well, noting once again the calming, soothing properties in the tea. "Perhaps we will get along, this rancher woman and I," she speculated.

Her father raised a skeptical eyebrow, and then took another sip, quiet with his own thoughts. After a few moments, he turned to her. "I'd like to see this new home of yours, and see you safely settled. May I come with you?"

Cha'risa studied his lined face. It tugged at her heart, that he wasn't ready to say goodbye just yet. She pulled her father into her arms, holding him tightly, aware that he was no longer the strong, hale man from her youth. Despite all the power that came with their healing gifts, life had not turned out the way either of them had expected. As she held him, she looked up again at the night sky. Another shooting star arced across the constellations. Its fall mirrored the tear trailing down her cheek.

Chapter 2

Caleb watched Ahote running full speed down the road from the mesas. Leaving the Hopi pueblo was a big step, but even from this distance, the smile on Ahote's face was easy to spot. Clearly, the boy wasn't having second thoughts.

"And 'tis a good thing," Caleb muttered, still trying to convince himself that taking Ahote away from his people was for the best. No matter how he looked at it, he was offering the boy a chance to chart his own path. How could that ever be wrong? It was precisely what he and Zachariah had done nearly twenty years ago, when they left their home and family in Ireland. It had taken the two of them nearly fifteen years to raise enough money to realize their dreams. They'd worked laying track for the railroads, in lumber mills, and on various construction crews, but they'd done it. Three years ago they'd purchased several acres, with beautiful views of the San Francisco Peaks, about ten miles outside the town of Flagstaff. Their first act as landowners had been to buy horses and build a barn. It hadn't taken long for Zach's reputation as a horse breeder and trainer to spread as far as Prescott and beyond.

Caleb allowed a small, satisfied smile, as he remembered how beautifully things had fallen into place after that. Caleb had taken on an extra job teaching carpentry at the Indian School in Keams Canyon. With that money, they'd managed to fence in the property, and buy their first few head of cattle.

They'd still been a ways off from having enough saved up to afford building a ranch house, when they'd met Daniel Cranston in a saloon in Flagstaff. Daniel had been happy to sit a while, drinking beer, listening to Zach and Caleb's stories of life in the Wild West. The three of them had taken an immediate liking to each other, and before the evening was out, Daniel had accepted an invitation to come see their ranch.

It was still as vivid today as it had been three years ago, that sight of Daniel standing on a small rise, looking out at where they planned to build their house; taking in the view of the ancient pine forest to the east, a view of the San Francisco Peaks to the north, and all that wide open space for the animals to graze. Daniel hadn't needed words to convey what he was feeling. He saw what they'd seen when they'd first laid eyes on this parcel: this was a place that spoke to the soul.

When Daniel returned for a second visit, several months later, he brought along his daughter, Katherine, and a business proposition. He wanted to create a conjoined ranch house and guest lodge on the property, one that would cater to city folk, offering them a taste of western adventure. Zach and Caleb had loved the idea. They'd set to work immediately hammering out the details of an agreement, and within six months they were using Daniel's seed money to break ground on the joint enterprise. It was doubly sweet, to Caleb's way of thinking, that Zach had fallen in love with Katherine, and married her, linking their fortunes to Cranston's even more tightly.

"You brought Big Red!" Ahote's cry of pleasure cut short the memories, bringing Caleb back to the moment. The boy ran straight for the horse, and Caleb had to smile at the way the two greeted each another. Big Red didn't give his affection easily, but he was as devoted to Ahote as he was to Zach. Ahote rested his forehead against the temperamental stallion, who blew a warm puff of air right into his face. The young man laughed and patted the horse fondly. Looking excitedly up at Caleb, he exclaimed, "We're really doing this, aren't we?"

"That we are," Caleb assured him. "Where's your mother?"

"She's coming. So is my grandfather, just to see us there safely. I hope that's okay."

"'Tis a long way from home for him." Caleb's Irish lilt often became more noticeable when he was taken by surprise.

Ahote shrugged. "I think he's not quite ready to say good bye."

"Are you? Ready, I mean? It's no small step you're taking."

Ahote didn't hesitate. "My grandfather clings to the past. I'm reaching for the future."

Caleb laughed. "That sounds like something one of your teachers told you."

Ahote looked him in the eye. "I do believe it was my carpentry teacher who said it to me first."

"I probably did at that. It's certainly true that for some people traditions and places are sacred, while others must risk everything to be satisfied."

"Is that what it was like for you and Zach?" Ahote asked.

Caleb nodded. "My Ma didn't want us to go either, but she understood we had to try."

Ahote looked thoughtful. "My mom is trying to understand. I'm hoping when she sees our new home she'll approve of what I want for my future."

Caleb put his arm around the boy. "It might be, once your grandpa sees the ranch, he will understand too."

Ahote looked doubtful. "My grandfather doesn't put great value on worldly success. For him, what's important is maintaining our spiritual legacy."

"Does he think the world will stop spinning if you skip your prayers?" Caleb was joking, but Ahote's eyes remained serious.

"Something like that," he mumbled.

Caleb studied the boy, who, for the first time, looked uncertain. Caleb patted his shoulder reassuringly. "It's important for you to do your own growing, no matter how tall your grandfather is."

Ahote nodded, and then looked away, down toward the mesas. Caleb followed the boy's line of sight, and saw two figures walking briskly along the dusty roadway, each carrying heavy bundles. While Caleb had come to expect such stamina in Ahote, it surprised him to see an old man and a small woman with similar endurance. His eyes narrowed, studying the woman more closely. Even from afar he could make out her thick braid of hair swinging as she walked. It was the longest he'd ever seen, and as black as night, not a speck of grey in it.

Caleb followed her every step, until she stood at last in front of him. She was much younger than he'd been led to believe. Around her waist, an elaborately embroidered belt emphasized a very feminine contour. It wasn't just her waist that was small; Caleb towered over her. Her eyes were big, though, and bold, too. She didn't hide from his gaze, and in those dark brown depths, he saw something both compelling and secretive.

"Ahote, this is your mother?" his Irish accent was thickening again.

"Yeah." Ahote said, not noticing Caleb's shock. He'd already begun tying his belongings onto the back of Big Red's saddle.

"This is the tough old bird?" Caleb was struggling to reconcile Ahote's description with the woman before him.

Ahote paused and looked up "Umm, Cal?"

Caleb tore his gaze away from the woman and turned to her son. "Sweet Jesus, boyo! You made her sound like an old hag!"

"Cal…"

"You might have warned me!"

"Cal!"

"What?"

"She speaks English."

Caleb couldn't help himself. "Bloody hell!" he exclaimed. He turned back to the woman, who was quietly laughing. Even as he gave Ahote a stern glare, he could feel the rising heat of a blush. He turned to the woman. "My apologies, ma'am, if I gave any offense, but I'm thinking your son wasn't entirely forthcoming about your age or appearance."

"How so?" Ahote demanded.

Caleb faced him accusingly. "She's not old or ugly!"

"I never said she was."

"You said she was a tough old bird!"

"Trust me, she's plenty tough. You don't have to worry about my mom carrying her weight."

Caleb shook his head, exasperated. "This is not the first concern I'm having."

Ahote looked perplexed. "So what are you worried about?"

"You do realize she'll be around a lot of rough men?"

"She's more than capable of handling herself around a bunch of cowboys." Ahote searched Cal's face. "She can do this. Give her a chance. You won't regret it."

The grandfather was asking the mother something. She answered, and the old man chuckled.

"What's he find so funny?" Cal addressed his question to Ahote, but it was his mother who answered him.

"He's amused that you think your men might pose a problem for me."

"'Tis that so?" Caleb studied her closely. "You don't look so big and scary to me."

Ahote's mother smiled, though it wasn't a very nice one. "Here's what you need to know, Mr. McKenna. I can do this job for you. But more importantly, if I don't go, Ahote leaves without my blessing, and he isn't going to want to do that."

Caleb looked over at Ahote, and the boy looked down. Caleb turned back, locking eyes with the woman. She returned his gaze with a resolute one of her own. At last, Cal sighed. For better or worse, he'd already offered her the position. Clearly, the men in her family weren't worried about her ability to handle a lot of rough and tumble cowboys.

9

"Your ma can ride up on Big Red with you," he told Ahote. "Put Grandpa on the bay along with their gear."

Ahote nodded, and then said something in Hopi to the old man. Together they worked to get the belongings and the family situated on the horses. When they were at last ready, Caleb motioned his party forward. The day was already getting away from them, and he wanted to cross the wash and find a place to camp. They'd need an early start tomorrow. It was his plan to be in Flagstaff by noon of the following day, in plenty of time to meet the train bringing Daniel Cranston back out west.

Caleb was so absorbed calculating the details of the journey ahead that it was several minutes before he thought to check on Ahote and his family. Ahote's mother was focused on the road ahead, looking determined as she sat stiffly in the saddle, obviously not accustomed to horses. But the old man was looking behind, taking in one last glimpse of the mesas receding into the distance. When he turned forward once again, his eyes met Caleb's. They held such a look of regret and sadness, Caleb felt certain the memory of it would haunt him for the rest of his days.

Chapter 3

Ahote was hot, and his mouth was filled with grit from the road, but at last they'd come to Tanner's wash, a tributary of the Colorado River, running between towering, multi-layered black cliffs. They would stop here for a noonday meal before crossing to the other side and continuing their southwestward journey. They would camp that night somewhere on the far eastern side of the San Francisco Peaks, putting them in easy range of Flagstaff the following morning.

It stuck Ahote sometimes how fearless the Anglos were; that they'd dared to build at the foot of the place of the high snows, the home of the Kachina People. Once upon a time, Ahote would not have dared come so close to the sacred grounds of the spirit people, but he'd seen the white man build their homes in Flagstaff, cut the forests, bring in the railroads. The Anglos were unafraid to take what they wanted, even if it was from the Kachina People. It seemed to Ahote, with everything they took, they grew stronger. In the meantime, his people continued to live their lives according to a spiritual order, trying to hold themselves apart from the white man, but failing. At one time the Hopi path was all Ahote had desired; he'd been eager to make his pilgrimage and complete his initiation in the Powamu society. Then the night of the abductions had come. He'd lost his father that night. The soldiers had killed him as they carried Ahote away from his Hopi world. They'd brought him to Keam's Canyon, and put him in a school where he'd learned to see the world with a white man's eyes.

Ahote had resented them at first, resisted their attempts to change him, but that changed the summer he'd taken a job with one of his teachers from the Indian School. Caleb was different than most of the other teachers. He was a tolerant man, and a good teacher. He saw something he liked in Ahote, and trusted him enough to offer him a summer job on his ranch. Caleb and Zach had needed help fencing in their property, and they were impressed with Ahote's work ethic and his endurance. What they hadn't anticipated, and neither had he, was that Ahote also seemed to have a gift with animals. Zach had immediately set about to teaching Ahote how to care for all the livestock at C & M Ranch.

Caleb and Zachariah brought Ahote back the next summer as well, pulling him out of school early for the spring roundup, and keeping him through the cattle drive in the fall. Before he'd returned to school, Ahote had met Daniel Cranston and his daughter. Ahote had sat quietly amongst them as they prepared for the wedding, and discussed their plans for the lodge. They'd insisted he come to the wedding, and somehow, miraculously, as the plans for the lodge evolved, it was assumed that Ahote would be a part this grand scheme. They wanted him to help Caleb with the running of the cattle ranch while Zachariah and Katherine managed the lodge and the horses.

Out of the corner of his eye, Ahote saw his grandfather dismount and walk over to the edge of the tributary. The old man stared northward. Tanner's crossing closely followed the ancient Hopi pathway into the Grand Canyon, to the place of the sacred springs and the salt cave. Ahote knew what the old man was thinking because he couldn't help thinking it himself. His pilgrimage trail was supposed to have taken him along this route to finish his initiation and take his place among the men of his village. Instead when he crossed the river, he would be heading away from his people, leaving the Hopi path behind for good.

"Help me down, Ahote," his mother insisted. Ahote realized he'd been lost in his thoughts. Immediately he got off Big Red and then helped his mother dismount. There was a blessed relief as air rushed in to cool the damp where their bodies had been pressed together. His mother looked tired and saddle sore, but she smiled at him all the same.

"I'll take the horses down to the river to drink," he told her.

She nodded. "I'll get a fire going." She stretched, trying to ease some of the stiffness.

"Make some tea," Ahote teased. "Isn't that your answer to all life's problems?"

"As it so happens, I do have something that will help."

Caleb handed Ahote the reins to his horse as well. "Set them out to graze after they drink. I'll see if I can hunt something up to go with our trail rations."

Ahote pointed to his grandfather. The old man had been dangling his hand in the water for a few minutes. Now the hand flashed upwards with a silver fish firmly in its grasp.

Caleb's jaw dropped. "Good Lord! How did he do that?"

"He calls to them, makes them think his fingers are something delicious to eat."

"Well, that's a fine skill to have! I guess I'll be helping your mother get the firewood."

Ahote watched Caleb head off into the trees, his mother heading off in a different direction with the same purpose. He saw to the horses, and then set them out to graze. By the time he got back to the water's edge, his grandfather had already caught five fish. Ahote sat down beside him, pulled out his knife and began cleaning them. They sat quietly together looking out toward the gorge. With a quick motion, his grandfather pulled out another fish.

He smiled at Ahote. "The fish want us to eat well this afternoon."

They heard movement behind them, and turned to see Cha'risa returning with a stack of tinder and wood. They watched as she knelt down and began her preparations for the fire. The walk through the woods must have alleviated some her stiffness, for she was moving with greater ease.

"She is a strong woman, your mother," his grandfather said.

"Yes," Ahote agreed.

"When she was young, I told her that she must look among the men and pick only the strongest for her husband, for only a man of great strength could make a happy marriage with her."

"Was my father the strongest?" Ahote asked.

"Oh yes," his grandfather remembered. "He was the fastest runner too. No one could keep up with him. I remember how fast he was making his Powamu pilgrimage. He did it in less time than any man I have ever seen. He ran all that we have ridden today, and then some." He pointed north with his finger, up the river and into the canyon beyond.

Ahote followed the direction of his grandfather's finger, fighting off the bittersweet sensation of what might have been. "Sometimes, when I think of him, I find it hard to remember what he looked like," Ahote admitted, and then sat quietly, his thoughts troubled. "I wonder if he would understand why I am leaving the mesa. I wonder if he would think I let the white man shape me in his own image."

His grandfather studied him. "Is that what you think?"

Ahote looked away. "I don't know. The work I do for Caleb and Zachariah makes me happy. But as much as I love the work, I can't help but wonder if I can truly ever be part of their world."

"Then why leave Hoteville?" his grandfather asked.

Ahote hesitated, but there was no dissembling around his grandfather. "Because I'm no longer part of your world, either," he answered truthfully.

Istaqa turned away and looked back out into the river. He was silent a few moments before he spoke again. "As strong as your father was – and remember he was the strongest of all the men your mother might have chosen – your mother was also very strong. She was so powerful, he was only able to put a baby into her one time. All that strength that was theirs poured undiluted into you. Remember that when you doubt yourself. You are destined to grow into a man of great power."

Ahote laughed, but it was a bitter laugh. "How can that be? I'm a man whose trunk has been cut from his roots. I have no foundation."

His grandfather patted him reassuringly. "You are wise enough to see the challenge before you; you will be wise enough to find a place where your roots will once again grow."

Ahote met his grandfather's steady gaze. "How can you be sure?"

His grandfather smiled then and said, "Close your eyes for a moment."

Ahote studied him, wondering what his grandfather was intending, and then he complied.

"Good," his grandfather said. "Now, imagine your body is like a kiva. Climb down into the center of your being."

Ahote wasn't quite sure what his grandfather meant, but he visualized a ladder, and himself climbing down it. His grandfather started to hum, and the hum seemed to Ahote like some kind of pathway. He let his body relax, following the winding track of the song. The melody carried him along, like the river running beside them, until at last, he came to a place where his feet seemed to strike solid ground. He pulled himself out of brilliantly blue water, and onto the bank of a shore, shaded with desert willows and cottonwood trees. Smelling the richness of the earth beneath him, he sat there for a moment and ran his hands through the damp, fertile soil.

Something was breathing close by him, so close he that could feel its breath on his skin. He turned and found himself staring right into the golden eyes of a large gray wolf. The vision so shocked him, he tumbled back into the watery, blue melody. Flailing, he scrabbled his way back to full awareness. When he looked once again at his grandfather, he saw that the old man was smiling.

"Ah," his grandfather nodded. "I thought so. "You have seen the spirit of the pathfinder. You will not travel my road, grandson; but I promise you, you will not remain lost. You will find your own way."

Chapter 4

Though Cha'risa would never admit it to a soul, Flagstaff intimidated her. She'd never come so close to *Nuvatuk-iya-ovi*, would never have dared if not for Ahote. But here, the White Man not only dared to live at the foot of the mountain that was home to the Kachina People, they thrived in this shared proximity. Caleb had told her that Flagstaff was now the largest city on the main railroad line between Albuquerque and the West Coast. The main street they rode down was teeming with people, mostly cowboys and lumbermen. There were many businesses fanning out from the depot, a large number of them saloons, with their doors wide open, the music, drinking and gambling already lively, though the sun was still high in the sky. Saloon girls stood in the doorways, enticing the men to come inside, all of them wearing garish dresses that revealed more than they covered. In the pueblos, they would call such idleness *koyaanisqatsi*, chaos and corruption, something that would invite an avenger to destroy the wicked.

Cha'risa wondered what an avenger would make of her leaving the mesas and joining the people of this town. Caleb must have seen her discomfort, for he drew his horse closer to hers, a silent message that he would keep her safe. People seemed to know him, and many waved as he rode by. What people made of his party of Hopi Indians she had no idea; she only knew that they stared.

Caleb brought his horse to a halt in front of the Bank Hotel. "Ahote, I have to stop by the bank, and the general store before Mr. Cranston's train arrives. Can you run over to the livery stable and pick up my buckboard?"

"Sure."

Caleb handed Ahote some cash for the storage fee. "Take your grandfather with you. I'll keep your mother with me, and introduce her to Mr. Burnett. I'm thinking it will be good for her to see how we go about provisioning for the lodge."

Cha'risa watched her son and father ride off with some trepidation. She wasn't ready to be without her men quite yet. Perhaps Caleb sensed this anxiety in her, for he gave her a reassuring smile as they went into the big stone building that was both a hotel and a bank. After visiting the bank, he led her across the way to the smaller of two general stores in the town. The store was a lot like a trading post, Cha'risa decided, only instead of trading blankets and jewelry, people were using coins and paper money to acquire what they wanted. The woman behind the counter was the exact opposite of the saloon girls, wearing a brown dress that covered her from neck to toe. Mrs. Burnett was married to the proprietor, and Caleb told Cha'risa, in their introduction, that Kitty Burnett knew the inventory of the store even better than her husband.

Cha'risa could see how the woman's hazel eyes were alight with intelligence. Unfortunately, Cha'risa could also sense the woman didn't approve of her. Mrs. Burnett was polite enough to extend a greeting after Caleb's introduction, but her eyes kept darting back to Cha'risa as she filled Caleb's order, checking to make sure Cha'risa wasn't touching the merchandise or attempting to steal. Cha'risa stayed quietly watchful, observing Mrs. Burnett and her wares from a careful distance.

As they got toward the end of the list, Mrs. Burnett called for a stock boy to help collect the heavier bags of flour, sugar, beans, and coffee. Cha'risa watched the pile grow, and then pointed at a large bag of corn meal, quietly suggesting to Caleb they add that to the list, too. Mrs. Burnett stared at Cha'risa a moment, and then waited for Caleb to verify that the bag should indeed be added to the purchases. Caleb nodded. Perhaps it was petty of her, but Cha'risa stopped the boy and opened the bag first, inspecting its contents. The corn that produced this meal was different from Hopi corn, and it wasn't finely ground by hand, as she would have done. She gave Mrs. Burnett one of her own looks, one that said just what she thought about White Man's corn from a bag. Then she allowed the stock boy to reseal the bag and stack it on the pile.

The bells on the door jangled as two well-dressed women entered the store. Their long dresses rustled and swept up the dust from the floor as they walked over to an aisle displaying all kinds of fabrics and dry goods. Cha'risa turned back to focus on the final steps of purchasing the ranch supplies, but she could feel the women's eyes watching her from the back of the store. She heard their loud whispering, and made out the words "dirty Indian." As Mrs. Burnett added up the total, Cha'risa turned to Caleb and whispered that she would be right outside, that she needed a little air. He looked at her, and then at the women in the back of the store, who ceased their whispering when his eyes met theirs.

"You go ahead," he said. "Just don't wander off. I won't be much longer."

Cha'risa nodded, and then slipped quietly out the door onto the wide, dusty street with its noisy saloons and bustling traffic. She took in a deep breath. On the mesas, the air always smelled of dust too, but it was the air of wide-open spaces, not this close, pressed-in smell of humanity. For a moment, she wondered if she'd taken on more than she was capable of. While she wasn't well liked on the mesa, she was never looked down upon. In fact, the opposite was true; they respected her because they feared her. Here, it would be a very different dynamic. She wondered if Caleb had considered how the townspeople would feel about her working at the ranch and to her shopping in their town. If she had felt small that last night on the mesa, she felt even more so now, no more than a speck of dust adrift in this chaotic town.

Her thoughts were interrupted when a fight spilled out of one of the nearby saloons. The proprietor escorted a group of men out onto the street, where they continued shouting and waving their firearms wildly about. The arguing and shouting reached a fevered pitch, and the proprietor hurried back into the saloon, closing the door behind him. One of the men, in an unthinking rage, fired off a couple of warning shots, apparently unaware that a wagon was passing close by. Cha'risa watched, frozen in place as the details of the mounting disaster unfolded for her in slow motion. A bloom of red spread across the driver's shirt, and the horses screamed and bolted, frightened by the noise and the smell of blood. The wagon wheels screeched as the buckboard careened down Front Street, heading right for Cha'risa. As she began to back away from the disaster, she saw a man stagger out of the saloon located next to Burnett's General Store. He was drunk, humming a tuneless melody, and he stepped out onto the thoroughfare, heedless of the wagon hurtling toward him. Before she was even aware of doing it, Cha'risa ran out into the street, grabbed the drunken man, and tried to pull him out of harm's way. The man stumbled and fell, pulling her down with him.

There was a burst of pain as she hit the ground, and she felt something pop in her ankle. All the while the wagon was bearing down on them. She heard a hoarse, anguished voice call out her name, just as the noise and dust of the wagon overwhelmed her. She threw her body over the man, shielding him, bracing for the impact. It never came. Instead she heard a sickening crash, a man's cry, and the horses' high-pitched screaming. The next thing she knew, Caleb was at her side.

"Cha'risa, can you hear me? Are you all right?"

There were other voices now, the sounds of people running and yelling. She lifted her head and looked at Caleb.

"Oh thank God!" he exclaimed, and for a moment she thought he was going to hug her. Instead his gray-blue eyes narrowed and he studied her closely. "Are you hurt?"

"I think I sprained my ankle," she said, and tried to sit up. He was quick to help her, and his jaw tightened when heard her sharp intake of pain as she tried to move. "I'll be fine," she assured him. "Don't be angry. It was the only way to save him."

"Angry?" Caleb looked confounded. "'Twas terror I was feeling. I thought you were going to die!" He looked down at the man lying so still beside Cha'risa. The man hadn't moved since they'd fallen. Carefully, Caleb helped her turn the man over

"Oh, Sweet Jesus," he muttered when he saw the man's face.

"Who is he?"

"Eli Ferguson."

The name meant nothing to her. She bent close and noticed his breathing was regular, but that he stank of liquor; she put her hand on his chest, and felt a steady rhythm beneath the palms of her hands. She checked his eyes.

"It isn't a concussion," she observed. "He's passed out from the drink."

Caleb sighed, shaking his head. "'Tis no surprise there."

Cha'risa started checking Eli's extremities, feeling for any broken bones. "I think being drunk may be the worst of his troubles."

Just then, they heard the crowd around the wagon start shouting for someone to go get the doctor. Caleb heaved another sigh, and then called back. "He's over here."

Several of the men turned, and Caleb gestured to the man Cha'risa was examining.

Cha'risa looked up, surprised. "This is your medicine man?"

Caleb nodded, and then looked over at the men surrounding the overturned wagon. They were struggling to free the driver, who was trapped beneath the wreckage. "I'll be right back," he said, and then added, "Stay put."

Cha'risa pointed to her ankle. "I won't be going anywhere," she assured him.

He frowned again, then nodded, and went over to lend a hand. Cha'risa watched him go. He was a big man, taller than the others, and strong too. The muscles in his broad shoulders bunched and strained under the exertion, but at last the men had enough combined strength to lift the crushing weight off the fallen man. She heard Ahote call her name, and turned from the accident scene to find both her father and son hurrying toward her.

"You're hurt!" her father exclaimed.

"Yes, but just a sprain."

He looked at the ankle already swelling and turning purple, and concern wrinkled his brow.

"I'll be alright," she assured him. "But father," She pointed to where the men were just now pulling the injured man from under the wagon. "We need to help that man over there."

He shook his head. "Let them call for their own medicine man. I will tend to you."

"Their medicine man is here." She nodded at the man passed out on the ground in front of her.

Her father's eyes narrowed. "I see." He turned to Ahote. "Go get your mother's saddle bag, and mine too. We'll tend to her injury first." He raised a hand, when she started to protest. He looked over at the crowd of men and then back at her. "After, we'll see if they will accept our help."

In the end, the crowd in the street didn't take much convincing. A few came over with Caleb to watch as Cha'risa's father mixed the powdered Jimsonweed into an ointment. He spread the concoction around her injury, and then proficiently wrapped her ankle, singing a song of healing all the while. Almost immediately, Cha'risa felt the medicine's energy counteracting the throbbing pain. She looked over at the crush of people surrounding the wounded man. She couldn't see through the throng, and felt anxious on his behalf, wondering what was being done to help him.

"Are you some kind of medicine man?" an onlooker asked of her father.

Ahote translated the man's question for Istaqa, but it was Cha'risa who answered. "We can help," she offered. "We're both practitioners of medicine among our people."

Her father's eyes met hers, and then with a slight nod of acquiescence, he got slowly up off the ground, brushing the dirt from his pant legs. Cha'risa looked for Ahote to help her get up as well, but Caleb got there first, helping her to her feet. Her father stared at the tall Irishman, and then raised an eyebrow at his daughter. She frowned back at Istaqa, and motioned him over to the fallen man.

Ahote quickly inserted himself between her and Caleb. Draping his mother's arm over his shoulder, he said, "I'll take it from here, Cal." Istaqa called over from beside the fallen man. "If he wants to help, tell him to gather up some supplies for a splint." Ahote translated the request to Cal, adding a few suggestions for the materials his grandfather preferred.

Cal continued to study Cha'risa with a worried expression. "She shouldn't put any weight on that foot," he cautioned.

"I'll be fine," Cha'risa assured him. "You just find what we've asked for."

"Are you sure she should be helping?" Cal persisted, as Ahote helped her hobble over to the wounded man. Caleb was beginning to aggravate Cha'risa. She didn't like how he assumed she couldn't think or answer for herself. She considered using a few sharp words to shut him down, but then she saw the injured man lying on the ground, and immediately her brain started taking inventory. In addition to the gunshot wound to his shoulder, it looked like the weight of the wagon had fractured his femur. It was a bad injury. Automatically, she opened her mind, expanding her thoughts, and seeking out the guiding hand of the spirits. The path forward was like a prism, illuminating her intuition, filling her thoughts, and causing the song to rise up inside her.

Chapter 5

Caleb was running. He'd been quick to find the items Ahote had asked for. He was nearly back to the accident scene when he heard the wail of the approaching train.

"Sweet Jesus!" he exclaimed. He'd nearly forgotten about Daniel. He saw George Burnett heading back to the scene of the accident, and he shouted out, "George, can you help me?"

When George trotted over, Caleb handed him the wood and leather straps. "I need you to take these to the old Indian working on Joshua. I'm supposed to be meeting that train pulling in." Caleb looked over at the group still gathered at the crash site. "Tell them I'll be right back, will you?"

"Sure." George gripped the materials. "Thomas McMillan offered us a room at the Bank Hotel. I already put the doc in there to sleep it off. If we're not out on the street, that's where we'll be."

"That was kind of Tom," Caleb noted, and then added, "Thanks for the help." At the screech of the train's brakes, he looked back over at the station. "Gotta go!" he said, and once again he was running, heading for the platform, before the passengers had a chance to disembark.

By the time Caleb and Daniel arrived back at the scene of the accident, Ahote's family had already made good progress. They'd fed Joshua a tea that had sent him into a deeply drugged sleep. His shoulder wound had been cleaned and bound, and now Ahote was carefully holding Joshua's upper body in a firm but gentle grip, while Cha'risa and her father maneuvered the broken ends of the femur into alignment. All the while, the two of them sang, their focus delving deeply inward, as if they could actually see inside of Joshua's body.

Ahote saw Caleb return and gestured to him to come and help. As Caleb approached, Istaqa began speaking, and Ahote was quick to translate.

"He says to wash your hands in that herbal solution over there." Ahote nodded toward a leather bladder lying near one of their saddlebags. "Then come take his place, and help keep the leg stabilized while he binds it."

22

Caleb quickly washed, and then sat down beside Istaqa, carefully helping to stabilize where the bone had been set. All the while, Cha'risa kept singing. It was a low, sultry chant. Caleb didn't just hear her song; he felt it through his hands. He could feel the way it thrummed deep inside of Joshua It was a compelling sensation, full of warmth, and something that seemed so essentially her.

As the healing coursed throughout Joshua's injured leg, Caleb felt himself relax. At some point, he realized that same heat and thrum was starting to move up through his hands, and into his own body. Startled, he looked up, his eyes seeking hers, but she didn't notice him. All her focus seemed to be on saving Joshua. He wondered briefly if he should move his hands away, if he was stealing the healing intended for Josh. He hadn't realized he'd begun to lift them off, until the old man gave him a hard nudge, and gestured clearly to hold Josh steady. He placed his hands back down, and almost immediately the warm tingling of Cha'risa's chant began to wind its way up through his hands into the pulse and pump of his own body's rhythms. There was not much Caleb could do except give into the sensation.

His head began to feel full, as if it were expanding farther and farther outward. It seemed to him as if he watched from a great distance, as Istaqa worked the wood and leather into a splint, carefully wrapped around Joshua's thigh. At last, Joshua's leg was sufficiently set in place. The chanting ceased, and with it the odd connection that had linked Caleb to Cha'risa. He felt a little disoriented, as if he were waking from a powerful dream. Looking up, he saw George and Daniel just now returning with a cabinet door from Burnett's General store. They'd ripped it off its hinges so it could be used as a stretcher to carry Joshua up to the room at the Bank Hotel. Istaqa nodded his approval.

"I didn't even see you go." Caleb told George, as he carefully helped to place Joshua onto the makeshift stretcher.

George nodded. "You seemed very intent on what you were doing. But Mr. Cranston is a forward-thinking fellow. He suggested we were going to need some way to move Josh off the street."

Caleb got up and went to take the front of the stretcher. "Here," George said. "Let me help you with that."

Caleb waived him away. "I'm built like a horse and you know it," Caleb insisted. "We don't need you throwing your back out again. At least not until we have Doc Ferguson back among the living."

"Next time my back goes out, I won't be going to see Doc, I'll be sending for your Indians."

Caleb shook his head. "They aren't my Indians, George."

"Perhaps not, but now that you've brought them here, I won't be risking my health with that drunk any longer."

"He's a good doctor when he's not bolloxed," Caleb ventured.

"Yes, when he's sober, but that's not very often, now is it?"

Taking hold of the back corners of the stretcher, Daniel and Ahote called out. "You ready, Caleb?"

Caleb grabbed the front. "Ready!"

On the count of three, the men lifted Joshua off the ground, and people made way for them as they carefully moved the injured man toward the hotel. Most of the town folk, realizing the show was now over, started meandering back into the saloons and work places along Front Street. Caleb looked back, wondering where Cha'risa was, and found her watching him as she and her father gathered up their supplies. When her eyes met his, he smiled. She was the first to look away, and he thought he detected a hint of color in her cheeks. Perhaps she had felt that rather intimate connection too. His smile widened as he contemplated that little piece of information.

Eli Ferguson was groaning when they entered the room, and Caleb was pretty sure he knew what would come next. He helped to ease Josh down onto the opposite bed, and then he immediately went out to find a bucket. A maid was standing just outside the door, and, upon hearing what he needed and why, she handed hers over with alacrity. Ahote slid past him as he came back through the door.

"Where are you sneaking off to?" Caleb asked.

"I'll be right back. I have to get some hot water for tea."

"Tea?"

Ahote smiled. "For the doc. Mom's got a tea to help with his drunkenness."

"Is that so?" Caleb mused. "Might be she could make a fortune selling that remedy in this town. What's in it?"

"Some kind of yellow flower."

"Very informative."

"Ahote!" Cha'risa chided. "I need that water!"

"Sorry," Caleb muttered to the boy, and then let him run off on his errand. Caleb brought the bucket over to Doc Ferguson's bedside.

Cha'risa looked at the pail. "Leave it there," she gestured with her head to a spot near the bedside. He did as asked, and then tried to get out of her way. Istaqa was beside Josh, still chanting quietly. Caleb decided his best course of action was to sit quietly in a chair near the door, staying close in case they needed anything more.

Ahote came back into the room, carrying a steaming kettle and some cups. He helped his mother drop the dried flowers into the water, and a pleasant scent began to waft up into the room. As Caleb watched, it occurred to him that Ahote was a lot more like his family than the boy realized. Be it men or animals, all three Hopis shared the same kind of inner knowledge of what the body needed to heal. Caleb wasn't sure why, but it pleased him to see this connection between the boy and his mother and grandfather.

"What the hell is all that Goddamn singing?"

And another country heard from, thought Caleb, as Eli sat up cranky, and clearly badly hung over. Quickly, Cha'risa moved the pail closer to him, and not a moment too soon. The pleasant scent of steeping flowers was soon overwhelmed by the smell of Eli's vomit.

It wasn't long before Cha'risa's tonic started to have a positive effect on Eli. Within the hour, he was deemed fit to return home, and it fell to Caleb to see the doc back to his small cabin. A late day sun warmed Caleb's face, as he left the doc tucked into his bed, and started walking back toward the hotel.

As he wandered down the street, he found his thoughts drifting to the first time he'd ever seen this mountain town. It wasn't even a town back then. He and Zachariah had stumbled upon it while laying track for the new railroad. One winter day the work had come to a sudden halt, marooning the crew in the middle of nowhere for several months, as they waited for a bridge to be built. To break the boredom, they'd traveled west nearly 30 miles, along with several of the men on their crew, looking for a place to buy a drink. At last, they'd wandered into a rough collection of tents and hastily built saloons, gambling halls and brothels. Behind this encampment, white-capped peaks rose up, and snow fell gently on the surrounding pines.

Caleb and Zach had seen a good bit of the country by this time. They'd signed onto the railroad crews immediately after coming off the boat from Ireland. But nothing they'd seen had touched their hearts the way this stretch of land did. From this rough encampment, they watched the snows melt, and spring burst into bloom. It wasn't until the heat and monsoon rains of summer that the crews were once again ready to continue their arduous work of laying track the rest of the way to California. By then it was too late for Caleb and Zach. They were so in love with the surroundings at the base of these tall peaks that no amount of money could have enticed them to leave.

Fortunately for them, even though the camp shrunk dramatically after the railway crews moved out, a new enterprise opened up. Ayer's Lumber Company provided both men with a steady paycheck cutting down trees in the virgin pine forest. Flagstaff grew and thrived with the arrival of the lumber industry, and the two Irishmen did as well. In time they had enough money to turn their dream of owning land into a reality.

Thinking of the ranch reminded Caleb that Zach and Katherine were expecting him home shortly. He stopped in one of the saloons to see if anyone was heading out this late in the day, and if they'd be willing to deliver a message. He was lucky enough to run into Toby Willard, who'd stayed later than he'd intended, watching the exciting events of the afternoon play out. As they shared a pint, Toby agreed to stop by C & M Ranch on his way back home, and tell Zach and Katherine about the delay.

Caleb paid for young man's drink, plus some extra for delivering the message. After wishing Toby a safe journey, Caleb at last made his way back to the hotel. As he strolled, Caleb began humming a nameless tune. The melody felt good vibrating within him, but still he paused, wondering where it'd come from. Caleb often hummed and sang, but the melodies were mostly Irish. This was most definitely not one of the songs from his youth. Suddenly, it struck him the unusual pattern of notes was exactly the song he'd felt flowing into his body earlier today. This was Cha'risa's healing song. It was still with him, and apparently still affecting him.

Istaqa had laughed at Caleb's concern over all the rough and tumble cowboys Cha'risa would encounter at the ranch. It hadn't occurred to Caleb then to worry about himself in that regard. But now it was clear that something about both the melody and the woman had gotten under his skin. The thought gave him pause but only for a moment, and then he cracked a smile. Whatever Cha'risa did to frighten off unwanted attention, Caleb realized he was looking forward to the challenge.

When Caleb entered the lobby, he found Daniel at the front desk booking two rooms for the night, one for Ahote's family and one for Caleb and Daniel to share. Caleb was touched by Daniel's generosity, and grateful for it. He'd noticed the pain from the ankle injury was draining Cha'risa. Even Istaqa, tough as the old man was, had begun to look a little worn around the edges as the afternoon dragged on. Perhaps with this extra room they would be able to get some well needed rest. He was just about to invite Daniel to come with him to rustle up some dinner for Ahote's family when Kitty Burnett showed up in the lobby carrying a warm pot of stew and some fresh baked bread.

"It's for you and your new hires," she said.

Caleb's brows lifted in surprise. "Why, Mrs. Burnett, that's very kind of you."

Kitty looked a little discomforted. "Yes, well, it is the least I could do. I'm sorry for the poor reception I gave your new housekeeper this morning. She and her father were very charitable towards the people of our town today. And she with that hurt ankle, just working and working to help save Joshua and revive the doc. I judged her wrongly."

Caleb was moved by her admission. "I'm glad to hear you've had a change of heart."

She put the pot and the bread into Caleb's hands. "Well, you just tell her that she's welcome in my store anytime. And be sure to tell her about my stock of medicinal herbs. A woman like that is bound to need what is on some of my shelves."

"I'll mention it to her."

"Honestly, Caleb, I don't know how you stole away a woman like that from her people. And that father of hers, he is nothing short of a miracle worker. I thought Joshua was done for, truly I did."

"He's looking better now." Caleb assured her.

"Well, you just be sure those two eat up. They'll need a good hot meal after all that they've done today."

"I will, Mrs. Burnett. Thank you for the lovely food, and the change of heart."

She blushed a little and then smiled before turning and hurrying back out into the evening twilight.

"Well, what do you think of that?" Daniel said, as they headed up the stairs to the room.

"I'm surprised, is what I'm thinking."

"Well, whatever the first impression was, it seems like your new housekeeper has made a very positive second one."

"So it appears."

"That was a smart move, son, bringing those Indians into our enterprise. Our Wild West lodge will have even greater authenticity with two Hopi shamans on our staff."

"I think a shaman is different from a medicine man, Dan, and Istaqa isn't going to be part of our staff. He just came along to be certain Ahote and Cha'risa were well situated."

"He came an awful long way to say good-bye," Daniel speculated. "It might not be hard to convince him to stay." Without even pausing to take a breath, he continued. "I'll bet he could tell some great stories around the campfire. That would be something none of our guests would ever forget."

"He doesn't speak English," Caleb reminded him. "And it isn't likely Istaqa will choose to leave the pueblos for good."

"Well the boy did, and she did," Daniel pointed out. "And I'll tell you this, that man loves his daughter. A man might do many things he never intended, for the sake of his daughter."

Caleb held back a smile. "I suppose that's so."

"And I'll tell you another thing," Daniel continued. "That old man has his eye on you. You'd better behave yourself around "Cha'risa.""

Caleb turned and looked at Daniel as they reached the top of the stairs. "What is it you're implying, Dan?"

"I'm saying she's a pretty thing, and you've been on your own way too long. We got a good thing going with these two. Don't mess it up."

Caleb no longer bothered hiding his smile. "She is pretty, isn't she?

Daniel sighed with exasperation. "Is that all you heard?"

Caleb laughed, and then entered the room, carrying the fragrant stew and bread. Behind him, he could hear Daniel mutter, "Damn fool."

Chapter 6

It was after midnight, and the man they called Joshua was sleeping comfortably. Cha'risa let her hands rest gently on his body, placing them just above both injuries, one near his shoulders, the other near his thigh. As she hummed softly, she felt the wounds drink deeply from the energy. His body was making progress; he was beginning to heal. She made a note to herself to give him more of the decoction of winterfat when he woke. He was still free of fever, and she meant to keep it that way.

Satisfied he was doing well, she turned and hobbled back to the chair. Her ankle was throbbing, and she needed to take weight off it. She elevated her foot on a small nightstand, and then leaned forward, placing her hands around her throbbing ankle. The injury was very swollen and constricted, but still she could feel a trickle of energy snaking through, opening her ankle to the healing warmth. It stirred a memory. Caleb had drunk deeply of her power that afternoon. She hadn't had the time to wonder about it then, but now it made her curious. Why had he opened to her that way, especially when he wasn't the injured party? What was most intriguing was, even though he had drunk deeply of the flow, he hadn't held onto it. He'd fed it right back into the cycle, adding his own strength to hers. He'd not just received; he'd given. It surprised her that an untrained white man could have done such a thing.

There was a knock at her door. It seemed too early for her father to be relieving her. The door cracked open.

"Cha'risa?"

Not her father. It was Caleb. He poked his head inside the room, and when he saw she was awake, he came in bearing a kettle of hot water.

"I thought you might like to make some tea," he said in his lilting Irish tones.

Well he wasn't wrong on that account, she thought. A cup of her Hopi tea was just what she needed. She pulled out a bundle from her pouch. "May I make you some as well?" she offered.

His eyes crinkled up at the corners. "I could do with a cup."

She put two bundles into the hot water to steep. "Why aren't you sleeping?"

"I kept thinking of you. I figured you might welcome some tea and a bit of company."

Cha'risa sighed. This undercurrent between them had to stop. The man did not understand she was unlike other women.

"Mr. McKenna…" she began, but he interrupted her.

"Call me Caleb," he said. "I'm not needing such formality."

"Caleb," she corrected herself. "I appreciate the tea, but it would be best if you didn't take such an interest in me."

Caleb studied her closely. "You're about to become part of my household. That puts you under my protection."

"I can take care of myself," she assured him, and then pierced him with one of her most forbidding stares. "Also, I think you might be indulging in some wrong-headed thinking where I am concerned."

He was unprepared for her directness, but then he grinned. "Well, you got me there. I have to admit I find you very interesting."

"You barely know me."

"True," he agreed. "But I'd very much like to change that."

She frowned resolutely. "It's not a good idea."

His brow lifted, questioning. "And just why is that?"

"There are things you don't understand about me."

He leaned forward, looking even more interested. "Enlighten me, then."

"Well, for one," she began, "I'm a medicine woman."

His eyes twinkled. "I managed to figure that out all on my own."

She leaned forward, willing him to take her more seriously. "Most men are afraid of medicine women."

He smiled. "Well, I'm thinking I'm not like most men."

"Perhaps you're not scared because you're ignorant of what I really am."

His studied her even more closely. "And what would that be?"

He wasn't easily dissuaded; she could see that, but it had to be done. She sat up straighter, her eyes still locked on his. "In my village, they believe I have teeth here." She pointed between her legs. "That any man who beds me will have his manhood devoured."

Caleb was holding back a smile. "They say that, do they?"

"Yes."

"Why would they be saying such a thing?"

"Because they believe I'm a witch."

"Do all witches have teeth down there?" He kept his eyes on her face, for which she was grateful.

"I don't know. The idea of it comes from a popular story about a boy who encounters the Jimsonweed girls, and is fortunate enough to outsmart them."

"So witches can be outsmarted?"

She glared at him. "That's not the point."

"No?"

"No. The point is that people in my village believe I'm as dangerous and terrifying as a Jimsonweed girl."

"That seems to me an odd conclusion. You were married and bore a son. I imagine that required your husband's parts to be in working order."

Cha'risa turned from him, fighting off a smile. She decided she liked his persistence. After all these years of being doubted, it felt good to hear him take her side. Still, for his sake, the words needed to be spoken. She took a moment, and he waited for her, not uncomfortable with her silence.

She did not look at him when she spoke again. "You need to understand that the line between a medicine woman and a witch is a fine one. The knowledge I use to heal can also be used to harm. Truly, the only difference between the two is how one chooses to use that energy."

"I'm listening," he said, encouraging her to continue.

She took a deep breath and once again met his gaze. "My people are always aware of this. They notice when someone is no longer using this power for the betterment of others." She paused a moment and then admitted. "Four years ago, I gave my village a reason to believe that I had crossed over to the dark side of this power."

"Did you?" He sounded fascinated.

Obviously, Caleb McKenna was not a man who scared easily, but it only made it more imperative that he hear the full accounting. Cha'risa didn't like to think of that night, let alone speak of it, but still, she forced herself to relive the events so he would fully comprehend the darkness inside her.

"Four years ago soldiers came to my village in the middle of the night. They came to abduct our children and take them to the Indian School." She glanced at Caleb. She knew he'd been one of Ahote's teachers. Perhaps he knew already how her son had come to that school, but certainly he didn't know all of it.

She continued speaking. "They dragged Ahote out of his bed, all the while shooting their guns in warning. From all over the village, children were screaming as the soldiers grabbed them, threw them across their backs, and carried them over to their horses. I stood there screaming too. I was so afraid. I felt powerless with all their firearms pointed at us, but not my husband. He ran up to where a soldier sat upon his horse, holding our terrified boy in his firm grasp. Kwahu tried to grab the reins, to keep the soldier from riding off with our son. But the soldier raised his rifle and fired a shot. The soldier had let go of Ahote to shoot Kwahu, and my boy broke free of the soldier. Both of us ran to where Kwahu lay motionless on the ground. I could see the wound to his head. There was nothing for me to do; my husband was already dead. For a moment, the soldier sat there stunned, looking at Kwahu, looking at me, but then he looked at Ahote, and he dismounted from his horse and grabbed my boy. He pulled him right out of my arms. All the while my boy was screaming and struggling against him."

Cha'risa took in a deep breath to steady her trembling hands. After a moment, she squared her shoulders and looked back up, meeting Caleb's steady gaze. She was ready to tell him the worst part of her story.

"When I looked into that soldier's eyes, I was filled with such hatred. It burned inside me unlike anything I'd ever felt before. It exploded like wildfire, a crazy wind blowing in all directions, and I just opened my arms and let it go. Almost immediately, the soldier's nose began to bleed. You could tell he didn't think much about it. He wiped away the first trickles as he climbed back on his horse. He pointed his gun at me and told Ahote to come or he'd shoot me too. Ahote looked at me once and then reached up toward the man, who grabbed his hand and swung him onto the horse. With his rifle still trained on me, he rode away from our village and into the canyon. Soon our village was empty of soldiers, empty of children, and eighteen adults as well, who'd been arrested for resisting. They didn't arrest me, because they never realized what it was I'd done."

"It wasn't long before stories started coming back about some kind of terrible disease striking down people in Keam's Canyon. All of us were frantic with worry for our children. But when the men they'd taken from our village finally came home, they said the disease only ever affected those soldiers who'd raided Hoteville. They described the symptoms, saying every single soldier who'd participated in the raid began bleeding from the nose, the ears, and the eyes. Our returned men glanced at me as they finished their story. They said it was unlike anything they'd ever seen, and the agonized screams of those afflicted had been terrible to hear. Every last one of those men died."

With the last of her story finally revealed, Cha'risa let out a shuddering sigh, and then fell silent. The shame of her confession weighed heavily on her, but she knew she'd done the right thing. Now Caleb would understand the darkness inside her, and why he needed to keep his distance. After only a few moments of this heavy quietude, Caleb reached out and took her hand. She looked up at him, surprised.

"They killed your husband and kidnapped your child."

Was he defending her actions? Another tear escaped her, and she shook her head, not trusting herself to talk.

"I would have fought them too," Caleb assured her. "I would have killed them if it meant I could save my child."

"But don't you see?!" she cried. "I didn't save him. I didn't save anyone!" She bowed her head. "That's the worst part. I had the power to stop them, and I waited until it was too late. I killed those men when it served no purpose, except to vent my own rage."

More tears fell now, a steady flow that she didn't even bother to wipe away. Once again she lifted her face and met Caleb's eyes. "I've never said this to another living soul, not even my father, but it is not the killing I regret, or the turn to the dark side of the power. What I regret is that I didn't save my husband and I didn't save my boy."

Caleb leaned in closer, his eyes searching deep into hers. "Next time," he said. "You won't hesitate."

That shocked her. "Are you suggesting I should freely use my dark power?"

"No. I'm saying I understand why you did, and if you ever do need to protect someone you love again, you will know what to do, and have the courage to do it."

She dropped her gaze from his, shaking her head. "This is a dangerous power to let loose. I have the ability to cause great harm."

"I'm thinking if you put a gun in my hand I can kill as well as you."

"You don't understand," she persisted. "Every time I open to that power, the darkness will lay a stronger claim within me. How can I risk that? Even I'm not sure if I'm a witch or a medicine woman!"

He put his hand under her chin, lifting her face to meet his. "You've given me many reasons why I shouldn't be interested in you, except for the one that actually matters to me."

"And what's that?" she asked.

"You haven't told me you're not interested in me." Then he leaned in even closer, kissing her on the mouth.

Perhaps she should have stopped him, but it had been many long, lonely years since a man had touched her like this, and had kissed her so tenderly. Without thinking, she wrapped her arms around him, responding to his kiss with a hunger of her own. It was Caleb who at last rested his forehead against hers.

"Can I take that to mean you might also be interested?"

Cha'risa laughed. "You are a fool, Caleb McKenna."

He cracked a smile. "You wouldn't be the first to have said so."

"No good can come of this."

"Depends on what you mean by good, because I thought that kiss was a lot more than just good."

She didn't know what to say, because she had, too.

He sighed and stood up, putting a little distance between them. "I'd better say goodnight to you, while I still can." Reluctantly, he walked over to the door, and then turned. "You and your father were a credit to me and mine, today, Cha'risa. Thank you for saving Josh and Doc Ferguson."

Cha'risa shrugged. "It's in our nature. It's what we do."

He smiled at her kindly. "You see, now there's your answer to whether or not you're a medicine woman or a witch."

Cha'risa looked up sharply, locking her eyes on his. "How so?"

"Without thinking, you put their interests before your own. Would a witch do that? One mistake doesn't define you, Cha'risa. You just need to have faith in the truth of who you really are." Then he exited the room, shutting the door firmly behind him.

Cha'risa wasn't sure how long she sat there pondering their encounter, but it came as a surprise when she looked up and saw her father standing nearby, studying her closely.

"Is my time up already?"

"Yes. I'll help you to the room so you can get some rest."

She stood up and put her arm around her father.

"How is the patient?" he asked as he helped her hobble down the hall.

"He's doing well. He's due for some more winterfat tea when he wakes."

Istaqa nodded. She paused a moment and then added. "I saw Caleb tonight, after you'd gone to bed."

"Oh?"

"I had the talk with him. I told him every frightening thing there is to know about me."

Istaqa nodded. "So now he can turn his attentions elsewhere."

"I don't think so," she admitted.

Her father stopped and stared at her. "Why do you say that?"

Cha'risa felt her face grow hot. "Because he kissed me, and then told me it wasn't in my nature to be a witch."

Her father stopped walking. At first he stared at her, his face unreadable. "He thinks he knows you well enough after only two days to make that assessment?"

"Apparently so."

Slowly, a wide grin spread over Istaqa's face. "The man's as strong as a mountain; but perhaps he's not as dense as one." And then he burst out laughing.

1899

Skillet Cornbread

Ingredients
1½ cups stoneground cornmeal
1 cup unbleached all-purpose flour (or blend ½ cup whole wheat flour and ½ cup all-purpose flour)
4 teaspoons baking powder
1½ teaspoons kosher salt
½ teaspoon baking soda
¼ teaspoon freshly grated nutmeg, optional
12 tablespoons (1 1/2 sticks) unsalted butter, melted and cooled slightly
½ cup maple syrup or honey
2 cups buttermilk
3 large eggs

Directions
Heat oven to 375º F. Place an 11" or 12" cast iron skillet (or other heavy ovenproof pan) into the oven to heat.

In a medium bowl, whisk the cornmeal, flour, baking powder, kosher salt, baking soda, and nutmeg until well combined.

Set aside 1 tablespoon of the butter to grease the skillet. Whisk the remaining butter in a large bowl with the maple syrup, then whisk in the buttermilk. Whisk in the eggs.

Add the dry ingredients to the bowl in two batches, stirring gently but thoroughly. Do not over-mix.

Remove the hot pan from the oven, setting it on a heatproof surface. Coat the pan with the reserved butter, then pour in the batter and return to the oven.

Bake until the top is golden brown, about 30 to 40 minutes. Cool in the skillet 10 minutes before slicing.

Serves 8-10

Chapter 7

Katherine wasn't doing well. Cha'risa examined her, praying for an encouraging sign, but about the only positive thing she could say was that Katherine was resting comfortably, for the moment.

"You are exhausted." Istaqa said. "Go and rest while you can."

Cha'risa had mixed emotions about being alone with her thoughts. In a quiet room she would never be able to silence them. However, there wasn't really a choice. He knew it, and she did as well. She needed to be strong for what was to come. "You'll get me if anything changes?" she asked.

Istaqa walked her to the door. "She'll sleep for a while now. You should too." She looked back at the bed, at Katherine, face pale against the pillow. Istaqa gave her a little push. "Go," he said, and then shut the door firmly behind her.

Just outside, Zach and Daniel were hovering, hoping for some encouraging word.

"She's resting now," Cha'risa said.

"But is everything okay?" Zach asked anxiously.

Like Caleb, Zach's Irish brogue got heavier when he was troubled, but even without such a telltale sign, the worry and fear on his face were clear to see.

"She's holding her own," Cha'risa assured him, wishing she could give him more, but careful not to give him false hope.

Zach's eyes locked on hers. There must have been so much he wanted to ask, but instead he just said, "You look knackered. Can I get you a cup of tea, or something?"

"Actually, I was just on my way to my room. My father has ordered me to lie down."

Zach nodded, taking her arm in his. "I'll walk you there." He turned to his father-in-law. "I'll be right back."

Daniel nodded. "I'll be here."

Zach walked with her silently until they arrived at her door. "Cha'risa," he said before leaving her, "I know you think you're to blame for all this, but the God's honest truth is the fault is more mine than yours."

37

She shook her head stubbornly. "I interfered with something I didn't fully understand."

The smile he gave her was tentative. "How about this?" he suggested. "We forgive each other, right here and now, before we know how it will end. We don't take it back, no matter what."

She stared at him, uncertain what to say, uncertain how to even go about such a thing.

"Cha'risa," he said taking her hand in his, "We all took a chance. Maybe it was a mistake, but one thing I know for certain, you gave Katherine hope. She's been so happy these past months. Even if she knew from the start she might be risking her life, she'd have chosen this."

"But I wouldn't have," Cha'risa said, "and neither would you."

He looked away, turned the knob on the door for her, and then sought her gaze once more. "Even so, I'll not be blaming you for what happens, understand?"

She looked back him, and then placed a hand on his shoulder. "She's not going to die, Zach. I'm not going to let it happen."

His eyes welled up when he saw her determination. He took her arm and ushered her into the room. "Get some rest." He'd meant to sound authoritative, but his voice was raw with emotion, and before the door shut she saw him wiping away a tear.

Cha'risa lay down on her bed, the image of his heartbroken face seared in her mind. Zach was a tall, ginger haired man, not quite as big as Caleb, but strong all the same from the years of hard labor he'd shared with his brother. He was a calming, nurturing man; much more even-tempered than Caleb. It took a lot for him to give in to despair, and she hated being the source of it.

She laid her head down on the pillow, relieved to get off her feet. Her ankles were swollen from the long, sleepless night, and her body ached. Her eyes closed, but before she could begin to relax, her thoughts started circling. The first image that settled in her mind was of the two brothers; so different, but so closely bound by the love they had for each other. They weren't brothers by birth. Zach had been born the son of Mary Clare's best friend, Gillian Conner. Mary Clare and Gillian had given birth within months of each other, and Mary was still nursing Cal when she'd learned of her friend's accident and untimely death. She'd taken Zach in because Gillian's husband was more interested in drinking away his grief than in caring for his son.

The baby was often left hungry and in dirty diapers. Mary Clare had plenty of milk for two babies; and all the love she'd once given Gillian, she poured into her friend's small boy. A few months after Zach had come to live with the McKenna family, Zach's father left Ireland, never to return, and never to inquire after his boy again.

Perhaps the bond between Caleb and Zach had started there, sharing their mother's milk, but over the years it had only grown stronger. It pained Cha'risa to know her presence in this house had strained their relationship. She'd managed to smooth things over, and steer everyone away from anger and recriminations, but not before making a critical blunder, one that now left Katherine clinging to life.

It'd been just over a year since she'd stood in that hallway, hiding in the shadows, and listening to the three of them argue. As the memory presented itself, she realized she would have to once again watch herself make that wrong turn. But maybe, if she studied the memory closely enough, she would see beyond the mistake, and perhaps, somewhere in there, she'd find an answer to her prayers.

Katherine paced the room, agitated. "I don't understand? How could this happen?!"

Caleb was just barely containing his anger. "I'm thinking you know quite well what's required."

Katherine's face turned a furious shade of red. "The picture is all too clear in my mind," she spat. "Good Lord! You've known her barely four months!"

Zach took his wife's hand. "Darling, you must calm yourself. Let him finish what he's come to say."

"It doesn't matter what he says. That woman has no decency, and she has no place here with us!"

It was clear Caleb was about to erupt, and Zach wisely put some space between the two, leading his wife over to the sofa. That brought the couple closer to the entryway, so Cha'risa backed away from the door, remaining unseen. Caleb had asked her to let him handle this. He wouldn't be happy to discover her eavesdropping, but she didn't feel right leaving him to face this on his own.

Zach sat down next to his wife, tucking a loose strand of auburn hair away from her face. Katherine responded to his touch, and she started to relax. "Honey," Zach ventured, "don't you think you're overreacting a wee bit?" he asked.

That was clearly the wrong thing to have said. Katherine tensed again, looking at her husband in disbelief. "Are you daft? What's going to happen to our business when people find out?"

Caleb's eyes focused on her, narrowing, but Zach looked at him and shook his head. Cha'risa could see how hard it was for Caleb to stay silent; still he allowed Zach to handle it, turning to stare sullenly out the window.

Zach took Katherine's hand in his. "Sweetheart, you know there's no rhyme or reason to how people fall in love. Look at you and me."

"This is about a whole lot more than simply falling in love!"

"I know it happened fast, and it isn't what either of us anticipated, but I've known Caleb my whole life. This woman is important to him."

Katherine shot back, "He can declare his love from here to kingdom come, but people will still think she's a whore!"

In her dark, hidden spot, Cha'risa flinched, and Caleb spun back to them, his eyes blazing. Again, Zach stopped him. "Just give me a wee bit more time with her," he pleaded. Then he turned once again to his wife, using his gentlest voice possible, heavy now with his Irish lilt.

"Honey, think about your father. Do you think he will be judging Caleb and Cha'risa this harshly?"

"My father is not the issue here!"

"Well, I'm thinking he might be worth taking a look at. He loves being around Ahote's family, wants to hear their stories, wants to drink Cha'risa's tea. He swears it makes him feel young again. Right now he's sitting out by the barn sharing a pipe with Istaqa. Your dad has said it often enough, our Hopis are going to make our ranch much more of an authentic Wild West experience."

"Zachariah, surely you must see it is one thing to enjoy the company of some Hopis working our ranch, and quite another to accept that one of them is marrying into our family."

Caleb had stood by long enough. He stalked up to where Katherine sat on the sofa, leaned in dangerously close, and allowed the full force of his displeasure to press Katherine back against the cushions.

"It's kind of you to remember I'm family," he fumed. "But make no mistake; it's not your permission I'm asking for. I'm simply doing you the courtesy of sharing my good news. Cha'risa is carrying my child, and we will soon marry. If God is willing, this will be one of many half-breed babies running around C&M Ranch. If you cannot wish me well, you at least better get used to it!"

Caleb straightened, preparing to storm out of the room, but just then Katherine burst into tears. He stopped to stare at her, completely thrown off balance. "Jesus, Mary and Joseph!" he swore.

Zach glared at him, and then turned back to his wife, drawing her close. "Hush, my darling. It'll be all right," he soothed, "I know it will." He nestled her against him, and slowly her crying eased. He spoke again, in that soft, reassuring tone of his. "You know, we've often talked about how nice it would be to have a wee one running about."

"That was when we were talking about children of our own," she said through her sniffles.

"Well, maybe you'll grow to love this little one, just like it was one of our own." He didn't realize his mistake until she again began to cry. Cha'risa shook her head at the ineptitude of the two men, and stepped into the room.

Caleb's face turned white when he saw her. Quickly, he took her by the arm, trying to usher her out.

Cha'risa kept her feet firmly planted. "I will speak with her."

"Chari, I'm not so sure that is a good idea right now." Caleb tried again to steer her back out into the hallway

She remained unmoving. "It's important," she insisted.

Katherine looked up through her tears, and studied Cha'risa guardedly. Cha'risa met her gaze, hoping the woman would see that she meant her no ill. Katherine didn't look away; instead she dried her tears.

"It's okay," she told her husband. She blew her nose in one of her hand-embroidered hankies. "I want to hear what she has to say."

"Are you sure?" Zach asked. "It can wait 'til you're feeling better."

"Just go," she scolded, shooing both men back to the spot by the window.

Cha'risa watched them hesitantly retreat, then carefully she approached the sofa, sitting down on the edge. Katherine was huddled into the farthest corner, her arms crossed protectively against her chest. That body language was not unknown to Cha'risa. She'd grown used to being rejected over the years, and had learned that being direct and confident was the best way to counter that kind of a wall.

"This is not just about my morals," Cha'risa began.

"It *is*..." Katherine started to object.

"No." Cha'risa put her hand up forestalling any further protest. "It's about my being pregnant."

Katherine went still. Cha'risa kept talking, but she allowed a gentler tone. "I had no idea that I would conceive when I was with Caleb. I didn't think it was even possible."

Katherine's face started to turn red again. "You knew what would happen!" she challenged. "What kind of medicine woman doesn't understand the implications of when a man beds a woman?!"

Cha'risa continued to speak from her heart. "I wasn't speaking in general terms, but very specifically about myself. I've never had an easy time conceiving. I had to make a special kind of tea just to conceive Ahote. After he was born, despite drinking many servings of this same tea over the years, I never again became pregnant. Finally, enough time went by, I had to acknowledge he would be the only one."

Katherine remained wary. "Why are you telling me this?"

Cha'risa found she needed to take a steadying breath. Without realizing it, her hand gravitated protectively to her belly. "This baby is a shock to you, but for me, it's a miracle." She looked up then; meeting Katherine's questioning eyes with her own. "When my husband, Kwahu, was killed, I didn't think there would ever be another man in my life." Cha'risa turned then to look at Caleb. As she held his gaze, the tension melted from his face, and he answered her with a warm smile.

"He is not of my people," Cha'risa said, still holding his eyes with her own, "but this baby tells me with certainty that Caleb is the man I'm meant to love."

Katherine's voice softened. "You love him?"

Cha'risa looked back at her. "I do."

Then Katherine's face set stubbornly once again. "Not many people are going to care about that."

"Probably not," Cha'risa acknowledged.

Katherine sighed with exasperation, and Cha'risa tried again to find the right words. "I know this is hard to accept. I was supposed to be a help to you, and instead I have complicated your life immensely. Even if I hadn't gotten pregnant, I'm not at all the kind of help you needed most."

Katherine studied her, clearly wondering where Cha'risa was headed with these observations. "Cha'risa," she offered. "It's true, you aren't what I expected, but I do know you've been trying, that you work very hard."

"But it's not the work I was hired to do, is it? When someone calls me to help with a sick animal, or a hurt ranch hand, I always go." Katherine seemed about to respond, but Cha'risa wasn't finished. "Also, I know my cooking skills are a big disappointment to you."

Caleb called out from his spot at the window. "I love your cornbread! You know I do!"

Cha'risa allowed a smile. "I can make cornbread. But it doesn't change the fact that most of the ranch recipes are unfamiliar to me. Katherine has had to invest a lot of time trying to teach me, and my progress has been slow. But that is not really the issue here today, is it?" she said, turning back to Katherine.

"No, it is not," Katherine agreed, her indignation rising once again. "This is about your promiscuity."

"No," Cha'risa countered. "This is about my conceiving a child when you cannot."

Katherine gasped, and then slowly she sank against the arm of the sofa, the fullness of her anger punctured by the truth. Cha'risa continued speaking urgently. "I could help you," she persisted. "There are things I know, things that could perhaps help a baby take hold."

Katherine's green eyes locked onto Cha'risa. Her desperation was clear to see. "Are you referring to that tea?"

Cha'risa nodded. "I've seen those same plants growing at the winter ranch."

Katherine looked at her then. "Why would you help me, especially when I've judged you so harshly?"

Cha'risa's hands rested on her womb. "These brothers link us, and this unborn baby links us. And if God is willing, your babies will link us as well. We are going to be a family now."

Katherine stared at Cha'risa. It was a long, uncomfortable moment before her expression shifted from disbelief to hope. "The winter ranch," Katherine mused, and then her eyes shifted to watching as Cha'risa cradled her unborn child. When Katherine looked back up again, it was with a spark of hope. "When can we go?"

Cha'risa wasn't certain just when her memories had turned into dreams, but she must have slept, for she opened her eyes to a room no longer bathed in sunlight; it was darkened now by a mid-morning storm. Outside the monsoon thundered and lit up the sky, while rain pounded against the windows and on the rooftop. Cha'risa pulled the blankets up around her. Her brain was still sluggish and fixated on the dream; remembering in particular that look on Katherine's face when Cha'risa had offered her the possibility of a child.

Cha'risa was reminded of something her father had once told her; that when someone opens their heart to you, it's much like a flower blossoming. It becomes an invitation for all your senses to become immersed in that person's light and beauty. That really was the best way to describe what happened last summer, when Katherine decided to open her heart to Cha'risa and become her friend.

An early morning sun warmed the ground of the winter ranch garden, and the air was filled with the scent of ripening melons. Cha'risa sat in the midst of all that warmth and fragrance, her fingers working swiftly, as she made small herb bundles from the desert plants they'd collected over the past two days. She finished another bundle, placing it with the growing pile inside the pouch at her side. She'd found many plants among the towering red rocks and along the dry washes; not only those needed for Katherine's tea, but also several others she could use for fever, pain, and digestive upset. She even found one she thought might help with Daniel's arthritis.

Cha'risa looked up from her work to see what Katherine was doing, and found her nearby on her knees in the dirt, heedless of the fine fabric of her dress. Her head was buried deep into the tomato plants, as she worked to reinforce the individual wells around each root. Harvest baskets full of cucumbers, tomatoes and peppers lay near where she worked. As Cha'risa watched, Katherine finished reinforcing the dirt around the last plant, and then filled its well with a ladle of water from a bucket she kept close by. At last Katherine stood, brushed the soil off her hands and apron, and then looked around at her handiwork.

"Well that looks better," she said, coming to sit down near Cha'risa. "Bobby Dickenson did a decent job keeping things watered, and I can't complain about the harvest, but I don't like that he let those wells get so eroded."

Cha'risa understood her concern. It was a delicate balance growing plants in the desert. There was more than one way to do it, but one always had to be mindful of the use of water.

"Istaqa will be traveling back here frequently. Maybe you should show him how you like the wells to be kept up. He could keep an eye on them for you."

Katherine looked surprised. "Why does he want to go back and forth in this heat?"

Cha'risa smiled. "He's used to the heat, and he wants to keep an eye on the Hopi corn he planted last May. I think he also planted a peach tree or two."

Katherine chuckled. "He did, did he? Perhaps my father's badgering paid off. That sounds to me like a man planning to stay a while."

Cha'risa gently caressed her belly. "I think the baby may have helped."

Katherine paused, the longing in her eyes clear to see. "Do you really think this tea will work?"

"You're young and healthy. I think your chances are good."

Katherine grew thoughtful. "I wonder if my father will leave Boston for good if I get pregnant."

Cha'risa chuckled. "I'm not sure a baby is required to get him to stay with us. I haven't heard him once talk about leaving, especially now he has a new best friend."

"Our fathers," Katherine mused. "It's the oddest thing, isn't it? They can't share more than twenty words between them."

"They manage well enough," Cha'risa observed.

Katherine looked up, "Did you say Istaqa planted a peach tree? Does he really think it will grow here?"

Cha'risa looked over toward the deep wash that ran through the property. "You'd be surprised," she said. "There's lots of growing potential here if you know where to look."

"He used the wash?"

"Either that, or he found an underground spring. He's good at locating those."

"He's something of a marvel, isn't he?"

Cha'risa grinned. "I've always thought so."

Katherine hesitated, and then said, "My dad's been right all along about the two of you." She looked away then, her cheeks coloring. "I'm sorry for my behavior the other day. To be honest, I judged you poorly from the start. I was so focused on what you weren't, I never left room for the ways you might be more than I expected."

45

Katherine's admission touched Cha'risa. It wasn't often someone cared enough to find the woman within. "Thank you," she said. "It's rare for someone to have the courage to say such words."

Katherine blushed at the praise, and then declared, "You know, you and I really aren't that different."

Cha'risa looked at her. Katherine's work clothes were more delicate than sturdy. A broad rimmed sunbonnet shaded her face, protecting her from the freckles that were the bane of her fair skin and auburn hair. She was a creature of a sheltered city life, not of the desert. And yet she thrived here, and her gardens did too. Even her beloved lavender found a way to blossom, despite the wind, and the dust, and the heat.

Cha'risa placed her brown hand in Katherine's pale one. "We're different on the outside," she said, "but maybe not so different when you look beneath the skin."

"We both like gardens and recipes," Katherine expounded.

That surprised Cha'risa. "I thought you didn't like my cooking."

"Well, it's not so much the cooking I'm talking about, as the ability to create recipes. Every medicinal tea you make is a recipe, you know?"

Cha'risa nodded.

"And we have other things in common, too" Katherine continued. "We both love those two brothers."

"And we're both lucky those two brothers love us," Cha'risa added.

Katherine giggled. "That's a good one. I should have started with that." She grew quiet then, deep in thought. At last she looked up and said, "Cha'risa, would you like to share this garden with me?"

"What?"

"I think we should cultivate some of your medicinal plants here. We know they grow well in this climate."

It took Cha'risa a moment to understand Katherine's was making a gesture of goodwill.

"Where do you suggest putting it?" she asked.

"Here," Katherine pointed. "I could put in two more beds right along the southern border."

Cha'risa followed her finger, and then agreed. "That's a good spot."

"Good! It's decided then." Katherine picked up two shovels and handed one to Cha'risa. "Let's start by laying in the new beds before we head back up north."

Chapter 8

The rain stopped, and the wind grew quiet. As the sun poked back out from behind the clouds, the atmosphere in the room began to get steamy. Cha'risa shook off thoughts of the past, and then got up to go open a window. Fresh, cool air entered the room, along with the sharp scent of the spent storm. Cha'risa breathed in deeply, and then set about straightening her clothes and smoothing back her hair. Her breasts felt heavy with milk, a sign that baby Sam was likely hungry. She was just putting on her boots to go find him, when there was a knock at the door.

"Come in," she called, assuming it was someone bringing the hungry baby to her. Kitty Burnett poked her head through the doorway. Cha'risa looked up in surprise.

Kitty bustled past her into the room, a pot of tea in her hands. "I've brought you tea," she announced.

Cha'risa raised an eyebrow. "What are you doing here? Who's watching your store?"

Kitty chuckled. "George is quite capable, you know, and I figured I'd come and lend a hand around here until your new housekeeper has a chance to recover from her long journey."

Caleb had run up to Flagstaff first thing this morning to meet the train bringing Daniel's housekeeper from Boston. Daniel had suggested sending for Esme as soon as he realized all was not well with Katherine's pregnancy, but he'd also needed the woman to prepare the Boston residence for an extended vacancy. Everyone had figured she'd still get to the ranch with time to spare, but no one had counted on the likelihood of Katherine going into early labor. Now, it appeared Esme's arrival was not a moment too soon.

Cha'risa smelled the fragrant blend of her special Hopi tea wafting up from the kettle. She looked at the pot with regret. "That smells wonderful," she said, "but I can't share a cup with you right now, it's past time for Sam's feeding."

Kitty smiled, and then set the tea down on the nightstand. "Sit," she commanded. "Sam is already taken care of."

Cha'risa raised an eyebrow. "I'm pretty sure I'm the only one carrying around a supply of mother's milk."

Kitty chuckled. "That's true, but the boy was starving, and Esme made him a bowl of grits."

"Grits?"

"Relax, it's a porridge made from corn. He loved it. His eyes went wide at the first bite, and then he just kept eating and eating. His little tummy got so full he fell right off to sleep."

"So where is he now?" Cha'risa wanted to know.

"Caleb put him in your sling and then took him to down the barn to check on the horses. Ahote's been down there all alone, and Caleb wanted to lend him a hand for a while."

"That's good, he's looking after both my boys," Cha'risa smiled, but then her thoughts turned to her own responsibilities. "But I still should go check on Katherine."

"Katherine's still asleep," Kitty said. "And we sent Istaqa to his room to get a little shut eye as well."

Cha'risa tensed. "You left Katherine alone?"

"Of course not! Doc Ferguson is with her."

"Doc Ferguson? You mean the drunk I saved?"

"Would you please sit down?" Kitty pleaded. "I promise he's sober as can be. He hasn't had a single drink since the accident. He's a reformed man because of you, drinks your teas religiously. Anyhow, he's just keeping an eye on things so you can rest. He promised to come get you and Istaqa when Katherine wakes."

Cha'risa stared at Kitty a moment, and then sat down, accepting a cup of tea. "Drink up," Kitty ordered. "A nursing mama needs to keep up her fluids."

In the wafting steam of her cup, Cha'risa could smell both the greenthread and the lavender. "This blend came about because of Katherine," Cha'risa admitted then. Fighting back a lump in her throat, she added, "Greenthread and lavender are two things that ordinarily would never meet, just like Katherine and me."

Kitty put her cup down, searching deeply into Cha'risa's eyes. "She's going to be okay," Kitty insisted.

Cha'risa fought to keep her tears from falling.

"None of that," Kitty said, taking Cha'risa's hand in hers. "Katherine wants this baby more than anything in the world. She won't give up. She'll see this through."

"She is strong willed, isn't she?"

Kitty laughed. "Good lord, yes! She never gives up. Do you remember how hopping mad she was when that minister refused to marry you and Caleb?"

Cha'risa smiled. "I remember."

"She told that story to anyone in town who would listen. I was in the store, helping Jenny Taylor when Katherine came storming in to tell us all about his suspect integrity."

Cha'risa laughed. "I remember. She was more outraged than I was. The man had married them after all, a Methodist to a Catholic. But when he learned I was Hopi, he started quoting lines from the bible. He said it would be a sin for Caleb to marry a woman who didn't share similar religious or cultural common ground with her husband."

"Oh, I remember," Kitty assured her. "Katherine was boiling mad when she told me about it."

"Caleb was really upset too. I remember suggesting we perform the ceremony according to Hopi traditions, since they don't require someone to officiate, but Caleb didn't want there to be any doubt as to Sam's legitimacy. He wanted that certificate."

"It was a lucky thing Jenny Taylor heard the whole thing," Kitty affirmed. "She'll never forget what you did for her husband; that he's alive, and he can walk. When you saved Josh, you made her your friend for life."

Cha'risa smiled remembering both Jenny and Katherine's intervention. "Katherine had to explain to me what a Justice of the Peace was, after she told us about Jenny's brother being able to perform the ceremony." A memory stirred of her wedding ceremony, and she mused, "He did a really lovely job that day, didn't he?"

"Well, Charles Whipple and Josh Taylor were best friends before Josh and Jenny fell in love," Kitty commented as she refilled Cha'risa's cup. "He had a lot to thank you for as well."

After visiting a while, Kitty suggested Cha'risa might like a hot bath. "It'll perk you right up," she said. Cha'risa didn't even try to argue. The tea had helped some, but the previous night had been grueling. It'd turned out to be an episode of false labor, but the stress on Katherine's heart had been real enough. When it was all over, Cha'risa was left with a strong premonition the baby would come today.

She sat in the tub now, the steamy, hot water reviving her muscles and her spirit. Kitty's words about Katherine's passionate nature kept replaying in Cha'risa's mind. It was true, with Katherine she either loved you or she couldn't stand you, but thing of it was, once Katherine decided to love you, she held nothing back.

Memories stirred of how Katherine had brought the full force of her fervent nature to bear when she helped Cha'risa plan her wedding. Throughout, Katherine had been so full of ideas, and so curious about Hopi wedding customs. It'd been Katherine's idea to have the wedding at the winter ranch. Caleb had always been drawn to the stunning red rock formations, and Cha'risa felt a strong affinity with that high desert terrain as well. Once Katherine mentioned the idea, they both knew there could be no better place for them to proclaim their love.

Cha'risa sank even deeper into the hot water, her mind submerging at the same time more fully into the past. She found herself once again among the rough collection of tents that made up the living quarters of the winter ranch. Katherine stood by her side, watching the night sky fade away, until all that was left was the moon and the morning star.

"It's so beautiful." Katherine murmured. "It never ceases to take my breath away."

Cha'risa reached for Katherine's hand, as together they greeted the birth of this special day. The morning star had been low along the eastern ridge when they'd started their work in the camp kitchen. It had presided over their pre-dawn efforts, and now sat high in the brightening sky. In the camp kitchen, a pot now sat on the coals, filled with coffee that sent tendrils of aroma throughout the camp. Beside the fire sat the tub of soapy water they'd made from yucca roots, ready for the ceremony that would begin as soon as the sun fully crested the ridge. The wedding guests were all up and about. Some already had a cup of coffee; all were dressed in their Sunday clothes. Looking around, Cha'risa felt a rush of excitement. Before the morning shadows were gone, she'd be married to Caleb. It was a big leap they were taking, and it was likely to ruffle some feathers, but even so she was eager to join her life to his.

Istaqa and Ahote came over and grabbed the handles of the tub. "Where do you want it?" Ahote asked.

Cha'risa led them up a rise to an outcrop of red rock. From this spot there was a good view of both the prominent mountains to the north and the softer curves of the green mesas to the south. Istaqa nodded his approval, seeing what she saw; the spot was perfectly situated between masculine and feminine energies.

When the sun finally crested the ridge, all the guests joined them at the location where the tub had been placed. Everyone watched solemnly as Istaqa divided the soapy water from the tub into two bowls. Ahote carried one bowl over to where Caleb stood.

"This is traditionally a woman's job." Ahote said to Caleb, but loud enough for everyone to hear. "Your mother-in-law is supposed to wash your hair. But you will have to settle for my grandfather."

Caleb turned to Istaqa. "Tell him I consider it an honor."

Ahote translated for his grandfather, who studied his new son-in-law and then extended his hand. Caleb locked palms with him. With the clasping of their hands they acknowledged the bond that now bound together.

Then Ahote picked up the second bowl, and carried it over to where Katherine and Cha'risa stood. "Katherine has agreed to represent the groom's family," he spoke to the assembled crowd, as he handed her the bowl of sudsy water.

"Is there a certain way I should begin?" Katherine asked as she took the bowl.

"Well," Ahote said, "the bride and groom are stripped to the waist, and then you must wash them very thoroughly."

Katherine looked at him admonishingly. "Very funny, Ahote. Stop joking around."

He stared back at her, perplexed. "I'm not joking."

"I'm sure your mother would have mentioned such a thing to me."

"Well," Cha'risa said. "He's not incorrect. You're supposed to wash me."

"I was under the impression that I would be washing your hair. This is the first I've heard about washing... body parts!"

"Is it a problem?" Cha'risa asked.

Katherine's face turned bright pink. Lowering her voice she said, "Chari, you are asking me to touch you rather intimately; to bathe you half-naked in front of everyone!"

Cha'risa studied her friend, whose face had now gone from pink to red. Katherine was now looking around for someone to help her better explain the problem. Her gaze stopped on Zach and Caleb. Cha'risa followed her glare. Caleb was already unbuttoning his shirt and there were wide grins on both men's faces. He handed his shirt to Zach, then looked over, caught her watching him, and winked.

Now Cha'risa understood Katherine's distress. Clearly, both men were filled with wrong-headed ideas about the nature of this ceremony. She looked at her father, who was gesturing to Caleb to kneel by the bowl. Istaqa had seen the wolfish grins too, and it was clear her soon-to-be husband was in for the scrubbing of his life. She turned back to Katherine and nodded her head slightly, just enough to indicate she was ready. She knelt down so that she was eye-level with Caleb. Then, pointedly staring at him, she firmly tucked the towel around her neckline.

"We make our own traditions today," she said, and then bent her head over the bowl. She heard her man laugh, and then yelp with surprise, as Istaqa forced Caleb's head down abruptly into the soapy water. Katherine was chuckling when she bent her head close and whispered, "Thank you." Then Cha'risa relaxed as Katherine's hands began to thoroughly massage the suds through her scalp and hair.

The bride and groom were well scrubbed, their heads soaking wet, and Caleb's skin still red and stinging from Istaqa's vigorous washing, when Istaqa helped them offer up corn meal and prayer feathers to the sun. The sun climbed higher, and the early morning cool burned off. All the women immediately went to work, laying out the wedding breakfast. Delicious smells began to waft through the camp as the picnic tables quickly became laden with food. There were peach and apple muffins, biscuits and gravy, eggs, bacon and thick sausages, and a big pot of porridge, swimming in butter and maple syrup. Sitting center place among the many dishes were platters of *tsukuviki* and *somikivi*; traditional Hopi wedding foods of both sweet and savory boiled corn meal, wrapped in rehydrated husks. Cha'risa and Katherine had worked painstakingly over the course of many hours on these delicacies.

When breakfast was over and put away, it was time for Cha'risa to dress for the second ceremony, the one where they would speak words in front of Charles Whipple that would legally bind them according to white man's law. Katherine was doing up the last of the buttons on Cha'risa's simple white dress, when Caleb asked if he could enter the tent.

"I've a gift for you," he said as she lifted the flap. He entered and stood before her holding a large bundle.

"I liked what you told me of how the men in your village prepare wedding clothes for their brides," he said. "It appealed to me greatly, the idea of giving you something I made with my own hands." With eyes clearly expressing the love in his heart, he handed her the bundle.

As she opened it, soft ivory fabric fell in rustling folds all the way to the floor.

She looked up at him. The robe was unlike anything she had ever seen or touched before. It felt like flowing water in her hands, and the beadwork along the collar was beautifully wrought in the colors of the sky. He watched as she traced her finger along the design.

"Katherine and your father helped me," he offered. "Turns out, I have some talent at bead work." He shrugged, grinning. "Who knew?"

She looked up at him, fighting the lump in her throat. "It's perfect."

"Well, here," Caleb said. "Let's put it on you and see how it looks."

He was so proud as he wrapped the robe around her. Katherine stood nearby, smiling with tears in her eyes, watching as Caleb hooked the beaded collar that secured the robe. The fabric all around Cha'risa felt deliciously soft and enveloping.

"I've never felt anything like this before," she said. "Where did you get this material?"

"We made it from my wedding dress," Katherine explained.

Cha'risa looked up at her. "This came from the dress you wore to your wedding?"

Katherine nodded.

"You altered it for me." Cha'risa's voice caught. "Why?"

Katherine smiled, even as she wiped a stray tear from her eyes. "We wanted to wrap you up in something that undeniably linked you to our family."

Caleb nodded. "Istaqa liked it. Is it okay? Do you like it?"

Tears were flowing openly down Cha'risa's cheeks. "It is more than okay. It is the most precious thing I've ever worn."

The sun bore down on them under a bright, cloudless sky, when Cha'risa stood beside Caleb in her flowing white robe. Before all their guests she listened as Charles Whipple declared in a clear voice, "With the power vested in me I now pronounce you man and wife." His rich baritone reverberated against the red rocks, and Cha'risa felt the vibration of it in her blood and in her bones. Her eyes locked on her husband. She could see he felt what she did. This man had just used his power to make their union legal. Their futures were now sealed together.

"You may kiss your bride." Charles said, and Caleb pulled her close. She could feel everything; the pressure of his lips, the hint of tears on his lashes, the gentle reverent touch of his hands. She could sense the unfolding awareness in every muscle of his body, that she was now his to hold for as long as he lived. It was the most delicious, tender kiss she'd ever received. It filled her entire being with a warm golden glow, and she felt certain it was a kiss she'd remember for the rest of her life.

On the last day of her wedding weekend, when the guests had all finally left, and the family was enjoying a last cup of coffee before they broke camp, Zach and Katherine made an announcement.

"I was waiting for the wedding to be over to tell all of you," Katherine said. "I think Cha'risa's special tea has worked!"

Her father's face lit up with surprise. "You're pregnant?"

"I think so."

His eyes got dewy, and he pulled her into his arms, hugging his daughter tight. Then he turned to Cha'risa and kissed her right on the lips. "You are the reason this happened!" he crowed. "You, and your marvelous teas!"

Chapter 9

Katherine's news had brought tears of joy that day, but now, eight months later, Cha'risa was haunted by Daniel's words. "You are the reason this happened." Cha'risa got up out of her bath. Wrapping herself in a towel, she zeroed in on her memories of when it all began to go wrong. Her own sweet baby, Sam, was only a few days old when she first noted the troubling symptoms in Katherine; the shortness of breath, the dizziness, the heart palpitations. Why had she never thought to ask Katherine more questions; to look deeper before offering up that tea? Only when it was too late, did she and her father hear the story of a childhood illness with a fever so high it had damaged Katherine's heart. Cha'risa's private hell had begun the moment she looked into Istaqa's eyes, and saw all her worst fears confirmed.

Now, with the impending arrival of Katherine's baby, Cha'risa stood naked in her room, and forced herself to ask the question she'd been avoiding for the last eight months. In giving Katherine that tea, had she once again crossed the line from medicine woman to witch? Had she used her skills for Katherine's benefit, or to ensure her own place within this family? The darkness she felt inside was like an abyss, and she felt herself standing at the edge. Oddly enough, it was the memories themselves that held her back from that step into the void. Over and over they replayed in her mind, and they were like that flower her father had talked about. Every memory had focused on moments when hearts had opened, when they'd been able to show one another the light and beauty within.

There was a knock at the door. Before she had a chance to respond, Caleb peered inside, holding a fussy Sam in his arms. He smiled widely when he saw her standing there unclothed. Her baby's thoughts seemed to run along similar lines when saw her. He arched away from his father, using his entire body to express his desire to nurse.

Caleb handed her their baby. "I guess the wee boyo wins this round," he said. "But it won't stop me from wishing I was the one nuzzling you."

Cha'risa smiled at her husband, and then at her baby, already rooting around her chest, searching for her nipple. When he latched on, she felt the milk begin to flow and sighed with relief. Missing the morning feeding had left her breasts overly full and tender. She carried Sam over to the bed, sat down, and then smiled up at her husband. "Come sit beside me."

Caleb joined her on the bed. He wrapped one arm around her naked body, the other he used to gently caress the soft hairs on his son's small head. "It's only for you, my little boy, that I am showing some self-restraint." He tucked Cha'risa up closer against his body, sharing his warmth. "How is Katherine?" he asked.

Cha'risa stopped smiling. "Not well. I didn't want to leave her, but Istaqa insisted I rest for a while."

"Well, at least there's one person you'll listen to."

Cha'risa examined him closely. He looked tired, and lines of worry creased his face. She was sorry for the toll these last few weeks had taken on him. She reached up with the hand that wasn't cradling Sam. Gently, she brushed away some hair that had fallen across Caleb's brow. "I listen to you, too," she said. "It's just I need to be there."

"I know."

There was another knock at the door. "Just a minute," Caleb called out. Quickly he retrieved Cha'risa's dressing gown, helping her hastily into it. Before Sam had a chance to complain at his interrupted dinner, Cha'risa sat down in a chair, placing him back on her breast. Caleb discretely placed a shawl over the nursing infant, and then called out, "Come in!"

Esme, Daniel's housekeeper from back east, came into the room carrying a lunch tray, along with a pitcher of milk. She was an older woman with gray hair and tawny colored skin, but her movements didn't reflect her age. She placed the lunch items down on the table with quick efficiency; setting out an appealing spread of bread, cured meat, a wedge of cheese, and pickles made from the cucumbers in Katherine's garden.

She looked up then, meeting Cha'risa's gaze with sharp hazel eyes that seemed to miss nothing. She straightened her ample form, speaking in an accent that was nothing like Caleb and Zach's Irish lilt. The words moved slowly over her tongue, with long, drawn out vowels. Cha'risa remembered Katherine mentioning Esme had originally come from the Deep South.

"It's good to meet you, Ma'am. Your husband here has told me lots about you. He's assured me my girl is in good hands, that you know what you're doin'."

She'd referred to Katherine as "my girl," and Cha'risa recalled now that Katherine's mother had died in childbirth. Esme had been the one to raise Katherine. "I'm going to do everything I can," Cha'risa assured her.

Esme's eyes locked onto Cha'risa's. "I can't lose that child, 'specially not that way."

Cha'risa could feel the woman's fear, and so she promised once again today something she had no right to. "She won't die."

Esme held her gaze a moment longer, and then nodded.

"Esme," Caleb said. "I thought you were going to rest."

"I never said that; that's what you said. All I needed was to get my apron unpacked. Then Daniel showed me around enough to make a start at things. I already got some cornbread cookin' that'll go real nice with that beef stew Miss Kitty brought you all. In fact, I best be checkin' on it. Wouldn't do for it to burn to a crisp."

She was about to leave the room, but then she paused. Turning, she focused her attention once again on Cha'risa. "My girl once told me she didn't think life would be worth livin' if she couldn't be a mama. You did good, helpin' her get this far. Some things are worth fightin' for, so that's just what you got to do; you got to help her fight."

Cha'risa's voice was thick with unshed tears. "With everything I have," she assured Esme, who nodded, and then fled the room, before her own threatening tears could escape.

Cha'risa lifted the shawl off Sam after Esme left. It had grown hot between their bodies, but he didn't seem bothered. His tiny belly was full now, and his eyes were closed, though he still hadn't completely given up the nipple. She watched him a moment longer, her heart filling with intense love. Perhaps all the memories today had been trying to show her exactly this. Being part of a family made you strong; being a mother made you even stronger. That much love and faith and desire might hold enough power to carry them through.

She turned to her husband. "What is it you always say to me?"

He scooted his chair closer to her. "I say lots of things to you. Can you be a bit more specific?"

"Love will find a way." The words had suddenly come to her.

Caleb studied her for a second, and then popped a piece of cheese into her mouth. "Eat," he said. "You need to ready yourself for round two."

Chapter 10

Another contraction ripped across Katherine's distended figure. She lay there pale and barely conscious, too exhausted any longer to even acknowledge the pain. Cha'risa looked at Istaqa and then down at the potion in her hand.

Her father put his hand on top of hers. "I will do it," he said.

"No." She shook her head. "I began this, I'll finish it."

She opened the vial and began to rub the contents over Katherine's heart. It was a risk to stimulate the heart when it was already under so much strain, but Katherine needed to push now or they would lose both the baby and the mother. As she rubbed, Cha'risa sang a low, demanding melody that wove itself through Katherine's body and into her consciousness. Suddenly Katherine gasped and tried to sit up. Istaqa held her firmly in place.

"We need you to push," Cha'risa said. "Push for your baby."

Katherine's eyes met hers. There was a little color in her face now, a dawning awareness of where she was, followed by a growing spark of determination in her eyes. "You make sure that baby lives, you hear me?"

"I'll make sure you both live," Cha'risa insisted. "Now push!"

It was a weak effort at first, nowhere near enough, but Cha'risa began her deep toned melody once again. She let the full force of her own being envelop Katherine. Together, they met the next contraction head on.

"Follow the song," Cha'risa urged. "Let it flow through you." She started the hum again, and felt the exact moment Katherine and the melody became one. All Cha'risa's strength became Katherine's now, and together they pushed again. The song flowed down into the baby, a boy child, still strong enough to make the passage.

"Again!" Cha'risa commanded, and together they threw themselves into the wave of pain, driving the boy farther forward.

"I see the head now," Istaqa told Cha'risa. "She's almost there."

Cha'risa looked into Katherine's eyes. "We can do this!"

Katherine nodded. Again Cha'risa wrapped her energy around her sister-in-law. She unfurled the energy, holding nothing back. When the contraction came they were both ready for it, and the chant became a battle cry. With everything they had they met the contraction. But not before Cha'risa felt Katherine's heartbeat faltering.

"NO!" Cha'risa cried, and she threw even more of herself into the link between them, forcing Katherine to stay conscious, forcing her heart to pump.

"Cha'risa! Stop!" she heard Istaqa cry out. She felt his hands upon her, his voice chanting insistently. She wondered what that healing melody was; she'd never heard it before. That was her last thought before she knew no more.

Chapter 11

Cha'risa heard singing. It was not her father's voice. Perhaps it was the song of one of her ancestors guiding her home. She listened more closely, following its lure. Eventually, she realized the song did not belong to one of her ancestors. She knew this warm tenor voice. It conjured up feelings of safety and love. It drew her back into her body, bringing her closer to the solid warmth of her husband, synching her into the rise and fall of his chest as he sang.

The cool shades of evening their mantle were spreading,
And Chari all smiling was listening to me;
The moon through the valley her pale rays was shedding,
When I won the heart of the Rose of Tralee.

Though lovely and fair as the Rose of the summer,
Yet 'twas not her beauty alone that won me;
Oh no, 'twas the truth in her eyes ever dawning,
That made me love Chari, the Rose of Tralee.

She opened her eyes. Caleb held her close against one side of his body, and had baby Sam tucked safely against the other. He smiled down at her, his face dimly illuminated by the moon outside the window.

"There's my sweet rose," he said, leaning over to kiss her.

She smiled as she felt the warmth of his lips on her brow. But then her memories came crashing back, and she sat up abruptly. Her movement startled the baby, waking him.

"Where's Katherine?" She was almost too afraid to hear the answer. "What happened to her and the baby?"

Her own child began to wail loudly, but she couldn't look away from Caleb, not until she knew. "They both made it through," he said, but then he looked away, and it was clear there was more he wasn't saying.

"What's happened?" she demanded.

Sam's wail now became piercing. Caleb handed her the baby. "He's going to wake the whole house," he said. "Feed the little fellow, for he hasn't eaten in hours."

Cha'risa brought her son to her breast. He whimpered just a little, followed by a small hiccup of relief, and then he latched on. Caleb watched his son's greedy guzzling. "He was inconsolable. We tried the grits again, but all he wanted was you."

"Caleb, please!" Her eyes fastened on him, and this time he didn't look away.

He sighed. "You saved her, and the boy is strong and healthy, but Istaqa says there is noticeable damage to Katherine's heart. He fears she may never fully recover."

Cha'risa started to pull Sam off the nipple.

"Don't," Caleb ordered. "Istaqa gave me strict orders you were to rest too. Honestly, Chari, I've never seen him so upset."

"I should go to him," she persisted, attempting to get out of bed.

Caleb kept a firm hold on her, and his tone was adamant. "Your father is sleeping now. Eli Ferguson is watching over Katherine and Michael, and I promised your father I'd see to it you rested. I'm meaning to keep that promise." His eyes locked on hers, and Cha'risa met his determined gaze. She hadn't quite made up her mind what to do when he raised his voice despairingly. "You nearly died, Chari!" His pained outcry startled both her and the baby.

She looked searchingly into her husband's eyes, and she saw then how she'd hurt him. He wanted a life with her, and she'd risked it all for Katherine. She reached up, gently caressing his cheek. "I'm sorry," she said, "I didn't know how else to put things right."

He didn't speak, but his arm around her relaxed. She set the baby onto her other breast, and then snuggled back in against her husband. They sat together quietly, Caleb still struggling with his emotions. At last, he broke the silence. "Chari, what exactly did you do to save her?"

"The only thing I could do," she said. "Her heart wasn't going to make it, so I gave her mine."

Chapter 12

Katherine and Cha'risa sat on the porch rockers, looking out at the meadow and the majestic San Francisco Peaks just beyond. The first hint of a fall chill was in the air, but Esme had ordered them outside nonetheless, wrapping them firmly in blankets, and placing a pot of Cha'risa's Hopi tea beside them. She had taken baby Michael, returning him a short time later, freshly cleaned, diapered, and firmly bundled. She handed him off to Katherine, and then was off again on some other time-sensitive household chore.

"Does she ever sit still?" Cha'risa asked.

Katherine smiled. "Not in all the years I've known her."

"I don't know why you didn't just bring her here in the first place. She's much better at cooking and housekeeping then I'll ever be."

"Yes, but for all her talents, she could never have made this happen." Katherine looked down at Michael tenderly. The baby yawned and stretched a little, then nestled into his mother's warmth and fell back asleep.

"He's so perfect." Katherine mused, studying his tiny face.

Cha'risa watched them for a moment. Katherine might never fully recover her strength, but mother and son were both alive, both here to experience this knowing of one another. Cha'risa looked over at her own little boy, who was currently on a blanket in front of them, pushing up onto his hands and knees, rocking back and forth, and then toppling back down.

"He's only five months old and look at him, he'll be crawling soon," Katherine observed.

Cha'risa smiled. "He's going to be a big strong boy."

"Just like Caleb." Katherine said.

And indeed, Sam did bear a striking resemblance to his father; though his eyes were not Caleb's laughing blue-gray, but a warm shade of golden brown.

Ahote strolled over from the stables, and sat down on the blanket next to his little brother. "Look at him go!" he laughed, as Sam started another attempt to create some forward momentum. "Hey, little guy, like this!" Ahote got on all fours and demonstrated how to crawl.

Zach had followed Ahote up from the barn, and immediately went to pick up his son. "What do you think of your cousin's foolishness, wee Michael?"

"Hey!" Ahote protested. "Someone has to show these little guys the ropes. Look how Sam is watching me!"

Sam made another attempt, but he still wasn't ready to lift any of his appendages off the ground. He rocked back and forth until he tipped over again.

"Don't worry, little fella, you'll get the hang of it," Ahote said, patting his baby brother on the back.

Esme came out with a tray of molasses cookies. "My own special recipe," she announced, "fresh out of the oven."

"Esme, you need to sit down and catch your breath!" Cha'risa insisted.

"I'm tending to you, not the other way around." Esme scolded.

"I can tell your back is hurting you," Cha'risa persisted. "Sit."

"Come on, Esme, share a cookie with us." Ahote pulled up a rocker for her, and then put a cookie in her hand.

"You all don't need to fuss over me. I'm nearly indestructible."

Cha'risa arched a brow. "No one is indestructible."

Esme harrumphed. "Look who's talkin'." Then Esme turned to Katherine. "Why aren't you eatin' those cookies? They're your favorite. I made them 'specially for you."

Zach plucked a cookie off the tray, handing it to Katherine, "Eat," he instructed, and then turned his attention back to Michael, who'd grabbed onto his finger and was holding on tight. "That's my little soldier boy," he said, bending to kiss his son's forehead. He looked back at his wife then. "I'm going to miss you guys."

"I don't see why you men keep running down to the winter ranch in this hot weather." Katherine said.

"It's all for you, and don't you know it," he insisted. "We can't have you coming to the winter ranch with the babies if we haven't a proper roof to put over your heads."

Ahote added, "We're building you a real ranch house that will keep out the cold winds, and Daniel has ordered a cook stove, the likes of which you've never seen. The place will be toasty warm, even when it storms."

"You'll be safe and snug all winter long once we get this finished," Zach promised. Then he noticed she was still holding the cookie, and he raised an eyebrow. "Are you going to eat it or admire it?"

She laughed and took a small bite. He gave little Michael another kiss, and then handed the baby over to Esme.

"Hey!" Katherine objected, "You should have given him back to me!"

"Finish that cookie first," Zach ordered, and then he turned to Ahote. "Come on, the day's not getting any younger. We need to hit the trail."

Ahote gave his mother a quick hug, and then stuffed a couple of cookies in his pocket for the road. "You heard the man, I have to run, but you won't be alone for long. Caleb and Daniel should already be on their way home."

"We'll be fine," she assured him. We don't need babysitting."

"Well, maybe you don't," Zach said, "but the cattle and horses need tending, and neither of you is well enough to take on the ranching chores yet. Just admit it, you need your menfolk." He gave Cha'risa a wink, and then bent over giving his wife a very enthusiastic kiss good bye.

As Cha'risa watched him head back toward the barn with Ahote at his side, her mind grew troubled. "I'll be right back," she told the women. Entering the lodge, she could hear Esme say to Katherine, "This baby's gettin' hungry; you better finish that cookie so I can give him back."

When Cha'risa returned a short time later, Esme was gone again, and Katherine was nursing Michael. Cha'risa sat down in her rocker and put a small pouch of tea onto the table.

"What's this?" Katherine asked.

"I think it's time you started drinking this daily."

Katherine looked at her. "What's it for?"

Cha'risa stared frankly back into her eyes. "It's so you won't have another baby."

Katherine stared at her a moment, and then her face colored a little. "We haven't done anything," she said.

"Not yet." Cha'risa amended. "But you're feeling much better, and from the look of him, he's over the worst of the shock."

Now Katherine's face did noticeably redden. "Well, I suppose it's a wise precaution until I am stronger."

Cha'risa locked eyes with Katherine. "This tea will have to be taken every day."

"Yes, I understand."

Cha'risa took hold of Katherine's hand, willing her to see. "You'll need it for as long as you have your monthly cycles. No more babies."

Katherine gasped and pulled her hand back. "No!"

"Your heart is too weak…" Cha'risa tried to explain.

"Yes, but I can work to make it strong again, stronger even!"

Cha'risa looked at her but said nothing.

"You can't know for certain!" Katherine exclaimed.

Cha'risa sighed. "Another baby would be a terrible risk, no matter what we try. Can't you just be happy being Michael's mother?"

"I am happy being Michael's mother!" Then she fell silent for a moment, her eyes starting to well up. "I always thought I'd have lots of children."

Cha'risa studied her friend quietly, and then sighed deeply. "Some things are just not meant to be."

Katherine's eyes sought hers. "I'm not giving up without a fight. I'll get strong again, you'll see."

"And I'll help you." Cha'risa said. "But in the end, you must be prepared that no matter what we do, it may not be enough."

Katherine paused, and then nodded.

"Promise me, you will accept what I say."

"I will, I promise. But you have to promise me something too."

Cha'risa met Katherine's earnest gaze. "What?"

"You have to believe it's possible."

Cha'risa paused a moment. For as much as there were mistakes, there were also miracles. Her friend was asking her for a leap of faith, and because Cha'risa loved her she nodded and said, "I'll try."

1903

Blackberry Pie

Ingredients
5 cups blackberries, rinsed and lightly dried
1 cup sugar, plus a little for the top
1 tablespoon freshly squeezed lemon juice
1/4 cup instant tapioca
Pinch of salt
1/4 teaspoon ground cinnamon
1/8 teaspoon freshly grated nutmeg
1 teaspoon minced lemon zest, optional
1 recipe pie crust, enough for a double crusted pie
2 tablespoons unsalted butter, cut into bits
2 tablespoons milk, to brush on top

Directions
Preheat the oven to 450º F.

Gently toss the blackberries in a mixing bowl with the sugar, tapioca, salt, and spices. Stir in the lemon juice and the zest.

Roll out two thirds of the pastry and line a 9-inch pie pan; leave the edges untrimmed. Spoon in the berries, mounding them higher in the center, and dot with the butter.

Cover with the top crust and crimp the edge decoratively with a fork or your fingers.

Put the pie on a baking sheet and brush the top lightly with milk; sprinkle with sugar. Use a sharp paring knife to cut several 2" slits to release steam.

Set on the center rack of the oven and bake for 10 minutes. Lower the heat to 350º and bake until the crust is golden brown and the filling is bubbling, another 40 to 50 minutes.

Cool on a rack before serving.

Serves 8

Chapter 13

Esme sat along the embankment, watching as Sam flapped his small hands in both fear and excitement. Slowly, he was inching his way to the edge of the stock pond. Caleb was just a few feet out in the water, his arms outstretched, encouraging his son.

"You can do it, boyo! It'll be grand, you'll see. Just take the leap!"

Michael paddled around Caleb, calling to Sam. "Don't be such a sissy! It's nothin' but a wee bit of water!"

A flash of determination sparked in Sam's eyes. Esme knew that look well. Here it comes, she thought, and sure enough Sam backed up, took a few running leaps, and then launched with a battle cry into the water. He only needed a single stroke to arrive safely in his father's embrace.

Sam's entry into the pond had created a very satisfying splash, and Michael must have taken the brunt of it. He was sputtering now, and flailing in the water. Esme stood, realizing the boy was panicking, but Caleb was immediately by his side. He had Sam propped up on one hip, and with a firm grip, he lifted Michael onto the other. Sam leaned over, patting Michael's back, and Esme heard him say in that sweet child's voice, "You're safe now." Moments later, confidence restored, both boys were back in the pond, splashing and laughing, drawn to the big Irishman like bees to honey.

Esme sat down again. For a few moments she relaxed to the sounds of the boys, the water, and the warmth of the day. She allowed herself a moment of forgetting what was waiting for her up at the main house. She let her mind wander, and soon memories stirred of the lake where her own father had taught her swim. That had been so long ago, before the bad days had come to the plantation, before her place in the family had changed. But she'd never forgotten what it felt like to be held the way Caleb held those two little boys; to feel so safe and certain of her place in the world. Even now, practically a lifetime later, swimming could bring her back; make her remember that carefree girl, who was too young to realize her skin was a shade too dark, and that the color of her skin could matter so much.

Esme hugged her knees to her chest. Remembering the innocent girl always stirred up painful memories of how her father had turned his back on her. She was quick to remind herself that even if he'd abandoned her, Uncle Daniel had not. She wondered if Daniel had ever looked back on those early days, if he ever had paused to remember how it once had been before her father had married Evangeline.

A cold splash shocked her out of her reverie. Caleb and the boys were standing in the water near her, dripping wet with wide grins on their faces.

"Come in, Esme!" Michael demanded.

Caleb's smile broadened. "He's confessed your secret. He's knows you can swim."

Esme frowned at the little boy. "Why are you telling Uncle Caleb all my secrets?"

"Swim with us!" the little boy insisted.

"Do I look like I'm dressed for swimmin' to you?"

"Swim! Swim!" both boys started chanting.

"Not all of us can lollygag about all day in the water."

"But you're lollygagging too!" Sam pointed out.

Esme looked nervously back at the house. When she turned back around, Caleb was watching her.

He turned to Sam and Michael. "I'm thinking you boys should've filled those buckets with blackberries by now. If you had, Esme would already be working on a pie for our dinner."

The boys looked over at the pails sitting on the shore. Quickly they scrambled out of the water, grabbing them up. Sam skipped toward the bushes, swinging his pail and singing the first words that came into his head. "Blackberry pie, blackberry pie, I'm gonna eat some blackberry pie!" Michael started singing the little ditty as well, but skipping wasn't his style. He ran toward the hedge, reaching it first. It wasn't far to run; Katherine had planted the hedge close to the southern shoreline. It seemed to Esme as if that planting had happened only yesterday, but it had been almost three years ago now, just after Michael turned one.

"You know," Caleb said, interrupting her thoughts, "when Daniel first proposed building this tank, I thought he was crazy."

"I remember," Esme said. "You told him it was too expensive."

Caleb smiled. "That I did, and then before I could say another word, Istaqa said, 'I know just the place.'"

Esme smiled. "Those two were always so full of ideas."

Caleb met her eyes. "They were."

Caleb and Esme looked out over the pond. Grasses grew all around it now, and Zach's horses were lazily grazing by the water's edge. Katherine's blackberry hedge was having a bumper crop this year, and the two little boys, laughing among the bushes, already had purple lips and fingers from the juice. It was a beautiful place, serene and pastoral. It was the last project the two men had ever undertaken. Daniel's health began to fail shortly after its completion. The first troubling sign had been his loss of appetite. Esme had tried every favorite dish of his that she could think of, but there was not much that tempted him. Istaqa and Cha'risa also tried various teas and healing songs. Their remedies brought some vigor back, but it never lasted. Little by little, he kept slipping away.

It was Istaqa who finally understood that Daniel's time was drawing near. Even now Esme was surprised it'd taken all of them so long to see it, but sometimes you just don't see things when you're in too close. Then, early last year, Istaqa started slowing down noticeably, too. Cha'risa fussed over him the same way Esme was fussing over Daniel, but it was a battle neither of them could win.

Daniel passed quietly on a warm spring night. Esme had been the one to find him. She'd come into the room just after dawn, bringing him his cup of Hopi tea. He'd looked so peaceful, sitting near the window, with the first light of day shining on him. As Esme was running down the stairs to tell the family the sad news, Cha'risa had been running up, to tell her Istaqa was gone; literally gone. He must have left sometime during the night. Esme couldn't even begin to guess where he'd vanished to or why, but Cha'risa had Caleb saddle up horses for them both, leaving Sam at home with Katherine and Esme. They'd returned three days later, solemn faced, with the news that Istaqa had also passed away. They'd found him not far from the winter ranch. They hadn't brought Istaqa back for burial. Cha'risa said he'd chosen his final resting place, and she and Caleb had buried him there, in a red rock canyon near the base of the tall mountain, looking out at the green mesas just beyond.

Esme never could look at the pond without remembering these two remarkable men. But it was the loss of Daniel in particular that'd left her so emptied out. He'd always been there for her, and the world felt dark and heavy now that he was gone. For the first time in her life, Esme felt old.

Caleb looked up at the house. "How's it going, do you know?"

"She's sleeping now," Esme said. "But, I'm scared, Caleb, real scared. It was a rough night."

"Sam knows something's up," Caleb said.

"He reminds me of Istaqa," Esme observed. "He sees things. Maybe he even sees too much." She fell silent then, overwhelmed with all the thoughts running through her mind. If only she could've glimpsed this future, she would've done things differently. Caleb continued to sit quietly beside her. She knew he was waiting for her to speak, because he also had this way of seeing clearly, and right now he knew her heart needed unburdening.

"I raised that girl like she was my own," Esme looked away, trying to hide the tears she couldn't keep from falling. "I can understand why she wanted another child, after losing her dad like that. She needed something life affirming." Cha'risa looked at Caleb then, ready to confess the worst of it. "When she first told me, I was happy for her. I should have been mad, the way she went about things, but I guess I needed something to fill the pain of Daniel's loss, too." Her eyes bored into his. "I never thought this would happen. She'd been looking so strong and healthy. I thought everything would be okay."

Caleb looked over at the main house. "Katherine's a fighter, and so is Cha'risa. They'll find a way to get through this, I'm certain of it."

"My sweet girl's lips were blue this morning when I went to check on her, and her face was so pale and clammy. And I don't have to tell you what your own wife looked like."

Caleb met her frightened stare. "There's nobody in the world more motivated to save to Katherine than Chari," he assured her.

Esme held his gaze a moment longer, and then nodded. "I just wish I knew what to do to help."

He stood and took her hand, pulling her to her feet. "I'll tell you what you're going to do. You're going to help me clean up these two wee scallywags, and then you're going to check on Katherine and Cha'risa, and make sure they eat something, and then you're going to make us some blackberry pie for our supper tonight."

She laughed a little, despite her tears. "Food is your answer?"

"It is, but not before we deal with that." He pointed over at the four year olds, up to their knees in mud, and covered in berry juice.

Chapter 14

The pies were in the oven, a hearty stew simmering on the stove, when Esme heard the wagon wheels pulling up in the front yard. They'd been expecting one of the Burnett boys to bring by a load of supplies from the store, but as she stepped out of the kitchen to greet the wagon, she was surprised to find Kitty Burnett with little Madeline sitting on the seat of the buckboard. Sam and Michael had gotten themselves dirty again, and they clamored now around Kitty and her daughter. Esme winced at the thought of either of those boys getting close to Maddy in her pretty dress. She wiped her hands on her apron, and then hurried out to rescue the Burnett women from her two ruffians.

"Miss Kitty!" she called as she rushed over. "I was expecting one of the boys." Kitty handed Madeline over the side to Esme, and then climbed down off the wagon herself.

"I thought maybe I could make myself useful around here, with Katherine feeling poorly. I hope that's all right."

"Well, that's very thoughtful," Esme said, hefting Maddy onto her hip. "You've had a long ride. Come inside and let me make you some tea. I have some cookies too." This last part she directed at Maddy, but the boys heard and started pleading, "What about us, Esme? We're hungry too!"

Esme took the horse's reins from Kitty and handed them to Michael. "You two take this horse down to the barn, and help Ahote get him situated. Then you wash up real good before you come back to my kitchen. After that we'll see about cookies for you."

"Are there enough for Ahote too?" Sam asked.

"Of course," Esme assured him, then she shooed the boys along, and ushered her guests into the kitchen.

Cha'risa was at the stove, already heating a kettle of water for tea. She offered up a tired but genuine smile when they entered. "I saw you ladies ride up," she said. She reached out for little Maddy, and the girl happily went to her. "I haven't seen you since your birthday," Cha'risa remarked. "Look how big you're getting."

"I'm three," Maddy said, holding up three fingers.

"I know," Cha'risa said. "Who do you think baked your cake?"

Maddy smiled and pointed to Esme. Cha'risa laughed, "Smart girl."

"Don't trouble yourselves with tea." Kitty insisted. "We're here to help, not be entertained."

"You don't work until we've fed you, and that's the end of it," Esme declared, and there were no more protests.

"How is Katherine?" Kitty asked.

"She's sleeping now, but she had a hard night," Cha'risa said.

"Will she be all right?" Kitty asked.

"The pregnancy is taxing all of Katherine's strength. I keep wondering if I ought to encourage the little one to come early, while Katherine is still strong enough."

Esme looked up. "Can you do that?"

"It's not something I like to do."

Esme locked eyes with the medicine woman, praying for her to understand what she dared not speak. Cha'risa gave an almost imperceptible nod, but it was enough to show she was thinking the same thing. If a choice had to be made, she wouldn't sacrifice Katherine for the baby.

At that moment, all of the menfolk strode into the kitchen wanting tea and cookies. Esme turned her attention to the horde. Given how hungry everyone looked, she decided to add some bread and cheese to the late afternoon spread.

When the afternoon tea was finished the men helped unload Kitty's wagon, and then headed back out to finish up the end of the day chores. Esme and Kitty set to work in the large kitchen pantry, storing the supplies she'd delivered from her store. Then Esme showed her the shelf where herbal remedies were packaged and ready for market, and Kitty was pleased at how many had been prepared. There was a steady demand for Cha'risa's tisanes in Flagstaff, with both the Burnetts and Doc Ferguson offering them for sale on their premises. Esme left Kitty shortly after that and headed to the front porch where they'd left the Burnett's personal belongings. She took a moment to catch her breath. She was feeling awfully stiff and tired today, but there was a household to feed, and she needed to get Kitty and Maddy settled before the dinner hour was upon her.

It was only one small overnight bag and a satchel, easy enough for her to carry even if she was feeling a might puny. She figured she'd put the Burnetts in the blue room. It was one of her favorites, mostly because of the watercolors that hung in there. They were paintings

Katherine had done of wildflowers from the meadows and the mountains.

Esme was about to head back into the house with the bags when she heard the children arguing near the barn. Maddy's dress was all crumpled and smudged with dirt, but it wasn't the state of her clothing that had the little girl upset. Esme put the bags down, uncertain if she needed to intervene or not.

"I want to be a princess!" the little girl demanded.

"But we're pretending to be Indians," Michael insisted. "You can't be a princess if you want to play with us!"

Maddy's eyes welled up and her lower lip trembled.

"Maddy, don't cry," Sam begged.

"You said after we played train robbers, I could pick the game!"

Michael raised an eyebrow. "I never said that."

"I have an idea," Sam said.

The little girl wiped away a tear. "What?"

"You can be an Indian princess! That way everyone can be what they want most to be." Michael started gesturing wildly, trying to veto this line of thought.

Maddy looked intrigued. "Well, who would be my prince? A princess is supposed to marry a prince."

"Oh, I know of something much better than a prince," Sam insisted.

"What?"

"You can marry the Indian Chief!"

Michael let out a loud squawk. "I'm the Chief!"

"I know." Sam agreed.

"Well, I'm not marrying Maddy!" Michael argued. "That's just plain stupid and I won't do it!" Maddy looked like she was about to cry again.

"Aw, come on Michael," Sam pleaded. "Just give it a chance."

Michael glared at him. "You can't make me, Sam. I refuse!"

"But, why? She'll be happy, and we'll be happy too."

Michael fumed. "Just get that fool idea out of your head. I won't marry Maddy Burnett, and that's final!" Michael stormed off toward the barn.

Esme shook her head, chuckling, and then turned to the house with the bags, leaving Sam to deal with Maddy's tears.

Chapter 15

It was well after midnight before Esme found her way to her room. Her head was pounding as she sat on the bed and kicked off her shoes. It'd been another rough evening and she felt unbearably tired. Dinner been cleaned up, and the toddlers all tucked into bed, when Katherine had started another series of contractions. They'd subsided without any intervention on Cha'risa's part, but they'd left Katherine short of breath and shaking. Esme had sat with her for a long time after that, rocking her, and singing her songs, keeping a vigil just as she had through all of Katherine's childhood.

A tear escaped, and memories flooded Esme's mind of watching baby Katherine take her first breaths, while her mother lay nearby breathing her last. More memories flowed of all the late nights she'd spent at Katherine's side; the colds, the coughs, and then worst of all, the scarlet fever. But her little girl had survived them all, and had grown up into a strong-minded beauty. Esme was sick at heart to look at her sweet niece now. Cha'risa had been right all along; the risk had been too great. Too tired to change into her nightclothes, Esme laid her head on her pillow. Her heart felt fluttery, and she expected she would never fall asleep. She was wrong.

She was cold and covered in blood; her mother's and her own. Daniel knelt beside her and wrapped her in a blanket, covering her nakedness.

"Esme, sweetheart, look at me!" he pleaded.

Slowly, she lifted her head and stared into his eyes. His face was pale and his hands were shaking as he bundled her more tightly.

"Momma doesn't look right," she said

Daniel's eyes welled up with tears. "She's gone, Esme. Your momma's in heaven now."

"No!" she shook her head, unwilling to hear those words. He tried to hold her close, but she pulled free of his arms, dropping the blanket as she ran to her mother. She shook her and cried, "Momma, he's wrong, tell him he's wrong!" Her mother lay silent and unresisting in her arms. "Answer me, Momma," Esme pleaded. "You said it would be all right! You said so!"

Daniel came up beside her, wrapping the blanket over her again. His eyes when he looked at her were filled with such sadness, anger too. "What happened here, Esme? Who attacked you?"

Esme couldn't answer. She just sat staring at the blood pooling around her mother's head, praying this was a bad dream. Momma had tried to stop the man from coming after Esme, but he'd pushed Momma hard, and she'd fallen, her head making a sharp crack on the table's edge. Esme looked away from the blood and into Momma's sightless brown eyes. If Daniel was right, and Momma was in heaven, those eyes would never look upon Esme again.

"Esme, please, tell me what happened," Daniel begged.

She turned to face him, her hazel eyes locking onto his green ones. In many ways Daniel looked like her father, but the two saw the world very differently. Daniel had been outraged when her father had sent Momma and her down to the kitchen house. Father never came to visit after that, but Daniel did, almost daily, bringing stories and treats, making Momma laugh and Esme giggle. Esme couldn't trust Father any more. He always took the side of his new wife, and Evangeline hated Momma. But Esme felt certain Daniel wouldn't get angry if she spoke. He wouldn't blame her for telling the truth.

"It was that overseer, the one you said Father should fire," she said at last.

She heard Daniel swear under his breath. He looked over at Momma's crumpled, naked body. Esme was twelve now, old enough to understand what it was the man had done to Momma, what he had done to her, but the words were hard to say. She let their nakedness and the blood speak for her.

Daniel's jaw was clenched with anger, but he was gentle when he scooped her into his arms. Esme could feel the storm of emotions growing stronger within him as he strode through yard. He unleashed that anger with frightening force when he kicked open the front door of the big house.

"I'm not allowed in!" Esme cried, but he didn't heed her, didn't stop.

"William!" he bellowed as he neared his brother's study. His shouts brought Evangeline running from the parlor. Her face turned a furious red when she saw Esme bundled in his arms.

"Get that filthy child out of my home!" she screeched, just as the door to the study opened and William took in the scene before him. His face paled when he saw Esme.

"What's happened?"

Evangeline opened her mouth to speak, but Daniel beat her to it. "Sarah's dead, Bill. Raped and murdered by Jud Cook. He raped Esme, too."

A shocked gasp escaped Evangeline. "I had no idea he would go that far!"

Visibly shaken, William turned to his wife. "You knew about this?"

She took a step away. "He... he asked me if Sarah was still off limits."

"What did you tell him?" Daniel's voice was low and threatening.

Evangeline stiffened. "I told him the truth; that William no longer came to her bed." She looked imploringly at William. "I never knew he intended this kind of violence. I swear it!"

Esme felt cold sink deep into her bones and she started to shake uncontrollably.

Daniel felt the trembling and turned his attention back to her. "She's in shock," he said. "We should send for the doctor." He turned and headed up the stairs with her.

"Where are you taking her?!" Evangeline demanded.

"TO HER ROOM!" Daniel bellowed. "She should never have been sent down to the kitchen house, Bill! You've always known it was wrong, now you need to make this right!"

William flinched. "I couldn't know it would come to this!"

Daniel stared hard at his brother. "I'm leaving, William, and I'll be taking Esme when I go. I'm heading north as soon as she's well enough to travel." He was breathing hard, enveloping his brother with his outrage. "You should never have let it come to this!" Then his voice grew loud again. "Get those papers drawn up, you hear me? Esme is going to leave here a free woman!"

William looked at his daughter, and the grief in his eyes was sincere. Esme longed for him to reach out and take her in his arms, as he had when she was little. But instead he turned from her, looked at his brother, and then nodded. Esme started to cry. Something inside her just knew she would never see him again, and that was exactly how it had turned out. He hadn't survived the war. What had survived was the memory of him turning his back on her. That had stayed with her all these long years.

The strong emotions of the dream woke Esme, the after effects leaving her weak and trembling. It'd been years since she'd had a nightmare like that. Her many years living as a free woman in Boston had dimmed those memories. Daniel's kindness had come to mean more to her than the bitterness she'd once felt for her father. But even so, her father's abandonment had left wounds that had never healed, and so had Jud Cook's brutality. She got out of bed, not willing to go back to sleep.

She grabbed her shawl, deciding as long as she was up, she might as well check on Katherine and Cha'risa. When she opened her door to leave, she was startled to find Caleb standing there. He had one hand ready to knock, the other holding onto a very somber faced Sam.

"Come," he said. "It's time."

Esme looked at Sam. "You're bringing him?"

"It's more like he's bringing me," Caleb said somewhat ruefully. "He's the one who told me the baby's on its way."

Esme stared at the little boy. There was no point asking how Sam knew. That boy just knew things. He'd been that way from the start.

When they got to the room, Caleb tried to get Sam to wait outside the door. Sam didn't even bother to argue, he just ran into the room, straight to Katherine's bedside.

"What's he doing?" Katherine asked when the little boy pulled up a chair. She watched bemused as he climbed up beside her, and laid his hands lightly on her distended belly. His eyes closed in concentration, he began to hum, and then to sing. Cha'risa came up beside him, studying him closely.

"What's gotten into him?" Katherine wondered.

"Should I take him?" Caleb offered.

Cha'risa put her hand up. "Wait. I know this song."

Caleb listened closely, raising his eyebrows. "That sounds like a Hopi chant."

"It is," she agreed, "A very old one."

Caleb looked at her in surprise. "I didn't know you'd started teaching him to heal."

Char'isa met his gaze. "I haven't."

Esme moved closer to the bed. "Is it doing anything?" she asked Katherine

"It feels kind of warm and tingly," Katherine said.

Cha'risa placed her hands next to Sam's. She was very quiet a few moments, and then looked up, mystified. "He seems to be giving strength to both Katherine and the baby." She looked over at her husband. "He's helping."

"So, should he stay or go?" Caleb asked.

"Leave him," Cha'risa decided, and then added. "But can I ask you to wake Kitty? She wanted to know when Katherine went into labor."

"Sure," Caleb said.

"I sent Zach and Michael down to the kitchen. Can you check on them as well?"

"I'll take care of things," Caleb assured her. "You just focus on what you have to do here."

Cha'risa came to his side. Standing on her tiptoes, she reached up and gave him a kiss. Thank you," she said.

Caleb stared back at her, his face a mixture of love and worry. "Don't do anything stupid," he cautioned.

She raised an eyebrow. "We'll be fine," she assured him. When he left, she returned to Katherine, placing her hands just above her son's, and joined her sultry voice to her son's clear, high-pitched tones.

Esme stood there a moment, feeling the power of their song, and then she turned back to Katherine. "How are you feeling?" Esme asked, speaking softly so as not to disturb the singers.

"Surprisingly good," Katherine admitted.

Esme examined her more closely. She was looking better. Her cheeks and lips were pink, and her eyes were bright.

"That song…" Katherine said.

Esme waited for her to finish, but Katherine was lost in some far away thought. "What about it?" Esme prompted

"I can feel it," Katherine said, turning to her. "It's like my blood is humming right along with melody."

"So it's working?"

"I don't know. I just feel very relaxed… and safe."

Well, Esme figured, relaxed was good. It wouldn't last, that much was certain, but for now she sat quietly by her girl and let the melody work its magic.

How long Cha'risa and Sam sang, Esme really couldn't say, but at some point she became aware that dawn was breaking and that Katherine had fallen peacefully asleep. There was a knock at the door, and then Kitty poked her head in the doorway, carrying a tray with a pot of steaming Hopi tea and some biscuits. Esme got up to help her.

"I thought you all could use a little sustenance," Kitty said.

The singing stopped. Sam looked up, smelling the fresh biscuits, and came running. Cha'risa made sure Katherine was still sleeping comfortably, and then she too followed. "Thank you, Kitty," she said. "Obviously this is just what we needed." She looked over meaningfully at Sam, who drank thirstily, and then shoved an entire biscuit into his mouth all at once.

"Healing must be hungry work," Esme said, and then she made Cha'risa sit as well, placing a cup in her hands. "You need to keep your strength up, too" she advised, and then added a buttery biscuit to the offering in front of Cha'risa.

"That smells good," Katherine said, waking from her catnap. "May I have a cup, too?" Esme quickly carried some tea over to Katherine's bedside. Cha'risa followed, and together they helped prop Katherine into a sitting position. Katherine took a few sips, and then sighed contentedly. The next moment though, she stiffened and her face grew pinched with pain. Cha'risa took the cup from Katherine's hands. "Everything okay?" she asked.

"The contractions are getting stronger," Katherine said, looking into Cha'risa's eyes. "But I feel good, Chari. I'm ready for the baby to come."

Cha'risa met Katherine's hopeful gaze. "You are looking better," she agreed. She glanced over at Sam; he was covered in crumbs and butter, happily consuming a second biscuit. "I think he's got something to do with it," Cha'risa admitted. "I haven't thought of that particular healing song in years. I can't figure out how he knew it, let alone understood it was the right one to use."

Katherine took her hand. "Maybe he had a feeling, just as I did." She searched Cha'risa's eyes, willing her to understand. "I know I upset you, that I made you a promise and then broke it. I can't explain it, other than I felt so strongly this was what I needed to do."

Cha'risa held her gaze. "You took a terrible risk, but I understand. Losing our fathers left a void in us both. It's natural to want to fill that space with something meaningful." She looked over at Sam again. "We have a long way to go before this baby is safely delivered, but that song Sam brought us is a good sign." She looked back at Katherine, giving her hand a squeeze. "I think it means our fathers are watching over us."

Esme had sat quietly by, listening to their conversation. Now as the contractions returned and strengthened, Esme whispered her own small prayer of thanks. Whether it was heard by her God or the Hopi's, she didn't much care. Someone up there was listening.

Chapter 16

Though dawn was only the faintest gray in the sky, the fact that no one had been sleeping was evident when Kitty and Esme walked into the kitchen. They'd been sent down to boil water for the birthing. There they found Caleb at the stove making up a pot of hot chocolate for Michael and Maddie, both of whom were wide awake, sitting at the table on Zach's lap.

"I'll keep an eye on that for you," Kitty told Caleb, making it clear he needed to get out of her way.

"How's Katherine?" Zach asked worriedly.

"Her time is getting near," Esme said, filling a big pot and placing it on the stovetop. "But she's holding up real good."

Ahote came in just then, carrying a bottle of Irish whiskey. "I found it!" he said, before noticing Caleb trying to signal him to be quiet.

Esme and Kitty looked at the bottle and then at the men.

"It's just one glass," Caleb assured them, "to calm Zach's nerves."

Esme went to the cupboard and pulled out three glasses. "You can all partake a little," she said, then warned, "But nobody better be drunk when that baby is born, you hear me?" There were no protests from the men. They all knew better than to argue with her. Kitty brought the children their hot chocolate as Caleb poured out three whiskeys. "Slainte," he said, lifting his glass to his brother and Ahote. "Slainte," they answered, clinking the glasses together. Ahote took a careful sip, but Zach and Caleb each took a long swallow.

"Dad?" Michael asked, "Are you going to finish that story?"

"What story is that?" Kitty asked.

"It's the one about the Irish hero, Cuchulainn," Michael told her.

Kitty wasn't familiar with it, but it was a legend Esme knew well. You didn't live with two Irishmen for this many years without hearing the tale repeated many times.

"Where'd we leave off?" Zach asked his son.

"You were getting to the part where Setanta was about to kill the dog."

"No!" Maddy's eyes welled up. "I don't want a story where the dog dies!"

Hiding her smile, Esme looked over at Zach and said, "Looks like you need to find a happier ending for Culann's hound."

Zach looked at her, and then back at Maddy. "Right you are," he said, and then he took another sip of whiskey, and cleared his throat. "Let's see," he said, "As I said earlier, Culann's hound was indeed a very good dog, but he'd frightened Setanta, who feared for his life, and unfortunately killed the dog." Maddy tensed in his lap. He looked down at her, adding, "but then, something remarkable happened."

The children stared back at him wide-eyed. "Was it a miracle?" Michael asked.

"Aye, a miracle," Zach decided, then looked up, meeting Caleb's eyes. Caleb lifted his glass and Zach raised his own as well. "To miracles," they both agreed, and then took another deep drink. Zach's hand was shaking when he set his glass down, and he needed a moment to settle his emotions. Esme had no doubt he was thinking of Katherine and the new babe.

"Did the dog stay dead or not?" Michael demanded.

Caleb picked up the story. "Here's what happened, Michael. Just at that moment a beautiful Indian woman came walking down the path. She saw Setanta overcome with grief for killing Culann's hound." Caleb's voice grew more theatrical as he spoke. "'Did you kill that hound?' the woman demanded, and Setanta said he did, but that it had been in self-defense. He confessed to the woman that he was heartsick because Culann's hound had been a devoted companion and protector."

"So what did the Indian woman do?" This came from Zach, whose eyes were now locked on his brother's.

"Well," Caleb said. "That beautiful Indian woman knelt down beside the hound, put her hands on him, and started singing. The sound of her voice was deep and alluring, and Setanta was drawn in by the melody. He felt as if he wasn't alone, as if someone else was standing close beside him."

"Was there someone?" Michael asked, sipping at his cocoa.

"There was, and you'll never guess who."

Michael put down his cup. Both he and Maddie looked up at Caleb wide-eyed. "Tell us!" they cried in unison.

Caleb leaned in dramatically. "It was the hound itself, its spirit, you see?"

Michael and Maddie nodded.

"And Setanta said to the hound, 'I'm sorry for killing you. I wish you didn't have to die.' And the hound said back to him, 'If you give me a year of your life, I will come back and live for seven more.'"

"Could he really do that?" Maddie asked.

Caleb nodded. "He could, as long as Setanta agreed to the bargain before the Indian woman finished her song."

"Well, did he?" Michael asked.

"He did," Caleb assured him, "and the hound came back to life. The Indian woman stopped singing, and told Setanta from this point on his name must change. He was linked now to Culann's brave hound, and he should now be known as Cuchulainn."

"That means Culann's hound," Michael informed Maddie. Turning to his uncle, he said, "I liked that version a lot. It's way too sad when the hound stays dead."

Caleb smiled. "Then give your thanks to Maddie. She had the idea of it."

The water started boiling. Esme made ready to lift the heavy kettle, but Caleb got there first. "I'll carry that up for you," he said. As Esme left the room, she saw Michael yawn, and lay his head against his father's shoulder. The story had taken away some of the boy's anxiety, but not his father's. Esme watched as Maddie also snuggled against Zach. Automatically, he pulled her in close, but his mind was somewhere else, somewhere dark, and filled with worst-case scenarios.

"Zach," she said, before heading up the stairs. "Maybe it's a miracle, maybe it's something else, but whatever it is, things are going well upstairs. There's reason to hope."

Chapter 17

Katherine smiled when Esme entered the room, and then she grimaced as another contraction gripped her. "She's progressing rapidly," Cha'risa said. "This baby's in a hurry."

Katherine laughed weakly from her pillow. "That's a Cranston trait," she said. "Always ready for the next adventure."

Esme cracked a smile too. "Another willful child is what you mean."

Just then another contraction broke over Katherine like a wave. She caught her breath, and then remembered to let it go. "That's right, Kat, just keep breathing," Cha'risa coaxed. "It won't be long now." Another contraction hit, and Katherine told them she could feel the baby coming.

Esme smoothed Katherine's damp, red hair off her brow. "You ready to bring this baby home now?" Katherine's eyes locked on hers, and she nodded. With the next contraction, Cha'risa told her to push. Sam started chanting again, and Esme placed herself shoulder to shoulder with Cha'risa, at the foot of the bed. Together they watched as the crown of a tiny head appeared. With the next push the little head was through. Esme helped to clear the nasal passages. On the third push Cha'risa eased the small shoulders through; and then, in the space of a breath, a tiny little girl was born.

The baby barely had time to cry before Cha'risa laid the child on Katherine's breast. Katherine held her close, and the baby snuggled in, calmed by the sound of her mother's heartbeat. Katherine looked up at Esme and Cha'risa. "I have a girl!" she laughed, and then cried. "She's beautiful!"

"Let me see!" Sam insisted. He leaned in close to where the baby lay on her mother. "She's all bloody," he said.

"I'm going to clean her right up," Cha'risa assured him.

Sam watched as the little girl was wiped clean, wrapped in a warm blanket, and then handed once again to her mother

"She has a tiny, tiny nose!" he said.

"That she does," his mother agreed.

"And a tiny mouth, and tiny ears too!"

"She is indeed a very little girl, but she will grow."

Esme listened to Cha'risa and her son, but her main focus was on Katherine, so she was the first to see her skin turn a bluish hue. There was a wild look in Katherine's eyes as she began to struggle for breath. Esme let out a strangled cry, and then grabbed the baby from Katherine just seconds before the spasms began.

"Quickly, bring more hot water." Cha'risa ordered Kitty. Kitty stood in shocked horror for a moment, and then pulled herself together and ran to the kitchen for the hot water that had been left sitting on the wood stove. Esme paced with the baby and watched Cha'risa work. Katherine wasn't moving now, and her face was drained of all color. Cha'risa laid her head on Katherine's chest, her expression grim. She placed her mouth over Katherine's, held the nose closed, and then blew into Katherine's mouth. She took in another big breath and did it again.

Esme own heart was pounding so hard she could feel the force of it in her throat and in her head. She turned and paced the other direction holding the baby tighter to her. It was only then that she noticed Sam had moved closer to his mother's side studying the situation, and trying to anticipate how best to help.

Cha'risa straightened, lifted her hand, and brought it down hard on Katherine's chest. Esme and Sam both flinched at the sound. Cha'risa lowered her head to Katherine's chest again listening, and then administered two more breaths. She brought her hand down one more time, another loud smack, and then laid her hand over the heart, massaging, waiting, and singing a song of pulse and rhythm. Sam got back up on his chair, placed his small hands on Katherine's chest and joined his voice to the song. Kitty re-entered the room with the hot water.

"I need you to prepare a tincture from the clary cup cactus root," Cha'risa instructed. "It's in my satchel over there." Cha'risa nodded her head toward the bureau. "Steep it in hot water and then bring it to me." Kitty quickly went to do as she was told.

At last Cha'risa and Sam stopped chanting. Esme searched deep into Cha'risa's eyes looking for the truth, relieved to see it so clearly. Her niece would not die today. Esme forced herself to inhale, and noticed she was shaking badly. Suddenly, she felt unbearably weak.

"Sam, would you like to hold the baby?" she asked.

He looked very tired, but still his eyes lit up, and he climbed off the chair holding out his hands.

"Let's have you sit in that chair by the window." She gestured with her head over to the wing back chair, and he ran over and scrambled up. As she handed him the baby, she noted the sun fully up in the sky. "I need you to watch her, to keep her safe and warm. Can you do that?"

Sam nodded. He folded his arms around the baby and held her close, studying her intently. The baby's eyes focused in on his. He looked up at Esme, grinning widely. "I think she likes me."

Esme offered up a weak smile. "That's because you're her hero."

He looked surprised. "I'm a hero?"

Esme nodded. "You saved the day, Sam. You helped bring her safe into this world."

He looked very pleased with that assessment, and started humming happily. Not a Hopi chant, but one of his father's favorites, The Rose of Tralee. Esme sat down on the settee. She needed just a few seconds before she returned to Katherine's side, but at least for now, both her girls were in good hands.

Kitty carried over the steaming solution of cactus root, and handed it to Cha'risa. Esme watched from the settee as Katherine breathed it in. Cha'risa took some of the cooled liquid and dribbled a small amount of it down her throat. Soon, Esme heard Katherine's breathing normalize, and a little color returned to her cheeks.

Finally, Esme forced herself out of the settee, and went to check on Sam. He hadn't relaxed his vigil. He still held the baby with great care, although his small body was slumped with fatigue, and dark circles ringed his eyes. Esme came and sat by him. She was still tired but she felt steadier now. "I can take her." Esme offered.

He let her take the baby. He might have curled up right there beside her and fallen asleep, but Esme felt the need to ask him something first. "Sam," she asked. "Where did you learn the melody you were singing to Katherine?"

"My grandfather taught me," he said. "He told me to sing it to Aunt Katherine and the new baby."

"You mean Istaqa?"

Sam nodded.

Esme studied him closely. "How can that be, Sam? He's been dead over a year now. He never even knew there was going to be another baby."

Sam yawned, and then looked at her. "You're being silly, Esme. Grandfather didn't teach it to me before he died; he taught me just a few days ago."

Esme tensed. "That can't be!" she exclaimed, but the words sounded hollow even to her. She believed in ghosts, and she knew all too well the strange nature of Sam's gifts.

Cha'risa had been listening to their exchange. "Sam?" she asked, "When did you last see your grandfather?"

Sam looked at her. "Last night. He told me the baby was coming, that you would need my help, and that I should sing the song with confidence."

Esme looked at Cha'risa. "Is that possible?"

"Apparently so," Cha'risa said with a hint of a smile

Sam yawned widely, and Kitty went to him, lifting him tenderly into her arms. "I think this little guy has earned his rest. Shall I put him to bed?"

Cha'risa nodded, and then kissed her son on his forehead. "I'll come and check on you soon," she promised, then added, "You were very brave and strong today, Sam. You made us all proud."

"Is Grandpa proud too?" he asked.

"I think especially Grandpa."

The door didn't even have time to close when Kitty left the room. Zach had been waiting right outside, a pot of Hopi tea in his hands. "May we come in now?" he asked.

Caleb stood next to him carrying cups for the tea. "Is Sam okay?" he asked Kitty.

"He's fine," Kitty assured him. "He just needs some sleep."

"Guess what, Dad?" Sam said before Kitty carried him off.

"What?"

"I'm a hero. Even Mom says so."

Caleb smiled widely. "Is that a fact? I'd like to hear more about that when you wake up."

Esme felt badly. She should have gone to the men as soon as the danger had past. They'd been left to worry for so long. As Kitty left and the men entered the room, she went to Zach.

"I'll trade you," she said, and exchanged the baby for the tea. "You have a daughter."

As he gazed into his baby's eyes, Esme could read the relief on his face that his wife and daughter had both pulled through. That wasn't the only emotion she saw there, as clear as day was the look in his eyes, offering up to his new born daughter all the love in his heart.

Zach walked over to his wife's bedside. She lay there pale and still, but the regular rise and fall of her breath gave proof she was alive. "Is she going to be all right?" he asked.

Cha'risa stood beside him. "She did well with the labor and delivery, but there was trouble at the end. She is sleeping now, and is very weak."

"But everything's okay now, right?"

"She will live," Cha'risa assured him, as he studied his wife lying so peacefully asleep. "However, I fear this baby has weakened her heart greatly."

Zach looked up at her, alarmed. Cha'risa met his gaze with an unwavering stare. "There can be no more children, Zach, no matter what she says." Zach nodded, swallowing hard. "She went to great lengths to convince us she was still drinking the tea," Cha'risa continued. "If she tries something like that again, I don't think she'll survive."

"I'll make certain she doesn't," he vowed. Then he looked down at the sleeping infant in his arms. "Is the baby okay?"

Cha'risa's demeanor softened. "She's a strong, healthy little girl."

Zach gazed up at her. "Really?"

"Really."

Cha'risa was quiet a moment, letting the truth of her assertion sink in. "What will you name her?" she asked.

Zach cleared his throat, and brushed an errant tear from his eye. "If it was a girl, Katherine said we should name her after her mother, Eleanor. Ellie for short."

Esme wasn't sure why, but the mention of Katherine's mother unleashed a flood of emotion. To her own horror, she began crying unstoppable tears.

Caleb gave her a funny look, then took her by the arm and turned her around toward the wing back chair. "You've overdone it," he declared. "You need to sit and put your feet up." He deposited Esme into the chair and slid a stool up under her feet.

Cha'risa came up behind him and pressed a cup of Hopi tea into Esme's shaking hands. "Drink," she ordered.

Esme raised the cup unsteadily to her lips, and took a small sip. She felt Cha'risa's warm touch on her shoulders and looked up. She tried to tell Cha'risa to go sit down, that she didn't need anyone fussing over her, but she just couldn't seem to string the words together.

She felt the healing warmth of Cha'risa's touch flow into her. It was just like Katherine had said, very relaxing. She took a deep, steadying breath, and then looked around at all the people in the room. She blinked, unable to account for what she was seeing. It was like nothing she'd ever experienced before. Each of them was bathed in a brilliant, golden light. It seemed to Esme as if the best of all they were, was shining through for all of heaven to see.

Maybe it's because of all the miracles, she thought. It was a miracle that Katherine was still with them, and there was the miracle of Cha'risa's extraordinary healing gifts. There was also the miracle of Istaqa offering his help from beyond the grave, and having it manifest through a miraculously gifted little boy. But most of all there was the miracle of this family. In this light, she could see all the ties that bound them together, and she could see how those ties bound her too into their circle of love and protection.

Her eyes focused on Zach holding their family's newest miracle, Ellie, safely delivered, strong and healthy, fully enmeshed in this circle of love. The light was so clear, so strong, that Esme could see it all. The truth of all those miracles swelled her heart with gratitude. The moment lasted a second, or maybe a lifetime, then the light exploded, the stroke swept through her brain, and it left nothing in its wake.

1910

Caleb's Beef Jerky Marinade

Ingredients
2 pounds flank steak
16 ounces Guinness ale (or other dark beer)
1/2 cup soy sauce
2 tablespoons Worcestershire sauce
2 cloves garlic, smashed
2 tablespoons honey
1 teaspoon dried mustard powder
1 teaspoon hot pepper flakes
1/2 teaspoon coarsely ground black pepper
Juice of ½ lime

Directions
Remove any visible fat from the flank steak and thinly slice the meat (against the grain) into long strips.

Mix the remaining ingredients in a large bowl. Combine the marinade and sliced steak and chill at least 6 hours and up to overnight.

Finish the jerky following the directions of your smoker or dehydrator.

Chapter 18

Ahote groaned in his sleep. The nightmare was starting again. Part of him knew it was a dream, and he struggled to fight his way back to consciousness. Another part of him was just so tired, he hoped he would never wake again. But in the end, it wasn't a choice. He couldn't bear to dream of the anguished faces of the people he loved best. He woke feeling the hard earth beneath him, and when he sat up, all he could see were miles of the inhospitable Colorado Plateau stretched out before him.

He got up and began to run; running was the only way to escape the agony. But no matter how fast or far he ran, the pain was never far behind. In the beginning, he'd been aiming for *Nuvatukya'ovi*, the San Francisco Peaks. Why he'd picked that northern point he couldn't say, perhaps because it was home to the Hopi spirits. But if that'd been his original plan, it wasn't any more. He hadn't stopped when he'd gotten to the mountains. In his head, he'd kept hearing the voice of his grandfather, telling him once again what a fine runner Kwahu had been; recalling the story of how his father had run all the way from the Hopi Pueblos to the *Moqui* trail, and then on to the sacred sites within the walls of the Grand Canyon. It wasn't a command, this voice of his grandfather now dead for seven years, it was more of an urgent whisper, but it was enough to keep him running northward.

It occurred to Ahote he'd lost hold of his sanity. He'd run for days now on little water and only a handful of Caleb's beef jerky. He'd eaten the last of the jerky two days ago, and now his strength was ebbing. His feet were blistered and bloody, his muscles throbbing, his entire body flushed and feverish, but every time he stopped to take a break, he would fall asleep and the dream would come. As soon as he saw the grief-ravaged faces he had to wake, had to push on, had to try somehow to outrun the horror he had wrought on his family. And as he ran, as constant as the dream was the voice of his grandfather, urging him toward the canyon.

His feet pounded a rhythm on the dry earth beneath him, and his nose filled with dust, and the scent of juniper and piñon. His mind wandered, lulled by a world that had been reduced to the next stride, the next breath. If the funeral was the ending, then Branna was the beginning. He remembered exactly the day it'd all started, with the telegram from Mary Clare.

"Sam! Watch out now. Don't turn your back on her!" Ahote strode into the center of the corral, correcting Sam's stance as the boy lunged the mare.

"When's it my turn?" Michael called from the railing. "You said I'd have a chance, too!"

"You will, little man, you will. Be patient."

Ahote had judged Sam's calmer nature would make a better introduction to captivity for the mare. Michael had a tendency to come on strong, and Ahote wanted to give the boy time to plan his approach before putting him in the ring. Still, it wouldn't be fair to make Michael wait much longer. It had, after all, been Michael's idea to save the wild horses. He'd been outraged when he heard of the government's plan to destroy the herd living on the mesa near the winter ranch. Zach had agreed it was a shame, but allowed the horses were causing a problem for everyone using that area for winter grazing. Michael felt there were better ways to handle the problem, and quickly drew Sam into a hastily conceived plan. Originally, the boys wanted to rescue all the horses, break them with Ahote's help, and turn them into mounts their fathers could sell. Ahote persuaded them to start with just one.

While nights were still chilly up the mountain at the lodge, spring had already arrived at the winter ranch. Ahote brought the boys to the mesa top one weekend in early April, planning to camp out a few nights while they searched for horses. When they found the herd, Ahote helped the boys separate out one very pretty mare.

The boys had been exhausted but proud when they led that wild horse into the corral back at the lodge. At first Zach had raised an eyebrow, but when he discovered the mare was pregnant, you'd have thought the whole plan had been his idea all along. Now Zach was considering bringing in a few more from the herd, to see if this crazy plan of Michael's might actually work.

Ahote was just about to swap out Sam for Michael in the ring, when he heard the sound of the buckboard approaching. It was Zach and Katherine returning from Flagstaff.

"Find Caleb!" Zach called out. "We have a telegram from Mary Clare!"

Ahote sent Michael running to the barn, while Sam tied the mare to the hitching post. Ahote gave Sam a carrot to hold out to the mare. She was wary, but accepted it.

"She sure is sweet, isn't she?" Sam said.

"She's making good progress," Ahote agreed.

Both Ahote and Sam looked up at the sound of a little girl's laughter. They saw Cha'risa coming up the path from the barn, with Ellie happily skipping ahead, swinging a basket filled to the brim with dried lavender. When Ellie saw her mom, she dropped the basket and immediately ran to her.

"Mom! You're home!" she cried, flying into her mother's arms.

Cha'risa smiled at Katherine. "She's been helping me."

"Were you, sweetheart?"

Ellie nodded. "I heard Mrs. Burnett say she wanted more sachets for the store. And Maddy wants some, too. She says they make her clothes smell so good. I thought I could help you make them."

Her mother smiled. "Well, we have our work cut out for us then, don't we?"

Ahote watched as Ellie continued chattering excitedly, telling her mom about the rest of her morning, and asking if she could come along the next time a delivery was made to the store. She really was a sweet kid, and the spitting image of Katherine, with her auburn curls and her mother's bright green eyes. Still, Ahote could never look at Ellie without thinking about the price this little girl had cost the family. Even now, six years later, he felt the hole left by Esme's death. He remembered her unstoppable energy, and the way she cared for everyone but herself. And no one in the family ever forgot the amazing meals she used to make. Katherine had made sure of that, writing down every recipe of Esme's she could remember, and then binding them all into a book.

Esme's death had been hard for the family, but that was not the only price they'd paid. Katherine's health had never fully recovered, and she was losing ground. Lately, she grew tired easily, and was often out of breath. Zach was worried, and what was worse, so was Cha'risa. There was no herb or chant she knew that could stop the deterioration of Katherine's heart. Not for the first time, Ahote wondered why Katherine had risked so much to have this child.

Ahote caught his mother staring at him. It was uncanny how she always knew his thoughts. Ahote looked down, catching sight of his little brother who was still standing close beside him. Now Ahote felt doubly ashamed. Sam adored Ellie, and had from the first moment he'd laid eyes on her. There was no use speculating on whether Katherine should have taken the risk or not. Even Ahote wouldn't want a world that didn't have Ellie in it.

Ahote hid his shameful thoughts by turning to Ellie and pointing a finger at her. "You!" he announced. "You're coming with me!" He plucked her from her mother's arms and placed her on top of his shoulders.

"Where are we going?" she laughed.

"We're going to see if we can get Uncle Caleb to stop mucking about, so we can all hear what's in this telegram!"

He began to run, and Ellie shrieked with excitement. "Faster!"

"What? Am I your horse?"

"Yes! Giddyup, you old horse!"

He snorted and pawed the ground with his leg, and then galloped toward the barn as Ellie's peals of laughter filled the yard. Ahote stopped as soon as he saw Caleb striding toward them, Michael running alongside to keep up.

When Caleb reached the family, the first thing he did was to kiss his wife. It was not a thoughtless peck, it was warm and tender. Watching the two of them filled Ahote with a bittersweet feeling. His mom could be stern, and she could be scary, but in Caleb's arms she was simply a woman in love. Ahote couldn't help but wonder if he would ever love someone that way.

"So where's this telegram?" Caleb asked.

Katherine pulled it out of her handbag, and Caleb ripped it open as he walked toward the rockers under the veranda of the lodge. He sat down with a frown, and his eyes darkened as he continued reading down the page. Zach sat down beside him.

"What's happened?"

"There's been some trouble with Branna."

Zach's eyes narrowed. "What kind of trouble?"

"It's exactly what you're thinking" Caleb said. "That drunk she calls a husband beat her up again, badly."

"Jesus! Surely the boys didn't stand for it!"

"No, they didn't. They caused enough ruckus that the whole lot of them landed in jail."

"And what did Ma do?"

"While all the boys were locked up, she took Branna to Dublin, and put her on the first ship headed to America."

"She's on her way *here?*!"

"She is. She's to telegraph us once she arrives in New York"

Zach sat back on the bench and whistled. "Do you think Aengus will give Ma any trouble?" he asked.

Caleb shrugged. "He might, but my guess is he'll be regretting it if he does."

"Who is Branna?" Michael asked.

"She's our sister."

"So she's my aunt?" Michael was still trying to put all the pieces together.

"She is." Caleb assured him. "She's an aunt to all three of you, and I'm thinking she'll like very well the sight of so many children to love."

"She might not," Sam fretted. "You're always saying we're a wild bunch."

Caleb laughed. "Branna has six brothers, all older than she. She knows how to handle a wild bunch."

"Then why did her husband beat her?" Michael asked. "Why couldn't she handle him?"

Caleb's face sobered. "I don't know the answer to that, Michael. All I know for certain is that Branna needs a new start, and she'll be making that start here with us."

"And, Michael," Katherine interrupted, "When Branna gets here, don't be pestering her with a million questions. If she wants you to know something, she'll tell you in her own way, understood?" She gave her son a stern look, and he nodded.

"Come on, boys." Ahote urged. "Last I saw, we had horses that needed feeding and grooming."

He put Ellie down, and was about to send her back to her mother, when Sam asked, "Can Ellie come too?"

"Yes!" Ellie clamored. "Can I go too? Please!"

Ahote looked at Katherine, and she nodded her head.

"And can I be the one to give them their oats?" Ellie begged.

"Sure," Ahote said, but then Michael erupted.

"Hold on there, just a minute! I didn't get a chance to lunge the horse. I should be the one to give out the oats!"

Ellie was about to object, but Sam took her by the hand. "You can help me with the hay, how does that sound?"

"Fine. But I should get to help brush them." Ellie negotiated.

"I don't think Michael would object to that, would you, Michael?"

Michael just rolled his eyes. "She's got you wrapped around her little finger," he sighed.

"Come on, all of you," Ahote said, leading them all off to the barn.

Later that evening, when the children were being readied for bed, Ahote walked back down to the barn. He often liked to enjoy a few quiet moments with the horses at the end of his day. He went first to Big Red; the old horse was still his favorite. Ahote was about to offer him an apple, when he heard voices coming from the loft.

"Do you think Mary Clare had other reasons for sending Branna here?" Zach asked.

"I told her," Caleb answered.

"You did?" Zach didn't sound surprised to hear it. "What exactly did you tell her?"

"What we both know, that the ranch work is getting to be too much for Katherine."

Zachariah sighed deeply.

"Don't blame yourself, Zach."

Zach's voice grew loud. "Who else is there to blame, Caleb? I'm the one who put those babies in her!"

Ahote walked up to the ladder, debating with himself whether or not he should interrupt them.

"I don't think your wife would change one moment of her life with you or those two lovely children," Caleb assured him. "None of us knows how long we have on this earth, Zach. We can only make the best of each day given to us."

Ahote heard a quiet sob, and realized Zach must be crying. Caleb's Irish brogue became more pronounced as he continued trying to comfort his brother. "You've made your wife's life a happy one. And now Ma has come up with a way to help make the going easier for both Katherine and Branna. And that's what we've got to do too, you see? We've got to do our part to take care of our women."

"How do I do that, Caleb? I can't keep her safe; I can't fix her heart!"

"I'm thinking you already do it every day, just by loving her. There's no better medicine than that."

Zach's sniffling quieted. "Well, it won't be a hardship to do more of that."

Ahote climbed into the loft and sat down by the men. The air was warm up here, and filled with the scent of drying plants, his mother's medicinal herbs, and Katherine's floral ones. Together they combined to make a heady aroma. Ahote looked up at the bundles hanging from the rafters. He wished he had something helpful and wise to say, but the only advice he could think to offer was, "Make sure she keeps drinking my mom's teas. That will help, Zach. She must drink the teas."

Chapter 19

Ahote stopped running and bent over, trying to catch his breath. In his head, he could still hear his voice echoing, "the teas, the teas." He hadn't taken much from home that night when he felt compelled to run. He had his rifle, a knife and a small pack filled with just a few things; the jerky, and some bundles of his mother's Hopi tea. Near the bundles of tea had been her prized sacks of Hopi corn, the ones she reserved for planting. He'd grabbed one of those as well. Why he took the corn, he couldn't say. It was the action of a man who believed in a future, who had faith he would be there to plant come spring. Ahote wasn't sure he wanted a future any more, but maybe the corn said something more; maybe some part of him wasn't ready to declare defeat.

He sat down and opened the pack, pulling out the sack of corn. He felt the weight of it in his hand, and then set it aside to search deeper in for the bundles of tea. They were just beneath where the corn had sat. He took one out, bringing the bundle to his nose. A sharp aroma emanated from the tea, reminding him vividly of the smell of desert plants in the rain. With that thought, a hundred more stirred, of red rocks drenched in monsoon rains, of wet horses and cattle, of Sam, Mike and Ellie splashing through puddles as they chased a rainbow. He saw Caleb caught in the rain and not caring as he held his wife under the deluge and kissed her.

The sun pierced through the mounting clouds, spreading its rays of light across miles of plateau. For a few moments Ahote sat there feeling the warmth of the sun, and breathing in the fragrance of his mom's small bundle of herbs. He decided he would try to sleep again, and when he woke he would build a fire and drink some tea. If he was strong enough, he might even try to hunt. Apparently, he wasn't prepared to die just yet.

He closed his eyes and thankfully the heart-wrenching dream did not come, but neither did sleep. As tired as he was, he could not quiet the memories. He could see it all so clearly, that first day Branna arrived, a dark haired beauty sitting beside Caleb in the wagon. At first she hadn't seen the family waiting on the veranda by the front door.

She'd been watching the flight of a hawk as it circled in front of the majestic backdrop of the San Francisco Peaks.

Caleb brought the team to a halt beside the barn, and helped Branna down from the wagon. She turned to her brother, her face filled with wonder. "You live here?"

He smiled, "Do you like it?" he asked.

"Jaysus," she exclaimed in an undiluted Irish lilt. "It looks like a whole other world."

The sun took that moment to flood the surrounding meadow and pine forest with light. She clasped her hands to her heart, at the sight of the landscape all aglow, and then began to turn full circle to take it all in. Halfway through the turn her sights set upon the well-built lodge, and then finally on the entire family, standing on the veranda watching her.

It was Zachariah she noticed first, and with a cry she ran into his arms. He held her tightly, and then wiped away a few of her stray tears before introducing her to Katherine. Ahote stayed silent, tucked back into the shadows, just watching as Branna was introduced to all three children. She exclaimed over each one of them. And then, she was introduced to Cha'risa.

She studied Cha'risa closely and then commented, "Well, you aren't at all big or scary."

"I never told you she was big," Caleb corrected.

Cha'risa looked at him. "Does that imply you told her I was scary?"

"I told the folks back home nothing but the truth about you, and the truth is you can sometimes be a wee bit terrifying."

"You have nothing to fear from me," Cha'risa assured the young woman. Then she looked at Caleb. "You, on the other hand, might want to think twice about the stories you tell." Then she turned from him, and brought Branna face to face with Ahote. "Branna, this is my oldest son, Ahote."

When Branna met his eyes, Ahote felt like he was falling from a horse; first a dizzying tumble, and then an impact that took his breath away. He must have looked like an idiot, staring tongue tied into those unsettling gray eyes, but he couldn't look away and couldn't speak a word.

Caleb thumped him on the back. "Get a hold of yourself, man."

"Um…hello." Ahote managed. He held out his hand and she clasped his firmly.

"It's nice to meet you, Ahote." Then the women were ushering her into the lodge, and he was left standing on the porch, still unable to form a single, coherent thought.

"Best stop thinking about it, son," Caleb said gently.

Ahote turned to him. "What?"

"She's a married woman. Whether she left her husband or no, what was done before God cannot be undone."

Ahote stared at him. "What are you talking about?"

"Good Lord, Ahote! Must I spell it all out for you? You're looking at her the way I look at your mother. And she's not free, son. She'll never be free."

The Colorado Plateau grew increasingly overcast, but Ahote hardly noticed. He just sat there with the disturbing words playing over and over in his mind. "She'll never be free." Ahote knew the words held true for him as well. There were consequences for loving a white woman. He should never have let it happen. He'd heard the unkind things people had said about Caleb's marriage to Cha'risa. And what better evidence could he have had of people's intolerance then the entire State of Arizona censuring their marriage. A law had been passed shortly after Caleb and Cha'risa married declaring all inter-racial marriages null and void.

Caleb hadn't been deterred, though. He'd taken Cha'risa to New Mexico and renewed their vows there. He'd also taken some trouble to draw up additional legal documents protecting her property rights and Sam's as well. While he was at it, he'd even preserved ten acres for Ahote at the winter ranch. He'd done what he could to protect his family, and Ahote admired Caleb's outright refusal to let people's bigotry get in his way. But Ahote had learned in the hardest way possible that an Indian man seeking the love of a white woman provoked an even stronger reaction. No, Branna wasn't free and neither was he.

He liked to think he might have done a better job managing this ill-fated attraction, if this hadn't been such an unusual time for C & M Ranch. Any other summer, he would have been mostly alone at the winter ranch, fulfilling his caretaker duties. Branna would have been busy up at the lodge helping everyone manage the seasonal increase in guests. They would have barely seen one another. But what he hadn't counted on was how the wild horse venture would create a degree of fluidity between the two ranches that had never existed before.

Ahote watched the wagons rolling toward him, and braced himself for an end to the peace and quiet of the winter ranch. Soon there would be a frenetic onslaught of setting up, and then would come an even worse hullabaloo when the tourists arrived, looking for their adventure up on Wild Horse Mesa.

Caleb came up beside him, and put his arm sympathetically around the young man's shoulder. "It's not that bad, son."

Ahote gave him a look. "What in blazes is Zach telling them that makes them all want to come here?"

"Well, Zach was always a very able story teller, and that pretty mare and wee colt are a powerful visual when he goes to sell these tours." Caleb grinned widely at him. "You showed him the value of those wild horses, and he just took it from there. Nothing makes Zach more content than the possibility of making money at both ends."

Ahote grunted. "Nice that someone's happy."

Caleb ignored the sullenness. "Who'd have thought these tourists would pay for the chance to help catch a wild horse? And what's more incredible is that people are interested in buying them. Truly, it's a credit to you. You've done a fine job helping Zach turn these wild animals into respectable mounts."

"I could do a better job if I could manage to get some peace around here. This is the fifth wild horse adventure he's sold this summer!" Ahote was speaking to Caleb, but now his attention was fixed on the lead wagon heading onto the property. Branna was driving the team with Ellie by her side.

Caleb followed Ahote's gaze, and saw immediately what was really troubling Ahote. "Is it hard for you, that she likes your company?"

Ahote gave him a pained look.

Caleb met his gaze with compassion and understanding. "You need to look at it this way, son. Branna is going to be with us for a long time. You'll never be able to solve this problem by avoiding her, she being my sister and all." He drew Ahote closer and gave his shoulder a light squeeze. "You'll find your way through it. I've never known you not to keep a level head."

"You make it sound easy, but it's really not."

Caleb nodded. "I know, but it's hard for her too, you see. She's a young woman trapped in a bad marriage. There will be no great love in her life, no children. All she can have are good friends. Couldn't you be that for her?"

Ahote looked away for a moment, considering, then straightened his shoulders and met his stepfather's direct gaze. "You're right," he said. "I'm being an idiot."

Caleb smiled. "You're no idiot, Ahote. And it's okay to love her; just love her like a brother."

Ahote nodded, and thought perhaps it really could be as simple as that. As he approached the wagon, he pointed right at little Ellie and said "You!" She was already squirming and laughing when he scooped her off her seat and up onto his shoulders. "What are you doing back again so soon?!" he demanded of the little girl.

"We're going to catch more wild horses, Ahote!"

"Yes, we are." He turned to face Branna and met her radiant smile with one of his own. "How many are coming tonight?"

"Ten," she said. "A gentleman, a family of five, and two couples."

"You want me to set up four tents or five?"

"Normally I'd say let's give the parents some privacy, but those boys of theirs are wilder than the horses we'll be chasing."

Ahote rolled his eyes. "I can't wait to meet them," he muttered.

She laughed and Ellie gave a kick from up top her mount. "Giddyup!" she demanded. He grabbed the little imp off her perch and set her on the ground.

"No," he said. "Today we're playing hotel, and you and I have some tents to prepare!"

"Oh yay!" she cried. "I like that game too!"

By late afternoon, the tents were raised, the beds were made, and Ellie had left a sprig of lavender on every pillow. Branna and Cha'risa had fresh loaves of bread cooling and were cooking a hearty stew over the fire pit when Zach and Katherine rode in with the new guests. It was the part of the excursion Ahote dreaded most, being introduced, along with his mother, as the resident Hopi Indians. From here on out, there would be stares and impertinent questions. It wouldn't end until the evening campfire, which always culminated with Hopi legends and stories of what life was like on the Hopi Mesas. Apparently his mother was keeping count, because she'd informed him tonight was most definitely his turn to lead the storytelling.

"Don't look so glum." Branna came up beside him, having just finished helping with the dinner preparations.

"Not glum," Ahote asserted. "Taciturn. Didn't you know Indians are supposed to be taciturn?"

She regarded him kindly. "You don't like being on display, do you?"

"Not much," he agreed.

"I know a little something about what that feels like," she admitted. She was quiet a moment then added, "I like your stories, you know? You know how to tell a good tale."

Ahote shrugged modestly. "Mostly I just tell the stories my grandfather told me."

"My gramps used to tell me tales too, Irish ones though."

"Caleb and Zach have told me quite a few as well. They're good stories. Maybe we should do Irish legends around the campfire tonight."

"Lord, no! These people are here for a Wild West experience, not a fairy tale from across the water."

Just then Sam came running up to him, breathless. "Ahote! Guess what?!"

"What?"

"It's about the mare!"

"Yes? What about her?"

"She's mine! Uncle Zach just gave her to me!"

Ahote looked at Sam's sparkling eyes and flushed cheeks. He'd never seen Sam look more pleased.

"She's yours to keep?"

"Forever and ever!"

"Just yours? What about Michael?"

"He picked the colt. He said he'd rather wait and have himself a stallion to ride, but I wanted the mare anyway. You have to help me pick a name for her!"

Ahote smiled. "Well, of course I will. You're a lucky devil. She's a fine horse."

Sam beamed. "Uncle Zach says it's no less then we deserve, since this whole idea was ours in the first place."

"Well, he's right about that."

"So what should I name her?"

"What kind of name are you looking for?"

"I don't know. All I know is that it needs to be special, just like her."

Ahote thought a moment. "Do you remember the story of the Wind God?"

"The one who lives at Sunset Crater?"

"That very one. The Wind God is named Yaponcha. Your mare runs pretty fast; you know, like the wind. Maybe you could name her that."

"Yaponcha," Sam said, considering.

Michael walked up with Ellie in tow and said, "My colt's gonna be faster, you can tell already."

"Do you know any Irish stories about horses, Aunt Branna?" Sam asked.

Branna's eyes twinkled, "Only if you like scary stories."

"You know I do!" Sam exclaimed.

"Well, has your dad ever mentioned to you anything about the Pooka?"

Sam shook his head.

She gestured all the children over to the seats near the fire pit, and Ahote followed, each of them crowding around to hear her story.

"The Pooka," she began in her thick Irish brogue, "is a most fearsome fairy creature. It only ever comes out after nightfall, and it causes all kind of mischief when it is about. It looks like a horse, a very sleek, dark horse, except that its eyes glow like molten lava."

Sam's eyes grew wide as she described the devilish creature, and Ellie huddled in next to him. She almost put her thumb in her mouth, but stopped herself and grabbed Sam's hand instead.

Branna leaned in dramatically. "The mere sight of the Pooka causes the hens to stop laying their eggs, and the cows to stop giving their milk. But the Pooka is especially known for bein' the curse of all late night travelers."

"Why?" Ellie asked, never taking her eyes off of her aunt.

"Well, because that demon Pooka with its fiery eyes will swoop those travelers right up on to its back. It runs, with those poor travelers clinging on for dear life, until it comes to a muddy ditch or a miry bog hole, and then it throws them right in."

"At least it doesn't kill them or eat them," Michael said.

"Well, no. I've not heard it said it does anythin' like that, but what I have heard is that the Pooka has the power of human speech, and it has been known to stop in front of certain houses and call out the names o' those it wants to take upon its midnight dashes."

"It calls for them?" Michael moved in a little closer to Sam, too.

"Aye, it does. And it's a haunted, horrible cry that it makes. Michaaael! Michaaaaaaael! And if he calls your name, Michael, you have to go to him or he will destroy something you love."

"Why does he do that?" Ellie's green eyes were as round as could be.

Branna leaned in close. "Well, because it is most certainly a very vindictive fairy."

Sam smiled broadly. "I love it! I'm going to name my mare Pooka!"

"But your horse isn't dark!" Michael protested. "Pooka would be a better name for my colt."

Sam shook his head. "I claimed it first. Besides, the colt will never know what it's like to be wild and free. My mare does though, so she will be Pooka, and that's the end of it."

Ahote smiled. Sam didn't often assert himself over Michael, but it was clear he wasn't budging on this. Ahote looked at Branna, grinning a little devilishly himself.

"I'm sure there must be tons of Irish legends about horses," he said and then turned to the children. "If Aunt Branna tells the campfire stories tonight, maybe she'll find us another great name to suit that little colt."

Branna put up a hand. "Now, hold on there. The people are here to listen to Hopi stories, not Irish legends."

"But, Aunt Branna, do you know more scary horse stories?" Michael asked.

"There are a few," she admitted. "But, "she added looking straight at Ahote, "I'm certain there are some interesting stories about horses in the Hopi legends as well."

Ahote shrugged. "Not really. The Hopi aren't traditionally a horse people."

He met her gaze, not even trying to hide his smile, as all three children started clamoring for her to tell more of her scary horse stories around the fire. She glared back at him.

"It looks like it's time to get this horde of visitors fed," he said before she had a chance to argue further.

"What about the stories, Branna? Will you please tell them tonight at the fire?" Michael pleaded.

"For the love of God!" she swore, and then looked Ahote right in the eye. "Wipe that smile off your face. I'm sure I'll find a way to repay you." Then she turned and headed over to the cook fire, looking back once to give him a final scowl.

Ahote allowed himself a satisfied grin. He'd made his first foray into being Branna's friend, and by all accounts it had gone very well. This was going to be easier than he'd thought.

Except that it hadn't been. Ahote stood up from the hard ground. There was no use hoping for sleep anymore, not with rain starting. He looked around for shelter from the coming storm. The plateau was very exposed, but he found a small copse of pinion trees. He crawled under their low-lying branches, and tried to make do as best he could. He huddled in misery as the wind picked up, and the rain began to fall in torrents. Soon, he was soaking wet, but he was also exhausted and weak with hunger. Despite the uncomfortable conditions, he succumbed to sleep.

Ahote helped Caleb load the boxes into the wagon. Another large group of tourists would soon be descending on the winter ranch, and Katherine had sent the three of them into town with a very long shopping list. Mr. Burnett and Branna came out of the general store with the last of the packages. All four of them breathed a sigh of relief when the last of the items were loaded onto the wagon bed. It was hot, especially for Flagstaff, and they all were drenched from their efforts. Branna's face was an alarming shade of red. She still wasn't used to the desert climate, and Flagstaff, at 7,000 feet in elevation, was a big altitude change for someone who'd spent her entire life at sea level.

Eli Ferguson came strolling down Front Street and waved a friendly hello at the group.

"Eli!" Caleb shouted and gestured the doctor over. "I have a new batch of teas for you, from Cha'risa."

As Ahote watched Eli approach, he thought back to the first time he'd met the doctor, twelve years ago, lying face down in the dirt, too drunk to realize that a tiny Hopi woman had just saved his life. Eli had done a lot with his second chance at life since then. Once he was sober, he'd demonstrated that he was actually a very talented physician. He was a respected man with a thriving practice now.

Eli peeked inside the satchel Caleb had given him. "Oh, there's more than just the Hopi tea in here!" He looked up, smiling.

"Cha'risa added a few other remedies she said you'd been asking for. There's a list somewhere in there to let you know which is which."

Eli clasped his hands together in anticipation. "Wonderful! You have no idea how quickly her remedies fly off my shelf. He rummaged deeper, looking for the list of the other medicinals. He looked up once he found it and said, "Come to my office, so I can pay you for this lot."

Caleb nodded, and then looked over at Branna, who was still flushed with heat. "Ahote, get Branna out of the sun for a bit." He pulled some coins from his pocket. "Go buy her something cold to drink."

"I've got some sasparilla sitting on ice in the store," Mr. Burnett offered.

"Perfect!" Branna declared, and Ahote led her over to a small group of tables the Burnetts had set out in their new soda parlor. From their seats by the window, they were able to watch Caleb and Eli heading off to Eli's small medical office. When Ahote finally turned back, he found Branna watching him.

"What?" he asked.

She looked away, blushing a little. "Nothing."

Perhaps he should have left it at that. No, not perhaps, he *should* have left it at that. But instead he said, "It doesn't seem like nothing."

She looked up, their eyes met and they just stared at each other, unable to look away.

At last she broke the awkward silence. "It's just that sometimes when I look at you, I think of those stories you tell, and I wonder what you might have been like if you'd never been taken away to the Indian School."

"What do you think I'd be like?"

"I think you'd be happy, that you'd have a beautiful Hopi wife and little children. You would be unfettered, and not so all alone."

He studied her closely. "Do you wish that for yourself as well, Branna?"

She stared back, unable to answer him.

Mrs. Burnett came by just then with two glasses of sarsaparilla weeping with condensation. She gave them both a curious glance. "Is everything all right here?"

Branna forced a smile. "We're fine." She reached for the cold glass of soda, and her smile turned genuine. "In fact we're better than fine." She pressed the cold glass against her cheek. "I'm thinking you must be a saint, Mrs. Burnett, because this feels like heaven!"

Mrs. Burnett laughed. "Well, it's even better when you drink it."

Branna lifted the glass to Mrs. Burnett, and then to Ahote. "Slainte!" she said, and then brought the glass to her lips, taking a long drink.

Mrs. Burnett smiled at Branna's pleasure over the cold soda, and then walked back behind the counter. Ahote never saw her go. He couldn't tear his gaze away from the look of utter satisfaction on Branna's face.

"What are you looking at, boy?" It was a stranger's voice, and the man's tone was filled with censure.

Ahote turned. Here, he thought, was trouble. He knew from experience that it was best not to say much in these situations, so he simply stood and placed himself between the man and Branna. However, Branna was a McKenna through and through. He heard her chair scrape the floor and felt her take a stand beside him.

"Excuse me, sir, but you are interrupting my nephew and me."

The man looked at her disapprovingly. "You don't look like his Aunt to me, Missy. If you're looking for some male companionship I'm sure I'd be a better choice."

Ahote's hand drifted toward his knife. At the same moment, Mr. Burnett approached the man. "Sir, these are good friends of mine. There is nothing untoward going on here."

The man turned to Mr. Burnett. He used his greater height to intimidate the smaller man. "I know what I saw, shopkeeper. And this here Injun has got no business looking at a white woman that way. Not even if she is white trash."

"White trash? White trash!" Branna's lilt grew heavy with scorn. "You shouldn't be callin' me trash when your own mind sees nothin' but filth!"

Ahote groaned inwardly. There would be no saving this situation. He pushed Branna behind him, and he heard Mr. Burnett urging her away. Ahote addressed the man. "I think you and I need to take this outside, Mister."

The man's eyes narrowed, and he pulled his gun. It all happened so fast. Ahote remembered staring down a gun barrel, surprised the man

109

had drawn his weapon in the store. Then he heard a war cry, and Caleb came hurtling toward him. The gun went off and there was the sound of glass breaking. Ahote hit the floor hard, shards of glass crunching beneath him, and the weight of Caleb's body on top of him. He heard Branna screaming.

"Caleb! Oh sweet Jaysus! Caleb, don't you dare be dyin' on me, you hear!"

Ahote felt something warm seeping onto his clothing. Then he heard Doc Ferguson's voice.

"Don't move, Ahote. Let me get to him first."

He was wet, so wet, from Caleb's blood spilling over him, from his own cuts all along his backside, from Branna's tears falling. The dampness chilled him, and he was dizzy and nauseated by the swirl of activity around him. He saw Eli's face when the doc got his first good look at the wound; he saw the shooter trying to run, only to find a crowd of angry, horrified locals penning him in. He saw Kitty Burnett trying to staunch the flow of Caleb's blood with her towel. She was crying, and the towel quickly turned bright red. But the worst thing was Caleb was conscious, and knew he was dying. He kept saying, "Promise me, Ahote, promise me you'll look after them." Ahote began to see even then it would be hard to keep that promise, that as long as he tried to live in the white man's world, there would never be an end to the blood and the tears.

Chapter 20

Ahote woke to find the rain had stopped falling. He was no longer huddled on the ground under the pinion trees, he was astride a horse. A blanket was draped over his shoulders, warming him, and a man held him from behind, keeping him steady as they rode toward the edge of the plateau. The man felt Ahote stirring and spoke to him. It wasn't a language he knew. The man spoke again, this time in the Hopi language.

"You are very weak," the man said. "I am going to help you, do you understand?"

Ahote nodded.

The man's face broadened into a wide smile. "You're Hopi! Welcome, brother, welcome!"

"Where are we going?" Ahote asked.

"You are safe now, the storm is past, and we are making our way to my village. We'll be there in just a few hours."

"I was trying to get to the Grand Canyon, am I far from there?"

The old man chuckled behind him. "I am Havasupai," he said. "The Grand Canyon is my home."

A memory stirred in Ahote's mind, of when he was still a child in Hoteville. He remembered some men coming to trade and attend the Hopi bean dances. His grandfather had bartered with them for their beautiful baskets and their red ochre paint, which Istaqa used in his sacred ceremonies. He had called them the people of the blue waters, the Havasupai.

The old man passed a water skin to Ahote, urging him to drink. It was hard to swallow at first, but the water loosened his throat, and he began to take big gulps.

"Go slow," the old man cautioned, and he took the water skin away. A moment later he handed forward a small piece of *pika* bread. Ahote was so hungry he nearly swallowed the piece whole. The old man kept alternating, giving him sips of water and bits of bread, as the horse made its way along a beaten path leading to the rim of the canyon. Ahote was filled with questions, but was too tired to talk. He chewed the bread more slowly now, savoring its taste and texture, allowing it to stir up memories of his childhood and of his mother.

111

At last they came to the rim of the plateau. A steep trail snaked down a wide gorge, and the horse began a precipitous decline into painted canyons that were beautiful and vast, as far as the eye could see. They reached the bottom of the gorge, and continued riding in terrain that reminded Ahote achingly of the winter ranch. After a while, the canyon walls began to close around them. By then the energizing effects of the pika bread had worn off, and it was all he could do to keep his eyes open.

Finally, something pierced through his fog of exhaustion; the spiced scent of desert willow. He sat up in the saddle and looked around. A single tree broke through the harsh, arid terrain, and then another. The landscape was changing, turning greener. Soon he saw a creek flowing alongside the path with water so blue it hardly seemed of this earth.

They began to pass irrigated fields where Ahote could see corn growing, along with melons, beans, and squash. At last the old man brought his horse into the center of a small settlement, nestled deep inside the canyon walls. Ahote looked around, amazed. He'd never seen anything quite so beautiful and untouched. The village rested between the majestic, tall cliffs of the canyon, separate from all the rest of the world.

The old man stopped his horse in front of an earth and timber dwelling. He climbed down and then helped Ahote dismount, ushering him into his small abode.

"I will start a fire," the man said. "Sit." He pointed Ahote toward a rabbit skin blanket. Ahote did as he was told, sitting quietly, studying the man who'd rescued him from the storm.

The man broke the silence first. "I am called Baa Naa Gj'alg," he said, as he coaxed some sparks into flames. "And you?"

"I'm Ahote, son of Kwahu, grandson of Istaqa."

The man looked up. "I knew your Grandfather," he said. "Your father too, before his untimely death." He paused. "I knew your mother too, the witch."

Ahote met the man's steady gaze. "She's not a witch, she's a medicine woman."

"She killed all those soldiers the day your father died."

Ahote nodded. "She did, the day they carried me away to the Indian School. She made a mistake in her anger and grief. She's never crossed that line since. She's devoted her life to helping others."

Baa Naa Gj'alg continued to observe him, and then nodded. "You speak true, I think. So tell me, Ahote, son of Kwahu, what brings you to us?"

Ahote looked at him a moment, then bowed his head. "I didn't know I was coming here. I was running away, running from something terrible that I am responsible for. I didn't know where I was running to, but as I ran, I heard my grandfather's voice always urging me in this direction."

"Ah." Baa Naa Gj'alg sat down beside Ahote and warmed his hands by the fire. He did not speak for a few moments, but he did continue to consider Ahote.

"You and your mother left the Hopi mesas long ago," he mused.

"Yes. I've been working on a ranch just south of Flagstaff. My mother married one of the owners of the ranch."

"Is this where Istaqa went as well? No one ever told us exactly what happened to him."

Ahote nodded. "My grandfather never meant to stay at the ranch. He was worried about my mother's decision to come with me. I think originally even she only came so someone would be there to guide me home if I grew tired of that life. But she hadn't counted on falling in love with Caleb."

"Caleb must be a brave man to court a woman like that."

Ahote smiled sadly. "From the moment Caleb saw my mother, he was drawn to her. It didn't take either of them long to fall in love. Anyhow, to answer your original question, when Istaqa learned my mother was with child, he decided not to go back to the mesas."

"I see," Baa Naa Gj'alg mused, and then his eyes locked with Ahote's. "Were you happy there?"

"Very happy for a long time, but then I messed everything up."

"How?

"I fell in love with Caleb's sister, and it cost Caleb his life."

The old man's brows creased in puzzlement. "I don't understand."

Ahote looked away, ashamed, but then the words started to flow out of him. He told the old man about his closeness to Caleb and Zach, and of his disastrous attraction to Branna. He went on to describe those final moments in the Burnetts' store. "I saw myself staring down the end of a gun barrel. I remember thinking what a crazy way to die, and then, in that next instant, Caleb was there, lunging between that bullet and me. It killed him, but really it was me that killed him, because I never figured out a way to be Branna's friend and nothing more."

Baa Naa Gj'alg did not look away. "Your stepfather must have loved you very much."

Ahote felt a lump form in his throat. "I loved him, too. He taught me so many things. Not just about horses and ranching. He taught me how to live a good life, how to be a good man."

Baa Naa Gj'alg took Ahote's hands in his own. Ahote could feel the way the older man measured the warmth of them, the pulse in them. Then Baa Naa Gj'alg looked into Ahote's eyes, searching deeply.

"You know," the old man said at last, "when I found you, I had been out singing the song to call the storm, but it wasn't only water I prayed for."

"What else did you want?" Ahote found he couldn't look away.

"I think what I prayed for was you."

"Me?" Ahote was shocked. "I'm of no use to anyone."

Baa Naa Gj'alg shook his head. "Istaqa sent you to me. And your stepfather thought you were worth dying for."

Ahote shook his head. "I really don't think I'm the answer to your prayers. What you found up on the plateau was nothing more than a lost soul."

The old man would not look away. His eyes held Ahote's, willing him to see more. "My people are struggling," he said. "Every year the white man comes along with some new restriction, trying to hold us in this small canyon, to keep us from our winter lands up on the plateau. But the canyon cannot support the people in the cold months. There is not enough sun to grow crops, not enough wood for fires. To force us to stay here is the same as killing us."

"So what can you do?" Ahote asked.

"I was unsure. That is why I prayed, and I think that is why you came. You have lived the life of your ancestors, and the life of the white man. It might be good to have one among us who sees both sides."

Ahote looked at him, and then said, "You do realize, I made a mess of living among the white man. I wasn't such a good Hopi either."

Baa Naa Gj'alg put a pot of water on the fire, setting aside a bundle of tea. As he waited for the water to boil he spoke again. "This past winter, when my people tried to go to the winter lands, ranchers chased us away from our traditional springs and wells. They said the water was theirs now, and that we had to leave. When we hunted on our lands, we had to keep a constant eye out for government officials. They said the land was theirs now, and that they needed to protect the wildlife on it. It made for a hard winter. My people were very hungry, and the children and the old folk were falling ill. One day some of my people were gathering up pine nuts when they ran into people from the Forest Service. The rangers yelled at them. They said the squirrels needed those pine nuts to survive, and we could not have them."

Baa Naa Gj'alg paused a moment, his eyes still locked on Ahote's. "They want us to die, Ahote, so they can have this land for their park. To them a squirrel is more important than we are."

Ahote grew quiet and thoughtful. He'd walked away from his own people, trying to embrace the white man's way of life. He'd run away from that world as well, but not before hurting the people he loved the most. Baa Naa Gj'alg thought Ahote could be the answer to his prayer, but what if he was wrong? What if Ahote ended up hurting these people like he'd hurt everyone else? As he tried to consider the right thing to do, he remembered a long-ago conversation with his grandfather, as they'd sat on the shore of the Colorado River cleaning fish. He recalled now Istaqa saying Ahote's path would be different, but that he would find his way. And it had been his grandfather's voice he'd heard whispering to him all along this journey. Now the message was quite clear. His grandfather wanted him to finish what had been interrupted so many years ago. He wanted him to find the salt caves, and Sipapu, the Hopi place of emergence.

Ahote turned to Baa Naa Gj'alg. "Is it far from here to the Hopi sacred sites?"

"It's not hard to get to."

"Could you show me the way there?"

Baa Naa Gj'alg nodded. "I can when you are stronger."

Ahote returned the old man's steady gaze. "I'll think about what you have said, and when I go to those sites I will pray. I'll ask for guidance."

Baa Naa Gj'alg smiled. "Good. We will go together, and we'll both pray."

Chapter 21

Cha'risa stood by Sam's bedside. He was crying out again in his sleep. She sat down on the edge of his bed and smoothed the hair back from his sweaty brow. He woke and looked up at her. "You were dreaming again," she said.

Sam sat up. "It was the dream about Ahote," he said.

Cha'risa fought back tears. These days they were never far from the surface. "Was it the same as before?" she asked.

"It started like the others," Sam said. "He was all alone and running, still sick and bleeding, sometimes stopping to cry at the moon. But then it changed. Something different happened."

Cha'risa was afraid to ask, but she also had to know. "How did it change?"

"Someone came to him. It was a man, but somehow more than a man."

"More than a man?"

"There was wind swirling all around him, and bolts of lightning too."

Cha'risa tensed. She'd been having dreams too; dreams where her father spoke to her and told her Ahote would at last find peace. Being at peace did not necessarily mean being alive, and she very much needed for Ahote to be alive.

She gathered up her courage. "So what happened when this man found Ahote?"

"He fed him, and brought him to his home." Sam's eyes grew wide with wonder as he continued to talk. "Mom, I've never seen a place like this. There was this waterfall with water so blue it didn't look real. And Ahote walked up to a pool at the base of the falls, watching all these people who were swimming there. And then, he just walked into the water and joined them."

A tear escaped Cha'risa, the first in a month that wasn't one of sadness but of joy. "I think I know what your dream means, Sam. I think I know where Ahote is."

"You do?"

"Yes."

"Is he alive?"

"Yes, I think he is."

Sam stared at her with wide eyes "Are you sure?"

"I know this place you just described."

"It's real?" he asked, still not taking his eyes off her.

"It's very real" she assured him. "It's in the Grand Canyon, in a place that is home to a people who have always been good friends to the Hopi."

He sat up. "Well, then let's go get him and bring him home!"

Cha'risa placed a hand on his shoulder, stopping him. She wanted Ahote back too, but there was more to consider. "Sam, your dream has shown us Ahote has at last found a place where he is accepted. What if this is a place where he could be happy?"

The child in Sam didn't want to believe Ahote could be happy elsewhere, but he was more than a child now, on the cusp of manhood, and he had to acknowledge the possibility. Sam's eyes welled up. "He belongs here with us, doesn't he?"

Cha'risa sighed deeply. "I don't know, son. I just don't know."

"So I won't ever see him again?" His tears began to flow.

"Oh, we will see him again," she promised, pulling Sam close. "He's alive and I know how to find him now, thanks to you." She smiled down at him, "But we need to wait before we go, and give him some time to figure things out."

"Mom?" Sam asked. "Why didn't I see all of this coming? Why didn't grandfather warn me?"

"I wish I could say, Sam, really I do." But, some things are just not knowable."

Sam got angry. "What good is this gift then?" he cried. "It can't even help me save my father and brother!"

Cha'risa felt her own tears start to threaten, but she forced them back. "I don't know why there was no warning of your father's death. Maybe some events are just so random; they even take our ancestors by surprise. But Istaqa is speaking now; and what he's showing us is good news. The first good news we've had in several weeks. We should be grateful for it."

Sam crumpled back on the bed. "I'm not grateful!" he sobbed. "I just want my dad back!"

Cha'risa's couldn't hold back her tears any longer. She gathered her boy in close again, and together they shared their grief and tears. After a while, Sam quieted, and then he turned to her and asked, "How do

117

you know my dream about Ahote wasn't telling us he fell in with strangers? How can you be sure he doesn't need us as much as we need him?"

She met his worried gaze. "That's a fair question," she said. "But here is what I do know. You have seen him get into the pool with the People of the Blue Waters. They are good people, Sam."

"But they're still strangers," he persisted.

Cha'risa sighed deeply. "Sam, you need to understand that Ahote's life here was incomplete. It was hard for him to find love and make a family of his own among the white man."

"Because he's Hopi?" Sam asked.

Cha'risa nodded. "Yes, because he's Hopi."

Will it be hard for me too?"

Cha'risa continued to look him straight in the eye. "I don't know."

"It wasn't hard for you, though." Sam observed.

Cha'risa felt the tears threaten again. "There aren't many men in the world like your father, Sam. I was lucky to find him, lucky he loved me, lucky to have you. I wish it could have been for more years, but even short as it was, it was a wonderful gift."

Sam grew quiet, considering, and then asked, "So, it really was a good dream?"

Cha'risa smiled. "Yes, I feel very certain it was a good dream."

1921

Peach Cobbler

Ingredients
Filling
6-7 ripe but firm peaches (about 2 1/2 pounds)
1/4 cup granulated sugar
1 teaspoon cornstarch
1 tablespoon lemon juice
Pinch kosher salt

Biscuit Topping
1 cup unbleached all-purpose flour
3 tablespoons granulated sugar
3/4 teaspoon baking powder
1/4 teaspoon baking soda
1/4 teaspoon kosher salt
5 tablespoons cold unsalted butter, cut into small cubes
1/3 cup plain whole-milk yogurt
1 teaspoon granulated sugar

Directions
Preheat oven to 425º.

For the filling: Peel the peaches, then halve and pit each. Cut each half into 4 wedges. Gently toss the peaches and sugar together in large bowl; let stand for 30 minutes, tossing occasionally. Drain the peaches in a colander set over large bowl. Whisk 1/4 cup of the drained juice (discard extra), cornstarch, lemon juice, and salt together in a small bowl. Toss this mixture with peach slices and transfer to an 8-inch-square glass baking dish. Bake until the peaches begin to bubble around edges, about 10 minutes.

For the topping: While the peaches are baking, in a medium bowl, whisk flour, 3 tablespoons sugar, baking powder, baking soda, and salt to combine. Add the butter and mix in with your fingers until the mixture resembles coarse meal. Add the yogurt and stir with a spatula until a cohesive dough is formed. (Don't overmix dough or biscuits will be tough.) Break dough into 6 evenly sized but roughly shaped mounds and set aside.

To assemble and bake: After the peaches have baked 10 minutes, remove from the oven and place dough mounds on top, evenly spaced. Sprinkle each mound with a little sugar. Bake until the topping is golden brown and fruit is bubbling, 16 to 18 minutes. Cool on a wire rack and serve warm.

Serves 6

Chapter 22

Ellie looked out the open window at Lee Mountain, a vibrant slash of red against a gray, cloudy morning. It was so hushed out there. Not even the birds disturbed the stillness, and the air hung heavy with the sharp scent of threatening rain. Ellie didn't spend too much time studying the mercurial weather; what she needed to focus on was cleaning up breakfast. There was a lot of cooking ahead for her today; a group of fifteen tourists were due to arrive at the winter ranch tomorrow. Her dad had booked yet another tour to witness the miracle of Istaqa's tree.

Ellie turned and studied her father, still sitting at the breakfast table picking at his eggs. He didn't look like a consummate storyteller at the moment; he looked troubled and uncertain. That was unusual for him. He was generally good-natured, always a song on his lips or a story to tell, and certainly no one else could tell the story of Istaqa's tree the way he could. He would begin by describing a tree that grew in a place no other fruit tree could survive, and how a long dead Hopi shaman named Istaqa had planted it there. With his eyes wide, he'd tell about all the sightings of Istaqa's ghost, and how that old Hopi's spirit dwelled in the wash and guarded the tree. He'd explain how the tree had grown tall, and every year its branches hung heavy with fruit. Then he'd lean in close and mention the two hawks always present at harvest time, and ask if it wasn't just a wee bit uncanny, those birds always circling round, preventing all the smaller birds from ruining the peaches? The tale grew more elaborate with each telling, and the result was that C & M Lodge ran a lot of tours to see that tree, especially when the peaches were ripe and ready for picking.

Ellie loved the way her father could excite people simply by telling a tall tale about a tree and its crop of peaches. She also loved that every tour her father booked was another opportunity for her to come down to the winter ranch and be with Sam.

Sam had moved out of the lodge over a year ago. He'd only been home from the war a short while when he announced his intention to take over running the winter ranch. He'd made it sound like a logical choice, but Ellie knew there was more to it. The war had changed Sam.

He'd returned to them physically whole, but even now, two years later, he had nightmares that left him pale and shaking.

Aunt Chari had told her Sam needed time to heal, and Ellie had tried to be patient, but she missed what the two of them had once meant to each other. She wanted that closeness again. She wondered if she'd have a chance to be alone with him during this trip, and if so, if she would be brave enough to broach what had become such a sensitive topic between them. There hadn't been an opportunity to see him this morning. Sam had left early to fill the buckboard with barrels of water from Oak Creek, and he still wasn't back.

Ellie scanned the long dirt road one last time, and sighed. It was no use waiting any longer for Sam's return. She had her own work to attend to. The capstone of the whole peach adventure was eating the pies and cobblers made from Istaqa's peaches. Usually, Auntie Branna was in charge of this task, and Ellie was her helper, but this trip Ellie was doing it all on her own. Her aunt wasn't feeling well, and she was trusting Ellie to see it done right.

Ellie would do just about anything for Auntie Branna. Both Auntie Branna and Aunt Chari had tried in their own ways to fill the gaping hole left by her mother's death. Of course, nothing truly could, but they never stopped trying and their love had saved her, had helped her find her way through the loss and the grief. Aunt Chari was always there for Ellie when she wasn't well, or was sorely troubled, but Auntie Branna had a very different way of caring. She was the one who'd first brought Ellie into the kitchen.

It had been a very specific project her auntie had in mind. Katherine's cookbook had gone missing right around the time of her death. When Auntie Branna realized it was gone, she'd torn up the lodge from one end to the other searching for it, but it just couldn't be found. At last Branna had said there was nothing else to do but start all over again. She'd sat Ellie down at the kitchen table, and declared that Ellie must help her. Together they would reconstruct the precious recipes Katherine had preserved over the years, especially the ones she'd learned from Esme.

Esme had died the day Ellie was born, so Ellie had never known her, but she knew that recipe book. It had grown thick over the years with recipes that came straight from her mother's memories as well as her heart. The book was as much about love as it was about food, and it became Katherine's way of making certain Esme's legacy lived on.

Auntie Branna had learned all the lodge recipes from its pages, as had Aunt Chari. But it was Auntie Branna who intuitively understood the recipes were much more than just instructions on a page. She not only mastered Esme's southern cooking, she also expressed her own way of loving and nurturing the family through food.

Auntie Branna had grown up on a dairy farm, so the first tastes of Ireland she'd shared with the family had been tangy cheeses and clotted creams. But soon the family was eating barmbrack, and boxty, coddle and corned beef, and the book continued to grow as Katherine added her sister-in-law's recipes to its pages.

At ten years old, Ellie had found herself tasked with writing down each ingredient and measurement, as Auntie Branna set about trying to reconstruct the book from memory. She made Ellie taste everything, and confirm it was exactly right, before Ellie could put the final version of the recipe into the new family cookbook.

All that time working with her aunt was healing for Ellie. She began to see that this was about much more than just recipes; it was an inheritance passed from Esme to her mother and from her mother to Auntie Branna. In time Ellie realized these recipes were being passed down to her too; she was part of this legacy. Soon it wasn't enough to just copy the recipes, she wanted to follow the instructions and actually cook something.

She started out cautiously, trying out a favorite recipe for molasses cookies. Sam and Michael had shown up when the smells of baking began wafting through the lodge. But it wasn't long before there was a much bigger crowd lingering around, waiting for her trays of cookies to come out of the oven. Her cookies had been a success, and Ellie had loved that feeling. It emboldened her to try other recipes. When Ellie turned eleven, Auntie Branna told her she had a real talent for cooking, and began Ellie's culinary education in earnest. She'd given Ellie increasing responsibilities over the years, and Ellie had never once given her a reason to be disappointed.

Ellie turned to finish clearing the table and found her father still sitting quietly with his breakfast mostly untouched. Something was definitely eating at him this morning.

"Are you feeling all right, Dad?"

"I'm fine," he assured her, but he seemed anxious and kept looking toward the door.

When Aunt Chari walked back into the kitchen carrying a pail of sudsy water, a look of relief flooded his face. Aunt Chari was always the one he turned to when he was worried.

"Are you going to eat your breakfast?" Ellie asked him.

He looked at her as if he was only now remembering she was still in the room.

"Ellie, I need a word with your Aunt Chari. Could you be finding some other chores to tend to?"

Ellie tried not to bristle at being sent away like a small child, but the very fact he wouldn't talk about it in front of her told Ellie exactly what it was he'd been stewing over. She'd been worried as well, and was anxious to hear what he had to say, but nobody would consider she was old enough to be part of that conversation. What nobody realized was that Ellie already knew Auntie Branna's secret.

A few weeks ago Ellie had been in the pantry when both her aunts had come into the kitchen. Neither of them was aware she was tucked back among the food stores, and so Ellie had inadvertently overheard Aunt Branna's desperate confession to Aunt Chari. She was going to have Doc Ferguson's baby.

Ellie hadn't been certain if she should make her presence known at that point. In the end, she stayed silent, figuring it would only embarrass everyone to reveal herself. That's how she learned Doc Ferguson was willing to do the right thing and marry Auntie Branna. It should have been enough to make the problem go away, but Auntie Branna was already married to that horrible man in Ireland. Aunt Chari had advised her to set the Irish man aside. In the Hopi culture a woman could do that, but Auntie Branna reminded her it was different for Catholics. She was married for life to Aengus, and therefore her child with Eli Ferguson was doomed to be a bastard.

Ellie hadn't heard any more about the baby in the weeks since, but something new must have happened. If only her father would confide in her. Why did he have to send her off like a child? Auntie Branna was important to Ellie, too. If there was more to worry about, they shouldn't keep it from her.

She looked out the window. It was still early, and the clouds were hanging around, keeping the desert heat from mounting. There was a little time to spare before she had to get to work in earnest, so Ellie made a decision. This time the eavesdropping would be deliberate.

"Well, I guess I can go pick some peaches." She could hardly believe how easily the lie fell off her lips. "I'll clean up breakfast when I get back," she offered.

"I'll take care of it." Aunt Chari said.

"Thanks," Ellie said with a smile, but since Aunt Chari seemed also to be conspiring to keep her in the dark, it only served to strengthen her resolve. She grabbed her straw hat, and a couple of big baskets. As she made ready to go her father said, "Just a minute. Where's my kiss?"

Ellie dutifully kissed her father and Aunt Chari goodbye, and shut the kitchen door behind her with a deliberate click. She made her way quietly alongside the house, into a copse of scrub pine just under the corner window. From here it would be easy to hear their voices, with the windows open to capture the cool of early morning.

Ellie settled into the thicket just as her father started to speak. "I've had a letter from Mary Clare." Usually Ellie's father looked forward to letters from his foster mother in Ireland, but his Irish brogue had thickened, a sure sign he was upset.

"Is that what's been bothering you?" Cha'risa asked.

Her father's chair pushed out from the table, and his footsteps clumped as he walked to the sink, setting his plate down with a clatter. Then Ellie heard him say, "She's afraid I've damned my soul to hell."

"That doesn't sound like Mary Clare," Cha'risa observed.

"Well, it's more like she's asking me if I've committed a mortal sin, and if I have, she's begging me to seek absolution with the church."

"Have you done something I'm unaware of?" There was a growing uneasiness in Cha'risa's voice now.

"I have," he admitted, "and you're the only one I'll confess it to. I'll not do penance for something I'm not sorry for."

Ellie risked peeking inside. This she needed to see as well as hear. She saw her father still by the sink, his dark blue eyes locked on Aunt Chari's. Cha'risa met his gaze unwaveringly as she waited for Zach to explain. After a moment he sighed, then returned to the table. As he sat, he reached out his hand to her, and she took it.

"When you told me about Branna being with child, I wrote to Niall." He paused, weighing his next words, then continued. "I picked him deliberately because I knew of all my brothers he was by far the most hot headed. I told him about the babe, and about how hard it's been for Branna all these years to be denied love and a family. I told him how Eli Ferguson was a good man who wanted to marry her, and give the child his name. In short, I said everything I could think of to manipulate my brother into taking action, and now in this letter, it's clear I achieved what I set in motion."

Cha'risa's eyes widened. "What's happened?"

"Aengus has drowned. They're calling it an accident, but Mary Clare suspects her boys had something to do with it. David and Eamon were seen buying him several rounds of drinks the night he died, and Niall came home late wearing very muddy boots."

"Does anyone else suspect Aengus was murdered?" Cha'risa asked.

Zach shook his head. "I don't think so. She says most people are saying good riddance. He never was anything but a drunk and a bully." Zach continued to hold Cha'risa's hand, as if it were some kind of lifeline. He seemed desperate for her understanding. "Branna's lived with an impossible situation for so long, and how can it be right for that little baby to be born in sin? It's my job to protect my family, but did I have the right to suggest a man should die?"

Cha'risa said quietly, "I've done worse then you, Zach: remember?"

"I do. That's part of why I'm asking you. You understand better than anyone exactly what I've done."

She closed her eyes briefly, searching for the right words to say. Then she looked at him again, her eyes filled with compassion. "When I killed those soldiers, my people turned from me, believing I'd turned evil. I accepted their censure, because I also thought that one act had changed me irretrievably. It took me a long time to accept that sometimes love drives us to extremes."

Zach dropped his head. "But still, it changes me, doesn't it, no matter what drove me to it?"

Cha'risa lifted his chin, making him once again look her in the eye. "It's not easy to learn how to forgive our darker impulses, Zach, but it's important to remember those urges don't have to define us, or who we choose to become. You made a difficult choice to protect Branna, and her life will be better for it. Now you need to find a way to make sure it doesn't ruin yours." A tear fell down his cheek, and Cha'risa wiped it away with her thumb.

He shut his eyes, clasping her hand against his cheek, as he silently struggled with his emotions. At last he sighed deeply, looking once again at her. "How is it you always know what to say?"

Her smile was bittersweet. "We've known each other a very long time, Zach. We mourned Caleb together; we mourned Katherine.

You've been a father to Sam, and I've been a mother to Mike and Ellie. I know what to say because I've lived close to you for over two decades. I know exactly who you are."

Zach moved closer to her. "We've shared a life, haven't we?"

"We have."

He studied her for a long while, and his stare was uncomfortably deep and searching. Never once did she drop her gaze. At last he said, "I've another confession to make."

"Oh?"

He drew even closer, until their lips were barely an inch apart, and then whispered. "I don't want to be your brother anymore. I want to be your lover."

Their faces were so close that Ellie should have seen it coming, but still it was a shock when her aunt closed the gap, kissing him on the lips. Ellie stood in full view of the window gaping. But they never saw her, because the next thing that happened was that her father pulled Aunt Chari hard against him, deepening the kiss.

Ellie was on her feet and running. All she could think was "oh God, oh God, oh God!" It was a few moments before thoughts began to form. He'd kissed her! He'd kissed her after admitting he'd engineered a man's murder. How could he admit to a mortal sin one minute, and then express an unnatural lust for her aunt in the next? And how could Aunt Chari encourage him?

Ellie's knees buckled, and she slumped to the ground. She couldn't bear knowing two of the people she loved best in the world had just betrayed her mother. She knew she should get up and move out of plain sight, but instead she just sat there and cried.

She hadn't sat there long when she felt something warm and furry lay down against her. Ellie snuggled against the dog, and Rhiannon's tail started thumping on the ground. She pulled the retriever closer, and didn't object when her dog started licking her tears. It took a few minutes, but Rhiannon's presence calmed her.

Ellie wiped the tears and dog saliva from her cheeks, then brushed the dirt from her skirt, and went to pick up the baskets she'd dropped. Even if the world had just turned upside down, it hadn't stopped. She wasn't going to disappoint Auntie Branna. Pies and cobbler needed to go in the oven, and her family still needed to be fed at mid-day. With Rhiannon trotting along next to her, Ellie headed away from the ranch, and down into the wash.

The sun was still struggling with the clouds, but more and more, the odd ray fought its way through, sending its light out across the desert. Ellie decided that's what she had to do too, just find a way through. Rhiannon made it look easy; her dog was always happy and ready for adventure. Even on this short walk, she'd scared up a dozen or so quail and a jackrabbit nearly half her size. To be fair, the jackrabbit had taunted her. It had been looking for a chase, and Rhiannon gave it one.

The peach tree was just around the bend, when the dog became alert again. Ellie felt it too this time. Something was watching them, a much bigger presence than a gaggle of birds or a rabbit. She gave Rhiannon a hand signal to fall in behind her. Then, walking slowly, she approached the bend with caution. What she saw caused her to stop still in her tracks. A low growl came from Rhiannon, but Ellie signaled her to be quiet. She didn't want her to frighten away the elk that was now looking right at them. It was resting on the ground between her and the peach tree, not twenty feet away.

Ellie motioned to Rhiannon, and they both walked slowly the rest of the way around the bend to have a better view. The elk followed their progress, and then majestically stood up, wary of their next actions. Ellie's heart was pounding. He was both beautiful and powerful. A beast like this had the advantage of weight and speed, and his massive antlers could be lethal, but he wasn't a predator. He never made a move toward them; he just watched.

Ellie sat down on a log nearby, making Rhiannon sit close beside her. When the elk's eyes locked with hers, she felt her whole sense of the world shift. This animal didn't know her father had encouraged his brothers to kill Aengus, or that he'd kissed Aunt Chari. He didn't know Sam screamed in his sleep, or that Auntie Branna conceived a child out of wedlock. For him none of that mattered, and soon Ellie began to feel that way too. What mattered was just this moment, just this connection with this wild creature. For a moment she felt totally free.

Chapter 23

Sam rolled into the yard with a wagon full of water and a team of hot, tired horses. He was surprised to find his mother just standing there, staring off into the wash. She looked uncertain, which was unusual for her. His mother always seemed to know what to do.

He jumped down from the wagon, and headed over to her. "Mom?"

He surprised her and color rushed to her cheeks. "Sam! You're back."

His mother blushing was also not an everyday sight. "Is something wrong?"

"I've upset Ellie. I'm not sure whether I should go after her or give her a little time."

"Ah." Upsetting Ellie was something Sam was uncomfortably familiar with. He was glad this time it wasn't his fault. "Can I help?" he offered.

His mother studied him for a moment, and then nodded. "She went to pick peaches."

Sam waited a moment for his mother to confide in him. "Mom," he ventured at last. "Are you going to tell me what happened?"

His mother shook her head. "I need some time to think about what to do. Can you just make sure she's okay?"

Again, he wondered what happened that had his mother so rattled, but he could see she wasn't going to say more, at least not now, and clearly she was worried about Ellie. He could take care of that much at least. "Sure," he said. "I'll see to the horses, and then head out."

"I'll take care of the horses. You go find Ellie." Cha'risa held out her hand for the reins.

Sam looked at her, beginning to sense her urgency, then gave her the reins and started off toward the wash. He moved quickly and silently through the desert, along the well-worn path to Istaqa's tree. He'd just rounded the corner when he saw them, the pup, Ellie, and the elk. He stopped in his tracks, not wanting to startle the beast with Ellie sitting so close by. Neither Ellie nor the elk seemed aware of his presence, but Rhiannon turned her head toward him. He signaled her to keep quiet.

It was rare these days that Sam had a moment to just look at Ellie without her being aware. It seemed to him that as she'd grown she'd become more than beautiful; she was like something woven from the earth itself. He wished for both their sakes he could be like other men, that he could ignore his dark dreams, and just love her.

He didn't usually allow himself to dwell on what might have been, but there was something in the way she looked at that elk that reminded him of the first moment he'd ever held her in his arms. She'd only been minutes old, but she'd locked onto him with all of her being. After all these years, he still remembered how that felt. From that moment on he was always aware of her.

As Ellie grew, it was clear she also had a sense they belonged together. It had never occurred to Sam something could change that sense of rightness between them. The first chink had come when his father had died, and filled with remorse, Ahote had fled from home. That was the first time Sam had realized just how much his Hopi blood set him apart from others. Still, it hadn't stopped his fantasies of marrying Ellie one day. Those ended when the war came. The war and his subsequent nightmares had changed everything.

The spell broke, the regal creature turned abruptly from Ellie, and in a few quick leaps he disappeared into the desert landscape. It wasn't until he was gone that she turned and saw Sam standing there.

She gasped. "Good Lord! I didn't hear you come up!"

Sam sat down beside her, stretched out his long legs, and started scratching Rhiannon behind the ears. "Your pup saw me, didn't you, girl?"

"Did you see the elk?"

"I saw him."

"Wasn't he magnificent?" Her eyes glittered with excitement.

"He's a special one," Sam agreed. The memories must have softened his resolve, because he then added, "just like you." Ellie's face lit up with happiness. It was dangerous ground, opening that door even a crack, so he looked back in the direction the elk had run, changing the subject. "I named him Sentinel."

Ellie scooted closer to him. "You've seen him before?"

Sam nodded. "Sometimes I come out here before sunrise, and I see him bedded down under the tree."

"Why Sentinel?"

"Because he protects the tree. While he's here, the other elk and deer won't get close enough to eat the peaches, or destroy the branches."

"So he's a loner?"

Sam nodded. "I think he likes being on his own."

"Kind of like you," Ellie said.

Sam looked at her, and again felt the need to change the subject. "Mom said I should come find you, that you were upset."

Ellie tensed beside him. "Did she bother to tell you why?"

He shook his head. "She wouldn't say."

Ellie sighed dramatically, but stayed silent.

"So what happened?" he prompted.

She threw up her hands, exasperated. "Jesus, Mary and Joseph! I finally get you alone, and she leaves it to me to tell the sordid tale! How in the world is that fair?"

"Who ever said the world was fair?" Even he could hear the prickliness in his voice, and he was immediately sorry.

She looked at him, surprised by his hurtful tone, and then turned away. "I don't think I can talk about it."

"Ellie, just spit it out." This also came out rougher than he'd intended, and he saw her spine stiffen.

"Fine, then," she said angrily. "My dad conspired to have Aengus killed so Auntie Branna could marry Doc Ferguson and their baby wouldn't be born a bastard, and then your mom kissed my dad."

"What?" He stared at her, and then said sternly, "That's not funny, Ellie."

She crossed her arms. "I'm not joking."

It was a shock when he realized Ellie meant every word. "Bloody hell," he swore, then remembered who he was talking to. "Sorry," he said, adding, "It's just a lot to take in. Do you think you could break that up into smaller bits for me?"

"Well, the kiss upset me the most," she offered as a starting point.

"Really? A kiss trumps murder?"

Ellie shrugged.

He studied her more closely. "What kind of kiss was it?"

She looked pained, "They were completely consumed with desire."

"Good Lord." Sam could hardly believe it. "Was there at least a declaration of love?"

Ellie shuddered with the memory, "They were too busy kissing for anything like that."

"Didn't your dad say anything to my mom?"

"Oh, he said something, alright," Ellie informed him. "He said, and I quote, 'I don't want to be your brother any more, I want to be your lover.'"

"What?" Sam leaned closer to her. "Are you sure those are the words he used? Maybe what he said was he wanted to be her husband?"

"There was no mention of love or marriage," she assured him.

Sam got up from the log and started pacing. Rhiannon looked up from where she'd been sitting and followed him expectantly with her eyes.

"Okay," he said at last, "I don't know what to think of that just yet, so let's move on. Auntie Branna is pregnant?"

"She is, with Doc Ferguson's baby."

"How come this is the first I'm hearing about it?"

There was an accusing edge in Ellie's voice. "How do expect to keep apprised of all the family news when you live down here like a hermit?"

He stopped pacing and frowned at her. "Ellie, don't start that again. I'm helping the family by running the winter ranch. Why does it have to be such a problem for you?"

Her face flushed. "You can't figure out why? Ahote and his family have been back for months; and since he's building a house on his inheritance, I think it's pretty clear he plans to stay. We have someone reliable now to look after the winter ranch. You could choose to come home!"

He saw the tears gathering in her eyes, and he sighed, sitting down beside her again. "A lot happened this morning, and we're both a little rattled, but don't be angry with me, okay?"

Ellie leaned against him. "I'm not angry, I just don't understand."

"Well, let's focus on today's events, and get through one crisis before we go borrowing another. Agreed?"

She nodded, and relaxed slightly.

"So," he said, "Your dad and my mom?"

"Yep," she affirmed.

They sat together quietly, each trying to imagine it. Then he recalled the other things she'd overheard. "Is Aengus really dead?"

She nodded.

"Does Branna know?"

"I don't know."

"And how exactly is your dad responsible?"

She told him then about the letter to Niall, and the circumstances around the subsequent drowning.

Sam got up again, extending his hand, and pulled her to her feet. "I do my best thinking when I'm moving," he said. "Let's pick peaches while we talk."

They picked up the baskets and went to the tree. Without even asking, he lifted her up onto one of the higher branches. He'd been doing that since she was about five years old, and he hadn't even stopped to consider she might be getting too big to be that far up in a tree. She didn't object. She just made sure the branch was strong enough to hold her weight, and then started filling her basket. Sam started picking as well.

They worked in silence, lost in their own thoughts, until Sam asked, "Are you upset about what your Dad did to Aengus?"

She picked a beautiful rose gold peach, sniffed it as she considered, and then looked down at him through the leaves. "I can forgive my Dad for riling up his brothers. He was just trying to protect Auntie Branna." She picked a few more peaches then added, "I'm more upset with the church then I am with him. A person should be able to set aside someone who hurts them. No religion should force anyone to live like that, or prevent them from having a life with someone they truly love."

Sam stopped picking. "Religion shouldn't prevent us from having a life with someone we love," he mused, and then he stared up at her. "What about us? Is it wrong if we stand in their way?"

She looked down at him again. "Are you saying our parents should be together?"

Putting a peach in his basket, he said. "Well, think about it. They've been through a lot, and got all of us through some very difficult times. And it never ends, does it? Branna is just the latest in a long line of challenges they've had to confront together. I guess what I'm saying is, I can see how it happened, and if what they're feeling is really love, and not just desire, than I'm okay with it."

She stopped picking. "Really?"

"Yeah," he said, "Although I'm still having a hard time believing your dad asked to be my mom's lover. He should have followed that up with a proposal of marriage."

Ellie shook her head. "I already told you, he didn't ask to marry her."

Sam frowned as he laid his full basket on the ground. He wiped dirt and peach juice from his hands, and then lifted Ellie out of the tree muttering, "He will once I've finished talking to him."

Chapter 24

Standing in the outdoor kitchen beside a growing mound of peach peels and pits, Ellie wiped at the perspiration on her face with a sticky hand. In the sweltering summer months she preferred this outdoor work space, because when the wood stove was lit, the inside of the house became unbearable. She arched her back and stretched, looking up at a sky, which was now mostly blue, except for a few huge cumulous clouds that were adding their humidity to the growing heat of the day. Feeling hot and grimy, she went over to where a couple of tall barrels of water stood. She ladled out some water, and dipping a rag in it, she sponged the sweat off her face. It felt wonderful, and she promised herself, at the end of the day, she would find time to do a more thorough washing.

She stopped by the fire pit before returning to her pile of peaches. Her father and Michael had built an uncommonly beautiful cook space out here. It was made of adobe and tumbled stones from the wash. They'd made it as tall as the indoor wood stove, and equally as wide. Ellie checked the coals, and then stirred the stockpot full of simmering black beans. Dinner was progressing nicely.

Ellie returned to her large pile of peaches, picked up her paring knife, and soon was back in the rhythm of peeling and pitting. She barely noticed as her baskets emptied, because she kept thinking of the conversation with Sam. Their parents' kiss had sent her running and crying like a child, but he'd been willing to see their perspective. She could see now how they could have come to care for one another romantically, and even how it wasn't wrong that they had. She smiled as she recalled Sam's final words, though. While he could understand their wanting to be together, he expected a ring on his mother's finger. Ellie was pretty sure her dad wouldn't argue the point.

It struck her that Sam had a very clear sense of right and wrong. At least, he did when it came to others. Ellie still couldn't understand why he wouldn't let the family help him. Why did he have to suffer those nightmares alone? That didn't seem right to her at all.

Even Michael couldn't get him to talk about it, and Sam and Michael had always talked about everything. But the war had changed even that. Michael had come home, and found a way to get on with his life, and Sam had not. Ellie wondered what had made the difference. They'd both been on the front lines, both in the trenches, but Michael had been in the infantry, and Sam had been a stretcher bearer.

Michael had once told her he wasn't sure how Sam had done it. He couldn't imagine running out on the battlefield with nothing but a stretcher in his hands. Ellie knew from Sam's letters that it had indeed been very frightening, but he'd also mentioned how glad he was that he was saving lives, instead of being part of the killing and destruction. Michael had not struggled with that aspect of war. There was an enemy to be driven back and he was a good with a rifle. His skill and his bravery had been rewarded with a silver citation star.

The other big difference between Michael and Sam's war experience was that Michael had a loving wife to come home to, and Sam didn't. That's the part that really stumped Ellie, because Sam could so easily have had that too. She thought back to that letter he'd sent her, the one where he told her he was afraid he wouldn't make it home. He'd also told her that he loved her and that if he died, his biggest regret would be never having asked her to marry him. He'd wanted to build a life with her, and that was what she'd wanted too. But now he wouldn't talk about it. Instead of growing closer, they were slowly drifting apart. She didn't know what to do. All she knew for certain was that she had to try something. He'd always been there for her, now she had to figure out a way to be there for him.

A light breeze started to blow, and though it was a warm wind, still it cooled her. Ellie closed her eyes, letting the wind dry her skin. She heard a rustling, and looked over to see Aunt Chari approaching. Her aunt didn't say anything; she just picked up a peach and a paring knife and started peeling.

Ellie knew she should say something. She was embarrassed to have been caught spying, and after her conversation with Sam she was no longer so certain she was the injured party. She was still searching for what to say when her aunt broke the silence.

"You watched us this morning."

Ellie blushed and then nodded.

Her aunt turned to face her. "I saw you as you turned and ran to the yard."

Ellie looked away. She couldn't defend her actions. It was a juvenile thing to have done. "I'm sorry," she said.

Her aunt put down the knife. "Ellie, look at me." Ellie turned back and their eyes met. "I am the one who's sorry," Aunt Chari said. "Your father and I have been too slow to acknowledge you're no longer a child. It's time we stop trying to shield you from unpleasant things. "

Ellie was surprised. "Aren't you mad at me?"

Cha'risa smoothed some errant tendrils of hair off of Ellie's brow. "I think you understand well enough what you did wrong. I see no use in getting mad. From this point on you will be part of all important family conversations."

"You mean it?"

"I do. In return I hope you'll do your best to respect others' needs for privacy.

Ellie felt her cheeks turn red. "I can do that."

Cha'risa smiled, picked up her paring knife again, and started working. "If there's anything you want to ask me about this morning, I'll tell you."

"Anything? Are you certain?"

Cha'risa's cheeks reddened. "This morning was a private moment between your father and me, but it also affects you. If you have questions, I'll answer them."

Ellie could tell this was awkward for her aunt, but she admired her candor. It was certainly a lot more honest than hiding in bushes. "I'm not upset anymore," Ellie admitted. "Sam helped me to see how it might have happened."

"So you have no questions?"

"I don't know, maybe one."

Cha'risa waited for her to continue.

Ellie took in a deep breath. "Do you love my dad?"

Cha'risa sought Ellie's eyes. "The truth is I've loved your father for a long time now. The first time I realized it, the boys had just gone off to war, and what I thought I wanted was for your father to comfort me, and he did. But then I found myself thinking about that moment often, and I realized the feeling must run deeper. I never said anything to him because I was afraid of ruining the close relationship we already had. I convinced myself it was simply a natural consequence of working so intimately with him, and it didn't need to be acted on."

"What made you take a risk today?" Ellie asked.

Aunt Chari allowed a modest smile. "It wasn't such a big risk once I knew he felt that way, too." She paused, and then added, "I really do love your father, Ellie. It's different from the way I loved your Uncle Caleb, or even my first husband. It is a quieter kind of love, and it kind of snuck up on your dad and me, but that doesn't make it any less real."

"Are you going to marry him?" Ellie asked.

Cha'risa looked surprised. "I hadn't thought about it," she admitted. After a moment she added, "If we marry, it will make it everybody's business. People are no more tolerant now than they were when Caleb was murdered."

"Sam won't be happy unless you make it official."

"He said that?"

Ellie nodded.

"Hmmm. My boy knows what's right for everyone but himself."

Her aunt sighed. Ellie did too, wishing Sam would stop standing in the way of feelings they both obviously shared. She understood then just how lucky her father and Aunt Chari were. It had been hard for them to admit their love, but it had been a risk worth taking. They were wise not to let it go. She leaned in then and hugged her aunt. When her tears began to fall she honestly couldn't say if they were tears of happiness for her aunt and father, or tears of regret for Sam and her.

Her aunt held her a few moments, then lifted Ellie's face to meet hers. "Thank you for understanding." A single tear fell down Aunt Chari's cheek and there was a catch in her voice when she spoke again. "Your mother was my closest friend, but you have become the daughter of my heart."

Chapter 25

Sam rode into Ahote's campsite, halting his horse near all the construction. His nephew, Moqui, dropped the wood he was carrying and ran to greet him. "Uncle Sam! Uncle Sam! Did you bring me anything?"

Ahote came up behind his son, giving him a whack on the head. "First work, then treats," he said, shooing Moqui back toward the discarded pile of lumber. "I could use another pair of hands," he told Sam, nodding towards the wagon bed, where a large pile of wood was waiting to be unloaded.

"Whatever happened to hello?" Sam asked, as he got off his horse and went to help.

Ahote smiled, handing his brother several planks of wood. "Stack them over there," he said, indicating the neat piles situated near the frame of the small house.

Sam wasn't at all unhappy about being put to work. He'd come to appreciate how nice it felt to just stop by his brother's and instantly get wrapped up in Ahote's life. When Sam had first moved to the winter ranch, all he'd wanted was quiet and solitude, believing that was what was needed for him to heal, and for a time it was. Alone day after day, he began to notice even the smallest changes in the desert, and that growing awareness helped him feel viscerally alive. Paradoxically, it was not so different from the way he'd felt in France during the war. Then it had been a mindfulness of breath and pulse, blood and bone, it was an awareness of life in the face of death. Now what he felt was the desert singing a song of life so potent, it rang in his ears and vibrated through his soul.

Ahote's arrival had brought an end to the solitude. He'd shown up at the lodge late one January night looking gaunt and bone tired. His wife Lena looked equally emaciated. They were carrying their two children, who were both very sick and running frighteningly high fevers. Cha'risa had sent for Sam immediately, and the entire McKenna-Connor clan had hunkered down, working tirelessly to save Ahote's children.

Sam had thought, after being so much on his own, it would be hard to be back in the nexus of family life, but the opposite had been true.

Instead of bristling at the crowd of bodies and the noise, he was comforted by the enfolding warmth of his family.

When Ahote began to talk of settling on the land Caleb had left him, the entire family had felt it was a good idea, especially Sam. It was something he'd been hoping to hear for years, and it was clear the situation on the Havasupai reservation was becoming untenable. Forest Service and National Park officials were getting more efficient at penning the Havasupai down in the canyon during the winter months, and with devastating results.

The previous summer the Bureau of Indian Affairs had tried to raise awareness in Washington of the life-threatening circumstances this policy was causing. The Bureau attempted to have 87,000 acres of the Tusayan National Forest granted back to the Havasupai, but the measure they put before Congress failed. The tribe now found themselves surrounded by officials even more hostile to the Havasupai's attempts to use their former plateau range and water sources.

After that defeat, Ahote began talking to his wife about leaving Cataract Canyon for good. It was more than just the trouble with the rangelands that had worn him down. Many Havasupai children had been lost in the flu epidemic in 1918, and Ahote's eldest daughter had been among them. The disease had decimated the tribe's entire population of school-aged girls.

Another tragedy struck just a year later when the community lost their most powerful shaman, Baa Naa Gj'alg; the man who had saved Ahote and had shown him a path of renewed purpose. Ahote had cared deeply for the rainmaker. He'd understood the shaman in ways others could not, and the old man's passing had been difficult for him.

Ahote hadn't been given much time to dwell on the shaman's death, when another worry manifested. Because the population of school children was now so severely reduced, the Bureau of Indian Affairs had decided they weren't going to add more grades to the local elementary school. Instead, they wanted to send children who were much too young to Indian boarding schools located off the reservation. Moqui was rapidly approaching the designated cutoff age.

It hadn't been easy for Ahote to say goodbye to the Havsupai and the wondrous beauty of the Grand Canyon, but he did leave. Reversing the path he'd taken eleven years ago, he led his wife and sick children back to the one place he could keep his family safe and together. He brought them home. All through January and February, Ahote and his family stayed at the lodge. Sam spent each day with his brother in the sickroom, singing songs of healing for Moqui and Tiva, and helping Cha'risa work her restorative magic. Ellie and Branna worked equally hard to return the children to health, providing never-ending pots of savory stews and soups. And they never stopped baking, tempting the children with a constant supply of cookies and fresh-baked bread.

In early May, when the weather grew warm again, Sam loaded his brother and family, along with their few belongings, into his pickup truck, and made his way down the rough roads to the winter ranch. For the first week, Ahote's family had stayed with Sam in the ranch house while Ahote built a wikiup over on his land.

While Sam couldn't offer them homemade cookies, it turned out everyone in Ahote's family loved his beef jerky. One day, after returning from the war, he'd found his father's recipe in Branna's cookbook. He'd remembered how much he'd loved it as a boy, and when he moved down to the winter ranch, he'd built a smoker, devoting a lot of energy to mastering his dad's technique. Ahote's family had eaten right through his modest supply the week they stayed with him. Once Ahote had moved his family into the wikiup, Sam had taken to visiting them frequently, always with an offering of jerky in his pockets.

As soon as the wood was stacked, Moqui accosted him, searching for the anticipated treat. Sam reached into his pocket, grinning as he pulled out a couple of sticks of the jerky. "I can't remember. Do you like beef jerky?"

"You know I do!" the boy exclaimed.

Sam laughed, handing them over. "There's some there for Tiva, too." he said.

"Can I give it to her now?" Moqui asked his dad.

Ahote nodded. "She's over by the seven pools, harvesting prickly pears with your mother."

Moqui turned back to Sam. "Can I have another piece for Mom?"

Sam gave him more, and then said, "Your cousin Ellie is here, cooking up a big dinner. She's expecting all of you around noon. Make sure you tell your mom that."

"What's she making?" Moqui asked.

"Can't say for sure, but I was out picking peaches with her this morning."

"Cobbler!" the boy cried, looking radiantly happy as he ran off.

As soon as Moqui disappeared into the scrub brush, Ahote turned to his brother and asked, "So is this purely a social visit?"

"Not that you aren't scintillating in your own right," Sam said, "but I came to ask if you'd help me get the tents set up."

Ahote looked up at the sky, and Sam followed his gaze. The sun had won out over the clouds at long last, though a few dark thunderheads could be seen gathering again to the north.

"It's going to rain," his brother said.

"Are you sure?"

Ahote gave him a look, and Sam sighed. There was no use arguing with a man whose mentor had been a rainmaker.

"We'll do it around dusk." Ahote said. "It should have rained itself out by then."

Sam nodded, and then sat down beside Ahote, handing his brother a piece of jerky. "It's been quite the morning at the ranch," he said, as Ahote bit into the treat. Then Sam proceeded to tell his brother all about Mary Clare's letter with its varied implications.

The first thing Ahote commented on was Aengus' death. "Branna is free to marry, then," he said.

Sam had never forgotten there'd been a time when Ahote and Branna had cared for each other. "Is it hard for you?" Sam asked. "Knowing Branna can move on now, and share a life with Doc Ferguson?"

Ahote shook his head. "I'm happy for her. She'll have a chance to know what I've known. I've lived a good life among the Havasupai, despite the hardships and the loss of my daughter."

"Will you ever go back to Cataract Canyon, do you think?"

"I'll visit in the summers, so that Lena won't feel too displaced, and the children won't forget their Havasupai family and heritage."

Sam nodded, then after a moment added, "Ellie heard more than just the contents of Mary Clare's letter."

Ahote raised an eyebrow, waiting for Sam to continue.

"Mom kissed Uncle Zach."

Ahote looked stunned for a moment, and then laughed. "Well, don't expect me to cry about that." He chuckled some more. "I would have loved to see Ellie's face. It serves her right for spying!"

"She was really distraught at first. I managed to calm her down, but not before upsetting her even more. I don't understand why I felt so short-tempered with her."

"Well, maybe it wouldn't hurt if you followed Mom's example. Why don't you just kiss Ellie and get it over with?"

Sam glared at his brother, and then sighed heavily. "What would you have me do, Ahote? You know why I can't marry her!"

"I know why you think you can't marry her. But I also believe your reasoning is flawed."

"How so?" Sam challenged.

"You're assuming these dreams are nightmares."

"Believe me, they're nightmares."

"I don't doubt they terrify you, but you're presuming this is happening because you aren't mentally stable. You've concluded that what happened to you in the war has broken you and overridden your ability to commune with our ancestors. But what if that isn't what's happening at all?" Sam looked at him, totally perplexed. Ahote sighed and then added. "Hasn't it ever occurred to you these dreams might actually be a message from our ancestors, a vision of the future?"

"Good God, Ahote!" Sam exclaimed, "How does that make things better? I see the world burning!"

"In this vision does everything burn? Is it clearly the end of the world?"

Sam cocked his head a little, trying to recall the dream. "Mostly I see burning cities, with the dead piled high." He was quiet a moment, and then added, "If it is a vision of the future, it would be bad, very bad."

Ahote pointed the remaining bit of jerky at Sam. "So here's a theory for you: what if the ancestors have been trying to show you the future. What if they keep trying to get the message through because it's dire, and because you have yet to recognize it as a foretelling? The warning could be drowning out all your other abilities."

Sam was thoughtful a moment. Losing his prescient dreams had been like losing a limb. It would be a relief to know he never really lost that capacity. But on the other hand, if these were visions, then nothing would change between him and Ellie. He hadn't proposed to her because he'd felt himself a broken man, but he equally wouldn't propose to her if there was to be no future.

"I see where your mind is going, little brother."

Sam didn't doubt it. Among the Havasupai, Ahote had grown into a man many sought out for his power of reason and his clarity of thought. "So tell me what to do," Sam said. "How can I know if this is a vision or a nightmare? And how, in either case, does that help me have a future with Ellie?"

Ahote's dark eyes were full of compassion. "You are asking the wrong question," he said. "What you should be asking is if that is indeed the future, what can you do between now and then to make certain each day counts?"

Sam didn't know what to say to that. That line of thinking hadn't occurred to him before.

"Wait here," his brother said, and Ahote got up and went into his wikiup. Sam could hear him rustling among his belongings. Soon he re-emerged bringing with him a small bag.

"What is that?" Sam asked.

Ahote poured the contents out in his hand, and Sam saw bits of blackened bones. He looked back at his brother questioningly.

"When Baa Naa Gj'alg died," Ahote said, "his power was so feared that the tribe cremated him out on the plateau, far from their homes. While they seemed to feel this was a good solution, I couldn't just leave him there like that. He'd saved me; helped me to find my own power and place in this world. I didn't ever want to forget him, or hide from who he was, so I took a few of the bones from his ashes, and I've kept them with me ever since."

"Does Lena know?"

"Good God, no. No one does."

"Aren't you afraid of the potential power that might dwell in his remains?"

Ahote shrugged. "Our mother is powerful, and you are too; I figure being around strongly gifted people is just part of my life's journey. I might as well embrace it."

Sam looked at him. "Why are you showing me this?"

"He helped me once when I was very lost. Maybe he can help you to find your way, too."

Sam looked at the bones then back at his brother. "What should I do?"

Ahote dropped the bones into Sam's hand. "Just ask him for help, and then be open to what happens."

144

Chapter 26

Rhiannon raced ahead of Ellie, bounding up the stairs and into the hayloft. Ellie followed, intent on retrieving a few of the peppers that had been left hanging from the rafters to dry. The chili she was serving for dinner needed a little kick. The aging planks creaked and groaned under her step, reminding her how much time had passed since her mother's death. Ellie's father had converted part of the hayloft into an art studio for Katherine. Later, he'd replaced the ladder with stairs, to keep the studio accessible to his steadily declining wife.

Ellie's mom had died in 1913, just before spring arrived to chase away the cold. It'd been a frigid winter, and as a result, very few guests had booked rooms at the lodge. Branna had sent everyone else down to the winter ranch so that Katherine could enjoy a warmer climate surrounded by family. Usually the kids attended school up in Flagstaff, but a special exception was made for them at the schoolhouse in Sedona that year. Ellie didn't remember much about her lessons, but she had many memories of being in the loft that last winter with her mother. As Ellie now stood at the threshold, she noticed childish pictures still hanging from the beams. She remembered drawing each one, along with the smile she got every time she gave one to her mother.

Rhiannon was already in the room, sniffing at everything in an agitated manner, but Ellie wasn't looking at her dog. She was staring out the big window, with its commanding view of Lee Mountain. The window had been another improvement of her dad's, to give the loft plenty of light for her mother to paint by. Her dad had placed it perfectly, to frame a view of the summit. Katherine had loved the mountains, and the view outside today was just the kind of scene her mom would have loved to paint. Dark gray cumulus clouds were gathering, threatening the sun, causing rays of light to streak out across the red mountain. The shifting weather reminded Ellie of the food she'd left cooking in the outdoor kitchen. She needed to get back, just in case those clouds decided to do their worst.

She turned from the window, intending to grab the dried chili peppers and return to work, but suddenly she felt very dizzy. She blinked, trying to restore her equilibrium. The dizziness passed, but it must have affected her vision, everything seemed illumined in an odd light. She heard Rhiannon barking, but she didn't pay any attention to it, because she was focused now on an odd glow coming from the far corner of the loft.

Ellie began to walk toward the light. She knew this spot well. This was where her mother's paintings were stored, those that didn't already hang in the lodge or at the winter ranch. The leftovers were all still here, stacked into the corner and covered with a sheet. After her mom had died, Ellie had often taken the sheet off and studied these hidden paintings. She'd copied her mother's style, and learned from it. She wasn't as gifted as her mother had been, but still she had a good hand.

Ellie was struck by an urge to look at the paintings once more. Forgetting about the peppers, she walked over to the corner, lifted the sheet, and began studying each one. When she finished looking at one, she would stack it to the side, continuing until there was only one painting left in the corner. As she lifted the last canvas to examine it more closely, she exposed a crevice in the farthest reach of the corner. The odd glow that had drawn her here seemed to be coming from inside. The thought of spiders or rodents crossed Ellie's mind, but still she stuck her hand into the opening, and immediately felt something, the contours of a book. It was wedged tightly into the wall, but Ellie was able to turn it, so that it slipped easily through the opening. When she at last was able to see what she held, she gasped. It was her mother's lost cookbook.

She sat down and opened it. Inside were all the old recipes. There were some that she and Branna had forgotten about entirely, but even more intriguing were all the sketches of the family tucked into the margins, and in the leftover spaces between one page and the next. She saw a buttermilk biscuit recipe, only a few ingredients long, leaving space on the page for a detailed sketch of Esme's smiling face. The molasses cookie recipe held a drawing on its backside of Michael and Sam caught in the act of raiding the cookie jar. Page after page held images capturing moments in time, linking the history of the family with the recipes that had fed them over the years.

Ellie hugged the book to her chest. "Oh, Mom," she whispered and then began to cry. After a while, she calmed herself enough to open the book back up for a closer inspection. As she opened the front cover, she noticed her mother's handwriting on the inside. It said, "For my family."

Chapter 27

Sam pulled up in front of the barn, tying Pookah to the rail. He brought the saddle into the tack room, and was just about to return and finish tending to her, when Rhiannon came bounding down the stairs from the loft, barking and backing up, trying to get him to follow her. Immediately, a dozen awful scenarios flashed through his brain, but all with one common theme: something terrible must have happened to Ellie.

He ran up the stairs two at a time, right through the threshold, and then stopped abruptly. Over in the far corner he saw Katherine holding a small girl in her lap. This was the first time he'd seen Katherine since her death. She'd never come to him in his dreams, but for some reason she was here now, in his waking state, looking right at him. Sam walked closer, studying the little tableau. The girl in Katherine's lap was absorbed in reading a thick book, but he could clearly see it was Ellie. She looked just as she had when she was five or six. He looked again at Katherine, wondering about the meaning of her presence and Ellie's changed appearance. Katherine met his gaze with a sad smile, and then she disappeared. As soon as she was gone, Ellie altered before his eyes, losing her child like aspect, becoming a woman once again. She seemed unaware of what had happened. She just looked up at him and said, "Sam, look what I found."

Sam reached for the book, but then his hands started to shake.

"Are you all right?" she asked.

'I'm not sure," he admitted.

"Well, come sit with me," Ellie urged.

"Not here," Sam said, and he helped her up, leading her over to a sunny patch of floor, warmed by rays of light streaming through the window. Rhiannon followed and settled near them, calm now that the ghost was gone. Sam searched Ellie's face as she sat beside him. "Ellie, do you realize what just happened?"

"I'm not really sure," Ellie said. "Only that somehow I was led to find this." She opened the book, showing him the inscription, and the first of the drawings inside.

He looked up from the book, meeting her eyes. "Ellie, when I walked in, I saw your mother. She was holding you in her lap as you read."

Ellie's eyes welled up. "I think I felt that," she said. "I could feel so much love." She took a moment to compose herself, and then said, "I want to show you something." She opened the book to a page of recipes for traditional Hopi wedding foods. Sam leaned over, and saw a loose sheet of paper inserted next to the recipes. It was a sketch of his mom and dad on their wedding day. His mom was wearing a beautiful satin robe with elaborate beading, and his dad was in his best suit of clothes. They stood on a rise, facing one another, with the familiar shape of Lee Mountain towering behind them.

Sam was silent as he stared at the drawing. There were a couple of framed photographs of his dad up at the lodge, but nothing like this. Tentatively, he touched the aged paper and ink. Somehow in this drawing, his dad seemed much more alive.

A knot formed in Sam's throat. "They look so young and happy," he said.

"You can see how much they loved one another," Ellie observed. "My mother's captured it so clearly." After a moment, in a voice that was barely a whisper, she added, "If you could just let yourself love me, I think it could be like that for us too."

Sam sighed, and then pulled her close against him. "I do love you. I've loved you from the day you were born. I sang you into this world. There has never been a day when you haven't been in my thoughts."

"Then why, Sam? Why can't we just be together?"

He was silent a moment, considering, and then said. "I've never tried to explain my dreams to you, but maybe I should. Do you want to know what makes me scream at night?"

Ellie stared at him. Her eyes were wide, but she nodded for him to go on.

"In my dreams, I see the world burn. I see bodies piled high, and all that is beautiful destroyed. What I can't figure out is if this is a vision of what's to come, or a symptom of deteriorating mental health. In either case, I have no future I can offer you."

Ellie was silent a moment, and then she leaned forward, planting a kiss on his forehead. "People marry all the time without knowing what the future will bring. If I only have one day as your wife it would still be better than a lifetime without you. And if the world does burn, you're the one I'll want beside me when the end comes."

Ellie put the book in his hands. "Look at the pictures," she urged. "My mother died before her time, but this book tells another story, maybe the one that matters most. It reminds us of how well she loved while she was alive." He looked at her, and she smiled shakily. "I have to go. I hadn't expected to be away this long. Let's just pray the pies and cobbler didn't burn." She left him then, grabbing a few dried chili peppers on her way out the door. Rhiannon waited to see if he was coming, and then bounded off after her.

Sam sat there a moment, uncertain what to feel or think. Then he decided just to follow her advice, and opened the book. Once he started, he couldn't stop. Sketch after sketch, he saw their lives through Katherine's eyes. There was a drawing of him, grinning as he fed baby Ellie straight from the raspberry jam jar. Another showed him sleepy eyed, sharing a cup of cocoa with his father late at night. His favorite was one of a family Christmas dinner. Auntie Branna was laying down a large turkey in front of his dad, who sat at the head of the table. Sam was sitting next to his mom holding toddler Ellie on his lap. Michael sat between his father and mother, poking fun at Sam from across the table. With the turn of each page, Sam saw the evidence of how safe and connected he'd once felt to his family, and the yearning inside him grew almost unbearable.

At some point, he became aware that the sun was no longer warming the floor planks. He looked over at the window and saw that the sky had grown dark and threatening. The storm Ahote had predicted was here. He remembered then that Pookah was still tied to the rail post. Leaving the book on his mother's work table, he ran down to tend to his horse.

By the time he finished with Pookah and arrived at the house, it was already starting to rain. He saw his mother frantically trying to get all the food from the outdoor kitchen indoors, and hurried over to help her.

"Where's Ellie?" he asked.

His mother handed him two potholders and the steaming pot of chili. "She didn't look well when she came back from the barn. I sent her inside to rest a bit."

As they were carrying in the last of the food, lightning lit up the sky, followed quickly by a loud crack of thunder. Not long after, the rain started coming down hard. Once they were back in the kitchen, his mom put up a pot for tea.

"I think Ellie could use a cup, too," his mother said.

Sam was pretty sure she could as well. He hadn't yet told his mother about the ghost in the barn, but while the water boiled, he related the whole tale. It was almost an after-thought when he told her the part about Baa Naa G'jalg's bones. He'd stuck his hand in his pocket and felt them still there. It was only then that he remembered that Ahote and he had invoked Baa Naa G'jalg's assistance.

"Is it possible, Mom? Could he have had anything to do with the appearance of Aunt Katherine's ghost?"

She put out her hand. "Let me see the bones," she said.

He took them out of his pocket and handed them to her. She held them in her hand a moment, and then her face paled. "You give these bones back to Ahote first chance you get." As she passed them back to him, she added, "We better check on Ellie."

They both walked quickly back to the room his mother was sharing with Ellie. There was no need to knock on the door. It was open and the room was empty. They stared at each other just as another crash of thunder reverberated through the sky.

I'll go look for her," he said.

She nodded and went to get him a slicker. "She probably didn't go too far," she said as she handed him the raincoat, but the expression on her face seemed far less certain.

Chapter 28

Ellie looked at the torrent of roiling water, then back at Rhiannon. It hadn't been raining when they'd first crossed the arroyo, so she'd never given the wash a second thought. Now, however, it was an impassable, raging current. "What an idiot," she muttered, frustrated because she'd seen the storm clouds when she'd left the house. But she'd been agitated. She'd needed movement and air to make room for all the thoughts circling through her brain. Before she'd even realized it, she was out the door, climbing the ridgeline and heading over into Jack's Canyon. She'd walked fast, and she'd walked far. She hadn't realized she was heading for Wild Horse Mesa until she was already halfway up its steep slope. At the time, she'd thought it a suitable place for her thoughts, high up, wide open, filled with family memories. But with lightning flashing and thunder shaking the earth beneath her, she knew it was the worst possible place to be. To make matters worse, she would have to climb even higher to find some place safe enough to cross over the raging wash.

Her clothes sodden, she ran alongside the arroyo, with her drenched dog loping along at her side. Rhiannon didn't like thunder, but she trusted Ellie to keep her safe. Ellie watched another flash of lightning streak across the sky, and felt like the worst person in the world for violating that trust.

They climbed for another half hour without finding a safe crossing. A crack of thunder ripped through the air around them, leaving the strong smell of ozone behind. They were now at the highest point around, and the storm was right over them. Their only hope of finding shelter would be to climb over the edge of the mesa, and hopefully find some outcropping along the side in which to take refuge. The overflowing arroyo blocked their access down the northern slope, but they could make a run for the eastern edge.

The lightning seemed to chase them as they ran, and Ellie's heart pounded with both fear and exertion. Eventually, she saw a slight dip down the northern side that didn't require crossing the arroyo. They headed off the mesa top, but it wasn't long before they encountered the raging wash once again. The wash was narrower here, but the water was still moving too swiftly to risk crossing. Thunder and lightning once again ripped the sky overhead. Ellie looked around for shelter, and found a small thicket of spindly scrub pines. It wasn't much, but it was better than nothing. She led Rhiannon over, and crawled under the low-hanging boughs. Wet and shivering, she pulled the dog close, trying not to cry as they hunkered down to wait out the storm.

She was so desperate, she began to think she heard someone calling her name, but it was only the wind howling, and soon the tympanic boom of thunder drowned it out altogether. The rain began to pelt down even harder, not that it mattered, as she and Rhiannon were already so saturated.

"Ellie!" She lifted her head. That wasn't the wind. She crawled out from under the brush and looked around. It was raining so hard that the figures on the other side of the arroyo looked indistinct, but she knew immediately it was Sam and Pookah.

"Sam!" she called waving her arms in a wide arc. He saw her, and then looked at the arroyo between them. "Don't move!" he shouted over the storm. He backed Pookah up, and Ellie knew at once he was planning to jump over.

"Sam! No!" she cried. The raging waters were nearly ten feet across. She watched, terrified, as Pookah launched from the muddy embankment, and flew over the churning waters, just as another flash of lightning lit up the sky overhead. The horse slipped as she landed on the opposite side, falling and bringing Sam down with her. He managed to prevent being pinned beneath her, but still their bodies hit the ground with a sickening thud.

Ellie ran to him. "Oh God! Sam! Sam, can you hear me?" She rolled him over carefully. He was breathing, but not responding. There was a gash on his forehead, turning the raindrops red as they ran down his face. Beside her, Pookah scrambled back on her feet, covered in mud but unharmed. The horse's recovery motivated Ellie. This was bad, but it wasn't by any means over. Having Pookah here gave her options. If she could get Sam to sit astride the horse, there was a shelter she knew of they might be able to reach.

There was another bright flash, followed by thunder shaking the ground around them. Ellie began patting Sam's cheeks and calling to him to wake up. Rhiannon whimpered, and then started licking his wound. Even Pookah leaned over, snorted, and then nudged him with her nose. Sam's eyes fluttered open.

"Oh, thank God!" Ellie cried.

Sam tried to sit up. "Go slow," Ellie warned as his face went pale. "You hit your head."

Sam looked at her, and then he groaned, leaned to the side, and threw up. Ellie got up and grabbed the water pouch off his saddle, handing it to him. He wiped his mouth, then took a swig, and spat out the sour taste of vomit. Another lightning strike reverberated nearby, and he seemed to remember the storm.

He tried to sit up again, moving slower this time. "You picked a great day for a walk," he said rubbing his head.

Ellie felt ashamed. "It was stupid of me, I'm sorry." She examined the gash on his head more closely. "Will you be okay? You hit your head pretty hard."

He began to nod, but the motion ignited fresh pain. He waited for it to pass, and then slowly managed to get to his feet. It was progress, but now he was seeing two of Ellie, both of whom stared at him with concern.

She continued to talk over the sounds of the storm. I don't think we should stay here." He looked over at the wash, which was steadily rising. Ellie said, "If you think you can ride, we might be able to make it to the kiva."

He looked at their current surroundings. If lightning didn't strike them when they rode across the mesa, the kiva would be a much better place to wait out the storm. "It's worth a try," he said. He took an unsteady step toward his horse, and then stopped because of the pounding in his head. He looked at Ellie, realizing for the first time he might not be able to make the ride.

She read his thoughts. "There's no choice, Sam. I'll take the reins, but you have to hold onto me. Just don't let go, no matter what." She helped him to walk over to Pookah. They had to wait a moment to let the dizziness pass again, but he managed to mount Pookah on his first try. She clambered up in front of him, shouting over the pounding rain. "Hang on tight, okay?"

"Okay," he said, and he wrapped his arms around her waist, just as another clap of thunder sounded overhead. Ellie whistled for Rhiannon, and then urged Pookah up the northern slope. Once they were on top of the mesa, she let the horse take off into a full-out canter.

As Pookah's hooves pounded the ground, Sam's head throbbed, but the proximity of the electrical storm overheard had his adrenalin pumping enough that he could handle the pain. The bracing wind and the deluge also did their part to clear his head. He noticed that the worst of the thunder and lightning was starting to move off to the east. He was about to heave a sigh of relief, when he felt the first prick of hail. By the time they reached the far side of the mesa, there was a constant sting of little ice pellets against his skin. Ellie jumped down, then reached up to help him dismount. He felt steadier now; more certain he could push through. He handed her a rope and his saddlebag, and then unsaddled Pookah.

"Don't overdo it, Sam." Ellie was getting hoarse from shouting over the elements, but even so he could hear the worry in her voice. He gave Pookah a pat her on the rear, encouraging her to find her own shelter from the storm. He watched as she loped toward a nearby copse of shaggy bark junipers.

"The cold air revived me some," he assured Ellie, "I'm okay now, really." Then he led the way off the mesa, down a narrow, muddied path along the southern rim. He was under no illusions about having put Ellie's fears to rest. She was keeping a close eye on him as he navigated the slippery path.

He made it without incident to the old Indian ruin. He hadn't been here in years, but they'd played here often as children. Ahote had showed it to Sam and Mike on that first wild horse expedition, the one where they'd captured Pookah. They, in turn, had shown it to Ellie and Maddie. He decided that someday soon he should show it to Moqui and Tiva. He realized then that he was stringing together coherent thoughts. It reassured him that the worst of the injury was now behind him.

The outer building was completely exposed to the elements, but the hole leading down into the abandoned kiva was still visible. There was no ladder; it had disintegrated ages ago in the harsh desert environment, but just as they had done as children, Sam anchored his rope around the trunk of a nearby mesquite, and then lowered Ellie and Rhiannon down into the hole. He followed soon after.

The ground was wet and pebbled with hail where the hole reached upward to the sky. There were also rapidly-forming puddles around the three of them as their rain-drenched bodies dripped onto the floor of the kiva. But for the first time in over an hour, the wind wasn't howling in their ears, and the rain wasn't pelting their skin or blurring their vision.

Ellie looked over at Sam. "Are you sure you're okay?"

"Much better," he assured her. "It's just a little headache now."

She still looked worried.

"Ellie, it's not the first time I've fallen off a horse."

She must have decided to believe him, because all of a sudden she let down her guard, taking in a very shaky breath. "Oh Sam! When you hit the ground like that…" She shivered and fought back her tears, "How did you find me in that downpour?" she managed at last.

He smiled, and then kissed the top of her head. "I'll always find you, Ellie." He held her close, but even so, her shivering continued. He frowned, stepping back to get a better look at her. Ellie was displaying signs of hypothermia.

"We have to get you out of these wet clothes," he said. Quickly, Sam helped her shuck the outer layers of her drenched clothing, and then his. The dog was shivering too, so he gathered them all into a far corner of the kiva, away from the sky hole, and they huddled together. Sam tucked Ellie along one side his body, and Rhiannon on the other. He covered them all with his rain slicker. It wasn't much by way of warmth, but it was sufficient to trap some of their body heat. He held her and her dog close, and began humming a song of healing. The melody felt good, easing the pain in his head, and spreading its warmth through Ellie and Rhiannon. Before long, they both stopped shaking and fell asleep.

 Sam lay quiet. He could feel the steady rise and fall of their breathing, and could hear the tapping of hail on the stone floor of the kiva. Outside, distant flashes of lightning lit up the ancient shelter through the opening in the roof. He was very aware of Ellie lying so close to him, and felt an overwhelming sense of relief. He'd found her in time, and the fall he'd taken hadn't done any lasting damage to him or his horse. There were other emotions he was feeling as well, ones that had once seemed complicated, but felt less so as he held her here in this shadowy, earthen womb.

At some point he must have fallen asleep too, because suddenly he awoke from a dream. His heart wasn't pounding in fear, though. This had been a new dream, one that had left him filled with love and a glow of well-being. He still held Ellie close against him. He shifted a little and she snuggled even closer, not fully awakening. He watched as she settled back into sleep. The darkened lashes against her cheeks reminded him of the babies in his dream; twins, a girl and a boy.

They'd looked like that when he'd held them in his arms. He couldn't help but smile. Finally he'd seen a vision of the future he could embrace. He leaned over and kissed her then, gently, on the lips. When he pulled away, she opened her eyes and looked at him intently. For a second time today, he was reminded of the day she was born, of that first time they'd ever laid eyes on one another. Both then and now, it seemed as if she could see all of him, everything, all the way down to his soul. And what she saw, she loved. It felt good to know she could see the best in him, even when he'd lost his way. It felt even better when she pulled him close and deepened the kiss.

1939

Corned Beef

Ingredients
5 pounds beef brisket
1 gallon water
16 ounces kosher (Diamond crystal) salt
¼ cup honey
1 tablespoon pink salt*
6 cloves garlic, minced
3 sprigs fresh thyme
3 tablespoons pickling spice

Directions
Bring the water, salts, honey, garlic, thyme sprigs, and pickling spice to a boil in a heavy-bottomed, deep pot. Remove from heat and allow to cool completely.

Add the meat, and weight it down to make sure it stays submerged in the brine. Keep in the fridge for 5-6 days.

Remove meat from the brine and rinse.

Add to a stockpot with just enough water to cover. Add the pickling spice and simmer gently for 3-4 hours till the meat is very tender.

Pink salt is an essential ingredient, giving corned beef its distinctive reddish color; it also kills botulism spores.

Chapter 29

Cal sat on the window ledge in his cousins' bedroom, taking in the view. It was something he, Sean and Eddy had done a million times growing up. From this window, one story up from the Burnetts' store, they'd perch themselves to watch the trains going in and out of town. As they grew older, and automobiles became more popular, that also had drawn their attention. At first there had been only a few among the horse drawn wagons, but now the main street in Flagstaff was part of a national highway, Route 66. The horses were long gone, replaced by a smooth, paved road and a steady stream of cars.

When they were younger, he and his cousins had liked to speculate on the people in those cars, hazarding a guess as to their circumstances and where they were bound. The visible belongings of vacationers often revealed if their final destination was a California beach, or a Grand Canyon adventure. The ones escaping hardships like the dustbowl or the depression were also easy to spot, their cars loaded up full with a lifetime of hard-used belongings. It always struck him that each driver traveling past him had made a decision to set his or her life in motion. None of them could know how it would all work out, but it had always seemed to Cal that it was hope, not just gasoline, that drove those cars.

"Cal, do you think I need my heavy coat?" Eddy was holding up his wool jacket. Both of Cal's cousins were packing to come down with him to the winter ranch for the spring roundup.

"It's still in the 40's at night," Cal said. "You should probably bring it."

Sean shut his suitcase and looked over at Cal. "I still can't get over Uncle Mike's news. Imagine being reassigned to the Philippines! I wish I was going!"

Cal cocked an eyebrow. "You do realize most of the family isn't happy about this news?"

Eddy added, "Did you see how quiet Mom got? That's never a good sign."

"She'll come around," Sean assured them, and then laughed, "What's she going to do? Tell the army they don't have her permission?"

Eddy chuckled. "Maybe she could get Mrs. Burnett to spit corned beef all over them."

Cal tried not to smile, but it had been funny. Not the part where Mrs. Burnett was choking, of course. When she'd heard her son-in-law's news, the piece of corned beef she'd been chewing on went down the wrong way, lodging in her throat. Her face had turned an alarming shade of red until Uncle Eli stepped in and gave her a solid thump on the back. He not only managed to dislodge the meat, the whack had been so strong it had sent the meat flying out of her mouth, across the table, and it had thwacked her grandson, Gabriel, square on the face. The toddler had picked up the chewed beef and offered it back to his grandmother, saying with all seriousness, "Grandma, it's not nice to spit."

The somber mood at the table had given way to laughter. Gabriel's reprimand had provided some much-needed comic relief, but when the laughter died down, Cal had glanced over at his dad, wondering how he was reacting to Uncle Mike's news. The look on his father's face made it clear the news wasn't resting easy. Cal had figured it wouldn't. His dad had been having disquieting visions lately, of a world consumed by fire. He'd had these dreams before, but not often. The dream was coming to him nearly every night now, ever since the news broke that Chancellor Hitler had formed an alliance with Japan.

Cal understood Uncle Mike's reassignment was tied to these worrying developments, and he had been expecting his dad to share the warning from his dreams with the family, but his father had kept his visions to himself. That left Cal wondering if he should stay quiet, too.

"Maybe I should enlist." Sean's shocking statement brought Cal immediately back to the conversation with his cousins.

Eddy rolled his eyes. "Oh, Mom would just love that."

"Well, I turn 18 in just a few weeks, and then it won't be her decision to make."

His little brother snorted. "Good luck trying to convince her of that."

Cal wondered if Sean would be deterred if he knew of the dreams. Everyone in the family understood it was unwise to ignore Sam's visions. Cal decided then he should speak to his dad. He must have had some reason for staying quiet earlier, but perhaps he'd feel differently if he realized his nephew was talking of enlisting.

"I need to gather up my stuff before we head home," Cal told his cousins, and then headed out of their room in search of his father. He wandered into the living room, where he found all the men deep in conversation. There was a hushed intensity to their exchange, and Cal could see now wasn't a good time to interrupt his dad. He continued walking through the front door of the apartment, and then down the stairs into Auntie Branna's restaurant. It was closed now because of this welcome-home feast for Uncle Mike and his family.

Cal rubbed his belly as he walked. All the unsettling news had upset his digestion. He burped up the sour taste of half-digested corned beef. Yep, Cal thought, it had been quite the party, and this was just round one of the celebration. There would be another feast this evening when they arrived back at the winter ranch. When he and his dad had left this morning to meet the train, his mother was already hard at work preparing one of Uncle Mike's favorite dishes. It was a recipe from one of her fancy cookbooks, and the scent of browning beef and rendering bacon had filled the kitchen. At the time, Cal had been anticipating a really good day of eating, but as he stifled another burp, he wasn't sure if he was going to have the stomach for his mother's rich stew.

Cal wandered through the small restaurant and into the Burnetts' attached mercantile. The store had changed a lot over the years. It still had grocery items, but more and more it had taken on the appearance of a gift shop catering to travelers motoring along Route 66. Having the store along this major route had made all the difference for the Burnetts, and so had the adjoining restaurant for Auntie Branna and Uncle Eli. None of them had suffered the same degree of upheaval during the depression that the rest of the family had.

Cal stopped in front of a prominent section promoting C & M Lodge and its authentic Wild West excursions. The sight made him smile despite his upset stomach. This was the first year in many they'd seen their way clear to cater to tourists again. The depression and the drought had forced them to reduce their herd by over half, and they'd turned the lodge and restaurant into a boarding house. But the biggest change had come during the worst of the drought, when Uncle Mike had enlisted in the army, in order to send additional wages home to help cover taxes and feed for the livestock.

At first it had been Uncle Mike's intent to leave Aunt Maddie home, keeping his expenses as low as possible so the money could all go to the needs of the ranch and the family. But Aunt Maddie had different ideas. It took nearly a year for her to figure out all the angles, but in the end she'd presented the family with a plan that allowed her to live in military housing with her husband, while still making sure the ranch stayed solvent.

Aunt Maddie had always been clever that way. It'd been her idea to run the lodge as a boarding house. She'd said it would help if they could always count on and plan for the income and expenses associated with that aspect of the family business. It had also been her idea for Auntie Branna to take over the Burnetts' small ice cream parlor, turning it into a restaurant. Aunt Maddie had correctly gauged that people would be looking for good places to eat along the new interstate highway. To Cal's way of thinking, Aunt Maddie was a major reason the family had managed to weather the hard times. She'd spent those lean years looking after everyone's welfare, and now it would be their turn to look after her and little Gabe.

Cal stopped in front of the rack of cookbooks featuring the food of C & M Lodge. Even this had been Aunt Maddie's idea, printing the family cookbook along with the illustrations created by his mom and grandmother. They sold the books both at the lodge and here in the gift section of her parents' store.

Cal opened the latest edition, knowing exactly what he would find. He was a bit of an artist himself, and when he was old enough, he'd been allowed to study the drawings from the original, which still sat on a shelf in the kitchen at the lodge. He'd never met his maternal grandmother, but somehow through the lines of her pen he felt as if he knew Katherine and what she'd loved. He flipped through, stopping to study the drawings of his namesake, his paternal grandfather, Caleb, another ancestor he'd never known. People always commented how much Cal looked like him. Cal wasn't so sure about that. He thought he looked much more like his father; more Hopi than Irish.

In this drawing, his grandfather gazed out at the viewer, hale and happy. He had his arms around a very beautiful woman dressed in an elaborately beaded silken robe. Cal hadn't looked at this drawing recently, certainly not since his sister, Kat, had gone through puberty. For the first time, Cal saw the striking resemblance between Kat and their grandmother. It was hard imagining Grandma Chari as being young, harder still to envision her loving anyone other than Grandpa Zach. But the illustration left no room for doubt; you only had to look at her face to see she'd loved Grandpa Caleb very much.

As Cal flipped the pages he watched his parents as well as Uncle Mike and Aunt Maddie growing older before his eyes. Before long he came to the later recipes, featuring his mother's drawings of his generation of the family. Her hand wasn't quite as skilled as her mother's, but still she had an excellent eye, and her drawings were vibrant on the page.

He thumbed through, looking for his favorites. He stopped at the one of Auntie Branna presenting a birthday cake to his cousin Sean. There were four candles, but they were no longer lit, because baby Eddie had blown them all out. Cal and Kat were sitting at the table, three-year-old twins with wide grins on their faces. Sean wasn't laughing, though. He was crying, and pointing a finger at his brother. Cal smiled. Those two may have grown older, but not much had changed between them. Sean was still expected to know better, and Eddy was always forgiven for being a clown.

Cal flipped a few more pages, stopping at the peach cobbler recipe. There he saw a pair of five year olds, comparing the size of their peaches as they sat on a branch in Istaqa's tree. It had always been a given, that he and Kat would compete over every little thing. But unlike Sean and Eddie, a lot was changing between him and his twin.

If he had to pinpoint when he'd first noticed things changing, it would have to be this past autumn, when Kat had been crowned Rodeo Queen. With the title had come a lot of unwanted attention. All kinds of men and boys had been vying for a dance with her that evening. When the last dance was called, a fight had broken out. The schoolboys had been wise enough to give way to the men who'd started the fight, many of whom had been drinking heavily. But Cal wasn't about to let men who couldn't control their tempers anywhere near his sister. The men, for their part, hadn't taken kindly to a seventeen year old telling them to move along. If his father, grandfather, and uncles hadn't quickly inserted themselves into the mix, it wasn't clear it would have ended well for Kat or for him. That dance had served as a wake-up call to all the men in the family.

It should have been a wake-up call for Kat too, but she refused to give it any further thought. Cal had tried talking to her, but he'd only managed to make her angry. She'd demanded to know in what world was she responsible for a bunch of grown men who had chosen to behave badly. In the end, Cal just kept a closer eye on her, and he noticed his dad, grandpa and uncles were doing the same.

162

The sound of someone crying brought Cal out of his reverie and back to the present. He returned the book to the display, and silently walked toward the muffled sounds coming from the restaurant. The room was lit up with the bright light of midday, but still he had to look a moment before he found Aunt Maddie sitting in a dark corner, sniffling and using her hand to wipe away her tears. He wasn't certain if he should approach her - she might prefer privacy - but then he thought about all she and Uncle Mike had told them at dinner. Once, she'd moved heaven and earth to make sure she could be with her husband, but that was before Gabriel was born, and there was no way she was going to Manila with a three year old in tow. Cal watched her cry for a few seconds more, and then decided maybe what his aunt needed most right now was just to be reminded she wasn't alone. He walked up to her and handed her his handkerchief.

She looked up at him as she took it. "Thank you," she sniffed, and then added, "I wondered where you'd gone off to."

Cal shrugged and then sat down beside her. "I just needed a little quiet."

Aunt Maddie wiped the tears from her face and blew her nose. "Were your cousins annoying you?"

"Not really. It's just they're pretty excited about Uncle Mike's reassignment."

Aunt Maddie studied Cal's face. "And you don't feel the same?"

He couldn't hold her gaze and looked away.

"Oh God," she swallowed hard. "What do you know?"

"Nothing," he said, but he knew the damage was already done. A lot of the family wondered if he saw the future, just like his dad did. He was glad he couldn't, but whether he could or not, he lived with someone who did, and that made him suspect.

She moaned, "Why did I let him re-enlist?" Tears began to fall again. "He asked me what I thought, back in the fall, before he signed the papers." She wiped at her eyes, and once again blew her nose into the sodden handkerchief.

Cal grabbed one of the cloth napkins from a nearby table and handed it to her. "Auntie, you couldn't have known they'd send him to Manila."

"I should have just said no," she continued. "We have a son now. What's going to happen to our little boy if Mike doesn't come home?"

Cal was quiet a moment, gathering his thoughts. He had no idea what were the right words to comfort her. "We aren't at war," he finally offered. "Uncle Mike is just going to help train Filipino scouts. He's not going there to fight."

Aunt Maddie shook her head. "Don't fool yourself, Cal. He's heading into harm's way. He's training scouts because we're anticipating some kind of aggression from the Japanese."

Suddenly Cal wished his dad had found her, or Auntie Branna. There was just no way for him to know if he was making things better or worse. Aunt Maddie sniffed again, but didn't speak.

Cal scooted closer to her. "We've missed you, you know? Mom especially. I can't tell you how many times she's wished you were here to ask your advice."

Maddie looked up at him, somewhat surprised. "Why does she need my advice?"

Cal looked at her incredulously. "Auntie, we've just restarted the vacation lodge and adventure excursions. That's a lot harder to do without you around to make sure we don't mess things up."

She sat up a little taller. "Your mom said that?"

Cal nodded. "On more than one occasion."

"You know, it turns out I've had some more ideas on that front," she ventured.

"Oh?" he encouraged her.

"I met some people out in California, the parents of one of the women I'm friends with." Her face grew more animated as she talked. "They're in the movie industry and they seemed very interested in our ranch."

Cal looked up, alarmed. "I hope you told them it wasn't for sale!"

She patted his hand. "They aren't looking to buy it, silly. I would never suggest we sell the ranch."

"Well, what are they interested in, exactly?"

"They're looking for a place to shoot some footage, and to rent out our cattle and horses. It could be a very good fit for the ranch; profitable, too."

"They want to make movies?" He was having trouble trying to imagine this whole scenario.

"Westerns," she clarified. She took in a deep breath, and then blew her nose one last time. She looked over at the stairway. "I suppose they'll be wondering where we are." She extended her hand so he could help her up.

As he pulled her to her feet she said, "You know what, Cal?"

"What?"

"You went and grew up on me."

Chapter 30

Cal bumped along in the truck bed with Uncle Mike and his cousins, as his dad drove back down the mountain from Flagstaff. Aunt Maddie and Gabriel were up in the cab with him, protected from the dust and the worst of the jostling. As the San Francisco Peaks gradually receded into the distance, Sean and Eddy hurled a stream of questions at Uncle Mike. How long would it take to get to the Philippines? What was Major General Grunert like? Would Uncle Mike meet Douglas MacArthur? What kind of weapons would he be using when he trained the Filipino scouts? They chattered on and on.

Eventually their voices became nothing more than background noise, along with the drone of the truck's engine and the wind in Cal's face. Leaning back against the cargo hold, Cal caught sight of a hawk circling overhead. He let his mind wander, wondering what the bird saw from so high up; what it might feel like to ride the wind. He relaxed a little and really tried to imagine it; catching the air currents, looking down at forests and meadows. His mind really seemed to take him there. In his imagined bird's eye view, he felt the perspective shift. His sight became uncannily sharp, and the colors became much more vibrant and varied. Suddenly he was aware of motion in the meadow below. The movement came from far beyond his normal peripheral vision; a rabbit scampering through the brush. He dove sharply, the ground coming up on him at an alarming speed. The shock of talons piercing flesh caused Cal to gasp.

"You all right there, Cal?"

The world righted itself, and Cal was once again bouncing along in the truck bed down the mountain road towards Sedona. "Yeah," he said, although he wondered if perhaps that big, heavy dinner had lulled him to sleep. He took a deep breath and then looked at his uncle.

"Yeah," he said again. "I'm fine."

Uncle Mike continued to study him. "You've been pretty quiet all afternoon."

Cal met his uncle's gaze, wondering again if he should say something about his dad's dreams. After talking to Aunt Maddie, he was beginning to understand why his dad had chosen to keep his visions to himself. Still, Aunt Maddie was one thing. Uncle Mike was

166

quite another. For him, being aware of the warning could make a difference, perhaps even save his life.

In the end, Cal decided just to put all his cards on the table. "Dad is having dreams about the whole world going to war. He thinks it's a vision of things to come."

Uncle Mike smiled kindly. "I know, Cal. He told me."

"He did?"

"Yeah, some months back, before I re-upped."

Cal looked at him, stupefied. "You knew and you still re-enlisted?"

"We exchanged some letters before I made my final decision."

"Doesn't it worry you, what he sees in those dreams?"

"Sure, it worries me. That's why I went ahead and re-enlisted."

"I don't understand."

Uncle Mike put his arm around Cal, drawing him near. "Cal, there's a reason the ancestors have been hammering this message at your dad so hard and for so long. The choices we make right now matter."

"He thinks the ancestors want us to go to war?"

"He thinks they're saying we have an important choice to make. We either stand up for what we believe in, or we let others remake our world into a place where there's no democracy and no freedom. As far as I'm concerned, that isn't even a choice. How can you keep your family safe in a world like that?"

Cal swallowed. "Is Dad going to enlist too?"

Uncle Mike gaze was deep and unwavering. "I asked him not to."

"Why?" Cal was disconcerted. "If his vision is about making a choice, how can you ask him to stand on the sidelines?"

"I didn't ask it of him lightly," his uncle assured him. "Part of my reasoning was simply acknowledging the military was likely to reject him. Your dad suffered shell shock after the Great War, and it was recorded in his medical files. Add to that how essential he is to the running of this ranch, and they'd most likely decide to just leave him where he is."

Cal couldn't understand how both things could co-exist: a relentless, strident warning, and a world where his dad couldn't take action. Uncle Mike stared deeply into Cal's eyes, correctly gauging the confusion there. "You know, Cal, the way I see it, your dad stepped off the sidelines the moment he shared his visions with me. He sounded a warning. Now it's my job to help make sure people heed it."

Cal still didn't know what to think, and Uncle Mike just kept staring at him. Then his uncle cleared his throat. Even so, his voice wavered when he spoke. "It's hard to leave Maddie and the baby, you know? It helps me to know he's here looking out for all of you."

"Yeah," Cal said. That part he could easily understand. It couldn't be easy for Uncle Mike to leave his family behind, heading straight into the nexus of Dad's dire warning.

"Can I ask you something, Cal?"

"Sure."

"Help your dad. Can you do that for me? Help him keep everyone safe."

Chapter 31

Dawn hadn't quite broken when Kat entered the kitchen, carrying a pail of fresh milk and a basket of eggs. Leotie toddled right behind her, holding a smaller basket with just five eggs nestled inside. Immediately Piglet wandered over, sniffing at the fresh food.

"Off with you, Pig," Kat said. "Honestly, Mom, that dog is a disgrace. You should send her down to the barn."

"She'll be working hard soon enough, as will you. You don't see me begrudging you your breakfast."

"No," Kat agreed, "but when I finish my breakfast, I won't hang around constantly begging for more." Then Kat urged Leotie over to where both their mothers were working. "Give those eggs to your mommy so she can put them in the corn cakes."

"And then she cooks them, and then we eat them!" The two-year old danced and spun around excitedly. The eggs rolled in the basket as she twirled, the dog watching intently, but sadly for Piglet, none of the eggs fell and broke.

Moqui's wife, Aunt Ana, scooped her daughter into her arms and rescued the basket in one smooth motion. "Awee," she cooed in Navajo, "would you like to help me crack the eggs?"

"Yes!" Leotie cried, at the same moment that Kat shouted, "No!"

The last time Leotie had been offered an egg to crack, she'd crushed the entire thing in her tiny fist, and had then thrown the whole mess into the bowl. It had been impossible to pick all the egg shells out of the batter.

Aunt Ana looked over at Kat and gave her a wink. "We're getting better at it, I promise."

Maddie entered the kitchen carrying Gabriel. She didn't look as if she'd slept well, but it was no wonder. That was some piece of news Uncle Mike delivered yesterday, although neither her parents nor her grandparents had seemed surprised.

Kat wondered briefly what it would be like for Uncle Mike living on a hot, humid jungle island. It was about as far from desert living as she could imagine. And then she wondered about Aunt Maddie, and what she must be feeling: sad, of course; probably afraid too.

169

"I see we are the last ones up. What can I do to help?" Aunt Maddie asked.

Kat's mom pulled a bowl out of the oven, filled with the corn mixture that had been left to rise overnight. "Here," she said. "Add five cups milk, and once Ana and Leotie finish cracking the eggs, mix them in good."

Kat smiled. She liked that about her family. No one ever dwelt overly long on the bad stuff. They always just rolled with the punches and got on with doing what they had to do.

Maddie handed Gabriel off to Kat, and then tied on an apron. "Leotie's cracking the eggs?" Aunt Maddie raised an eyebrow at that.

Kat was looking at the little boy she now held, who was studying her right back. "Just why exactly am I holding this child?" she asked.

Ellie smiled at her daughter. "Keep him out of trouble while we finish making breakfast."

Gabe looked over as Leotie tapped the first egg against a measuring cup. "Can I do that too?" he asked.

Kat figured it was only fair, so she carried him over and said, "Let Gabe do one, too."

"Have you ever cracked an egg before?" Aunt Ana asked him. He shook his head.

"Let us show you, then." She took the egg Leotie had just cracked. "You tap it just like she did so it cracks, then you give it to me." She demonstrated what came next by splitting the fractured egg the rest of the way open and dropping its contents into a porcelain bowl. Kat approved of this new method. Not a single shell had gotten into the bowl. Aunt Ana pulled a stool over for Gabe to stand on and said, "Now your turn."

Kat placed him on the stool, holding him steady as Aunt Ana handed him an egg. Piglet stood close by. Kat had to admit the dog would be useful if the little boy made a mess of things. But Gabe proved to be a much more thoughtful child than Leotie. He didn't rush right in; he studied the egg, and then cautiously tested the strength of the shell against the measuring cup until he at last applied enough pressure for a perfectly controlled crack.

"Nicely done!" Kat said, as he handed the egg off to Aunt Ana. He smiled up at her, pleased with her praise. Kat hadn't gotten the chance to know Gabe the way she knew Leotie. He'd spent much of his life in California. This was really the first time he'd been around and old enough to show some personality. There was something very open and sweet about him, and Kat knew in that instant it was going to be easy to love this kid.

It was getting late. Kat watched the rising sun light up the red rocks, and began to feel antsy. Breakfast was taking way too long. Usually, by the time the sun crested the ridge, they'd have hit the trail, but today she couldn't seem to roust her sisters and cousins from the breakfast table. They were the only ones still left eating. Her grandmother had stopped just long enough for a cup of tea before heading out to begin the annual planting of Hopi corn. Cal, her grandpa, her dad, and all of her uncles had left for the barn not long after that. Her mother and aunts had been the last to leave the table, heading to the outdoor kitchen to get a start on the midday meal. They'd left Kat in charge of the stragglers, with the expectation that everyone would be hard at work by now.

The problem was that Sean and Eddy had started this dumb competition of who could eat the most corn cakes, and Lissie, in an even dumber move, had decided to try to win it. There was no way a ten year old girl was going to win an eating contest against two teenage boys, but there was no telling Lissie that. Kat's sister was as stubborn as they came. Thankfully, Lettie, at the wise old age of six, had enough sense to stay out of it. It said something when the baby of the family had more sense than Lissie.

Finally Kat decided she'd had enough of trying to talk sense to this crew. If they wanted to ignore the roundup, let them. She was going to go saddle up her horse and show her dad she was ready to get to work. But first she had to do something with the little ones. She wasn't going to leave the toddlers with Sean and Eddy, when those boys clearly weren't demonstrating any common sense.

"Lettie, come with me. I'm going to bring Gabe and Leotie back to their moms."

Lettie looked at Kat imploringly. "What about Lissie?"

"Amaryllis is too busy making poor choices this morning." No one in the family ever used Lissie's full name unless they were upset with her. Kat hoped Lissie would take the hint, but instead, Lissie looked up unconcerned from her fifth corn cake and smiled with a mouth full of food.

"One more and I'll have it all tied up."

At that point Eddy deliberately put another cake on his plate and took a big bite.

"Looks like you'll need two more now," Sean smirked, and he and Eddy cracked up all over again.

Kat was disgusted. "I don't know how any of you are going to sit in the saddle with your bellies about to burst." She hastily wiped the stickiness off the toddlers, and then took Gabe in one hand and Leotie in the other. "Are you coming, Violet?"

Lettie noted the commanding use of her full name, but instead of snapping to, she started to cry. "I don't want to leave Lissie."

Kat sighed in exasperation and then turned her back on the whole sorry lot of them. With the toddlers in tow, she headed to the outdoor kitchen to find her mother. Her mom and aunts were in the midst of lifting the chuck box onto the cargo bed of the pick-up truck when Kat arrived. The water barrel and firewood were lying nearby, ready to load as well. "Can you give us a hand?" her mom asked as Kat walked up.

"Sure." Kat sat the toddlers down on a nearby bench, and Piglet immediately went to work, licking the remains of butter and honey off of Gabe and Leotie's sticky hands and faces. The children giggled and shrieked while Piglet gave them a much more thorough cleaning than Kat had. Kat wiped her own sticky hands on her jeans, and then went to help with the chuck wagon. Together they heaved the chuck box up over the tailgate and onto the cargo bed. Kat jumped into the truck to anchor a rope around it.

"Is everyone else down at the barn now?" her mom asked, climbing up next to her with supplies to load into the chuck box.

Kat shook her head. "No. I couldn't get them to stop goofing off."

Her mom stopped stuffing plates and flatware into the drawers, and looked at her. "What do you mean by goofing off?"

"They're having a corn cake eating contest. Lissie is trying to win."

"Kat! Why didn't you put a stop to it?" The annoyance in her mother's voice was unmistakable.

Kat was about to explain, when her dad and Uncle Mike came riding up from the barn.

"Where the heck is everybody?" her dad asked. "It's getting late."

Aunt Ana and Maddie were struggling, trying to lift the water barrel, and Uncle Mike got off his horse to give them the extra oomph they needed to get it up into the truck bed.

172

Her mom brushed back a loose lock of hair. "Apparently," she said to her husband, "the kids are having an eating contest and Kat didn't have the good sense to put an end it."

"I tried!" Kat protested. "No one would listen to me."

"Who's winning?" Uncle Mike asked, throwing another rope at Kat to help secure the barrel.

Kat grabbed the rope. "Possibly Eddy, but Lissie is giving him a run for his money. She might pull it off, if her tummy doesn't burst first."

"Oh, Kat!" Now her mother was truly exasperated. "You should have made her stop."

"I already told you, I tried! Nobody wanted to hear what I had to say."

"Kat," the tone in her dad's voice was absolute, "go in right now and tell them to get a move on."

"If they want to spend their day puking on the trail, it's their business."

"I just made it yours."

It was clear there could be no more arguing. He was angry with her; not the boys, not Lissie, but her! Kat jumped down from the cargo bed, flinging her long braid over her shoulder furiously. As she stomped angrily back toward the house, she at least made sure she had the last word. "They're idiots! Don't know how that got to be my responsibility!"

Uncle Mike laughed. "Quite the little lady," he commented.

"I heard that!" she yelled back, just as she reached the kitchen, and then banged open the door.

The four faces at the table turned toward her at once. Lissie looked decidedly green, and Lettie looked as if she'd been crying. The crash of the door flinging open wiped those stupid grins right off of Sean and Eddy's faces.

"That's enough!" Kat snarled as she grabbed the platter of corn cakes off the table. "You guys forget we have more cattle to round up today? Dad and Uncle Mike weren't happy to hear you dummies were in here eating yourselves sick."

"I wasn't!" Lettie protested.

Sean narrowed his eyes. "Just how did they know what we were doing, Kat?"

"I told him, knucklehead!"

Eddy at least had the grace to look guilty. He turned to his brother and said, "Come on, we better get to work."

Kat heaved a sigh. At last things were moving in the right direction. She watched them go, not saying anything until Lissie and Lettie tried to follow.

"Not so fast, you two," she said. The girls turned around slowly. "Let me have a look at you, Lissie." Kat put one hand on Lissie's clammy forehead and another on her distended belly. "You don't look so good. Are you going to be sick?"

Lissie stared at her a moment, then looked away and nodded.

Kat groaned, and then took both girls by the hands and headed for the door in search of their mother. Kat didn't have to look far; their mom was standing right outside, with Piglet by her side.

Kat handed Lissie over. "She thinks she might throw up. I'm not sure she should go with us today."

Ellie studied her middle daughter. "You do look a bit green around the edges there, Lissie. Maybe you should help your aunts and me with the chuck wagon."

"No! Wait!" Lissie cried. "I'll be fine in a bit!"

Kat tried to reason with her. "We don't really need you today. We're just going to find the missing cattle and bring them to the holding pasture. You can rest up a bit and then ride out with Mom and Aunt Maddie in the chuck wagon."

"Oh, can I do that too?" Lettie pleaded at the same moment that Lissie hollered, "That's not fair!" The effort Lissie expended in yelling was all that was needed to offset the fragile balance. She ran out the door to the closest bush and started retching.

"That's lovely," Kat said, feeling sick herself at the sight.

"Well," their mom said. "It seems you two are with me today."

Lissie turned from where she was still huddled over by the bush, trying to give Kat an evil glare, which was hard because Piglet had come over and was trying to lick her face. Meanwhile, Lettie was dancing up and down, delighted with the change in plans.

"You'll still have to help get dinner ready for everyone." Kat told Lettie.

"I know, I know."

"Okay, then." Kat turned to her mom. "Sorry about Lissie. I guess I should have done a better job watching out for her."

Her mom smiled. "Well, I imagine Lissie won't likely make that mistake again. She should be well enough to help Grandpa with the horses when everyone gets back."

Kat looked over at Lissie, who'd perked up a little at the mention of spending time with Grandpa and the horses. This day might turn out all right after all; that is if Kat got to the barn before all the men left without her. Kat pulled her cowboy hat up onto her head. "Well, I'd best be off."

"You can spare the time to give me a kiss," her mom said. Kat leaned in and gave her a quick peck, which her mom somehow managed to turn into a hug as well. "I know your cousins gave you a hard time this morning," she said. "Sometimes boys just need to blow off a little steam."

Kat looked up at her. "And Lissie, too, it seems."

Her mom smiled. "And Lissie, too."

Kat returned the smile and then whistled for Piglet, who came running. "You ready to put in a solid day's work, Pig?" The dog wagged his tail, and the two of them started off toward the barn. She turned after a moment and waved back at her mom. "I'll see you at dinner," she said, and then she ran down the dirt path with Piglet loping along beside her.

As Kat got closer to the barn, she could see her dad had already saddled up Storm for her. She wasted no time slinging herself up onto the mare. "I'm ready," she declared.

"Good," her dad said. "You're with Cal." He handed her a Winchester. "You remember how to shoot one of these?"

Kat stared at the weapon a moment. They didn't usually take firearms on roundups. "What's that for?"

Her dad looked at her for a moment, and then sighed. "Nothing I can put a finger on, just a feeling something isn't quite right."

Kat stowed the rifle behind her saddle. "Well, if there is something wrong, the sooner we hit the trail, the sooner we'll know."

Her dad nodded, adding, "I'm sending you and Cal into Jack's Canyon."

Cal looked decidedly unhappy. "We've already been through the canyon."

"Well, that's what's left. Ahote and Moqui left nearly an hour ago, heading off towards Turkey Hill, and Grandpa just left with Sean and

Eddy heading north toward Lee Mountain. Uncle Mike and I are taking Wood's Canyon, so that leaves the eastern quarter to you and Kat."

Kat was just as miffed as Cal. They'd been all over Jack's Canyon yesterday. But something was troubling her dad, and she wanted him to know he could count on her. "Come on, Cal," she urged. "Let's get going." And then she nudged her horse around Cal's, taking the lead.

That got his attention. "Hold on there! Who made you the boss?"

Their eyes locked, and then knowing smiles mirrored on their faces. There was only one way to settle this. With a shout they set their horses racing off toward the ridge. Behind her, over the pounding of hooves, she could hear her father calling, "Stick together, you two! I mean it!"

Chapter 32

Cal's horse crested the ridge first, but Kat was pleased all the same. Storm had nearly flown up that ridge. She'd done her very best, and Kat was proud of her. She let Cal lead the way down into the pine valley, as was his due. She noticed plenty of cattle sign along the way, but that didn't tell them anything, as the entire herd had passed through here on their way to the holding pasture.

They reached the valley floor, and then a short while later, a wash. Cal indicated he would search on the far side of it. Kat nodded, taking the northerly flank of the embankment. They fell easily into their work rhythm, working separately, but always aware they were in it together, sharing the heat and scent and wide-open spaces of the desert.

As Kat scanned for signs of the lost cattle, her thoughts roamed. She wondered what exactly was eating at her dad today. She'd learned enough over the years to know you ignored his hunches at your own peril. It was possible something bad was brewing, but she couldn't help wondering if he was once again being over-protective. He'd been doing that a lot recently, ever since the fight at the rodeo dance. The men in her family had put a quick stop to that drunken brawl, and that should have been the end of it. But there was no question being crowned queen of the rodeo had changed how people looked at her.

On the plus side, it had been nice to be admired, and she'd gotten to ride Storm down Main Street in the parade. Also, they'd let her keep the crown. She'd never admit it to Cal, but she did kind of feel like a princess when she put it on. But there was another side to being admired she wasn't quite sure what to do about. She was receiving a lot of unwanted attention from the boys at school. It was not the kind of behavior that warranted any intervention from her family. The boys were well behaved, but they were also persistent.

She'd talked to Cal about it, asked him what he thought would get those boys to settle down. He'd intimated a boyfriend might help calm the waters. Then he'd suggested Manny Gomez might be a good choice. She hadn't really thought about a boyfriend before that. She did like Manny. They'd spent a lot of time together, since he was one of Cal's best friends. If she had to choose someone, he wouldn't be a bad person to pick. He knew his way around a horse, that was for sure, and he loved ranching. But the thing was, she really couldn't say if she liked him in that way or not. It seemed to her she ought to know her own mind better before making a commitment like that.

Cal headed down into the wash studying the terrain, looking for some kind of sign, but he wasn't hopeful they would be the ones to find the missing cattle. On the other side of the wash, Kat was quiet, lost in thought, and soon the rhythm of Cal's horse and the lack of any telling signs lulled his mind, sending it adrift with his own thoughts. He kept replaying his conversation with Uncle Mike, and wondered if his uncle was right, that the military wouldn't accept his dad. If that was the case, what was the point of plaguing him with these awful premonitions? Why would the ancestors drive home a message of standing up for what was right if Dad was not going to be able to do something about it? Uncle Mike had felt it was enough that Dad was sounding the alarm. Were the ancestors just hoping to cast a wide net? Was that the point?

Cal was so distracted trying to puzzle it all out, he didn't see the low hanging branches of Cat's Claw up on the embankment. By the time he realized his mistake, the thorns had entangled him, tearing his shirt and digging into his flesh.

"Jesus!" he swore as the blood welled up.

Kat looked over at him, raising an eyebrow when she saw him trying to disentangle from the sharply barbed bush. "You need a little help there, Cal?"

He held up his hand. "Did you bring your med kit?" He knew of course that she had. Kat's saddlebag was always well stocked with first aid supplies. In that she was very much like their dad and grandma; she had a real talent for patching up both people and animals. It often came in handy when they were out working with the cattle.

She headed over and helped free him from the branches. Then she grabbed her first aid kit out of her saddlebag, guiding him over to a rock where he could sit.

"That looks like it hurts," she commented, as she inspected the wound and then took a clean cloth out of her kit, applying pressure to stop the bleeding. Kat looked at the overhanging branches and then back at him. "That's a pretty hard bush to miss, Cal."

"I know." he felt like an idiot. "I got lost in thought, and just wasn't paying attention to the trail."

She lifted the cloth. The bleeding had slowed, so she pulled out some antiseptic to clean the wound. "What were you thinking about?"

Cal hesitated a moment, and then just decided to come out with it. "Do you think I should enlist like Uncle Mike did?"

"What?" She stopped cleaning the wound and stared at him. "Are you asking me if you should join the army?" He nodded, and her eyebrows arched in surprise. "Why would you even want to?"

He shrugged. "It was something Uncle Mike said."

"Uncle Mike thinks you should become a soldier?"

"No. He wants me to stay here and help Dad keep an eye on the family while he's gone."

Kat looked perplexed. "You aren't making any sense. If he wants you to stay here, why would you think you should join the army?"

Cal met her gaze. "Mostly it's because of Dad's dreams. It's hard to ignore what's coming. I mean if something is wrong, if it threatens all you believe to be good in this world, don't you have a responsibility to stand up and resist?"

Kat didn't answer right away. She rummaged through her kit for some gauze and tape, and then began dressing the wound. Finally she said, "I don't know if it's our responsibility to go running off to some foreign war. I mean, we're not even old enough yet."

Cal tried not to smile. "You do realize this won't be something we do together? Women don't go to war. It isn't safe for them."

"It isn't safe for men, either," she countered.

Cal shrugged. "I didn't make the rules. I'm just saying there's no such thing as women soldiers." Kat looked away then, and he understood her frustration, he really did. She didn't want anyone telling her what she could and couldn't do. But this was different. War was different.

"Kat," he said after a bit, "we're not little kids anymore. I've grown into a man, and you've grown into a woman. There are just naturally going to be things I can do that you can't, and vice versa. It's just the way it is."

Kat finished dressing his wound. She held his hand between hers for a few moments, and he felt calm, soothing waves of energy traveling through him. He sighed and let himself relax. Kat had more than a talent for patching people up; his sister had the healing touch.

After a bit, Kat pulled away and began putting her supplies back in her kit. She looked at him then, as she clicked the lid closed. "I feel like you're rushing this man and woman thing. Let's just be our old selves for a while longer. Let's finish high school, and make plans for college, and let's leave the questions about state of the world to the adults."

He didn't say yes, but he allowed that he could give himself the extra year to finish high school before making any big decisions. He watched her stow the kit back in her saddlebag and was about to go mount up when something caught his eye.

"Kat! Look here!" She came quickly. "Look," he pointed, and showed her the fresh cow tracks and cattle dung veering away from the wash. She started, studying the ground more closely.

"Horse tracks too," she pointed.

He didn't like that development. Had someone deliberately driven cattle away from the holding area? Whoever they were, based on the trail sign, it had been less than a day since they'd passed through here. He looked at Kat and then they both ran for their horses. The least likely scenario had just panned out. They were going to be the ones to find the missing cattle.

They started following this new trail, and eventually came to an infrequently used forest service road. There they found tire tracks belonging to some kind of truck and a mishmash of cattle and horse prints.

"Cal? What's going on here?"

He looked at his sister. "Nothing good, that's for sure. If I had to guess, I'd say someone figured out a way to load our cattle onto a truck, and then headed off with them down a well-hidden road." He tried to picture it. There were so many ways a plan like that could have gone wrong, but somehow whoever these rustlers were, they'd pulled it off.

"How many do you think they could load up?" Kat asked him.

"I have no idea. If I had to guess, four, maybe five, but I've never seen a truck that hauls cattle before."

"We're missing closer to twenty."

Cal nodded. "All of them breeding stock, and babies we haven't yet branded."

They looked at each other, the picture becoming clearer to them both. "We need to show Dad," she said.

"You go." Cal said. "I can keep scouting on ahead. It might be their truck can't move that fast with a load of cattle on a beaten-up road."

"Just be careful," she warned. "No heroics if you find them. Stay hidden."

Cal looked back at her. "Same goes for you. Don't stop for anything."

She turned her horse, urging the mare into a full gallop. She headed on a northwesterly track, a faster route back that ran perpendicular to Lee Mountain. Cal watched her go and then started down the old road.

He'd traveled along for about fifteen minutes before he realized something wasn't adding up. He stopped for a minute, pondering, and then turned his horse around to look more closely at the road he'd already traveled. It wasn't until he got back to the start that he realized what had been nagging at him; the horse tracks didn't continue along with the tire tracks. Instead, they veered back around, and headed out of the trees on a northwesterly track; parallel to the one his sister had just taken.

He pointed his horse north, ready to ride out after her, when for the second time in two days, he lost all sense of his body. He was flying again, like some kind of bird, circling around the back side of Rabbit Ears. What he saw in a boulder field far below sent him crashing back into his body, and spurring on Kaibab like there was no tomorrow.

Chapter 33

On its front side, Rabbit Ears was an impressive red rock formation. Massive sandstone pillars rose so high, it seemed like they might just reach heaven. On the backside, however, it had a very different aspect. It was cracked and fragmented. Large portions of it had broken off ages ago, sending gigantic boulders crashing down into the valley below. Kat was approaching a field of these long-lost pieces of Rabbit Ears, when she saw smoke and smelled fire nearby. She slowed Storm to a walk. It was springtime; a dry, windy season in the desert, and even the smallest fire could quickly become dangerous. She turned Storm toward the smoke.

When she got a little closer she began hearing voices. That made her pause. Who in heaven's name would be stupid enough to light a fire out here? She tied Storm up to an old mesquite tree, and then silently made her way toward the voices. When she got close enough, she could see three men nestled inside a circle of the massive boulders, all sitting around a small cook fire. Carefully, she tucked herself into the shadowed crevice of one of the giant rocks to get a closer look. She saw a man with a big red beard and sweat-stained clothing boiling coffee. Another man, with greasy blonde hair and equally filthy clothing, was heating up a can of beans. A third man was counting out a wad of bills. He was as filthy as the others, but he alone looked up as she spied on them, as if he could sense her hiding nearby. Kat shuddered, not liking the glimpse she caught of his cold, calculating, pale blue eyes.

"There's fifty clams here for each of us," Mean Eyes declared. "Not a bad week's work."

Greasy Hair looked up from his beans. "I wonder how that cowboy plans to sell those cattle."

Mean Eyes shrugged. "Not our problem."

"He don't have to sell 'em." Red Beard said. "He could breed himself a whole new herd; put his own brand on 'em. Nobody'd know."

The other two nodded their agreement, while Red Beard poured the coffee into tin mugs. Greasy Hair stuck a filthy finger into the beans, stirring things around a bit. Then he brought the finger to his lips and sucked it clean. "Well, it was good work while it lasted," he commented. "Pretty clever, the way he rigged that truck up."

"Yep," Mean Eyes agreed. "Clever enough to make old cowboys like us obsolete before long."

Kat heard a hawk cry overhead, and realized she'd been here long enough. She needed to find her father and Uncle Mike. Silently she backed away from the men and their cook fire. She could feel her heart pounding. She'd never met anyone who'd deliberately steal from a neighbor. But of course, these men weren't neighbors. They were drifters, and apparently only one part of a bigger outfit. Carefully, she continued her slow retreat. When she felt she had gone far enough from the boulder field, she turned to make her way silently back to Storm. To her horror, she felt her feet slide out from under her on some loose shale. She went down with a loud thump, and the crackle of desert brush beneath her rump.

"What was that?!" Mean Eyes was up instantly, and heading toward her.

With no more thought of stealth, Kat scrambled up and started to run.

"Someone's spotted us!" Mean Eyes yelled. "Get him!" All three men started after her, and she ran as fast as she could, slipping and sliding down the loose rock toward her horse. The men were close behind her, as she hastily untied Storm from the tree. She leapt into the saddle and spurred the mare into a full gallop. Kat's hat blew off and her braid came loose, as Storm sensed her need and ran like the wind across the valley and towards the ridge.

"It's a woman!" One of the men yelled in surprise.

"Don't just stand there!" Mean Eyes roared. "Get the horses!"

Storm was running full-out towards their ranch, but the men were riding stallions, and were excellent riders. It wasn't long before Kat heard the pounding of hooves on the trail behind her. She bent low in the saddle and urged even more out of her mare. Storm gave everything she had, but the leader of this small gang was gaining on her. Kat pulled out her rifle, turned, and fired off a shot, but it was hard to aim from the saddle of a galloping horse. The bullet missed Mean Eyes and hit a tree. She saw him snarl at her, urging more speed on his stallion. Within moments he was alongside her. His arm wrapped around her waist, hard and unyielding, and she lost her rifle as she struggled to free herself from his grip. With a final sudden motion, he yanked her off her mount and onto his. Kat screamed in fear and frustration. Terrified, Storm kept running, and Kat began to understand just how very stupid she had been.

Red Beard and Greasy Hair pulled up beside Mean Eyes. Greasy Hair stared at her slack-jawed and Red Beard whistled.

Mean Eyes dismounted pulling her along with him. "Who are you?" he demanded, spinning Kat around to face him. His pale eyes widened slightly as he got a good look at her face. "It's McKenna's girl!" he exclaimed.

"I'd heard that half-breed had himself a beautiful daughter." Greasy Hair brought his face up close to hers, studying her with interest. The smell of his pungent breath was sickening.

"Well, she sure is pretty enough!" Red Beard said.

Greasy Hair reached out, fingering a lock of her hair. He swallowed hard, and then said, "Just look at that, will you? It's black as a raven's, and hanging all the way down to her waist."

"So what now, Boss?" Red Beard asked.

Mean Eyes scowled. "Well, we can't let her go. She knows too much."

"What a shame," Red Beard said. "She's such a pretty little thing."

Mean Eyes' grinned. "Well, I ain't sayin' we can't have ourselves a bit of fun before we get rid of her."

Kat felt a wave of nausea rise in her stomach, but she forced it down. She wasn't anywhere near ready to give up. The rifle was gone, but she had her knife. It was in her boot, easy to access if she was fast enough. She used the nausea to her advantage, and bent over double, clasping her middle. "I think I'm going to be sick," she said and sank to her knees. The men didn't stop her. In a flash she had the knife, and rose up slashing at Mean Eyes. She was fast, but his reflexes were faster, and he raised an arm to block the blade plunging toward his neck. She felt the knife sink into flesh, but it was his forearm, not a fatal wound. She could see immediately all she'd done was make Mean Eyes very, very angry.

"You bitch!" He swung his bloodied arm at her, hitting her hard in the face. The blow knocked her to the ground. She still held her knife, and she slashed again at him, as he clambered on top of her. This time he caught her wrist, slamming her hand down hard on the ground. She didn't let go of the knife, and he did it again with more force. Kat screamed as felt a sharp pain and heard the sound of bone cracking. The knife fell from her fingers.

Mean Eyes picked the knife up off the ground, and looked at her, his pale eyes furious. "You like to play with knives?" he taunted.

Kat saw the knife plunging toward her, and she screamed again, certain it was the last sound she would ever make. Instead the knife slit open her shirt, and cut into the skin between her breasts. A line of blood welled up from the top of her sternum down to her stomach. Around her, the men grew still and silent. Every last one of them stared at the sight of her laid open, red blood running down white flesh. Kat looked at Mean Eyes still sitting astride her. His first move shocked her. He buried his face between her breasts and began nuzzling and sucking on her nipples. His face and hair became covered with her blood. His sweaty skin sharply stung her cut flesh, and the stink of him was enough to make her gag. The urge to run overwhelmed her. She began bucking underneath him, trying to shake him off.

He sat up and laughed with her blood streaked all over his face. "Look how bad she wants it, boys!" Then he pointed at Greasy Hair. "Leroy, go get me some rope from my saddle bag." Leroy wandered off to a thicket of trees where their horses had wandered to graze.

Red Beard came up and grabbed her wrists. "I'll just hold her down for you, boss."

The pain made her cry out, and her vision blurred as he pressed down on her broken bones. Mean Eyes smiled. With his filthy hands, he tore off the rest of her shirt, and then started fondling her breasts again. His mouth came down on hers, his bad breath and body odor forcing her senses to return and take note of every nauseating detail of his body. She tried to struggle again, but Red Beard held her firmly, pressing her broken wrist harder into the ground. She gasped from the pain, nearly blacking out. She was still seeing stars when Mean Eyes pulled her jeans and panties down around her ankles.

He sighed when he saw her naked on the ground before him. "I think I may have just died and gone to heaven."

Kat couldn't think straight, couldn't register anything except for this one horribly foul man standing over her, loosening his pants. Hot tears welled up in her eyes.

"You're not dead yet, mister, but you're about to be."

Mean Eyes started at the sound of Cal's voice. Through a haze of pain, Kat turned her head and saw her brother standing near the copse

185

of trees; his rifle cocked and ready to blow Mean Eyes to Kingdom Come.

Cal signaled with his head to Red Beard. "Let go of her and move away or I'll kill him now." His face was grim, and the tone in his voice left no doubt he meant what he said.

Still, Red Beard hesitated, and Mean Eyes snarled at him. "Do it!"

Red Beard released his painful hold on her, and Kat quickly rolled away, scooting toward her brother, her pants still wrapped around her ankles. She found her knife as she scrambled through the desert brush, grabbing it up with her unbroken hand. As she got closer to Cal, she noticed Greasy Hair lying on the ground, his throat slit. Cal had killed a man to save her.

"Pull your pants up, Kat," Cal said, as he gestured with the rifle to direct Red Beard over alongside Mean Eyes.

Kat was shaking and bleeding, and her right hand screamed in pain, but still she tried to lift her pants back over her hips. The effort made her so sick and woozy, she collapsed with a small moan. Cal looked down at her, his face stricken. That was all it took for both men to make a run for their rifles. Cal took a shot at Red Beard, winging him. The man screamed and fell, just as Mean Eyes reached his weapon.

Cal was rapidly reloading, but not fast enough. Kat could think of only one thing to do. She stood, placing herself between Mean Eyes and her brother. By the time she was upright, Mean Eyes had cocked and aimed his rifle. He lowered his weapon for a split second, when he saw her blocking his intended target. He took notice of her nakedness, and the knife she held tightly in her left hand. He winked at her as he raised his rifle once again, and aimed right for her heart. She heard a shot ring out, waited to feel the impact on her body. Instead she watched with surprise as Mean Eyes crumpled at the knees, then fell face down in the red dirt, his blood slowly dampening the earth beneath him.

Kat was still trying to figure out how had Cal gotten that shot in time, when a big black dog came charging into the clearing. It snarled and bared its teeth at Red Beard, who hesitated in another attempt to reach for his gun.

."Hold it right there, Mister." Cal said, pointing his rifle at the man. Red Beard's good hand dropped to his side. It was then Kat realized the angry dog was Piglet, and it wasn't Cal who had killed Mean Eyes. She looked up and saw her dad and Uncle Michael thundering toward her on horseback. It seemed too good to be true. With her uninjured hand, she touched her chest right where Mean Eyes had aimed. There was no bullet hole, but still her hand came away wet and sticky. She made the mistake of looking down. Her blood was everywhere, and she sank to her knees, just as her father jumped down off his horse and ran to her. She wanted to run to him as well, but instead she toppled over and her world went black.

Chapter 34

Cal kept his gun trained on the bearded man while Uncle Mike bandaged the outlaw, and then tied him securely to a nearby tree. A low-throated growl let the man know that Piglet was watching him, too. When it was done, Cal lowered his rifle, looking over at his sister lying on the ground, pale and still. Their dad was staunching the bleeding from the long knife wound down her chest. Kat was going to need a lot of stitches.

Cal closed his eyes and dropped his gun. He'd really messed up. They should have stuck together. He groaned, dropping to his knees, only to come face to face with the man he'd killed. A thick pool of blood haloed the man's head, and a red gash gaped across his throat. Cal felt the bile rise in his throat, and then he began to vomit.

Uncle Mike came to his side and held him steady while he emptied his guts out. At last Cal stopped retching, sat back on his heels and wiped his mouth. Uncle Mike handed him a canteen of water. Cal took a swig and spat out the sour taste. Then he took another and swallowed, letting the water soothe the burning down his throat.

"The worst is over," Uncle Mike assured him.

Cal looked over at his Uncle, and then burst into tears. It was horrifying, crying in front of Uncle Mike, but he just couldn't stop.

Uncle Mike pulled him close. "It's best just to let it all out," he said matter-of-factly.

When Cal was finally able to pull himself together, he looked back over at his sister. His dad was still bent over her, bandaging her up carefully. Cal closed his eyes, taking in a shaky breath. "It's my fault she's laying there," he said.

Uncle Mike shook his head. "You're the reason she's still alive." Uncle Mike stared pointedly at the dead man beside them, and then over at the wounded man tied to a tree.

Cal looked over at the other dead man; the one Uncle Mike had killed. Cal had dragged the body into the thicket, so his carcass wouldn't be anywhere near Kat while their dad tended her wounds. "She stood up to that bastard." Cal said, his voice shaking. "She was going to take a bullet for me."

"She was buying you time," Uncle Mike agreed. "And it worked. The moment that rustler hesitated, he was a dead man. If I hadn't taken the shot, you would have."

Cal shook his head again. "I messed up. She should never have been alone when she ran into these men."

Uncle Mike was quiet a moment then said, "Why don't you tell me exactly what happened."

So Cal told him everything, how they found the trail of the missing cattle, and then the tire tracks along the seldom-used forest service road. He explained the logic of why they decided to separate, and then how he'd turned abruptly around when he'd found the horse tracks heading off in the same direction Kat had taken. The only thing he didn't mention was the part about his vision of being a hawk.

Uncle Mike listened to it all before commenting. "Cal, if you'd stayed together, wouldn't you both have returned to the ranch the same way Kat took today?"

"Probably," Cal said. "It was the quickest way back."

"So you'd have both run into the cattle rustlers at the same time, wouldn't you? There still would have been trouble."

"Maybe," Cal allowed, "but maybe one of us would have had the sense to ignore the campfire, and just get home with the news. They might never have known we were close by."

Uncle Mike looked at him curiously. "Is that what happened?"

"Yeah," Cal said.

Uncle Mike studied him with interest. "Cal, you guys were separated at this point, right?"

Cal nodded.

"So how could you possibly know she stopped to investigate the campfire?"

Cal sighed, realizing he was going to have to talk about the weird stuff after all. He took a deep breath, and then just let the rest of the story come out. "I saw it in a vision," he said. "I felt like I was bird flying overhead, and I could see her. I saw the whole thing, from the moment she got off her horse to the moment the rustlers realized they'd been spied upon."

Uncle Mike studied him a moment, and then sat back, a hint of a smile on his lips. "And you think that sounds crazy to me?"

Cal stared at him, "Doesn't it?"

Uncle Mike cocked an eyebrow. "You do realize I was practically raised by a woman with supernatural healing powers? I know there's some spooky blood on your side of the family, and I respect it. That's why when your dad couldn't shake the feeling something bad was going to happen, I understood we needed to turn around."

Cal looked up at him. "So that's why you showed up when you did."

Uncle Mike nodded, then said, "Cal, do you want to know what I saw when I rode over that ridge today?"

"What?"

"I saw my nephew holding two outlaws at gunpoint, a third one dead. It was a bad situation, but you did what was needed to protect your sister." He paused, but when Cal stayed silent he spoke again. "Maybe you and Kat should have stayed together, but whatever decision you made at the start of your day, you were very brave when it counted most, and I'm extremely proud of you."

Cal looked at him in disbelief. "I nearly wet my pants with fear, and you just saw me cry like a baby."

Uncle Mike smiled, "Trust me, I've seen much worse. Brave doesn't mean you aren't scared. Brave means you are scared and you come through anyway." He put his arm around Cal, and they sat for a minute quietly watching Sam work on his daughter.

Cal was the first to turn away. "Do you think she'll be okay?"

Uncle Mike nodded. "Those men hurt her badly, but her injuries aren't life threatening."

"So she'll heal?"

Uncle Mike turned to him. "How can she not? Look who she's got patching her back together." He paused for a moment and then added, "Do you know what they used to call your father when we served during the Great War?"

Cal shook his head, and Uncle Mike continued. "They nicknamed him the Magician. It was the doctors who started it. No other medic did a better job stabilizing the wounded than your dad. The men he helped would often talk about how his very touch had felt healing to them. The doctors started saying he had magic hands, and from there it wasn't long before someone called him a magician, and it stuck."

Cal smiled a little. "He never told me that story."

Uncle Mike took a deep breath. "Well, he doesn't like to talk about it much." Uncle Mike looked over at the surviving cattle rustler. "Cal, can you keep an eye on that guy for me?"

Cal nodded. "What are you going to do?"

"I'm going to ride back to the ranch and get the truck so we can get Kat home. I also need to send someone out to fetch the sheriff. We got to get this guy taken into custody, and if what you suspect is true, someone out there is still trying to get away with our cattle. We're going to need some help with that as well."

"Go," Cal said, and he picked up his rifle. "I got this."

Chapter 35

Cal sat by his sister's bedside. She was sleeping now. Dad had given her something before he'd stitched her up. He'd told Cal it might be a while before she woke, and had suggested Cal might try and rest a bit too, but Cal had stayed by her side, just wanting to be near her, content to watch her breathe. He'd come very close to losing her today. You'd never know that just underneath that clean, white nightgown, she was sewn up from her sternum to her belly. She looked better now than she had lying on the desert floor. That wasn't to say she looked great. Her hair, though tied back, was still matted with dirt and blood. Her right hand was in a splint, and her left eye was bruised and swollen shut from where the rustler had hit her across the face.

Cal thought about the man he'd killed today. He understood he no longer was the same boy he'd been when he got up this morning. One moment that man had been alive, shocked to see his own blood pumping out onto the ground. He had struggled as Cal restrained him. Cal had felt the man grow weak in his arms, and had heard man's final breath. At some point, Cal realized, he'd have to come to terms with that, but not now. Now he wanted to sit here, watching the rise and fall of Kat's chest, and just be grateful for it.

The door opened and his grandma came into the room carrying a pot of Hopi tea. "She's still sleeping," Cal said.

"This tea is for you." His grandma poured a cup and handed it to him. Then she sat down beside him, and poured one for herself. They sat together, quietly sipping. She was studying him thoughtfully, and Cal didn't shy from her scrutiny. At last she said, "The sheriff's here. They're making plans to look for the missing cattle. I told them to wait and let me talk to you first."

It took a moment for Cal to realize what she was going to ask him. He set down his cup. "I don't know how I did it," he said. "It's not like I can just say 'show me the cattle,' and expect to have a vision."

His grandma patted his hand reassuringly. "No, I realize that. In time you will be able to control it, but meanwhile, I could help you."

"Let her, Cal." Kat's voice was a scratchy whisper.

Both he and Grandma looked down at her, surprised to see her awake. Kat tried to sit up, grimacing from the pain. Immediately

Grandma was at her side, helping to gently prop her up against some pillows. "Take it slow," Grandma cautioned.

Kat noticed Cal's cup of tea. "Can I have a sip of that?"

Grandma handed her the cup she'd been drinking from. "Take mine."

Kat took a few sips. "Thanks." She took several more swallows. "My throat just feels so raw."

It was raw from her screams. Cal doubted he could ever forget the sound of them. He knew then that he'd make the rest of that rustler gang pay for the harm done to his family today. "Grandma," he said, "Show me what to do. I want to try."

Cha'risa took his hand, squeezing it, and smiled approvingly. "This won't be hard at all," she promised. "Just close your eyes and follow the sound of my voice." He shut his eyes, ready for her direction. "Breathe deep," she said. "With each inhalation feel yourself expand, and when you exhale, let go. Let your body and your mind relax."

As he breathed, she began to hum, and he followed the sound of her voice. The melody snaked around him, urging him along its own path. Almost immediately, an image of the forest service road came to his mind. He could see the rutted path with the layered on tire tracks, and began to imagine himself walking alongside it. With each step, he felt the melody encouraging him to feel lighter, see farther. He relaxed even more deeply, allowing this impulse to sweep him up and carry him into the air. Just like that, he was flying again.

His grandmother had stopped humming, but it didn't matter now. He was already one with the bird, and his vantage point was climbing. The tracks left the forest service road, and joined up with the old Black Canyon stagecoach road, traveling along the southern end of the Bradshaw Mountains. The tracks entered the foothills, veered off of an old roadway, and then into a remote canyon. There, tucked far away from any surrounding civilization, was an impromptu holding pen filled with cattle.

He circled around to get a better look. There was a small cattle tank filled with water inside the pen. Two large trucks were parked nearby, next to a rough campsite, where a couple of men were sitting, boiling coffee over a fire. Cal swooped down close enough to get a good look at the herd. He could clearly make out the C & M brand on some of the cattle, and even noticed brands from some of the neighboring ranches.

With a gasp, he abruptly found himself back in his sister's bedroom, his body once again feeling quite earthbound. His sister locked eyes with him and he grinned. "I saw them!" He knelt, taking her good hand. "We did it, Kat! We found our missing cattle and then some!"

"Well, what are you waiting for?" Grandma prodded. "Go tell Grandpa and your dad where they are."

Chapter 36

Once word spread of the cattle rustlers and the attack on Kat, the house swelled with people. Auntie Branna and Uncle Eli drove down from Flagstaff, arriving right around the time the sheriff and his men showed up from Prescott. The news must have spread quickly around the valley as well, because many of the local ranchers started showing up, ready to help. From her bedroom, Kat could feel their presence and hear their outrage. They were angry about the cattle, but they were incensed about what had happened to her. She couldn't face their outrage or their pity just yet, so she kept to her room.

Her mom stopped by in the middle of the gathering, offering Kat some soup, but Kat told her she just wanted to sleep. And so she had, for several hours. The setting rays of the sun, piercing through her window, finally woke her. She'd slept away an entire afternoon.

The men were long gone following Cal's lead, and the house was much quieter now. Kat decided she had had enough of lying around. She eased out of bed. There wasn't much that didn't hurt, but she persevered. She understood the best way back to the business of living was to get on her feet, and take it one step at a time.

Getting her body moving was one thing; getting her mind to stop churning was quite another. Her thoughts kept circling back to the attack. She had assumed that with the protection of her family, little could harm her. She had assumed most people were decent and good, but today she'd learned you couldn't assume anything. There were people out there who would enjoy hurting her. She'd learned that you didn't have to be that far from home for someone like that to cross your path. She'd learned that in no time at all her world could change from a safe, secure existence to one where she didn't exist at all. What she was going to do with all that new knowledge, she didn't yet know. She decided, much like putting one foot in front of the other, it was best to focus for now only on the present.

When she got to the kitchen, Kat could see her mom sitting at the table. Grandma was sitting on one side of her, Auntie Branna on the other, and Piglet lay at their feet. Her mom's head was resting on Grandma's shoulder, and all three were staring out the window, as twilight filled the room with a rosy glow. None of them noticed Kat, until Piglet began thumping her tail loudly against the floor.

"Kat!" Her mom was out of her chair in an instant, searching Kat's face with red-rimmed eyes. "How are you feeling?"

There was no easy answer to that question, so Kat just said, "I'm fine. I just needed to move around a bit." To avoid any closer scrutiny, Kat bent down to pet Piglet, but even that proved to be painful. Suddenly, even petting the dog was a multi-step process. Piglet, oblivious to her struggles, stretched out fully, anticipating a good belly rub. That made Kat smile. This was the same dog that'd charged Red Beard this morning with teeth bared. "Piglet the Brave," she murmured, and then used her left hand to oblige Pig with as good a tummy rub as she could manage. Kat glanced back up at her mom. "Did Dad tell you what she did?"

"He told me all of it," her mom said, unable to meet Kat's eyes. Then she inhaled deeply, straightened her shoulders, and looked back up to face her daughter. "What can I get for you, some tea perhaps, or soup?"

"I am a little hungry," Kat admitted.

"Good! That's real good. Soup it is."

"I can make a corned beef sandwich to go with that," Auntie Branna offered.

"That sounds good to me, too" Kat said. "I'll be right back. I'm just going to visit the outhouse before I eat."

Her mom hesitated. "Maybe I should go with you."

"I'll be fine," Kat insisted, and left before any of them could voice more concerns. When she entered the yard, Lissie saw her and came running up.

"Finally you're awake! Nobody would let me see you!"

"I'm just on my way to the outhouse."

"Oh, I have to go too. I'll go with you." The family privy was a two-seater, and the girls were used to sitting there together. Usually Kat didn't mind the company, but Lissie was often chatty on the potty, and Kat didn't feel like talking about what had happened, most especially not with Lissie. How did you explain such a shameful attack to a ten year old? She lifted her nightgown with her good hand, and then realized she couldn't use her broken hand to pull down her panties.

"You need some help?"

Kat looked at her sister. "I can do it." She shifted her nightgown to her injured side, freeing up her functioning hand. Lissie shrugged and went about her business. She was on and off the seat before Kat even managed to get her panties down. When Kat finally sat down, Lissie hovered nearby, and it was obvious she was just dying to talk.

At last Lissie ventured, "That's going to be some black eye."

"Yeah," Kat said, and then having finished, she stood and started the struggle all over again putting herself back together.

"Does it hurt?" Lissie went on, still fixated on Kat's eye.

Kat turned to her. "Lissie, I kind of have to focus here."

Lissie noticed her struggle with the underpants and then exclaimed, "Oh for crying out loud, just let me do it!" She yanked the panties back into place. "Come on," she said. "Let's go see what Mom has for supper."

"Soup and sandwiches," Kat said quietly, humbled at having to rely on her little sister for something as basic as the outhouse. Lissie must have sensed her discomfort, because she was quiet again as they walked through the yard. When they got to the back door, however, she turned and hugged Kat. "I'm glad you're okay."

The hug hurt a lot, but Kat tried not to let it show, managing instead to just say, "Thanks."

Lissie looked up at her smiling, oblivious she'd caused Kat any pain. "You and Cal sure showed those bad guys not to mess around with the McKennas!"

Kat wondered how on earth Lissie came up with that assessment, but then she did the math for herself. Mean Eyes and Greasy Hair were dead, Red Beard was in jail, and Cal knew where to go to find the rest of the cattle-rustling ring. She felt like crap, and couldn't even go to the privy without help, but Cal was unharmed and she would heal. She couldn't deny their scorecard looked a lot better than the rustlers. She ventured a smile. "I guess we did, didn't we?"

"You sure did!" Lissie crowed with delight.

Kat gave her sister a heartfelt, albeit less exuberant, one-handed hug, and then she opened the door and ushered Lissie in, blinking back tears from her eyes.

The kitchen was full when she entered. Grandma and Lettie were setting the table, Aunt Maddie and Aunt Ana were preparing toddler sized portions for Gabe and Leotie, Aunt Lena was helping Aunt Branna make a platter of corned beef sandwiches, and her mom was filling up a soup tureen to bring to the table. It shouldn't have surprised Kat to see them all there. It was supper time, after all, and everyone needed to eat, but she also knew they were there because they wanted to see her; to make sure for themselves that she was doing all right. That was a good thing, she reminded herself. It was better they saw her upright, not lying like some weakling in her bed.

Kat sipped at her soup. It felt warm and soothing on her throat. She focused on that, not paying much attention to the conversations around her. Little bits came through anyhow, the high-pitched voices of Gabe and Leotie expressing the wanting of this, the not wanting of that. At one point, Lissie reprimanded Lettie for feeding Piglet from the table. Usually Kat was the one doing the scolding, but today she was feeling generous toward Piglet.

"I'm thinking of putting some water up for a bath. What do you think?"

It took Kat a moment to realize her mom was talking to her. "I'm sorry. What?"

"I said, how about a bath? We can't get the wound wet, but we could wash your hair, and give you a good sponging down."

Kat touched her hair, and it struck her then just how much she needed to get clean. She wondered how hard she would have to scrub to wash away the feel of Mean Eye's rough hands. She swallowed back that thought; it wasn't safe to go there. Then she looked at her mom and nodded her assent.

Kat thought she was handling everything just fine. She'd helped clear the table, and get the water heated. Then she'd scoured herself clean using a sponge and the warm water from a tub that had both Gabe and Leotie in it. They splashed and giggled, more than happy to share their bath water with her. For a moment she was struck by a divide between herself and them. They believed they were safe. They trusted no harm would come to them. They didn't yet know the truth about safety was that it was an illusion.

Mom was getting another batch of water heated, and when it was ready, she called Kat over to the sink to have her hair washed. Kat left the squealing little ones, and went and bent her head over the basin. She felt the warm water flow over her head, and her mom's hands start working through all the stuck-in dirt and blood. But as the water began to run red all around her face, something clicked inside, and not in a good way. Her heart began to beat rapidly, erratically. She could feel the wrongness of its rhythm. Panicking, she pulled up suddenly, flinging water from her long, wet hair all over the kitchen.

"Kat, what is it?" Her mom looked at her, alarmed.

The edges of Kat's vision began to blacken. She panicked even more, her heart speeding up even faster. She wanted to get out of the kitchen, needed air, and she made a move for the door, but then her grandma was there. She felt the familiar arms enfold her, and Grandma's heat pierced through the layer of terror that now separated her from everyone else.

"I have you, Kat," Cha'risa said, and then Kat felt and heard the deep, resonating hum of her grandma's healing song. She latched onto it, following its flow as it pumped through the chambers of her heart, and sent therapeutic vibrations pulsing through her blood. Kat helped urge it along, encouraging its spread all through her. The panic began to lessen. On her next intake of air, she helped guide the healing toward her irregular pulse, willing it to become less erratic, encouraging it to slow.

"That's right," her grandma approved, "just breathe deep and join with me." Kat could still hear and feel the irregular heartbeat, but she was no longer so afraid. Then with a final heavy thud, her heart clicked back into rhythm, and Kat just lay there drained of all energy in her grandma's arms. "It's over now," Cha'risa said.

Kat looked at her, and then over at everyone in the room. They were all staring at her. The little ones were wide eyed and frightened. Kat turned from them all and groaned.

Cha'risa pulled her closer, wiping Kat's soapy, wet hair from her eyes. "You're alright," Grandma soothed. "The bad effects of the day just caught up with you."

Aunt Maddie plucked Gabe out of the tub, wrapping a towel around him. "Why don't we get these little ones ready for bed?"

Aunt Ana scooped up Leotie. "Good idea. Lettie, Lissie, you come with us."

Lissie began to object. "It's not my bedtime!"

Aunt Lena took her by the hand. "Let's you and I get Lettie ready for bed, and let Kat have a little quiet, okay?"

Lissie looked like she wanted to refuse, but her mom didn't give her the opportunity. "Lissie, don't argue, just go." Lissie looked once more at Kat and then nodded. Suddenly the room emptied out, until only her mom, grandma and Auntie Branna were left.

"Well, we can't just leave her dripping soap and water all down her face and backside," Auntie Branna commented.

"Kat?" her mom asked. "Do you think you'll be okay if we finish rinsing you off?"

Kat nodded. There wasn't really a choice. They had to get the soap out. She started to stand, but her knees were too wobbly. Immediately her mom was by her side, supporting her as they made their way back to the sink.

The water didn't run red anymore as they finished rinsing her hair, but Kat remained wary, wondering if at any moment her body would betray her again. They stripped off her soaked nightgown, and Auntie Branna ran off to get her a clean, dry one. Then her mom wrapped her in a big towel, sat her down in a kitchen chair, and began the long, arduous task of detangling all the snarls and mats in her hair.

Kat's mind wandered again, as it had so many times since the attack. Those men had beaten a message home today. She wasn't in control of her life. What she'd wanted had meant nothing to them. They'd planned to use her and dispose of her like they would a can of beans. The beans reminded her of Greasy Hair, and she remembered the way he'd swallowed hard when he touched her long locks. He'd said almost reverently, "as black as a raven's and down to her waist." Not even an hour later he was dead, lying in a pool of his own blood; his throat slit by Cal. She remembered staring up at Cal; the look on his face had been both determined and frightened. She'd done that. She'd taken the last of his childhood just as those men had taken hers.

Suddenly, Kat felt like she couldn't stand it, not the men, not her stupidity, and especially not her hair. "We should just cut it all off!" She cried out.

It took a moment for her mom to realize what she was saying. Her eyes grew wide.

"You want to cut your hair?"

"Yes, get rid of it! I don't want to be admired for it ever again!"

"Kat, you're upset right now. Maybe we should wait…"

"I don't want to wait! I just want it gone!"

Auntie Branna had just come back to the room, with the fresh nightgown, followed by the rest of her aunts. They all hesitated now, uncertain if they were intruding. Her mom looked up imploringly at Grandma Chari, unsure of what to do or say. Her grandma was the only one who didn't hesitate. She came and sat down beside Kat, and said with certainty. "You can't cut away who you are, Kat. Even with short hair you'll be a beautiful woman. That's just how you were made."

"But every time I look at my hair I'll see those men. I'll dredge up their every word, and touch, and smell. They wanted me dead!" Hot tears burned Kat's cheeks.

Her grandmother wasn't deterred. She moved closer, turning Kat's gaze to hers. "I'm not saying don't cut your hair, I'm saying don't do it in an act of anger or self-loathing. That's the wrong reason."

"So what's the right reason?" There was a part of Kat that really wanted to know, but part of her didn't believe there could be a right reason.

"Cut it as a way of letting go," Grandma said. "Cut it as a way to make room for something better."

"Oh." Kat sat up straight, searching her grandmother's face for more.

Cha'risa held Kat's gaze firmly in her own. "Life can be harsh and nothing is ever certain, but a few minutes ago, frightened as you were, you made a choice to make room for healing. You helped me set your heart back on course." Kat grasped at her grandma's words, trying hard to understand. Her grandma smiled. "Some part of you already knows there is power in letting go. When you cut your hair, choose to understand how to open to what's possible from here," she touched her heart, "and here as well," and then she pointed to her head.

With her eyes still locked on her grandma's, Kat nodded.

Her mom said, "I'll go get the shears." She rummaged briefly in one of her kitchen drawers, and then returned to the table carrying the scissors. "So," she said, taking in a deep breath. "First you tell me what you're letting go of, and then I'll cut."

Everyone gathered expectantly around Kat, and she looked at each one of them wondering, what she should say. Then suddenly it was obvious. She would finish what those rustlers had started, but on her own terms. For the first time since the attack she felt certain of herself. "I am cutting my hair," she said, "because it is time for me to let go of my childhood. I want to make room to become a woman, to know more clearly what I want, and who I want to be."

"Well said!" Auntie Branna exclaimed.

Her mom sniffed back a few tears. "Yes, indeed, it was." Then she gathered Kat's long hair into a ponytail and made the first cut.

As her mom worked all of Kat's aunts and her grandma made comments and suggestions, until at last, Auntie Ana handed Kat a mirror telling her to take a look. Kat stared at herself. Once her mom had decided to cut she'd been bold, and Kat's hair was cropped very short. It was a bouncy, tousled bob, a little unevenly cut, but it felt wonderfully lighter.

"I want my hair cut too!" Kat looked up at the sound of Lissie's voice. Her sister was standing by the entrance to the kitchen.

"I thought we told you to go to bed," Aunt Maddie scolded.

"No, you told me to put Lettie to bed, which I did. She's sound asleep now."

Ellie looked at her younger daughter. "You can stay, but we don't cut anyone's hair without a good reason."

Kat added, "You need to be able to say what you're letting go of, and what you're making room for."

Lissie didn't even hesitate. "Well, that's easy. I'm making room so I can be more like Kat. She's the bravest girl I know. When I grow up I want to be just like her!"

There was some chuckling from her aunts, but Kat just stood there staring. She'd never stopped to consider how much her little sister looked up to her, and she found it touched her deeply. She got up, making room for Lissie on the cutting chair. Then their mom gathered up all of Lissie's thick, auburn hair and began to work. She cut it in a style very similar to Kat's, and Lissie was thrilled when she looked in the mirror. Kat leaned in to stare at their reflection together.

Lissie smiled. "We look swell, don't you think?"

"A couple of glamour girls," Kat agreed.

Lissie laughed and no sooner got out of the chair, when their grandma sat down.

"You too?" Ellie asked.

Kat looked at her grandmother, perplexed. "Grandma, what can you possibly need to let go of?"

A small, regretful smile tugged at the corners of Cha'risa's lips. "I need to let go of some very wrong-headed beliefs."

"Whatever are you talking about?" Ellie asked.

"I'm talking about my grandchildren, whom I love with all my heart. I'm sorry for things I didn't do, but should have."

Ellie stared at her in disbelief. "How can you have regrets? You've been an amazing grandmother."

202

Kat nodded, and Lissie took her grandma's hand.

Cha'risa gently cupped Lissie's cheek. Then she looked up, deliberately making eye contact with everyone in the room. "Growing up among the Hopi, I was taught a child of a mixed marriage belongs to the mother's tribe, not the father's. For years I have not forgotten that you, Ellie, are Irish American, or that Lena is Havasupai, or that Ana is of Navajo descent. I didn't step in to teach my grandchildren the things I know, because I thought they should learn the ways of their mothers. I didn't understand until today how big a mistake that was. Now I see I must make room to look beyond my traditional beliefs. Cal has manifested shamanistic gifts, and he will need help to understand them. And for a long time I have known Kat has inherited the gift of healing from my side of the family. She has a right to learn what it means to be a medicine woman." Cha'risa fixed her gaze on Kat. "If you wish it, I will teach you everything I know."

Kat knelt at her grandma's side. "Do you really think I could be a medicine woman?"

Her grandma took her hand and smiled at her. "You've already made a good start. Wouldn't you like to know more?" Kat nodded. "Good," Cha'risa patted her hand, and then let it go. "Let's cut my hair then, and make room for your education to begin." She turned then to Ellie. "Make it look good."

Ellie saluted, "Aye, aye, captain!" Then she got to work, cutting the silver ponytail off at the nape of the neck. Cha'risa's hair was so thick, it was harder to style. The hair itself dictated the lines of the cut, charting its own design, reflecting the free spirited nature of the woman herself.

When they were done, Ana stepped up to the chair and said, "I want to cut my hair, too."

Ellie had just stooped down to pick up the three ponytails from the floor. She placed them now on the table, one black, one dark red, and one silver. "You know the price for a cut in this kitchen," she said.

"What are you letting go of?" Aunt Lena prompted.

"We've set something in motion here," Ana answered. "We're making an effort to clear away harmful energies, and prepare the way for new and better things. I want to be part of that. I want to help cut away the harm done this day so Kat and Cal can fully heal."

As Ana sat down, the rest of the aunts showed their solidarity by lining up behind the chair. Soon Ana's ponytail was laid on the table.

Ellie, having learned her lesson with Cha'risa's thick hair, had kept the hair a little longer, and the styling minimal.

Kat listened as one by one all of her aunts sat down in the chair. They spoke of what they were letting go of, what they wished to make way for, and every sentiment was a prayer for Kat to heal and rise above the terrors of this day. The one exception was Aunt Maddie. Maddie had been last in line, and she'd had a lot of time to think about what she wanted to say. As Kat listened, she found perhaps the best advice yet on how to stay strong.

"We created a ceremony today to protect Kat and Cal from the after-effects of a very violent morning." Maddie took a steadying breath, but her voice still trembled from holding back tears. "Mike killed a man today. He needs that protection too. Maybe he needs it even more, because he's a soldier and it's not the first time he's killed somebody. Soon he'll be leaving for a part of the world that's on the brink of war. When I cut my hair I'm not only cutting away harmful energies, I'm also offering up a precious remnant of many fine years of loving this man. If you are all willing, I would like to make a talisman of our love and protection for Mike by twining together some hair from each of our severed pony tails. It will be something we can give him to keep him safe when he's away."

When Maddie stopped speaking, Ellie threw her arms around her, and the two of them just stood there crying. Kat felt a lump form in her throat as she watched. Finally Ellie straightened up, drew in a shaky breath, and sat Maddie in the chair.

Kat watched the amber brown ponytail fall. It hit the ground with a light thud, but for Kat it resounded through her like a bell. Aunt Maddie had gotten to the heart of this ceremony. The key to staying strong was to care about others, and to do your best to protect them. Kat realized her grandmother must have understood this when she offered Kat something she could devote her life to. A healer was also a protector.

When Aunt Maddie's hair was finished, she looked in the mirror, surprised to see that the short cut, despite its imperfections, actually suited her well. Ellie laid the light brown ponytail next to the others on the table, and then looked up. "Okay, who's going to do my hair?"

"I'll do it." A man's voice announced. Every woman in the room was startled when the kitchen door opened. Kat saw her dad standing at the threshold. Just behind him, all of the rest of their men crowded to get a look inside.

Ellie brought her hand to her heart to calm her racing pulse. "You scared me half to death!" And then, "How long have you been standing there?"

Sam walked up to her, and gave her a kiss. "Long enough," he said. He looked at all the women then, studying their new haircuts. "I can't promise to do as good a job as you, but I can cut clean and straight, and then you can fill in the fancier bits if you're willing."

She nodded, handing him the scissors as Mike, Ahote, Moqui, Eli, Cal, Sean and Eddie all piled into the room. For a moment the room was in chaos, as men went to kiss their wives and admire Ellie's handiwork. Sean and Eddie headed straight for a platter of corned beef sandwiches and dove in like a couple of starving men.

Ellie raised her voice and silenced the room. "You men have all arrived for the last cut of the day, the end of a ceremony we began to bring healing and protection to this family. We had one rule when we took the chair; we needed to be able to say what we were making room for in our lives. My reason for cutting my hair is to make room for all the love that is in my heart right now. This family is so full of people who are decent, compassionate and kind." She turned to Kat and Cal. "Today you saw the worst side of human nature, but you should never forget where you come from, or how you've been raised. You are loved by the finest people I have ever known."

She took the seat then, and Kat watched as her dad pulled her mom's hair back into a ponytail. Then he leaned down and kissed the nape of her neck. Her mom relaxed into the kiss with a happy sigh. He made the first big cut with the precision of a man who is comfortable relying on his hands. Kat watched her parents with tears in her eyes. Today had terrified her, but she wouldn't let it define her. She had better examples than Mean Eyes and his rustlers to help remind her just what a man could be.

Cal came to sit beside his sisters. "We have another twin," Cal joked when he saw Kat and Lissie's identical haircuts. He offered each of them a molasses cookie he'd snagged from a tray Auntie Branna had brought out. He studied their short hair again. "It suits you guys," he decided.

Kat touched her close-cropped curls. "Thanks."

"Did you get the rest of the bad guys?" Lissie was eager to know.

Cal grinned. "We did. They should all be enjoying some quality time at the county jail by now."

"And the cattle?" Kat asked.

"Safe for the night," Cal assured her. "The sheriff left some men to watch over them until we can bring them all home."

They were quiet for a few moments; eating the cookies and watching Aunt Maddie braid a bracelet for Uncle Mike from the locks of all their hair. "Maybe when your wrist is healed you can make me one of those," Cal suggested.

Kat smiled. "Oh, I think I know a way to make that happen right now. What do you think, Amaryliss, could you help me make one of those bracelets for Cal?"

A wide grin spread over Lissie's face. "Sure!" She ran over to the table and started collecting strands from each ponytail.

Kat watched her for a moment, and then turned back to Cal. "I guess we made a few mistakes today, but you know what, Cal? I'm also kind of proud of us."

He turned to face her, nodding his agreement. "We saved each other."

She took his hand with her good one. "We did." She paused a moment and then added, "Thank you for finding me."

He put his arm around her, drawing her close. "I will always find you, Kat." Lissie came back then with hair from all the ponytails. "I think we should make one for each of us," she announced. Kat and Cal nodded, and then pulled her into their close circle, bending their heads, working together to weave the strands of hair.

1945

Molasses Spice Cookies

Ingredients
3 cups all-purpose flour
1 1/2 teaspoons baking soda
1 teaspoon salt
2 teaspoons ground ginger
2 teaspoons ground cinnamon
1/2 teaspoon ground cloves
1 cup unsalted butter, (2 sticks), at room temperature
3/4 cup granulated sugar, plus additional for rolling
¾ cup dark brown sugar
½ cup molasses
2 large eggs, at room temperature

Directions
Preheat the oven to 350º F. Line two baking sheets with parchment paper.

Combine the flour, baking soda, salt, ginger, cinnamon, and cloves in a large bowl and whisk to combine.

In a large bowl, beat the butter, both sugars, and molasses with a wooden spoon until the mixture is fluffy and lighter in color. Add the eggs, one at a time and mixing each in well.

Add the dry ingredients in 2 or 3 batches, stirring each addition until just incorporated. Do not over mix. The dough will be sticky.

Chill the dough 30 minutes to firm it up.

Scoop the dough into balls about 1½" in diameter (about the size of ping pong balls). Roll the balls in sugar, then arrange them on the prepared pans, 6 per pan. Press each ball into a ¾" disk.

Bake for 10 minutes, rotating the pans halfway through the baking time. The cookies should be brown and have crackly tops. Let the cookies cool on the baking sheets until they're easy to remove, then transfer them to wire racks to finish cooling.

Makes about 24

Chapter 37

Kat woke up disoriented. The sounds were wrong. She had expected to hear the crashing South Pacific waves just beyond the canvas of her tent, but instead, she heard the wind moaning through pine trees, their branches knocking against the walls of a solidly built room. She tried to sit up to get a better look around, but a stab of pain in her left leg made her pause. It was only then she realized where she was. She was home, for the first time in over three years. The waves and the tent were just leftover memories of her time in Australia, Owi and Luzon. The South Pacific was far distant now. For her the war was over. She sat up more carefully; mindful now of her injury. Instantly, her grandmother awoke in the chair beside Kat's bed.

"Take it slow," Cha'risa cautioned.

"I'm fine," Kat assured her. "It was just an unsettling dream."

Cha'risa took her hand, and squeezed it tight. "Well, you're home now, and safe."

When Kat had come through the front door last night, she'd been exhausted by the long return journey. They'd put her directly to bed, and she remembered nothing after her head hit that pillow. But now she looked up at her grandmother, felt their hands clasped together, and for the first time in many days she felt immense relief. She'd missed her grandma so much over the past three years; but never as much as she had these past few months.

Her grandma's hand felt abnormally cold. Her touch usually had a warm, tingly feel, a side effect from her ever-present healing energy. Kat noted the chill in the room. The howling wind that had woken her had brought with it spitting snow that now pinged against the windowpanes. Kat was warm under a pile of blankets, but her grandma had fallen asleep in that chair without a single covering.

"Grandma, you shouldn't have let yourself get so cold!" Even as Kat chided her grandma, she started sending healing flows of her own through their clasped hands.

Her grandma stopped her abruptly. "None of that," she insisted. "You need to save your strength."

A smile teased at the corners of Kat's mouth. "Someone very wise once told me healing is like a flame; you can light another without extinguishing your own."

Cha'risa raised an eyebrow. "Are you throwing my teachings back at me?"

Kat's smile spread wide. "At least you know I was paying attention."

"Mom, I can watch her now. Why don't you go lie down?" Both women turned to find Sam standing in the doorway.

"Jesus, Mary and Joseph! Both of you stop your fussing!" Cha'risa dismissed them with a wave of her hand. "There'll be time to rest soon enough. Right now, I want to keep a close eye on my granddaughter, make sure this wound heals properly."

Kat watched as her dad approached the bedside. He pulled one of the blankets off the bed and wrapped it around Cha'risa. He wasn't going to argue, but he also wasn't going anywhere. He fully intended to keep an eye on both his mother and his daughter.

It had been Sam who'd come to San Francisco to meet the ship and bring Kat home. He'd taken good care of her on that long train ride, but now he just pulled up a chair and let his mother take the lead.

Cha'risa positioned the blanket around her shoulders like a shawl. "I was just going to inspect the wound," she said, "and then Kat was going to tell me about her dream."

"I was?" Kat didn't remember offering any such thing, but already her grandma and dad were lifting her nightgown, gently loosening the leg brace, and then removing the bandages over the wound on her thigh.

"It looks better than I thought it would," her dad commented. "The infection is nearly gone."

Her grandma focused her attention on cleaning the wound. "Looks like the medicine they gave her worked pretty well."

Kat's compound fracture had gotten infected on the voyage home, but while she'd been on the hospital ship, they'd given her injections of penicillin. She'd been making steady improvement ever since. She'd seen penicillin at work before, administered it herself to patients in need, but not many outside the military had access to the antibiotic. This was the first time her dad and Grandma had ever seen the drug work.

Her grandmother put a new dressing over the incision, and then her father helped re-fasten the brace. Kat understood their need to fuss over her. If she were in their position, she would be just as vigilant. The family had taken some hard knocks these past years; first Sean's death at Pearl Harbor, and then the news that Uncle Mike had gone missing during the Battle of Bataan. It felt good when you could finally use the gifts God had blessed you with to save what was left of your family.

She noticed her dad staring at her intently. "What?" she asked.

"I want to hear about your dream." He kept his tone light, but Kat knew it was already causing him to worry.

"It wasn't a nightmare," she assured him. "I dreamed of the vision I had; the one where I saw Uncle Mike."

Both her grandmother and father went utterly still, and then her father said, "I'd like to hear it."

"What difference does it make now?" Kat wanted to know.

"It's what started everything, isn't it?" her grandmother answered. "It might prove interesting to hear the details."

Just then, Ellie popped her head in the door, wearing her biggest smile. She was carrying a tray with a steaming pot of hot chocolate, a plate of fresh baked biscuits, and a bowl of homemade peach preserves.

"Hi Mom," Kat grinned. She'd missed that smile almost as much as she'd missed her mom's cooking.

"Thought you might be hungry," Ellie said. She placed the tray on Kat's nightstand and gave her daughter a gentle hug and a kiss. Cha'risa began pouring out four cups of cocoa. Sam pulled up a chair for his wife, and then together they divided up the biscuits and jam. Kat took a sip of the hot chocolate. This was officially her first taste of home-cooked food in three years, and she intended to savor the moment. Slowly, she dribbled a big dollop of the peach preserves onto the still-warm biscuit.

"Oh God," she sighed with pleasure at the first bite. There might be a winter storm outside, but right now she tasted the sun-warmed glow of summer. She was just about to take another bite when her mom asked, "What were you guys talking about when I came in?"

The food was so good; Kat had to think a moment before she remembered. "Oh," she said frowning. "Grandma and Dad want me to tell them about the dream I had."

"The dream about Mike," her dad elaborated.

Her mom had been just about to take a sip of cocoa, but she lowered her cup and looked at her daughter. "You mean the vision?"

Kat nodded, and Cha'risa added. "She dreamed it again last night. We thought it might be wise to hear if there were any new details."

Her mother's eyes sparked with avid interest. "I agree. Let's hear all of it, Kat, exactly how it happened."

It was useless to fight all three of them, and besides, Kat realized, they were right. It was important for them to hear the entire story. They might know the ending, but there were things they didn't know. She wanted them to understand what Cal had done for her, and maybe just as importantly, she wanted to tell them about Jack.

The jungle bore down on her with its relentless humidity and mud, but still she traveled through it with ease, moving on four legs, hitting the ground at a full and easy lope. She stopped by a river's edge and looked in. The distorted reflection of a big, black dog stared back at her. She knew from experience it was best to be completely at one with the animal, so she let herself merge with her spirit guide, and together they stepped into the river, swimming silently to the other side.

The dog climbed onto the embankment, shook the water from its coat, then cocked its ears and sniffed the air. There were men nearby, lots of them, and Kat could make out enough of their words to know what language they spoke. Her adrenalin started pumping, and the dog understood her fear. They moved quickly, hugging the tree line, making haste to leave the men's scent far behind.

The dog ran tirelessly. Soon the trees gave way to fields of tall cogon grass, and later to rice paddies. Her spirit guide didn't stop running until, at last, it came to a wide-open field. Peering out between tall stalks of grass, the dog stared fixedly across at a military encampment with wooden watchtowers and a high barbed wire fence. Despite all the military enforcements, its massive gate hung wide open.

The dog crossed the field, stopping cautiously at the gate to sniff around. The place smelled strongly of suffering and death, but there was another scent too, one that was familiar to them both. They crossed through the gate into a gray stillness. It seemed as if only shadows stirred here, but even so, the familiar scent lingered, and led them deeper into the compound. The dog passed by dozens of barracks, moving unerringly towards just one. Inside, a line of sleeping mats lay on the floor, all filled with indistinct figures, except for one. There a man lay who was clearly illuminated. The dog trotted up to this occupant, sat down on its haunches, and stared at the man's face. She wasn't sure if it was she or the dog who whimpered, but the noise woke the man and he opened his eyes. He didn't register surprise when he saw her; he just smiled weakly and whispered, "Kat."

With the uttering of her name, the dog disappeared, and Kat found herself back in her natural form, sitting beside Uncle Mike. She took his hand, not quite able to believe what she was seeing. It had been over three years since the family had received the news Uncle Mike was missing and presumed dead at the Battle of Bataan.

"You're alive," she whispered, and a few hot tears escaped her.

He had very little strength, but he tried to sit up. "Those better be happy tears," he said.

She laughed even as she cried, and then pulled him close, hugging him tight. "Dad never stopped believing," she told him. "He was certain he'd know if you were dead."

"Was he now?"

She nodded, but left the rest unsaid. Dad had never had a vision of Mike's death. He'd felt certain the ancestors would offer them a chance to say goodbye, just as they had when Sean had passed. Now it seemed her dad's reasoning had been sound. Uncle Mike was truly among the living, but just barely. He'd not been treated well. Dark circles ringed his sunken eyes, and his sallow skin was pulled taut, clearly displaying every bone.

He watched her study him, and then took in a deep breath, sighing heavily. "It's too bad I'll have to wake up from this dream."

"It's more than a dream," she assured him. "I really have found you."

"Don't mess with me, kiddo," he cautioned.

"I never would."

"Even so, dream Kat, what will you do next? You can't fly half way round the world to rescue me."

A small smile escaped her. "I'm not as far away as you think. I'm stationed on an island just off the coast of New Guinea."

He raised an eyebrow. "Really? You're a soldier?"

She laughed a little. "Not a soldier, a nurse. I'm assigned to one of the evac hospital units."

She could see the moment he started to believe. He tried to sit up straighter to get a better look at her, and she helped him. "We took back Leyte," she told him. "We have a foothold in the Philippines now; it won't be long before we take back Manila."

"I know."

"You know?" She was puzzled. He didn't sound at all excited.

"We hear rumors," Mike said. "The Japs don't intend to leave us behind for you to find, though."

She frowned. "What do you mean?"

"There are stories going around they're killing the POWs. They shipped all the ones who were healthy enough back to Japan. Those of us too sick to make the journey were left here in Luzon. It appears their plans for us won't include any happy reunions."

Kat was horrified, and then her mind started racing, looking for ways to stave off disaster. "Where exactly in Luzon are you?"

"I'm in Cabanatuan POW camp."

"How far is that from Manila?"

"It's about 60 miles north. But, Kat," Uncle Mike looked her straight in the eye, "Nothing you can do will change what's going to happen here."

Her face was grim. Her unit was packed and ready to go. Any day now they'd be sailing with the 7th Fleet, ready to take back Luzon. But while the 92nd evac hospital was scheduled to make that landing, it would be without her. The nurses were always separated out before a new offensive. And her uncle was right, the Japanese would be well aware when an army that size headed their way. If they were intent on killing the prisoners they'd have plenty of time to do it.

"You're alive, though," she mused out loud. "I wouldn't dream of you unless there was some purpose in finding you."

Uncle Mike gave her a weary smile. "Maybe it's as simple as a chance to say good-bye."

"No!" she exclaimed. But even as she denied it, she couldn't help thinking about Sean. Sean had been aware Dad was there with him at the end. He'd felt Dad's love, and Dad had said it had been enough so that Sean wasn't afraid when he passed over. Could this dream be the same, she wondered, a chance to comfort Uncle Mike as he lay dying?

"No," said firmly. She wouldn't accept that explanation. She wouldn't stop trying, not while there was still a chance. So she did what she always did when staring death in the face. She directed her healing sight deep within his body. She studied all his critical systems from the inside out, looking for something, anything that might have been missed before. "Aren't you taking quinine for the malaria?" she asked at last.

With a sad smile, he took her hand. "There haven't been any medications available for a while now. The Filipino resistance used to smuggle it in for us, but lately the Japanese have cracked down."

"But why?" Kat was aghast.

"They're getting desperate. The tide is turning against them; they're running short of supplies. Why would they waste precious resources on us, especially when they don't intend for us to live long enough to be rescued?"

Anger began to burn inside her. Uncle Mike was one of the bravest men she'd ever known. His life meant something, and yet they would kill him from neglect or worse, with no remorse.

"Kat," her uncle said, "I know you want to try and save me, but maybe we should just let this moment together be enough."

He was right, she realized, not to want to waste this moment. There would be time when the dream ended to search for options, but for now she rested her head on his chest, listening to his labored breathing, wanting to hear the reassuring beat of his heart. Uncle Mike wrapped his arms around her, holding her close.

"Do you want to know what I was dreaming of before you showed up?" he asked.

She looked up at him. "What?"

"Your mom. She was standing in the kitchen at the lodge, wearing an old apron of Esme's. She had on her oven mitts, and was just about to take a tray of molasses cookies out of the oven. I could smell them, Kat; I could almost feel them in my mouth, all warm and gooey, with a potent, gingery kick."

"Oh," she sighed, she could almost taste them herself. "That was a good dream."

"You're a better dream," he assured her, and tried to give her an encouraging squeeze, but his grasp was weak. His voice was rough when he spoke again. "I'm glad it's you who's come to be with me at the end." He started shuddering then, and Kat was quick to help him lie back down. She tried to make him more comfortable, but the trembling worsened, and soon his entire body was convulsing. Kat looked around for some kind of nursing tools, but there was nothing except the worn reed mat on the hard plank floor. Back on Owi, where she was stationed, she'd spent the last month helping to crate up every kind of medical supply imaginable. It would all be on its way here as soon as the fleet set sail. Help was coming, if she could just find a way to keep Uncle Mike alive long enough to be found.

She drew him close; enfolding him in her arms, and began to hum one of her grandmother's healing songs. Grandma had taught her that when you wanted to heal someone, you looked at what they could become, not just how they appeared. It was in those in-between spaces that you could move energy along pathways of healing.

She directed the soothing vibrations into his ravaged body, visualizing all Uncle Mike could be once more. She wished she could be with him in body, and not just spirit; and not for the first time, she wished with every fiber of her being to set sail with that fleet. After a while, Uncle Mike's trembling calmed. He began taking slow, even breaths, and his fluttering heart smoothed into rhythmic beats. He fell asleep as she held him, and for a long while she refused to let the dream end, uncertain what his future would hold, unwilling to let him go.

When Kat looked up, it took her a moment to remember this was nothing more now than a story she was telling her family. As she glanced about the room, she noticed a small crowd had gathered by the door; Grandpa was there, looking older, grayer, but still robust and in good health. He held onto Gabe's hand, and Kat was surprised that the youngster she'd left behind was now, at nine years old, a tall, serious-faced boy.

Lissie and Lettie stood just behind Grandpa and Gabe. The change in Lissie was also striking. There was nothing left about her that was girlish, and Kat realized in just another month her sister would be turning sixteen. The only thing that hadn't changed about Lissie was she was dressed in her usual work clothes, and her hair was still cut short, as it had been ever since that night long ago, when they'd had the hair cutting ceremony. Lettie, on the other hand, had not quite left girlhood behind. At thirteen she stood on the cusp, but was making every effort to give the impression she'd already crossed over into the world of adults. She was wearing an impractical pink dress, and her long hair was curled, with only a pair of rhinestone hair combs to pull it back.

Just over Lettie's head, Kat could see Aunt Maddie, a little older, and a little thinner, but it was hard to ignore how happy she was. The reason for her joy was clear. Standing close, with his hand clasped in hers, Uncle Mike grinned widely as his eyes met Kat's.

Kat couldn't help herself, she tried to get up and run to him, only to remember she couldn't. Instead he came rushing to her, and as he scooped her up into a tight bear hug, she cried, just as she had done in the dream.

At last she gathered herself together so she could get a better look at him. His skin was no longer sallow, and his eyes twinkled with the liveliness of a well-fed man, even if he was still far too thin. He'd only been home just over three weeks. It wouldn't be long before her family would help erase all signs of those years of abuse.

"Couldn't let me have all the good eating to myself, could you, kiddo?" he teased.

The others began crowding him, all wanting to hug Kat as well. Kat gave Mike one last satisfied glance, and then let the family enfold her with the warmth of their love.

Chapter 38

Except for Lissie and Lettie, the family dispersed after the grand reunion. Lissie had brought down a pile of Kat's clothing from upstairs, figuring Kat would need the downstairs bedroom long enough that they might as well settle her in comfortably. Kat's new room was the pretty blue one they all referred to as Katherine's room. There were a series of watercolors that hung on its walls. The paintings were all of mountain and meadow flowers that Grandma Katherine had seen and painted from this window during her long years of failing health.

"How does this look?" Lettie asked, holding up a dark green skirt, plaid blouse and light gray Shetland wool sweater.

"What's it for?" Kat asked.

"For you, silly! I'm helping you get dressed."

Kat considered the outfit. Not too colorful, she noted. Lettie was trying to be sensitive to her tastes, but still Kat couldn't help saying, "I'd rather wear jeans."

"We'd have to cut the leg open to get it around your brace." Lettie pointed out.

"Ah," Kat acknowledged. "Clever girl." Lettie's smile was so endearing, Kat decided to try to be more magnanimous. "Well, since it's been a while since I had to put an outfit together, how would you like to be my stylist, just until I can get back in my jeans again?"

"Can I do your hair too?" The excitement in Lettie's voice was hard to ignore.

"Why not?" Kat laughed. "In for a penny, in for a pound."

Their dad arrived a short while later, pushing an antiquated wheel chair. Her sisters had already helped Kat to dress, and now Lettie was focusing on the finishing touch, a pair of tortoise shell combs to pull Kat's hair back, in much the same style Lettie had used on herself.

Her dad stopped and stared when Lettie stepped back to show off her work. "Well, don't you look pretty!" he exclaimed.

The corner of Kat's mouth quirked up. "Gee, Dad, why do you sound so surprised?"

He laughed, then pointed to the utterly ancient wheel chair. "Your transport awaits, my lady," he said, with a sweeping bow.

Kat looked at it, horrified. "Where did you get that thing?"

"Uncle Eli."

"It's a monstrosity!"

"That may be," her dad allowed, "but look at this!" And then he pulled a lever and demonstrated how the chair could comfortably elevate her injured leg. He lowered the lever and then carefully picked Kat up off the bed, setting her in the chair. "Breakfast is ready. Should I push, or do you want to try maneuvering it yourself?"

Kat settled into the chair, adjusted her leg into the raised position, and then turned herself to face the door. "I guess I'd better get used to it," she said with a resigned sigh, and then turned the wheels, rolling haltingly out of the room, down the hallway, and into the kitchen.

Because the lodge's formal dining room was more for their paying guests, the family was in the habit of eating all their meals in the kitchen. They sat around a large table that had been built a very long time ago by Ahote and Grandpa Caleb. Outside the wind was still howling, and snow was accumulating, coating the windows with white. Inside the kitchen, though, the stove kept things nice and toasty, and the table was laden with eggs, bacon, more biscuits, butter and preserves, and pots of tea, cocoa and coffee.

Kat took it all in: the good food, and the joy of having her family beside her at long last. As she studied each of them, wanting to impress this homecoming in her memory, her gaze settled on Gabe. He was chatting away with his mother and Grandpa. Occasionally he would look over at his dad, but if Mike met his gaze, Gabe would turn away again quickly. It drove home to Kat another painful reality of how this war had hurt Uncle Mike. His own son didn't even know him. Mike caught her watching, and gave her a reassuring smile. Kat realized then that he'd do what Connor men knew how to do better than anyone: bide his time, just take it nice and easy, and let Gabe come to him when he was ready.

Her mom interrupted Kat's thoughts. "Kat, I want to hear more about what happened when you woke up from that dream. You never did say how you convinced anyone to let you go to Luzon."

"Yeah," Lissie added. "You said the nurses weren't going to be allowed to make that landing. So how did you manage it?"

"I never figured out how she did it, either" Uncle Mike observed. "All I know is that she was waiting for me at the end of that daring rescue, and she got me stabilized in record time, so I could come home to all of you."

Kat looked at them all watching her expectantly. It was true, the dream had been only the beginning; there was a lot more still to tell. She poured herself another cup of her grandma's special Hopi-lavender tea, and then opened herself to the past, letting it all come alive once again.

Kat sat up in her cot, smelling the ocean and hearing the waves crashing along Owi's shoreline. It had been hard to leave the dream and Uncle Mike, but if she was going to save her uncle, there really was no choice. If he didn't get help in the here and now, he would die.

Quietly, Kat got up, careful not to disturb her tent mates. She slipped into her fatigues, and then tiptoed out of the tent, gently lowering the flap down behind her. It was still dark outside, but dawn was just beginning to light the eastern edge of the sky. She walked down to the fencing that circled the nurse's quarters, and made her way to a spot in the enclosure where one of the boards was loose. Lifting it just slightly, she peered in both directions to make sure the sentries weren't making the rounds. Convinced the way was clear, she turned sideways and squeezed through the small opening. Then, carefully, she realigned the board before making her way to the water's edge.

She gazed out at the water, uncertain of what her next actions should be. The gulf between what she knew and what would be believed seemed awfully wide. But if she couldn't sound the alarm, Uncle Mike was lost. She was reminded of those awful days at the end of 1941, when the attack on Pearl Harbor, and the fall of the Philippines, had filled the airwaves. She hadn't been with family when she'd heard the news. She'd been in Tucson, in her second year of nursing school. Kat remembered that awful feeling of powerlessness. The world of her dad's nightmares had come to life. For its opening act, it had swept away both Sean and Uncle Mike. The worst part was she couldn't do anything to change what'd happened. There was no way to make this better.

She wasn't alone in her grief and despair. Everywhere she looked, as she traveled home for Sean's memorial service, people were in shock. But it was even worse when she got home and saw that haunted expression on the face of every member of her family.

Things had not gotten any easier during that brief stay home. The day after the memorial service, she'd gone with her family to the train station to see Cal off. He'd enlisted the day the news broke about Pearl

Harbor. Sean's memorial service had been timed to allow him to attend before heading off to basic training. Kat had stood on the platform, unmoving, long after the train was out of sight. Finally, her dad had put his arm around her, and gently coaxed her back across the street to Auntie Branna's apartment.

Kat had only been back at school a week, when a representative from the army had shown up, looking to recruit nurses to serve in the war effort. Without a second thought, she'd signed up. She figured she couldn't do anything for Sean or Uncle Mike, but she'd had enough of feeling helpless. She would do what she could for soldiers like Cal.

Now, as Kat stood looking out at the water, watching the stars fading from the night sky, she couldn't help thinking how every action cast its ripples, sometimes for better, sometimes for worse. She was reminded of a conversation she'd once had with her grandma.

"Sometimes I don't like looking at the stars," she'd said. "They make me feel small, like my life is of no consequence."

Cha'risa had harrumphed and pointed to the heavens. "You think you are separate from that?" Kat's brow furrowed. "You think I'm not?"

Cha'risa had smiled and took hold of Kat's hand. "This idea of being separate is an illusion. You need to look beyond yourself, until you can see how the Great Spirit dwells in all things. That which moves the galaxies and the stars also moves you and me."

Kat had remained unconvinced. "But even if I could see this connection, how would it change anything?"

Her grandmother remained patient. "When you understand how things are connected, you begin to see how every action we take sets off ripples throughout the cosmos. Whether we understand it or not, each of us creates the energies that surround us."

"Are you saying everything that ever happened to me, *I* made happen?" Kat remembered being ready to reject that idea outright, but her grandmother's gaze had been so deep and compelling, Kat had continued to listen.

"Things happen for a reason," her grandmother insisted. "If you are smart enough to figure out the why, you will hold the power of the stars in your hands."

That conversation hadn't made sense to Kat back then, but lately she was beginning to understand. If you survived adversity, you learned from it, you changed because of it, and sometimes you could even make a darn good case there was some higher purpose driving it.

Her thoughts of home had made her restless, and she began to walk along the sandy beach. Just ahead she could see the officer's quarters. The high tide was nearly upon their tents, and soon their floors would be flooded with sea water. It was one of the less charming aspects of life on Owi, but the island had much worse to offer than soggy quarters.

The army had moved the hospital to Owi because the situation with the enemy had continued to be extremely volatile on Biak, a larger island just four miles away. What nobody realized until it was too late, was they'd moved the hospital into something much more deadly than Japanese territory. The scrub brush on Owi was infested with a nasty chigger that burrowed into people's skin, causing a rash and carrying a terrible disease. Large as the numbers of wounded were from the fighting on Biak, the numbers of scrub typhus cases had been nearly four times that.

If it hadn't been for that virulent pest, however, Kat would probably never have gotten even this close to the action. She'd spent the first several months of active duty in Australia, far from the front lines. But the scrub typhus epidemic made the need for nurses out in the field an imperative, and the army had been forced to rethink their policy of keeping nurses so far from the front lines. Five months ago, Kat's excellent nursing record and recent promotion to first lieutenant had landed her this assignment.

She looked over at Owi's still-quiet runway. She was closer now to Uncle Mike than she'd been at any other time during her stay in the South Pacific. From this runway, fifty to sixty flights took off each morning, heading north to the Philippines. Lately they'd been setting their sights on Luzon. That's how close she was: a single tank of gas would get her there. All she had to do was figure out how to get this amazing military machine to direct some of that power Mike's way.

Kat understood that power had many ways of manifesting. It could be overt, but oftentimes it was subtle, and flowed through pathways not well understood by most of mankind. It occurred to her the path to saving her uncle would likely require more faith than force. She wondered if it was possible her grandmother could discern Kat had need of her advice. The existence of such a possibility inspired her to call out.

"Grandma!" Her voice traveled out over the ocean, and was lost in the wind and waves. She cried out again, "Grandma! How do I save him?" Her voice trailed off. "Grandma," she called again, but this time it was barely a whisper because a hard knot had lodged in her throat.

"Lieutenant McKenna?"

She jumped at the sound of a man's voice, and turned. Major Carter was studying her with concern. His dark blonde hair was tousled, like he'd just rolled out of bed, but his camera hung around his neck, so it was clear what had him up and about just before dawn.

"Why are you out here, alone and in the dark?" he asked.

The nurses were never supposed to leave their compound unescorted; it wasn't good that he'd caught her. Still, the major looked more curious than angry.

"I needed to walk, sir," she said. "I do my best thinking when I'm walking."

"Me too," he admitted, and then gestured for her to join him. "Perhaps it's best if you don't walk alone." Kat nodded and fell into stride with him. They had only walked a short distance when he ventured, "Is something wrong?"

The words were on her lips to assure him that she was fine, but then she paused. Over the past several years she'd gotten very good at keeping people at arm's length. But once she'd found herself on that ship, heading off to war, she'd wondered if that had been wise; if maybe she'd come to regret always holding herself apart. What was very clear now was that if she didn't reach out to someone, Uncle Mike would die.

"I do have a problem," she admitted.

He grew more attentive. "Is it something I can help with?"

She knew that look on his face well; she'd seen it many times in the operating room. It was the way he looked when he was preparing to assess a difficult case. His blue eyes would narrow, and his brow would wrinkle in concentration. He liked solving problems. She also knew he liked his reports to be brief and to the point, so she ordered her thoughts before she let the words come.

"My uncle was one of the men left behind when the Philippines fell," she began. "He's being held in a Japanese POW camp." She pointed north out over the water. "I'm afraid he hasn't much time left. If I don't get to him soon, the Japanese will kill him."

Major Carter's eyes widened. "Hold on. How do you know all this?"

Kat held his gaze a moment, and then turned away from the water's edge, walking slowly back along the beach, all the while gathering her thoughts. The major followed, waiting patiently for her to continue. While she couldn't say for certain how he'd react to her vision, she did trust him. They worked well together and trusted each other's professional skill and judgment. Hopefully that was a good enough place to start. She decided her best option might be to try showing, rather than telling him, so she took in a deep breath, closed her eyes, and opened herself to the flows of energy all around her.

A wind picked up and ruffled her hair. It had grown long again in the years since the rustlers' attack. Now the dark lengths were caught and swirled in the energies she was gathering. She opened her eyes then, and reached out her hand.

"May I?' she asked. He nodded, and then placed his hand in hers. Breathing in once more, she let herself fill with the familiar warmth of healing. Then she exhaled, directing that heat through their clasped hands, all the while praying for it to help pave the way for greater openness and understanding.

"Major Carter, I come from a somewhat unusual family. My grandmother is a Hopi medicine woman, a very powerful healer, and my father is not only a healer, but a man who sees visions. I'm very much like them." She paused a moment, gauging his reaction. He looked a little surprised by this confession, but also interested, so she took another deep breath and finished her explanation. "Last night I had a vision. My spirit traveled to where my uncle laid dying on a dirty mat, on a cold, hard floor. We talked for a while, and that's how I know he's on Luzon, in a POW camp called Cabanatuan. He believes the Japanese are planning to kill the POW's rather than let them be returned to us."

Major Carter stared back at her, silent for a few moments, considering her words. All the while, the heat between their hands continued to increase. Finally, he looked away, turning his attention to their clasped hands. "Your hand feels so warm." He didn't let go, instead he focused on the sensation even more intently. "I also feel tingling; it's vibrating all the way up my arm." Then he rubbed his chest. "I feel it here as well." He looked at her, the question clear in his eyes; he wanted to know if she was making it happen.

"Can you feel anything else?" she asked.

His brows narrowed in concentration. After a moment he said, "Nothing concrete, but I do feel very relaxed, which is odd, because I was out walking to clear my head, too."

"Oh," she said, dropping her hand from his, "I disturbed you, I'm sorry."

He shook his head. "I believe it was I who interrupted you, so you have nothing to apologize for. Besides, I'm glad for a chance to focus on something else." He paused a moment, massaging his hand, the one she'd just held. He turned from her, and took a moment to study the first golden light of dawn now striking the water. When he turned to face her again, his eyes were filled with compassion. "If everything you told me is true, then you know how to find the survivors from the Battle of Bataan. I was at Pearl Harbor when the Japanese attacked, but I could just as easily been in your uncle's position, abandoned, and sacrificed to the greater war effort." He grew quiet again, and then looked up, having made a decision. "Lieutenant, I'd like to tell the colonel about this."

"You believe me?"

His lips turned up in amusement. "That is what you wanted, right?"

"Yes, of course. I'm just surprised you didn't take more convincing."

He laughed. "We've worked closely together for how long now?"

"Five months, sir."

"So while I can't claim to have known you were prone to visions, or that your touch could spread an unusual sense of well-being, I did notice other things."

"Really? Like what?"

"Well, I noticed you can detect disease and infection long before the usual signs appear. I also noticed the rate of healing in your patients is way above the norm. And by the way, your patients talk about it, too. They tell me your touch feels like magic; that when they're with you, they believe it's possible to be well again."

Kat looked at him, surprised. She'd known he was an observant man, she just hadn't realized he'd also been observing her. Once, that might have made her uncomfortable, but not now. All she could feel now was deeply grateful and incredibly moved that he was willing to believe her. Her eyes welled up, and she didn't even try to hide it from him.

The major smiled, and offered her his arm. "Shall we?" he asked.

She took his arm, heaving a sigh. She'd crossed the first hurdle. "Do you suppose the colonel will be as open minded?" she asked.

"He'll at least listen," he assured her. "Colonel Harrison and I go way back. We've been together since Pearl Harbor."

Colonel Norman Harrison looked decidedly unhappy as he listened to the voice on the other end of the phone. It was obvious from the colonel's responses that Kat was in hot water, and what's more, she'd dragged Major Carter right in with her. When the colonel at last hung up the phone, he pinched the bridge of his nose, as if he were in pain. Then, sighing deeply, he looked up, focusing his attention back on Kat and the major. "It seems you two will be meeting with Colonel White this afternoon. There's a plane leaving for Leyte in half an hour. They want you on it."

"Sir?' Major Carter ventured. "What do you think is going on?"

"I couldn't say exactly. All I know for certain is that you've stirred up a hornet's nest. Pack all your things. Good chance neither of you will be coming back to Owi."

"The colonel turned his attention to Kat. "From here on, Lieutenant, you play by the rules, understand?" He didn't stop to hear her response. "Don't try to leave the nursing compound without an escort. One of the guards will escort you to the airfield."

Kat nodded. "Yes, sir."

"And don't talk to anyone else about this until you've had a chance to meet with Colonel White." Turning back to the major, he added, "We'll be shipping out any day now. Try to join back up with us if you can."

"Yes, sir."

"Sir?" Kat ventured, "What's happening with the nurses?"

His voice softened a little. "Most of our nurses are being sent to Biak, but I honestly don't know what's going to happen to you. That's why I'm asking you to be incredibly circumspect. Don't give them any reason to look at you sideways. We need you in our hospitals, not in a brig."

The colonel fell silent, and Kat could tell he was weighing his next words. After a moment he cleared his throat, and addressed Major Carter specifically. "Jack, I think it would be better for both your sakes if you try to avoid any mention of this other business." He looked meaningfully over at Kat, who was confused as to what the other business was, but then she saw the color rise on Major Carter's face.

"There is no other business going on, sir." Major Carter assured him.

"Good. I see we understand one another."

Major Carter looked like he wanted to say more, but already Colonel Harrison had gotten up and was walking toward him. Pulling Jack near, the colonel spoke in lowered tones, but Kat's sharp ears picked up most of his words.

"As a friend, I'm happy to see you finally putting Evelyn in the past, but if the high command suspects your relationship with the lieutenant is anything other than professional, it could cause problems for you."

It was clear Major Carter wanted to contradict the colonel's assumption, but he must have decided it was futile, and instead all he said was, "I'll be careful."

The colonel nodded and extended his hand. "I'll see you soon then."

"See you soon," the major reiterated, clasping the colonel's hand with his own.

Kat studied their faces as they said their good-byes. The bond between them was plain to see. Major Carter would come back, she promised herself. Whatever it took, she would make sure of it.

Major Carter walked with Kat towards the nurses' compound. Kat stopped him before they were within sight of the guard's station. She wasn't sure exactly how to thank him for sticking his neck out on her behalf, so she said instead, "I'm sorry, sir. I never meant to put you in such a difficult position."

He smiled reassuringly. "Don't worry about me. I'll be just fine, and you will too if you don't let yourself get too distracted."

"But now you're implicated in whatever they think I've done."

He shrugged. "No matter how they put the screws to us, neither of us has anything to hide. Hopefully they'll be smart enough to see that."

"Doesn't it worry you at all?" Kat persisted. "They're hauling us up in front of the head of intelligence for the whole Sixth Army!"

He looked around to see if anyone was listening to their exchange, then took her arm and continued walking with her toward the nurses' compound. "This isn't all bad," he said. "While they aren't inclined to trust you at the moment, Colonel White is someone who can help you save your uncle."

He was right, she realized. She was being hauled up in front of exactly the kind of person she'd been hoping to reach. She studied Major Carter more closely, admiring his ability to remain calm under fire, and logical where others might get emotional.

"Thank you for believing me," she said. Then, before she even knew what she was doing, she stood on her tiptoes and gave him a peck on the cheek. She knew as soon as she did it that this was the stupidest thing she could have done by far. She blushed furiously, and then turned and ran off towards the nurses' barracks before she did anything else she'd regret.

"You did what?!" Lissie's voice modulated up into a squeak. Kat stopped her story to look at her sister, and then at all the other faces around the table. That impetuous kiss had happened nearly three months ago. She still couldn't explain why she'd done it, and felt once again the heat rise to her cheeks. It was no less embarrassing now than it had been back then.

"So you *were* sweet on that guy!" Uncle Mike exclaimed. "I thought so!"

"It wasn't like that," Kat insisted. "He'd been so helpful getting me that far. I was just so relieved, I didn't even think."

She caught her Grandma and mother exchanging knowing glances. "For crying out loud!" Kat exclaimed, "You guys don't understand. That wasn't a romantic gesture; it was just plain dumb!"

"Was the major angry with you, honey?" her mom asked.

Kat looked down blushing even more. "No."

"So what did he do?" Lissie demanded.

"Nothing, really. Later, when we were on the plane, I apologized to him." Kat prayed that would be the end of the questions.

"And he accepted your apology? Grandpa continued the inquiry.

"Sort of."

"What does 'sort of' mean?" her dad insisted.

Kat sighed deeply. "He told me he was pretty sure that was going to be the nicest part of his day."

Uncle Mike laughed and slapped his hand down on the table. "I knew it!"

Kat turned to him, her face solemn. "You and I owe Major Carter a debt we can never truly repay. He stood by my side that whole time, all the way to the point where I was reunited with you. But that's the end of it. Shortly after you were shipped home, we ended up in that hospital in Manila and this happened," she gestured toward the compound fracture of her left leg. "The war is over for me, but it isn't for him. That's how this story ends. There's no romantic happy ending." A tear escaped, burning a path down her cheek.

"That's enough for now," her mother said, taking the wheel chair and moving Kat away from the table. "She needs to rest."

Chapter 39

Kat lay in her darkened room, listening to the wind blow and watching the snow swirl outside her window. She looked down at her injured leg, remembering once more the accident that had sent her home. It had begun with the shell-shocked patient who'd panicked at the sound of thunder outside. He'd ripped the IV from his arm, trying to run for cover. She'd caught up with him just before he made it to the stairs. When they'd made eye contact, it had seemed to her that he was beginning to remember where he was, so she'd reached out to him to help him back to bed. Her movement had startled him and he'd pushed her away. The next thing she knew she was falling down that flight of stairs. It had all happened so quickly. One moment she was a nurse, and the next she was a patient lying on the operating table. If it'd been anyone else staring down at her, as she was prepped for surgery, she might have been scared, but it had been Jack. She'd stared back into his eyes, saw his calm confidence, and felt certain the outcome would be a good one. Knowing she was in extremely capable hands, she'd breathed deeply into the mask and drifted away.

Kat must have fallen asleep while lost in those memories. It was actually the silence outside that woke her. The heavy winds had stopped, and as Kat opened her eyes, she saw outside the window that snow now blanketed everything in silence. Even the house seemed hushed and still. She was considering closing her eyes again when she heard the sound of a page rustling. She looked over and saw Lissie sitting in a chair, a single lamp lighting up the pages of one of Kat's favorite books, Zane Grey's *Knights of the Range*.

"Been raiding my bookshelves?" Kat asked.

Lissie looked up, surprised, and then smiled. "Actually, I brought several books down for you in case you got bored, but I think I'm going to hang onto this one for a while." Lissie set the book down on the nightstand beside her. "Are you feeling better?"

Kat nodded.

"I'm sorry, about earlier, "Lissie said, approaching the bedside. "I didn't mean to upset you."

Kat gave her a reassuring smile. "It's not your fault. Some parts are just harder to talk about than others."

"I still can't believe you kissed that major." Lissie paused, and then in her typical blunt fashion asked, "Did he ever kiss you back?"

"Goodness, Lissie!"

"Sorry." But Lissie didn't look particularly contrite. "I guess all I really want to know is do you love him?"

Kat was about to tell Lissie to mind her own business, but something made her hesitate. This seemed more than just idle curiosity. "What's going on here, Lissie?" she asked. "Why are you so interested in my feelings for Major Carter?"

"I..." Lissie swallowed and then forced herself to just come out with it. "I kind of always thought you had feelings for Manny."

"Manny Gomez?" Kat wasn't sure exactly where Lissie was heading with this questioning. She tried to prop some pillows up behind her, and Lissie was quick to help. "Whatever gave you the idea I liked Manny?" Kat asked.

Lissie shrugged. "I guess it just seemed like he was always hanging around here, always talking to you."

"He's Cal's best friend. Of course he hung around here."

"So you never liked him? You aren't interested in him at all?"

"Not that way." Kat gave her sister an assessing look. "What are you trying to get at, Lissie?"

Her sister sat down on the bed beside her. "Promise you won't tell a soul?"

Kat nodded.

Lissie's green eyes locked on hers. "I think I'm in love with Manny."

For a moment Kat was speechless. Finally she managed, "Does he love you back?"

Lissie shook her head. "He doesn't have any idea how I feel. I kind of figured he was your guy, so I kept it to myself."

"I see. And now that you know he was never my guy?"

Lissie looked up and grinned. "Well that kind of changes everything, doesn't it?"

"You know, he's quite a bit older than you," Kat pointed out.

"Well, how much older than you is Major Carter?" Lissie countered.

"Six years," she admitted.

"That's about the same age span as Manny and me."

"I see," Kat said, smiling. "So what do you plan to do about it?"

Lissie settled in even closer to her. "Well, I guess now that I know you aren't interested in him, I plan to marry him."

Kat raised an eyebrow. "Don't you think you ought to get to know him first?"

"Oh, I know lots about him already!" Lissie started ticking off on her fingers. "He loves horses as much as I do, and he's got an even nicer ranch than we do. But I think the reason I really love him is because he's suggested they allow women into the roping events at next year's rodeo!"

Kat tried not to laugh. "Well that is certainly an impressive list of attributes."

Lissie nodded. "Yep. Now all I have to do is get him to see things my way."

That was Lissie. If she loved someone, she was going to make sure he knew it. And the more Kat thought about it, the more she thought it really should be that simple. "You know what, Lissie? Maybe I need to learn to be more like you."

Lissie gave her sister a lopsided grin. "I'm the one always trying to be like you, so how is that going to work out?" They both started to giggle. When the laughter died away, Lissie rested her head on Kat's shoulder. "So do you love Major Carter?" she asked again.

Kat stopped to consider then said, "I think I do."

"Then you should write him a letter and tell him," Lissie decided.

Kat looked at her sister incredulously. "Just like that? Dear Jack, I love you? What if he doesn't feel the same?"

Lissie shrugged. "Then at least you'd know."

"I did write him a letter when I was on the hospital ship," Kat offered.

"What did you say to him?"

"I thanked him for being there for me when I really needed a friend."

Lissie made a face. "Yuck! That's not even a speck romantic!"

Kat laughed. "I know. I am pretty awful at this, aren't I?"

"You really are." Lissie was thoughtful a moment, and then asked, "Just what makes him so special, other than his willingness to help you?"

"Well," Kat answered, "he's very smart, and very good at what he does. But he's not arrogant about his abilities like some doctors are; he's very caring and compassionate."

"Is he handsome?" Lissie asked.

Kat smiled. "Actually, he is."

"More handsome than Manny?"

"Well, he's very different looking than Manny," Kat said, thinking how best to describe him. "He's tall," she offered, "and broad shouldered. He's thinner than Manny, not as wiry, but still plenty strong. And his hair is blond, where Manny's is dark brown. But the feature I really like most is his eyes. They're gray-blue, with flecks of gold in the center. When we're in surgery together, that's all you can really see of his face, just those eyes poking out behind the mask; like sunshine breaking apart the gray of dawn."

"Now see," Lissie teased, "you can be romantic when you try."

Kat laughed. "Maybe so."

"Still, I don't see why you would like him more than Manny," Lissie persisted.

"Manny's a really great guy, Lissie, but being with Jack just felt very different. He was so easy to talk to. I felt comfortable telling him things I don't usually talk about to anyone. I actually told him the whole story of the rustlers' attack."

Lissie lifted her brows in surprise. "You did?"

"Yep. And I think he must have felt comfortable with me also, because later he told me things too."

"Really?" Lissie sat up, very interested. "What kind of things did he tell you?"

"Well, I learned what had been troubling him when I ran into him on the beach that morning."

"You did?"

Kat nodded.

"Well don't stop there!" Lissie demanded. "Now you have to tell me all of it!"

The C-47 was ready for take-off, and Kat was already buckled into her seat when Major Carter finally showed up. He ran the last few yards to the plane, shoved his duffle into the cargo area, and then took the seat beside her.

Kat had been running through her head dozens of different ways to explain her impertinent kiss, but in the end she decided there was simply no explanation for her inexcusable behavior. She turned to him as he fastened his seatbelt, and took a steadying breath. "Sir, I believe I owe you yet another apology. My actions earlier were out of line."

He looked amused. "You're referring to the kiss, I assume?"

She blushed and nodded.

"Don't apologize," he said, now openly grinning. "I'm pretty sure that is going to be the nicest part of my day."

More color rose to her cheeks. "Oh," she said. "Well, thank you, sir, I think." She was so far out of her comfort zone she had no idea what to say next. There was an awkward silence until she remembered the bag by her feet. "I brought breakfast," she said, reaching in and pulling out some bread and cheese.

He was both surprised and pleased. "How did you even have the time?"

"I asked Doris to run to the mess tent while I was packing. There's also some spam in here, a couple of chocolate bars, and some dried fruit, too."

The major got out his pocketknife and started slicing the cheese. "I take it back," he said, holding up a thin slice; "this is now the best part of my day."

"I see," she laughed. "Food trumps kiss."

"It does when I've missed my breakfast," he agreed. He layered some cheese onto the bread, and handed her the first sandwich. Quickly, he fixed another for himself, took a big bite, and then sighed with pleasure. "Thank you for thinking of my stomach, Lieutenant."

"The least I could do, sir," she replied.

The plane started speeding down the runway, and then lifted off into the air. The major leaned over her to peer out the window. "This is only my second time flying."

"Mine too," she admitted, looking out as well. "Cal often tried to describe it to me, but it wasn't until I saw the tops of clouds that I understood what it meant to no longer be earthbound."

"Cal?"

"My brother,"

"Ah yes, the twin."

She nodded.

"Is he a pilot?"

"No, he's with the 6th Army. He's an Alamo Scout."

"Really?" Major Carter looked impressed. "I've heard stories. It takes some very specialized training to join their ranks."

Kat smiled. "Well, he's special all right, no doubt about that."

The major paused, and then asked, "Just what kind of special are we talking about?"

"My kind," she admitted, "only his gifts are more suited to scouting than healing."

The major studied her a moment, considering. "Would it be all right to ask just how your gift works?"

She put her sandwich down, weighing her response. She wasn't used to talking about her differences, but she'd already shown him some of what she could do. Also, she owed him an explanation. He deserved at least that much after getting tangled up in her quest to save Uncle Mike. "Well," she said, "I think the best way to describe it is that it helps me to see with great clarity." She paused and then said, "I can show you, if you like." He cocked an eyebrow and then nodded.

She placed her hand on his heart, and let her senses travel past his skin, into his body. "When I use all my senses I don't just feel the beating of your heart, I see the valves opening and closing, and the blood pumping through the chambers."

"I feel that heat and tingling again," he commented.

She nodded, and then let her hand fall from his chest. "That's not unusual. It's a side effect of the healing energy; it how you know it's flowing." She grinned at him then. "Your heart, by the way, looks very healthy and strong."

"Good to know," he said, once again amused, and then his curiosity returned. "Is that all of it? All of what you can do?"

She shook her head. "Once I can see it, I can fix it."

He leaned in, his interest piqued. "How? Is it something I can learn?"

"I don't know. It was something that just came naturally to me."

"But what exactly do you do?"

She paused, searching for the words to describe it. "I guess the best explanation is that I see what isn't working right, and then I visualize it operating as it should. I use my thoughts to direct the body toward a healthier state of being."

"But it's more than imagination," he asserted. "It evokes a physical sensation."

"Oh, it's very real," she agreed. "It may begin with a thought, but it takes on a form and substance of its own."

"One day, when all this is behind us," he said, pointing out toward Leyte, "I want you to try and teach me."

"I'll try," she agreed. "But if I fail, you must come to Arizona, and I'll let my grandmother have a go at you."

He gave her a look of mock alarm. "I'm already a little afraid of your grandmother."

She laughed, then took a bite of her sandwich. Major Carter picked up his as well, and then paused again.

"This uncle of yours; is he, you know... special too?"

Kat shook her head. "Not in that way. Uncle Mike's lineage is mostly Irish, with a little English thrown in. But still, he's an amazing man. He saved my life once, which is one of the reasons I fully intend to return the favor."

The major's interest was again piqued. "Care to share that story?"

Kat looked at him, then dropped her gaze and said, "It's not something I talk about easily."

"I'm sorry, I shouldn't pry."

"No, don't apologize. You should know something of Uncle Mike. If you know him better, maybe you'll feel as I do; that no matter what happens, it will have been worth it."

The major's eyes were full of compassion. "I'll feel that way whether you tell the story or not. He's one of ours, and I want him to come home."

She looked up into his eyes, grateful for his generous spirit. Then she took a deep breath and told him the story of a girl who was in no hurry to grow up. She described a world of ranches and rodeos, horses and cattle, and of cattle rustlers. She told him of her devotion to her brother, how Cal had saved her, and then she'd saved him. She introduced him to Uncle Mike, the sharp shooter, with the cool head and steady hand. And then she described her father, the healer and dreamer. She ended the story telling him something of the women in her family; of the ritual that began with cutting her hair, and had ended with the beginning of her journey as a healer.

He sat quietly when she'd finished. She could see on his face the story had touched him with its horror, but also with its beauty.

"What happened to Red Beard?" he asked at last.

"He's still in jail, but it's not a life sentence."

The major genuinely looked unsettled. "How long is his sentence?"

"He got twenty-five years. But it could be less with good behavior."

Major Carter frowned, shaking his head. "I don't like the idea of you having to live in a world where that rustler walks free."

Kat tried to reassure him. "I try not to hate him, or fear him. I try to think of him as part of what made me who I am."

"That man would have raped and killed you if he could," The major pointed out.

She nodded. "I know. He would have thought nothing of killing Cal, either. But he wasn't the victor that day, we were."

The major frowned. "So, it's okay as long as the good guys win?"

Kat realized she was doing a poor job of explaining this to him. She tried a different approach. "In the beginning my reaction wasn't that different from yours. I was really angry, and very afraid. But I had my family to help me, and of course the lessons with my grandmother made a huge difference. Eventually, she helped me to see that I was being my own worst enemy. My fear and anger would consume me, and keep me from living a good life. Once I understood that, I made myself a vow. Those rustlers were not going to have that kind of power over me."

The major grew quiet, lost in his own thoughts. His hand drifted toward his jacket pocket, and his hand pressed up against whatever it was that lay just behind the fabric. He looked back at Kat. "Can you really do that? Just turn it off and move forward with your life?"

She blushed a little. "I can only try. Sometimes it's hard not to let the crazy winds blow."

The major raised both eyebrows quizzically. "The crazy winds?"

"That's what my grandma calls it when your emotions run amok."

"I see." A hint of a smile teased the corners of his mouth, and then he asked, "But how do actually you stop those crazy winds? How do you suppress that kind of anger?"

Kat looked thoughtful a moment and then said, "It's not so much about suppressing, as it is about redirecting it. You focus on what you can do, and try not to divert too much energy to what is already over and done with."

She paused, studying him closely, and then added, "I don't want you getting the wrong idea. I know some helpful techniques, but I don't always use them. Today, for instance, my crazy winds blew plenty. The way those Japanese have treated Uncle Mike fills me with anger. How can they consider just snuffing him out? And I'm afraid, too. What if I get this close and I still can't save him?"

Major Carter sat back then in his seat, looking a little discomfited. "We're going to do our best today," he said, "but I can't promise you we'll win this one."

"It's enough that you're here," she assured him, "standing with me, vouching for me. I will always be grateful, no matter how this day turns out."

He glanced away, seeming uncomfortable with the direction of the conversation, and Kat was left wondering exactly what she'd said to upset him.

Lissie sat up, looking troubled. "Why did he cut the conversation off like that? Was he mad at you?"

"I wondered that too, at the time. I thought maybe I was putting too much pressure on him, expecting too much of him. Later, I came to understand there was something else troubling him.

"What was it?"

Kat pulled Lissie back in close to her. "Do you remember I told you he also had a problem; that he had something he was trying to work through?" Lissie nodded. "Well, it turns out, all my talk of the dangers of letting anger consume you had struck a chord in Jack."

The plane made a sharp descent, and Kat looked out the window, catching her first glimpse of the Philippines. The view below of San Pedro Bay was one that got her heart pounding, and her hopes spiraling high. The water was filled with maybe as many as a hundred American ships, all gathered as a prelude for the push to Luzon. She looked over at Major Carter. "You should see this," she said.

He leaned over to look out the window and then whistled. "That's not something you see every day!"

Just then the plane banked hard, throwing them against each other. He caught her, to steady her, and their eyes met.

"You ready for this?" he asked, trying to read her mood. Whatever had been eating at him before was clearly past. He seemed once again very approachable and genuinely concerned.

"I guess I'd better be." Kat said. Just then the plane dipped precipitously, and she latched onto the major's arm with a vice grip. "Good Lord!" she exclaimed. "What's up with our pilot?"

"Could be there are still some enemy aircraft in the area." They both turned their attention back to the window again, watching the plane line up with the airstrip.

"We're one step closer to finding Uncle Mike." She'd said it as a whisper, but still the major heard her.

He gave her hand a squeeze. "We've done all right so far. Let's pray our luck holds."

She looked at him and smiled. "The last time I prayed, I got you."

He laughed. "Well then, you might need to pray a little harder this time."

She considered it for a moment, and then shook her head. "I'm pretty sure I got it right the first time around."

They were met on the runway by a member of Colonel White's staff, and an escort of two rifle-bearing marines. Colonel White's aide led them down to the harbor and onto a transport, offering little more than his name and rank, Lieutenant Marvin Willis. Neither of the two marines introduced themselves, but Kat read their nametags, T. Wight and L. Blake. They saluted her, but did not engage any further. As they motored past the impressive array of amphibious assault ships, cruisers, destroyers, LSTs, and liberty ships, Kat and the major stayed silent. But when it became clear what their destination was, Major Carter shattered the quiet with a long whistle.

The USS Wasatch was a Mount McKinley-class amphibious force command ship. She was the flagship of the Seventh Fleet, commanded by Admiral Thomas Kincaid. She was also the command and control center for General Douglas MacArthur.

They boarded the ship below decks, and Kat found herself among a crowd of sailors all moving purposefully around the interior of the ship. Her presence turned more than a few heads, but the Marine guards and Lt. Willis created a path through the sailors, who all gave way.

Kat watched as Lt. Willis started up a steep ladder. His continued silence had unnerved her. She nudged Major Carter, whispering, "Do you think he's taking us to the brig?"

"I think we're okay. The brig is usually down, not up," the major whispered back.

T. Wight gestured with his rifle at the ladder well. "Keep moving," he said. Kat didn't argue. She grabbed hold of the rungs and followed after Lt. Willis, who continued to climb up several winding flights. It was hot inside the ship's hold, at least 100 degrees, and Kat could feel the sweat dampening her face and clothes as she climbed. Perspiring was a perpetual state in the South Pacific, but inside the bowels of the ship it was more than just steamy. The air was stagnant, and heavy with the smell of grease and men. She wiped at her forehead, and then grabbed hold of the next set of rungs, continuing to keep pace with Lt. Willis. At last, they exited out onto the main deck, and Kat was grateful for fresh air and a light breeze.

Major Carter came up beside her, and pointed up toward the bridge. "Look at that, will you? I've never seen so much communication equipment all in one place before."

Kat stared back up at all the communication towers. Every decision that was being made concerning Luzon was happening here, right now, on this ship. It made her hesitate. Yes, she'd come to the right place, but when faced with the gigantic flood of information coming in, would anyone even have the time to care about saving a ragtag group of POW's?

Just then sirens went off all around her, followed by loudspeakers blaring a call to general quarters. Willis looked up toward the sky, and then motioned for them to follow him, leading them quickly to the officer's wardroom, just a few doors down from where they'd stood. He ushered them inside as the loudspeakers continued the call to battle stations.

He turned to Blake and Wight. "Keep them here. I'll be back just as soon as the all-clear is sounded." Just then, a dog came barreling down the deck, and dodged right past Blake and Wight into the officer's wardroom.

"Wolly!" Willis stooped down to pet the canine. He turned to Kat and Jack. "This is Wolly, short for AWOL. He belongs to our XO, and is trained to come here when General Quarters is sounded." Willis was actually smiling as he bent to scratch Wolly behind the ears. "Such a good dog, yes you are," he crooned. Kat struggled to reconcile this warm, gushy side of Willis with the taciturn man she'd just met. He turned back to Kat and Jack. "You should be safe enough here until the all-clear is sounded." With one last pat for Wolly, Willis headed out the door, and then started briskly toward the ladder leading up to the flag bridge.

Kat knelt down beside Wolly. He wasn't as big a dog as Piglet. He looked like some kind of Border Collie mix with brindled black and white fur, and semi-erect ears. She offered him her hand, and Wolly sniffed her with great interest. After a moment, he looked up at her. He had the most intelligent eyes Kat had ever seen on a dog, but then he gave her a goofy doggy smile, and licked the palm of her hand. Kat laughed, and began to pet him. He wasted no time rolling over and offering her his belly.

"Wolly," Blake scolded. "You're embarrassing yourself." Wolly looked over at Blake, and then sat back up into a more dignified position. He cocked his head at Blake, as if to call him a killjoy, and then trotted over to a table by the window. He jumped up on a chair and then from there onto the table.

A voice thundered through the opening to the galley. "Wolly! You know better than to be on my tables! Get back in that chair!"

Kat was startled; unaware anyone else was in the wardroom. Wolly had the grace to look ashamed as he scooted off the table. A man came out from behind the mess line, and gave Jack and Kat a friendly salute. "Chief Commissary Steward Lucca at your service." Chief Lucca smiled then, and reached into a bag he was holding, handing Kat and Jack each a fresh baked shortbread cookie.

"Galley's battened down at the moment for general quarters. That's to tide you over until they sound the all-clear." He was about to offer some cookies to the two marines, when something caught his attention out the window. "Got ourselves an unwelcome guest," he said.

Kat turned just as the ack-ack guns on the neighboring USS New Jersey started firing. A moment later, a single Kamikaze plane exploded above the harbor. Pieces of it fell from the sky, crashing into the water below, leaving only a trail of black smoke behind.

"Nice," Blake commented, and then he nodded toward the bag of cookies. "I believe you were going to offer me one of those."

"You sure you can handle all that butter and sugar? This is much richer than your normal marine chow." Lucca teased. Blake was a big guy; Kat wasn't sure she'd have risked poking fun at him. There was certainly no question in her mind this guy could handle quite a large number of cookies. When Lucca offered him the bag, Blake looked the chief in the eye and took two, then passed the bag over to Wight.

"Does that happen often around here?" Major Carter asked, still fascinated with the scene out the window. Fireboats were now dousing the burning oil slick.

Chief Lucca followed Jack's gaze, nodding. "The Kamikazes did incredible damage during the battle of Leyte, but of course they're a one shot deal. Not many left around here now, not enough to be more than a nuisance."

"Just give it a few more days," said Wight. "Mark my words; we'll see them again in force when we get close to Luzon."

The major looked at the chief and the two marines. "You think Luzon could be as bad as the battle for Leyte?"

All three nodded.

The major's expression turned somber. "I read a report stating we had nearly 3,000 casualties."

Chief Lucca's brow furrowed with the memories. "We lost six ships. Three were destroyers, and the enemy took out over 200 of our planes."

"But that was nothing compared to the damage we did to the Japs," Wight interjected.

Blake started listing off the tally. "They had over 12,000 dead, and we took out a fleet carrier, three light carriers, three battleships, ten cruisers, 11 destroyers, and over 300 planes."

"I'd heard that there's not much left of their fleet," Major Carter commented.

"We made damn sure of that!" Blake enthused, and then turned toward Kat, "Sorry, ma'am, pardon my language." He offered her a cookie as an amends. Kat smiled and told him to keep it. Just then the all-clear sounded, and Chief Lucca got up, leaving the bag of cookies in front of Kat and said, "How about I make some tea to go with these cookies?"

Kat realized neither she nor the major had drunk anything for hours now. Not since they'd taken off from Owi. "A cup of tea sounds perfect," she said. "Thank you."

Wolly barked as the Chief started back toward the galley. The Chief turned back around. "Wolly. I nearly forgot!" He reached into his pocket and tossed a small cookie into the air. Wolly caught it mid-flight. Chief Lucca laughed. "He just loves those. It's my own special recipe created just for him."

Fifteen minutes later, Kat and Jack were seated once again at the table by the window, now covered with a white linen tablecloth, and they were drinking tea from bone china cups. Finger sandwiches and pastries lay between them on a china platter, with gilded navy insignia.

Across from her, Jack cut into a chocolate éclair with a sterling silver fork, and just under the table, by her feet; a very content Wolly was sound asleep. It had been months since either she or the major had been surrounded with such niceties. She'd had no idea that life at sea could be so civilized. One thing was for certain, if you discounted the watchful presence of Blake and Wight just outside the door, this was about as far from a brig as you could get.

The major had been quiet as they'd shared their tea, deep in thought, but now he paused before taking a bite of his pastry. "May I ask you something?" he asked.

Kat put down her egg salad sandwich "Sure."

"I can't stop thinking about something you said earlier on the plane, about how you made a choice not to let anger rule you."

She looked at him more closely. "What is it you want to ask?"

Jack put down his fork, and his eyes locked on hers. "I want to know how to do it."

Kat held his gaze for a moment, not sure how to respond. "Major Carter…" she began.

"Call me Jack," he said.

"Jack," she agreed. "And you may call me Kat."

He smiled. "I'd like that."

She took in a deep breath. "Before you ask me for advice, you should know I have a lot more experience being given advice than I do doling it out. In my family, whenever someone's spirit is sorely troubled, they usually go to my grandmother, or my father, or Uncle Ahote. I'm pretty far down on the list of people to seek advice from."

"Well, none of those people are here," Jack pointed out, "and clearly you've had some success with redirecting your anger. Can't you just describe for me what helped you?"

She looked into his blue-grey eyes. Whatever was troubling the major, he was sincerely looking for a way to make a change. She'd never tried to put something like this into words before, and she had to dig deep, searching hard to find the right ones. At last she said, "I think the best way to describe what I did was, I prayed. Each day I asked for help accepting what had happened, and for help in accepting the power I did have to affect positive change, and growth, and healing in my life. I prayed that my anger and hatred of these men would not become a foundation on which I built my life."

Jack leaned forward. "And that worked?"

"Not at first, but I kept with it. Over time I began to realize they weren't just words anymore, they'd become a solidly entrenched belief." Kat watched him thinking it over "Does that sound silly to you? I don't even know if you believe in prayer."

"Oh, believe me; I've done my fair share of praying. Being in the South Pacific has a way of encouraging a much closer connection to God."

"May I ask," she ventured, "who or what has made you so angry?"

Jack hesitated, and then reached into his jacket pocket and pulled out a letter.

Kat stared at the return address on the envelope. "Is that a letter from home?"

He nodded.

"You're angry with someone in your family?"

"I think, if I'm honest, I'm angry at all of them."

"Oh," His confession surprised Kat, but she didn't look away. "Well, go on. I'm listening."

Jack opened the envelope, and pulled out a photograph for Kat to study. "This here is my mother, holding my nephew, Johnny. That big guy there, the proud father, that's my younger brother, James. That woman holding the baby girl, that's Evelyn."

"Evelyn!" Kat looked back up and Jack. "*The* Evelyn, the one Colonel Harrison made mention of?"

Jack looked at her, his eyes full of hurt. "She was still my fiancée when she married my brother. She had to marry him, because she was carrying little Johnny there."

Kat was horrified. "Your brother seduced your fiancée?"

"I don't think it was seduction. Evelyn never did anything she didn't want to do. Anyhow, the picture says it all, doesn't it? They're happy together, have built this beautiful life, made this perfect family. They've moved on, and I'm still stuck in this dark, angry place, hurting no one but myself."

Kat was quiet a moment, considering. "And you're mad at your mom too?"

"I suppose I shouldn't be. She was the only one who had the decency to tell me what had happened, but just look at her now; she's fully part of that happy family scene." The hurt was evident on his face. "In the beginning she understood my anger, but now she thinks four

243

years is long enough, and it's time for me to forgive them. She wants me to let us all be a family once more."

"Her desire is perfectly understandable," Kat said, "but it's much easier to tell someone to do that, quite another to actually be the one to do it."

"What's worse," he continued, "is I know how hard it's been on her. She lost my dad not long after James and I became estranged. It would mean the world to her if I could find a way to give her back what's left of her family."

"Has James ever tried to reach out to you?" Kat asked.

"Once, but it was for Evelyn's sake. She was feeling guilty, but didn't have the courage to approach me. He wanted me to go easy on her, not to upset her too much while she was carrying his child. But he never said anything about being sorry, or asking for my forgiveness." Jack looked out the window then, lost in a world of painful memories. "I've had this argument with myself before, how I should be the better man. I tried to do the right thing before the landing at Hollandia, and again before Biak. But no matter what I try, I can never get past the arrogant tone of his letter." He turned to Kat then, and she could see his distress. "I'm not just angry with them, I'm angry with myself, because if I don't make it home, I don't want..." his voice choked. He looked away, took a sip of tea, and then tried again. "I don't want my mom to remember me as the guy with a heart of stone."

Kat put her hand on top of his. Immediately, she felt the heat flowing from her touch into him. He looked up at her, curious.

"You're doing it again."

"Yes."

"Why?"

She shrugged. "It started flowing on its own, as soon as I touched you."

"Will it help?"

"Well, it certainly won't hurt." She paused a moment. In a situation like this her grandmother would have something useful to say, but nothing profound came to Kat. Instead, she just kept wondering what it was his mother had written. At last she gave into her curiosity. "May I ask what the letter says?"

He heaved a sigh. "I don't know. I saw the picture, and found I couldn't bring myself to read what she had to say."

Kat's heart went out to him. It couldn't feel good to be all the way on the other side of the world, and feel like there wasn't anyone in your family who was on your side. "Your mom is still writing to you," Kat observed. "Even if she's disappointed you can't move on, she still loves you, still wants that connection with you. Shouldn't that count for something?"

He looked at Kat a second, and then picked up the letter and began reading. His eyes had traveled part way down the page when he stopped reading, his eyes widening in surprise.

Kat studied him closely. "What does she say?"

It was nearly impossible to describe the look on his face, there was both hope and hurt. When he spoke, his voice was hoarse from the mixed emotions. "She says they named the baby Jacqueline. They named her after me."

Just then Lieutenant Willis popped his head in the door. "Okay, you two, time to put aside the pastries. Colonel White will see you now."

Jack stuffed the letter back in his pocket, and it seemed to Kat that he tucked all those conflicting feelings back inside along with it. He stood and offered her his hand. "You ready?"

Her eyes met his as she let him help her up. "Are you okay?"

"Don't worry about me. We have other things to think about right now."

She nodded. "I know, but Jack?" He looked at her, and she held his gaze as she spoke. "Forgiveness and acceptance are two different things. For now it might be best to focus on accepting what happened, accepting the ways it's changed you. Look for the ways those changes have made you better, stronger. Those are the first steps to take toward freeing yourself. Forgiveness can come later."

Jack considered her advice and then cracked a smile.

"What?" she asked.

"For someone not accustomed to giving advice, that sounded to me like fairly sage council."

"Hey, you two," Willis interjected. "The colonel doesn't like to be kept waiting, and he definitely isn't the forgiving type either."

Jack's eyes locked on hers, "Are you ready to go save your uncle?"

Clearly, he was ready, and as she met his gaze, she found she was too. It was time to meet this Colonel White, and see if so many events had aligned because Uncle Mike still had more living to do.

When they headed for the door, Wolly followed. Willis raised a hand. "Not you, Wolly. You stay." Then Willis led Kat and Jack out the door and up the ladder leading to the flag deck. When Kat reached the top she heard the sound of doggy feet on the deck below. She looked down and saw Wolly standing at the bottom, wagging his tail expectantly. Lt. Willis saw him too and sternly pointed in the direction of the ward room.

"Go back," he ordered. But Wolly put his paws on the first rung.

"What's he thinking?" Kat said. "He can't possibly climb something so steep!"

"Wolly! No!" Lt. Willis, shouted, but Wolly ignored him. Kat and Jack both watched, astounded, as Wolly climbed up rung after rung, until he stood once again beside them.

Willis shook his head. "Commander Currier won't be pleased, but he won't be surprised either. This dog isn't called AWOL for nothing."

How did he climb up that thing?" Kat still couldn't believe it.

"Oh," Lt. Willis assured her, "if you think that's impressive, you should see him climb down."

"I really love that Wolly!" Lissie exclaimed.

Kat nodded, smiling. "He was something special. And he became very attached to me on that journey to Luzon. Every night he would show up at my door. He'd sit there expectantly until either Blake or Wight let him in.

Lissie laughed. "Don't tell Piglet, she'd be jealous." She paused a moment. "Did Jack ever find a way to forgive his family?"

"I think he tried. He posted a letter to them before leaving the Wasatch, but I honestly don't know how that story ends. I was wounded and sent home before the mail caught up to us in Luzon."

"Something else occurred to me while I was listening to you." Lissie said.

"What was that?"

"You already know the answer about how to be more like me."

Kat looked at Lissie sideways. "What on earth are you talking about?"

"You said you wished you could just come right out and say what you felt, like I do, right?

"I did." Kat said, now recalling that part of their conversation.

"Well then, just do like you did when you were mastering your anger. Pray every day, until you can accept you're ready to say 'I love you, Jack.'"

Chapter 40

As evening fell, big snowflakes began to blow and swirl outside the window. Kat sat in the parlor watching as the storm regained strength. Grandpa had gotten a nice fire going, but it was Gabe, not the warm hearth, that had lured her in here. He'd been sitting on the sofa with his mother, reading from his fourth grade reader, and had wanted Kat to listen to him, too.

It struck Kat that snowfall ought to seem astonishing after living three years on those hot, humid islands. So should sitting in a room with Gabe, who was now so much bigger and more accomplished than when she'd last seen him. Home had been a dream for so long, but now she was here, and it was wrapping itself around her so fully, it was her time in the South Pacific that was already beginning to feel like the dream.

Grandpa and Lissie popped their heads in, wanting Gabe to bundle up and come with them to the barn to check on the horses. He jumped up, gave his mom a quick kiss, and then gave Kat a shy smile. He remembered who Kat was; he had memories of things they'd done together before the war. That was the big difference between his reunion with Kat, and the one with his father. All he knew of Uncle Mike were stories he'd been told. It was hard to watch the two of them feeling like strangers; trying to find a way to make up for those lost six years.

When Gabe left, Aunt Maddie also got up. "I think I'll go see if your mom needs any help getting supper on the table."

"I could help too," Kat offered. "You could give me vegetables to chop."

"We'll put you to work soon enough," Aunt Maddie assured her. "But this is only your first day home. Just take it easy for now, give your body and your mind a chance to catch up with all that's happened."

Aunt Maddie had more than a little experience with returning veterans of war, so Kat didn't argue with her, but in her heart, Kat knew there was a limit to how much quiet contemplation she could tolerate.

"I'll sit with you," Grandma said, entering the parlor. "I need to get off my feet awhile anyhow."

"How is Mike?" Maddie asked. "Did you ever get him to take a nap?"

Cha'risa gave her a weary smile. "He's a hard one to settle down, but he did agree to sit and read for a bit."

Maddie nodded toward Kat. "I have a feeling this one isn't going to be any easier."

"It's a good sign," Cha'risa said, heading to the big wing backed chair by the fire. She groaned as she sat, putting her feet up on the footrest. "They're both anxious to get back to the business of living."

Kat rolled her wheelchair over to the hearth, parking herself beside her grandmother, who took Kat's hand in hers and squeezed it. Then she looked over at Maddie. "Go on, before you have a horde of hungry people clamoring for their dinner. I'm just going to sit here and spend a little time with my granddaughter."

"I can take a hint," Maddie pursed her lips into a fake pout. Then she grinned, and winked at them both before heading for the kitchen.

"It's good to see her smiling again," Cha'risa said as she watched her go. "You're responsible for that," she said turning to Kat. "You never gave up until Mike was returned to us."

"I can't claim responsibility for Uncle Mike's rescue," Kat insisted. "I think all I really did was to make a lot of noise."

Her grandma smiled. "Sometimes, it's that extra bit of noise that turns the tide." Cha'risa studied Kat, her eyes glinting with approval. After a moment she said, "When I first started training you, I had no idea you would end up being such a strong medicine woman, but you are, Kat. You are the most skilled healer I have ever known."

"I still have so much to learn," Kat objected.

Cha'risa nodded. "It's good you're not prideful or complacent about your gifts. Never stop learning, Kat. And don't be afraid to look at yourself honestly. If you don't understand the possibilities within you, it's easy to make mistakes."

Kat glanced up at her grandmother. A new ability had manifested while Kat was away. Kat had confided in Cal, during one of his visits, while she was still in Australia. She'd described it to him as a light shining down a pathway. It only ever showed itself in patients who lay near death, and the path always led to the same place, an end to the pain, a way to cross over. She was hoping Cal could help her decide if it would be merciful to use this new ability, or an act of extreme arrogance. She was worried she might lead someone down that path who wasn't quite finished with this world.

Cal had echoed her fear, and urged her not to explore any further until she'd had a chance to talk to their grandma. There was no easy way though, to have a conversation like that in writing. A new ability couldn't just be described. It needed to be examined. Kat had chosen instead to focus her energies on easing the pain of the dying, and she relegated this new aptitude to the farthest corner of her mind. She'd felt like it was the right call, burying it deep in her consciousness. When she thought about her experience with Uncle Mike, she felt further validated in her choice. What if she'd been swayed by his belief she was there to help him pass on? Just the thought of using that gift on him made her sick. What a horrific mistake it would have been!

But now here was her grandma telling her she shouldn't hide from any of her gifts. Perhaps it was time to let this ability resurface. They could study it together. She was just trying to figure out the best way to broach the subject, when Lettie popped her head into the parlor announcing that dinner was ready. Kat could hear the dinner bell sounding, signaling to those out in the barn it was time to clean up and come inside. Her grandma got up out of the chair, stiff and slow, and Lettie grabbed the handles of Kat's wheel chair, already halfway out the door with her, pushing her toward the kitchen. Kat sighed, realizing the moment had passed. She'd have to seek out another time and way to ask her grandma for guidance.

Kat stirred the food around on her plate, lost in thought. The decision to let the new ability resurface had left her uneasy.

"Is everything all right, honey?" Her mother had noticed Kat's lack of appetite.

"I just have a lot on my mind," Kat said, setting down her fork.

"Being home can take some adjusting," Aunt Maddie consoled.

Uncle Mike tried a different track. "Kat, just take a bite. When was the last time you had a meal like this?"

Kat looked down at the perfectly prepared beef brisket. "Go on," Uncle Mike urged, a corner of his mouth quirking up. "No dream ever tasted this good."

She laughed halfheartedly, and then obliged him. Her uncle was right; it was a delicious reminder that she'd left army rations behind for good.

When Uncle Mike was satisfied she was on the way to doing her dinner justice, he leaned in closer to her. "You ended your story this morning at the point when you were about to meet Colonel White." His eyes locked with hers. "I was really hoping you'd tell us more tonight."

"Honey don't pressure her," Aunt Maddie reproved.

"Nonsense," Cha'risa asserted. "She should finish telling the story."

Suddenly, it struck Kat there was no better way to explain the concerns about her new gift than finishing her story. She looked at her family, and it felt right to her, making this confession to all of them. "We were just getting to the interesting part, weren't we?" she said.

"Wonderful!" Mike sat back, pleased. "Now I won't have to imagine what you said to the colonel to get him to sit up and take notice."

Kat's face grew somber. "It's not at all what you think, Uncle Mike. I didn't save the day, not in the slightest."

"Since I'm sitting here, alive and well fed, I tend to disagree."

"Nevertheless, I'm not the hero in this story. I wasn't even clever enough to anticipate why the colonel was so insistent on meeting me. No, if anyone saved the day, I would have to say it was Cal."

When Lt. Willis escorted Jack and Kat into the conference room, Colonel White gestured for them to take a seat without even looking up. His head stayed buried in a stack of papers on the table before him. Neither Kat nor Jack dared break the ensuing silence. Kat had heard of Colonel White before today. Cal had mentioned him because of the colonel's involvement with the Alamo Scouts. He was General Kruegar's intelligence chief, and Cal had expressed real admiration, telling her the Colonel had a reputation for being very good at his job. Given the buildup, Kat had expected a more imposing figure. It surprised her that Colonel White did not appear at all intimidating, but when the colonel looked up, studying her with sharp, penetrating eyes, she quickly amended her assessment.

"I'm not going to beat around the bush here," he said, completely overlooking Jack's presence, focusing only on Kat. "The name McKenna is known to me. I've met your brother, Cal, and I've read the reports surrounding his unusual gift for scouting." He leaned forward, his eyes boring intently into hers. "Is that what I am dealing with here, Lieutenant? Do you have the same kind of abilities as your twin?"

Jack looked over and met Kat's gaze. He looked worried, and somewhat aghast that they'd never considered this possibility. Kat tried not to appear rattled as she turned back to meet the Colonel's compelling gaze.

"My gifts can also be described as unusual, sir," she answered, "but they're different than Cal's. What he sees is from the widest possible perspective, like a bird up in the sky. My vision grants me the clarity to see and sense the strength and vitality within people."

"I see," the colonel said, as he rifled through the papers in front of him, "but in your report, you talk very specifically about Cabantuan Prison. That is something beyond the strength and vitality of a single individual, wouldn't you say?"

"Well, sir," she offered, "my dreams will sometimes show me other kinds of details, but the part of my gift I can control is focused on the human body and healing."

The colonel pulled out a map and spread it on the table in front of her. "Just humor me a little here. Here's the city of Cabantuan." He pointed to a place on the map, and Kat leaned over, studying it. "When you look at the outlying terrain, does it bring to mind anything else that might be worth mentioning?"

Kat studied the details of the map and then offered, "I remember this river, sir. I crossed it in the dream, and felt afraid when I heard lots of men speaking Japanese on the other side."

The colonel raised an eyebrow. "Would you be able to pinpoint on the map where you crossed the river?"

Kat studied the map even more closely. "I can't say for certain, sir, but I do think I was heading in this direction." Her finger traveled from the north in a southwesterly direction.

The colonel made a big red circle on the map where she'd been focusing her attention. Do you have any idea how many men there were?"

Kat shook her head. "I heard their voices for a while, sir, as I ran past. It felt like a substantial gathering of soldiers, but as to how many, I really couldn't say."

"Anything else you can remember about the terrain or enemy troops?"

Kat frowned in concentration. "I remember the landscape changed, sir, a couple of times after crossing the river. I ran through tall grasses and rice paddies. There was a wide exposed field all around the camp. It had tall watch towers and lots of barbed wire."

The colonel rifled through his papers once again and then pulled out a photograph, handing it to her. She looked up at him in surprise. It was a picture of the prison camp. "You know where they are, already!"

He nodded. "The Filipino resistance has been keeping an eye on this situation and sending me intelligence. They've told me something similar to what you have; they fear the Japanese intend to kill the POW's. They've been suggesting ways to affect a rescue. Unfortunately, until we make this landing in Luzon, we just won't have the resources at hand to pull it off."

A sudden desperate hope rose up in her. "But you're planning to save them, sir?"

He didn't pull any punches. "I don't know. If this landing is anything like Leyte, it will be rough going for a while. But it's on my mind, Lieutenant, and if an opportunity presents itself I will seriously consider it." The colonel sat back down, considering his next words. "Lieutenant," he said after a few moments, "Have you ever considered that feeling and hearing the presence of a large number of enemy combatants is not that different from what your brother can do? It's possible you also may have a talent for intelligence gathering."

Kat shook her head adamantly. "Sir, I can't do what Cal does. I can't choose what I see in those dreams."

"Humor me for a moment," he persisted. "If you'd known that enemy troop movements mattered to me, might you have been able to pay more attention to those aspects of the dream?"

"I suppose it might have been possible, sir, but my dreams don't come at will, and they're always going to be more focused on people and their health issues, not on terrain and enemy positions."

The colonel tried a different track. "Could Cal always pick the things he wanted to see?"

"No, sir" she allowed.

"So someone showed him how to control what he saw?"

She met his gaze, and then nodded, "Yes, sir."

Jack looked at her, also troubled by this line of questioning. "Sir, may I ask a question?" he interjected.

The colonel looked over at him, as if he was only now remembering Jack was a party to this conversation. He continued to stare longer than was comfortable, at last giving a curt nod.

Jack cleared his throat. "Sir, if the lieutenant prefers to continue on as a nurse, will she have the option?"

The colonel turned and faced Kat again, saying bluntly, "I haven't decided." Kat felt her heart begin to thud, and fought hard to stave off the panic threatening to overwhelm her. It was even more difficult because of his unrelenting and unnerving study of her. "I honestly don't know what I want to do with you," he continued. "I have a lot to consider. But here's something I want you to think over. With some training, if you turned out to be even half as good as your brother, you would save a lot more of our boys than you ever could as a nurse."

"Good lord!" Ellie exclaimed. "He wanted to turn you into a spy?"

"It was a logical train of thought," Uncle Mike allowed. "And that's what Cal does. It does save a lot of lives."

Ellie glared at him. "Cal is naturally good at it that kind of thing. That's not the case at all with Kat."

Her dad interrupted them before they had a chance to really get into it. Turning to Kat, he   asked, "How did you convince that colonel to let you stay with nursing corps?"

"I didn't," Kat said.

Her dad looked at her, perplexed. "I don't understand. He let you rejoin the 92nd after the landing."

"He did." Kat agreed. "But it wasn't I who persuaded him, it was Cal."

"Cal?" her mother looked stunned.

"Just how did he do that?" Uncle Mike wanted to know.

"I'm getting to that part of the story."

"Let her finish then," Grandma scolded. "No more interruptions!" And a hushed silence fell around the table as Kat continued with her tale.

The landing at Lingayen Gulf had not been as bad as everyone had been anticipating; but it was still a nightmare. As they neared Luzon, Japanese suicide aircraft had materialized just off the coastline near Manila. General Quarters had sounded, and Blake and Wight had hurried Kat and Jack along to the officer's wardroom. Wolly had shot past them, ears flattened against his head, as the Wasatch began a heavy barrage of anti-aircraft fire from every gun in her battery. The noise from the big guns had been deafening. Explosions lit up the sky and the waters all around them. Wolly hadn't run to the window this time. Instead, he'd cowered under the table as a hail of torpedoes and Kamikaze aircraft attacked the allied fleet. Right off the bow of the Wasatch, Kat and Jack had watched, stunned, as a Nakjima Ki-43 slammed into the aircraft carrier, the USS Kitkun Bay. Almost simultaneously a five-inch shell struck the carrier's starboard side.

Kat's first and only naval landing had seemed to her a scene from hell. Even now, as she told the story to her family, she recalled vividly the choking smell of smoke and fire, the constant thundering of the big guns, and the ghastly visions of broken bodies floating in the water. A total of 24 allied ships sank, and another 67 were damaged by the time Kat disembarked with the Sixth Army onto the beach at Lingayen Gulf.

Those first few days after the landing Kat and Jack waited, still under military guard, expecting to hear word from Colonel White. Nothing ever came from his office, but on January 17, nearly a week after their arrival, they both received orders to report back to the 92nd, now camped on the northern side of Lingayen Gulf. Kat stared at the orders and then back at Jack in disbelief. "He's letting me go."

Jack reached for her orders, reading them for himself. He looked up at her, surprised. "I didn't expect that," he said.

"Me either," Kat admitted. Most of their conversations over the past week had been about ways they might launch an appeal, if Colonel White decided to transfer her to military intelligence.

It took Kat a moment before the full impact sank in. She would remain a nurse, and not only that, she would be serving with the 92nd, on the front lines, as the Sixth Army retook Luzon. A memory of the map Colonel White had shown her flashed through her mind. Cabanatuan was south of here, inland. She was close now to Uncle Mike. It couldn't be much more than a day's ride away. She looked over at Jack. "Do you think this has any bearing on Uncle Mike's rescue?"

"It isn't clear," he said, but then he grinned at her, "One thing's for sure, things certainly do seem to go your way."

She cracked a smile. "I told you, you're my good luck charm."

"Excuse me, Major." A young man approached. "I'm Corporal Nolan. I was instructed to deliver the two of you to the 92nd Evac."

Kat got up and the corporal shouldered her duffel. Jack grabbed his and all three made their way to the waiting jeep.

"Where are we headed?" Jack asked.

"Just a little north of here; not too far from San Fabian."

"San Fabian?" Jack didn't like the sound of that, and Kat understood his concern. While the Japanese had attacked them hard at sea, they'd largely spent themselves after three days. The actual landing at Lingayen Gulf had been fairly quiet. The only trouble had come from enemy forces awaiting their arrival on the northern side of the gulf, near San Fabian. Kat and Jack had helped with some of the casualties from that fighting. It had included several wounded from the 54th evac hospital. The unit had taken a direct hit by a shell their first night on the beach. It had been devastating, leaving behind more dead than wounded.

Corporal Nolan tried to put their minds at ease. "San Fabian should be safe enough now. Each day we're there it gets harder to attack our forces. You'll see," he added, tossing both duffels into the back of the jeep. "It's been quiet there the past two nights, and there is now a battery of heavy artillery set up around the perimeter."

"I'm sure we'll be fine," Kat assured him, winking at the major. "I'm bringing my lucky charm with me."

The terrain around San Fabian was a mixture of beach, coconut groves and rice paddies. Kat saw the battery of long toms the corporal had mentioned, set up between the forward-most camps and the town. The 92nd was located close to a blown-up bridge, just a little over a mile from San Fabian. Sleeping tents were set up in front of a large stockpile of hospital supplies, while foxholes peppered the landscape all around the encampment. When the jeep pulled to a stop, several of the doctors came to check out the new arrivals. Immediately, smiles spread across their faces as they encircled Jack and Kat, pleased to have them back with the unit. In the midst of all the hugs and back patting, Colonel Harrison appeared.

"You made it!" he exclaimed, throwing his arms around Jack. He took a step back then to get a good look at him. "Looks like you put on a little weight there, Jack."

Jack laughed. "We ate extremely well on the Wasatch. Had I realized the advantages, I might've joined the navy."

"And missed out on all our adventures together? Nonsense!"

Jack laughed, and then the Colonel turned to Kat. "And you! I swear you must have nine lives! No wonder they named you Kat."

"I've been extremely fortunate," Kat agreed, "although I'm more of a dog person, sir."

"Well, however you managed it, I'm glad to have you back with us, Lieutenant. It never made any sense to me, separating the nurses out just when we need them the most."

Kat grinned. "I never liked that policy myself, sir."

"We don't have separate nursing quarters for you here, but we'll set your tent up between mine and the major's, just so we can keep an eye on you."

The colonel invited the two of them to his tent for dinner. He'd picked up a few local delicacies to add to the army rations; palm hearts and a dessert made from glutinous rice and coconut, wrapped together in banana leaves. Smiling, he added one last element to the feast, a half-full bottle of scotch.

"It's the last of it," he told Jack. "Until someone sees fit to assign me to someplace more civilized."

He poured them each a drink, and then wanted to hear all about the meeting with Colonel White. Kat had seen for herself how close these two men were; Jack had every reason to trust Colonel Harrison, but still, she was uncomfortable when Jack described Colonel White's thoughts on transferring Kat over to army intelligence.

Colonel Harrison fixed his gaze on her. "Would it have been possible, do you think? Could you have developed skills like your brother's?"

Despite her discomfort, she didn't look away. "I think it might have been possible, sir, to some extent. But I don't think it's likely I'd have been as good as Cal. His ability to scout is rooted in conscious thought. Mine comes from dreams, which have a tendency to follow a direction of their own."

The colonel nodded. "Well, it seems we dodged a bullet." He raised his glass of whiskey. "Here's to Colonel White's excellent conclusion to leave Lieutenant McKenna with us!"

Kat and Jack both clinked their glasses to his. Jack and the colonel finished their scotch in a single swallow. Kat sipped hers slowly, watching as they refilled their glasses.

257

It was late when dinner ended, and the last of the scotch was polished off. It was mostly the men who were responsible for emptying the bottle, but other than laughing a little too much at each other's terrible puns, they seemed to hold their liquor well enough. Kat had nursed her one glass throughout the meal. She wasn't really much of a scotch drinker. Her big indulgence had been the palm hearts. For some reason she'd found them utterly irresistible.

Jack walked her to her tent, situated between the colonel's and his. Just ahead, by the broken bridge, they could see floodlights and hear the noisy rumble of a generator, as a crew of engineers worked to restore access over the river.

"You must feel good right now," he speculated.

"Actually, I think I ate too much. My stomach is about to burst."

He laughed, and then put his hands on her shoulders. "I'm talking about Uncle Mike. It must feel good to have done what you set out to do."

She studied his eyes, which had remained intent on hers. "It will feel better if Uncle Mike is saved, but I guess I have to leave that up to Colonel White and General Kruegar now."

He continued to hold her gaze. For a moment Kat wondered if he was intending to kiss her, but instead he leaned close, touching his forehead to hers. "Thank you," he said.

"For what?" His closeness made her feel a little breathless.

"For helping me find a way to get past my anger towards James and Evelyn."

"The praying worked?"

"Not exactly the way I expected, but yes." Now his lips were almost touching hers. The kiss, when it came, made her heart flutter. He felt good, and she pressed up close against him as he folded his arms around her and deepened the kiss.

It took a while for Kat to fall asleep. Her mind kept reliving the feel of Jack's lips on hers. She was glad it was Jack who was her first kiss, and she hoped, when he was more sober, he would want to do it again. She fell asleep remembering every detail of what it felt like to be held so close in his arms.

The dream, when it came, was puzzling. Above her a hawk circled, screeching a warning cry over and over. Then the black dog showed up, but he didn't try to guide her. Instead he stood there snarling and snapping at something approaching, something only he and the hawk

258

seemed to be able to see. Her dog's behavior was unusual, and it nagged at Kat's consciousness, until finally the sense of unease woke her up. The first thing she noticed was that it was dark and quiet outside her tent. The floodlights and generator had finally been shut off. But the sense of something not being quite right remained. She looked at her watch. It was just after midnight. She hadn't been sleeping for very long. Kat slipped back into her clothes, and then put on her shoes. She was just about to peek her head outside her tent when she heard rifle fire. Her rifle and knife were lying just beside her pack. She gathered them both now, and then crawled cautiously out of her tent, staying low to the ground. She'd just made her way to the nearest foxhole when she heard some grenades go off, and then the pop popping of machine gun fire.

Jack stuck his head out of the tent. "Get down!" Kat warned. Just then another grenade exploded in their encampment, and firing began all around the perimeter. Jack crawled to the foxhole, a knife in his hand. In the distance, Kat could hear Japanese calling to each other. More grenades were thrown, and one exploded near enough to throw dirt on Kat and Jack as they huddled in the foxhole. A tommy gun started firing nearby; joining its sound to the cacophony of automatic weapons.

Colonel Harrison crawled into the foxhole with them. "The supplies are on fire," he shouted over the noise.

"Jesus!" Jack exclaimed. "We can't lose that equipment!"

The colonel nodded. "You and I need to find some fire extinguishers."

Just then they heard a jeep come to a stop. The driver got out, yelling, "What the hell is all this firing?!"

"It's the Japs!" Colonel Harrison cried out. "Get down!"

"Well I'll be damned." The man got out, grabbing his rifle, just as a grenade landed and exploded in his jeep. The man made a flying leap into their foxhole, his leg spurting blood.

The red alert began to sound all through the camp and men were running, shouting and screaming, as the firing intensified. Kat peered out over the foxhole, noted the direction of the shots coming closest to them, and took aim with her rifle. She squeezed the trigger, and instantly the sound of the Tommy gun was silenced. "Go!" she said to Jack and Colonel Harrison, "get the fire extinguishers and my medical pack. I'll cover you!"

Jack and the colonel looked at each other, and then as Kat fired off the next shot they scrambled out of the foxhole. Seconds later, Jack threw down her helmet and the med kit, and then he was off again, running full speed. Kat put on her helmet, and then turned her attentions to the wounded driver, a major from a neighboring unit. Hastily, she cleaned and dressed the wound, then looked up out over the foxhole again, trying to spot Jack and the colonel over by the burning supplies. She found them struggling with malfunctioning fire extinguishers, dodging bullets all the while. She shouldered her rifle and medical pack and then crawled out of the foxhole, moving quickly, ducking among the trucks and trees. As she got closer, she could see more clearly where the shots were coming from. She took aim and fired several shots into a copse of trees near the supplies. The shooting from the trees abated, and Kat took the opportunity to make a run towards Jack and the colonel.

When she arrived, the colonel was rounding up men to help move boxes out of the worst of the fire. Jack had moved further away, and was calling out there were wounded. Kat made one more visual pass around; looking for more shooters, but the enemy must have cleared out of the trees, having achieved their goal of torching the supplies.

Jack had already begun to assemble a makeshift infirmary, and had sent litter bearers out to search for more wounded. Kat stopped a pair and told them about the major she'd left in the foxhole near the colonel's tent. Then she joined in with the other officers who'd heard Jack's call; helping to clean and dress wounds, and to administer morphine. Ambulances arrived and she helped load their wounded. They filled two ambulances to capacity; fourteen wounded in all.

Their medical administration officer, Roger Farquar, had somehow gotten the water trailer up to the fire. He and the colonel had started a fire brigade, with a line of men using their helmets as buckets to put out the fire. Jack, Kat and the other medical officers joined the line of men, adding their efforts to save the burning supplies.

Kat's world was reduced to one of smoke, fire, and water. Her movements became automatic, and she lost all track of time. At last, Jack put a hand on her shoulder, stopping her, and pointing out the arrival of a stronger guard for the camp. They were ordering all the medical staff to hole up and stay put. Kat stood there a moment, covered in soot, staring at the fire that still raged.

Jack took her arm. "Come with me," he said.

She let herself be led away, stopping to retrieve her pack and her rifle. "Do you think they're gone?" she asked.

He looked grim. "I don't know. But we already lost three good men tonight. We don't want to risk losing any more medical staff." They crawled back into a foxhole, and both sat there utterly spent, listening to gunfire in the distance. He broke the quiet after a while and said, "May I ask you something?"

"Sure."

"Most of our men panicked tonight. A lot of the wounds I treated were from friendly fire, but you…" He stopped, his eyes searching hers. "You were amazing. Where in God's name did you learn to shoot like that?"

She managed a weak smile. "You can thank Uncle Mike for that. After that attack by the rustlers, he made darn sure Cal and I would never miss a shot again."

Kat and Jack watched in the dark from their foxhole as shells streaked over their heads, bombarding the Japanese hiding out in the hills. Sounds of shooting continued echoing through the night, as infantry patrols combed the area, flushing out more of the enemy. And all through those pre-dawn hours, the fire continued to burn strong and bright, consuming the torched supplies.

"I thought Biak was bad," Jack said, "but I've never lived through anything like this. As a unit, we made a lot of mistakes out there tonight."

Kat turned to face him. "We'll just have to be more prepared for next time."

He stared at her a moment, and then chuckled a little. "You're something else, you know that?"

She smiled back at him. "That's a good thing, right?"

Jack put his arm around her, and pulled her close against him. She smelled the odors of smoke, sweat and blood clinging to him. "That's a good thing," he assured her. "Rest, if you can," he urged. "It's going to be a long night and an even longer day ahead."

She rested her head on his shoulder, thinking sleep wasn't likely, but a dream claimed her nonetheless. Again she heard a hawk's cry as it circled and called to her. Its voice was so strident she woke with a start.

"Is there a Lieutenant McKenna anywhere here about?" She heard a guard call out.

"Over here," she said, now fully awake. The guard approached the foxhole, with another man following close behind. She cried out in surprise when she got a better look at the man behind the guard. "Cal!"

He jumped into the foxhole and enveloped her tight in his arms. They were both still crying when he stepped back to get a better look at her. "You are a sight," he said.

She wiped away at some of the soot on her face. "It's been an eventful night around here."

"I know," he said. "I scouted ahead on my way over here; saw the Japs combing the woods. I've been trying to warn you."

Kat paused. "Warn me, how?"

"I tried to see if my spirit guide could call to yours."

"You might have succeeded," she mused. "Twice tonight I've dreamed of a hawk calling to me."

He raised an eyebrow. "Well, I'll be damned. We might have to experiment a little more with that, and see just how far we can get."

"Is that why you're here?" Jack probed, standing up as well, looming over Cal. "Did Colonel White send you?"

"Jack!" Kat admonished. Then she turned to Cal. "Cal, this is a friend and colleague of mine…"

"Major Jack Carter," Cal finished for her. Kat stared at him, her face turning pale, as she realized he must have spoken with the colonel before coming to see her. Cal met her eyes. "Let's sit, shall we?" He glanced over at Jack and cocked an ear towards the distant gunshots. "There are too many fireworks going on around here for my comfort."

Kat wasn't sure if he was referring to the artillery, or the rising heat coming off of Jack. She sat though, at his suggestion, and the men sat on either side of her; the narrow foxhole forcing them all to huddle shoulder to shoulder.

"I do have news for you from Colonel White," Cal informed them, lowering his voice. "First of all, he's not going to move Kat to army intelligence, so you can both just stop worrying about that."

"Oh, thank God!" Kat sighed with relief. She could feel Jack let go of some of his mounting tension as well.

"What's the rest of it?" Jack asked.

Cal looked at Kat excitedly. "He's sending me to Cabanatuan, to meet up with another team of Alamo scouts!"

Kat gasped. "He's going to do it!?"

"I think so. A lot will depend on what we see." His eyes were sparkling now. "You and your amazing dream! Look what you set in motion!" He hugged her close to him, and then kissed her cheek.

"This is good, very good," Jack said. "But there's one thing still bothering me."

Cal cocked an eyebrow at him. "The colonel told me you were a bit of a pain."

Jack arched an eyebrow right back at him. "Did he now?"

"He did."

"Well, the thing is," Jack said, continuing his train of thought. "It doesn't quite add up. The colonel obviously is aware Kat's vision was spot on, but he doesn't follow through with transferring her over to Army intelligence." He looked straight into Cal's eyes. "Why is that, do you think?"

Cal sighed, looked over at Kat, then back at Jack. "I made a deal with him, okay?"

Kat tensed. "What kind of deal?"

Cal's eyes when they met hers were full of regret. "I gave him a bird in hand."

"What does that mean?" she demanded.

"I told him I'd stay with army intelligence indefinitely if he'd let you continue on with your career in medicine."

"Cal!" Kat cried. "Why would you do that?"

"Shhh," Cal cautioned. "Lower your voice."

"Why did you tell him that?" Kat demanded in lowered tones.

"Kat, think about it. They would get to know a lot about your capabilities while they worked to help you expand on them."

Kat's stomach lurched. "What exactly are you saying?"

Cal gave Jack a measuring look, and then turned back to his sister. "How much does he know about what you can do?"

Kat's face went even whiter under the grime. "Not all of it," she admitted.

"What don't I know?" Jack prodded.

Kat looked over at him, looking for the words that wouldn't ruin everything between them, but while she struggled to find them, Cal answered for her.

"Kat's gift is growing, Major. In her efforts to ease the pain of others, a new pathway opened to her, one that allows her to give people a peaceful, easy end."

263

Jack looked at Cal aghast, and then at Kat. "You help people die?"

Kat looked away, shaking her head. "No, I didn't know if it was right to try. But I can see how it can be done."

Cal continued talking. "If that ability were discovered by army intelligence, they would try to exploit it."

Jack's eyes went wide. A look of horror crossed his face the moment he understood the meaning of Cal's words.

Cal drove the point home. "They'd try and turn her into an assassin"

Kat's head shot up, the fury in her eyes plain for Cal and Jack to see. "I'd never let that happen!" she exclaimed. "I'd kill myself first!"

Cal smiled sadly, nodding. "That's why I traded my freedom for yours."

No one around the kitchen table said a word when Kat finished her story. The only sound was the quiet sniffling of her mother's tears. Her dad put an arm around his wife, talking to her in soothing tones. "He did the right thing, Ellie."

"I know," she said, and then started to cry harder.

Cha'risa's eyes locked on Kat's. "When were you going to tell me about this new gift?"

"I was planning to earlier, but…"

"Tomorrow you will allow me to examine it," Grandma insisted. "Together we will figure out how you can best use it, and how you can protect against any attempts by others to misuse it."

Kat nodded.

"Jesus, Mary and Joseph," Uncle Mike exhaled under his breath. "I had no idea what you kids went through! I was just so darn happy to see Cal's face as he helped me escape from that hellhole." He looked over at Kat. "And you, when I got to that evac hospital in Guimba, and you were waiting there for me, it never crossed my mind what it might have cost you to get there." He got up and walked over to her, wrapped his arms tightly around her, and broke into tears as well.

When the tears finally stopped, and the room grew quiet, Lettie broke the silence, asking, "What happened to you and Jack?"

Kat looked over at her little sister. "We're good friends. I think we always will be."

"But he never kissed you again?" her little sister persisted.

Kat shook her head. "No, he never did."

"Why not?" Clearly this wasn't the romantic ending Lettie had been expecting.

"I'm not sure," Kat said, "but I think it was because he realized just how different we were."

"Well, that's one explanation," Grandpa said obstinately.

Kat cocked an eyebrow. "You have a better one?"

"As a matter of fact, I do. Did you ever think he might be ashamed of himself for getting bolloxed, and making a pass at you? That night of all nights, he should have kept his wits about him."

Kat felt a need to defend Jack. "Grandpa, people made worse mistakes that night. Bottom line, he did what he needed to do during that crisis. He saved lives."

"That may be," Grandpa maintained, "but my explanation works as well as yours. That's all I'm saying."

Chapter 41

That night, it was only her grandma who brought her to her room and helped her get ready for bed. After tucking her under her warm blankets, Cha'risa sat down beside her, taking her hand.

"You musn't be afraid or ashamed of this new ability," she said. "All healers know something of how to bring about death. It's impossible not to. What's important is that we make a choice to value and preserve life. That's what makes a medicine woman different from a witch."

Kat bowed her head. "That's why I chose not to use it. But, Grandma," she looked up, searching her grandma's eyes, "This isn't just an awareness of how to stop the body's functioning; it's more like an assertion that this is what's best for that person." A single tear fell from Kat's eyes. "How do you trust something like that?"

Her grandma sighed deeply. "I'm not sure. Tomorrow, when we are both rested and fresh, we will examine it more closely." Cha'risa was about to say more, but instead, when she drew in her next breath, she started coughing. It was a nasty, hacking cough that left her choking and struggling for air.

"Grandma, are you alright?" Kat sat up alarmed, automatically laying her hands on Cha'risa, searching for the source of the disruption.

Her grandmother pushed ineffectively at Kat's hands. "Not yet," she croaked, her voice shaky and thick with phlegm. Even then, soothing flows of healing were entering into Cha'risa, and the energy went where Kat had intended, calming the cough, soothing the voice. "Kat, please wait!" her grandma begged. "Give me a moment before you see the rest."

Her grandma's anguished plea shocked Kat. She looked up, and her grandma's eyes locked on hers. They were filled with such sadness that Kat's fear grew even greater. "What are you talking about?"

"I didn't see it myself until it was too late," her grandma said.

Kat didn't wait to hear any more. Already her healing sense was probing, searching deep within Cha'risa. After a moment she looked up, her face ashen, her voice barely a whisper. "Grandma, this can't be." Cha'risa dropped her gaze, and said nothing. As Kat continued her examination, she could see just how bad it was. This was late stage lung cancer. It wasn't just in Cha'risa's lungs, but in her bones as well.

"No one else knows," Cha'risa said quietly.

Kat stopped her searching, looking at her grandma in disbelief. "How can they not know? How does Dad not know?"

"I only found out myself just as Uncle Mike was heading home. I couldn't diminish their joy at having Mike returned to us, or add to their concern when we found out you were wounded."

"Grandma, we need to tell them! We need to focus on you now. Maybe there is still something we can do."

"Kat, you and I know better than to fool ourselves. This is not something we can heal."

"There is a difference between facing the truth and giving up. We need to at least make an effort."

"I have been trying. Nothing makes a difference."

"But you've been trying all on your own. Let me help, too."

"Fine," her grandma said. "We will try, you and I, but until we know more we say nothing to the others."

"What about dad?" Kat asked. "We'll have more luck if we include him, too."

"The more people who know, the less likely I can keep this secret."

Kat let her frustration show. "Why is it so important to keep this secret?!"

Cha'risa eyes held onto Kat's, silently pleading for understanding. "I want to have what time I can with your grandpa; just the way we are now, before he has to relive the horror of knowing another wife is dying."

Kat could understand this desire to hold back time with grandpa. Still, there was more at stake here, and she couldn't help insisting, "Dad can keep a secret."

For a moment Kat didn't know if Cha'risa would agree, but then her grandma nodded, saying only, "We will tell him tomorrow." She was silent a moment, and then added, "Kat, if you ever see that path towards an easy death light up inside of me, you must tell me."

Kat was horrified. "Grandma, don't even talk like that!"

"I'm serious, Kat. Tell me, but don't take me down it. When the time comes, I will take the final steps on my own."

Sleep did not come to Kat that night. So many thoughts crowded her head. Mostly they were of her grandmother and uphill battle that lay before them. But also, she kept thinking about Jack. She remembered her Grandpa's words at dinner. His explanation might not be the right one for why Jack had pulled away from her, but there was no evidence hers was the right explanation either.

Her thoughts then went back to her conversation with Lissie that afternoon. "Just write him a letter and tell him I love him," she mused, and then laughed. Lissie made such a complicated thing sound so easy. Despite her doubts, Kat found herself sitting up and reaching over to the nightstand for a pen and paper. As soon as she began writing to Jack, the words just poured out. Most of her letter was about the awful discovery of her grandmother's illness, but at the end she surprised herself by writing these final words. "This is the first time since Christmas that I've faced a crisis without you, and I find that I've grown used to your calm presence and thoughtful logic. I miss you, and wish you were here with me now. I wish you could be here with me always. Stay safe, Jack, and write to me when you can. All my love, Kat."

From the memoires of Leotie Connor

1945 was a significant year for my family. I was only eight years old, but there are several events that are still vivid in my memory. One was the family reunion following the dramatic rescue of Uncle Mike from the Cabanatuan prison camp. The stories of Kat and Cal's part in that rescue were thrilling to me. For years after, Gabe and I played games where we reenacted their daring and bravery, and their selflessness.

Another thing I remember clearly was the arrival of Jack Carter. My grandfather, Ahote, had moved the entire family up to the lodge after the spring roundup that May. That was not our usual pattern; we were the caretakers of the winter ranch in the hot season. I wasn't complaining, though. My mind was full of all the adventures Gabe and I could have over the course of an entire summer. One day, the two of us were playing out by the pond when a car pulled up. A tall man with blonde hair got out. A dog jumped out right after him, running over to sniff me.

"Wolly," the man said, "come here."

"That's okay, mister," Gabe said. "We like dogs."

The man smiled. "I can see that." He walked over and shook Gabe's hand and then mine. "I'm Jack Carter," he said. "I'm looking for Kat."

We turned toward the house, planning to run and tell her she had a visitor, but she was already on the veranda, standing as if frozen in place; her face an odd mixture of hope and disbelief. Wolly got to her before the rest of us did. She was so happy to see Wolly, but it was nothing compared to her reaction to Jack. I still remember that kiss, and how it made me feel; like the world had just shifted and something had been put right.

It was after Jack's arrival that I began to understand the real reason for our relocation to the lodge. My great-grandmother, Cha'risa, was very ill. Grandpa Ahote, Uncle Sam and my cousin, Kat had been trying all kinds of interventions, but none had been able to turn back the progress of the disease. Jack had arranged for some appointments with doctors in Phoenix, but every specialist they met with told Cha'risa the same thing; the disease was terminal.

Finally, my great-grandmother had had enough. By then her lungs and bones were riddled with cancer, and it was hard for her to breathe or move around without pain. "It's my time," she told the family, "No more doctors, and no more ceremonies. You need to let me go."

We were all told to say our good-byes; that great-grandma was going to stop eating, and use her gifts as a medicine woman to stop the functioning of her body. For two days the family congregated around her bedside. It didn't feel at all like a death watch, but more like a very special family gathering. I was in the room when Jack asked great grandma if he could have her blessing to marry Kat. What she said to him that day made a strong impression on me.

"Can you make her smile at least once every day?" Cha'risa asked.

Jack grinned. "I think I can manage that."

Great Grandma looked even more intently into his eyes. "Can you do at least one thing every day that shows your willingness to nurture and support her?"

It was then Jack understood these were vows she was extracting from him, and his face grew serious. "Yes," he said. "I will."

"Can you take a take a moment each day to appreciate her for exactly who she is?"

"I can," he promised.

"Jack," she said. "There are days it is going to be hard. Days when you will have to remind yourself of that divine spark of truth and love and beauty that lives inside of you both. But if you take time each day to be grateful for the love you share, you will always find a way to keep the promises you have made today."

Jack leaned in close to her and bowed his head. "So I have your permission?"

Great Grandma nodded, and then placed a hand on his forehead, shutting her eyes as she let the energy of her blessing flow into him.

I found out afterward that Jack wrote down those vows so he would never forget them. When I got married, I asked him for a copy, and they are what Gabe and I promised each other on our own wedding day.

Over the course of those final two days of her life, my great-grandmother made time to say a private good-bye to each and every one of us. When my turn came, she called me close to her bedside and took my hand. I felt the heat from her touch trickling into me. I'd felt this before, during the many times she'd nursed me back to health

270

from various childhood illnesses. But there was something different this time. Her life force was weaker, a shadow of what it once had been, but at the same time it probed deep.

"Leotie," she said at last, smiling wanly. "One day I believe you are going to offer the world something very special." She looked deeply into my eyes then, willing me to remember her words. "When that day comes, if you call on my spirit, I'll be there to help you walk that path."

Having once said all her good-byes, my great grandmother cut the strings holding her to this life, and died peacefully in the night.

I never forgot her last words to me. Over the years, whenever something big happened in my life, I would wonder if this was that special thing my great-grandmother had foreseen. That thought crossed my mind when I went to Washington in 1974 to help the Havasupai in their last and ultimately successful quest to get Congress to restore their winter hunting and grazing lands up on the Colorado plateau. I wondered about it again when I published my first book on the tribes of the Four Corners region, and then once more when my fictional novel about the Havasupai became wildly popular. But the moment my great grandmother had foreseen did not arrive until I was well into middle age, and I did not call Cha'risa. She came to me in my dreams, as did my grandfather Ahote, and my great, great grandfather, Istaqa.

Gabe and I had been out watching the stars before retiring to bed. Thousands of people had arrived in our small town of Sedona to witness a celestial event, an alignment of the stars that was supposed to herald a new age. So many people and vehicles had come that they strained the very limits of our town, but Gabe and I were well away from the crowds, spending a romantic evening together watching the harmonic convergence from the peace and quiet of the winter ranch. When I finally fell asleep that night, the dream that enveloped me was so intense, I could feel the power of it radiating all through me. Even in my sleep I knew that the moment I'd been watching for all of my life had at last arrived. The power and the certainty were so strong that I awoke with a start, still hearing the voices of my ancestors reverberating through my brain, saying over and over, "He is coming."

As with all dreams, it seemed less potent in the light of day. I began to doubt the import of the dream, especially when instead of feeling energized by its message I began to feel poorly. After two months of this malaise, Kat insisted I come in for a check-up. When she announced that at 50 years of age I was once again pregnant, I just stared at her dumb founded.

"This is that moment?" I'd asked in disbelief, "the thing Grandma said I was meant to do to change the world?"

There was a knowing smile on Kat's face. "It's never what you expect it to be."

I might have taken comfort in this shared experience with Kat, of Grandma and her prophecies, but this was just so far from what I'd anticipated it was almost laughable. All my life my grandmother's promise of a great destiny had spurred me on, causing me to take risks and pursue things I might not otherwise have dared. But in the end, what Grandma had seen wasn't about what I was capable of at all, it was about this baby. I sat there a moment, just trying to take it all in.

I put my hands on my belly. Apparently, the weight of the world belonged on this tiny baby's shoulders, not mine. That is when I first realized what this might truly mean for Gabe and me, and my heart sank. Knowing this destiny belonged to our child was going to be oh so much harder.

46922522R00155

Made in the USA
Middletown, DE
02 June 2019